# Praise for
# *Hotel Moscow*

"Talia Carner has a sharp eye for detail and a captivating story-telling eloquence. *Hotel Moscow* is a finely-drawn tale of a country emerging from its dark Soviet past into a present overshadowed by a new kind of terror and lawless corruption. Told from the point of view of an American woman, Brooke Fielding, who is in Moscow on business, this is a frightening journey into a world of violence and power struggles that will keep the reader mesmerized. A wonderful evocation of time and place and an insightful post–Cold War thriller that reminds us that in Russia the more that changes, the more that stays the same."

—Nelson DeMille, author of *Radiant Angel*

"*Hotel Moscow* is a tantalizing book full of corruption, extortion, and shocking treatment of women—and that is just the tip of the Russian iceberg. Talia Carner's engaging style draws you in with its powerful description of life in Russia twenty months after the fall of communism. I was mesmerized from beginning to end."

—Deborah Rodriguez, author of *The Kabul Beauty School*

"With the urgency of a thriller and the sharp, atmospheric lens of a great documentary, *Hotel Moscow* hurls you into the vortex of the corrupt, outlaw world of the Soviet Union morphing into modern Russia. A fascinating and ultimately gripping read!"

—Andrew Gross, *New York Times* bestselling author of *One Mile Under*

"*Hotel Moscow* is bold and breathless. A smart story about a fearless New York woman who arrives in Russia with more baggage than she knows, it explores both the personal and the political with compelling prose, heartfelt insights, and gripping action. An impressive achievement!"

—Ellen Meister, author of *Farewell, Dorothy Parker*

"Inspired by true events surrounding the fall of communism in the Soviet Union, *Hotel Moscow* follows a group of enterprising American businesswomen on their quest to teach Russian women about the opportunities available to them through capitalistic business ventures. Overcoming decades of rigid thinking, and navigating in a dark underworld controlled by a brutal mafia and a male-dominated, politically corrupt bureaucracy, makes the task a lot more challenging and dangerous than anticipated, at the same time it makes for a gripping read. Rich with insight and detail, as well as drama and emotion, through its multiple-character narrative this book deftly explores a chapter in history that is little understood much less written about, while telling a heartening story about the possibilities for change and empowerment that follow when brave women work creatively together to forge a better future."

—Rodney Barker, author of *Dancing with the Devil:
Sex, Espionage, and the U.S. Marines*

"Talia Carner is a born storyteller, and in her new novel, *Hotel Moscow*, her unique gifts are in abundance. She has written a compelling tale of life during the fall of the Soviet Union—engaging, exciting, and revelatory of what it was like for a woman to be there in a time of great danger, and great change. This is a stunning and very shrewd book that will linger vividly in the memory of every reader."

—Jay Neugeboren, award-winning author of
*Imagining Robert, 1940, The Stolen Jew*, and others

# HOTEL
# MOSCOW

Also by Talia Carner

*Puppet Child*
*China Doll*
*Jerusalem Maiden*

# HOTEL MOSCOW

## TALIA CARNER

WILLIAM MORROW

*An Imprint of* HarperCollins*Publishers*

P.S.™ is a trademark of HarperCollins Publishers.
"Russia Then and Now . . ." previously appeared on digitaljournal.com.

HarperCollins books may be purchased for educational, business, or sales promotional use. For information please e-mail the Special Markets Department at SPsales@harpercollins.com.

FIRST EDITION

*Designed by Diahann Sturge*

Library of Congress Cataloging-in-Publication Data has been applied for.

ISBN 978-0-06-238859-9

15 16 17 18 19   OV/RRD   10 9 8 7 6 5 4 3 2 1

To my mother,

*the artist Reviva (Lederberg) Yoffé (1924–2012),*

A VALIANT AND RESOURCEFUL WOMAN

WHO FILLED MY WORLD WITH COLORS—

AND TAUGHT ME NOT TO BE AFRAID

*Not I, not any one else can travel that road for you,*
*You must travel it for yourself.*
*It is not far, it is within reach,*
*Perhaps you have been on it since*
*you were born and did not know,*
*Perhaps it is everywhere—on water and on land.*

—Walt Whitman (1819–1892),
"Song of Myself," *Leaves of Grass*

# HOTEL
# MOSCOW

# DAY ONE

*Thursday, September 30, 1993*

# ❧ CHAPTER ❧

# *One*

THE PLANE HAD emptied by the time Brooke Fielding strode down the ramp tube of the Moscow airport, her burgundy-colored raincoat and overnight case strapped with an elastic cord to a wheeled carrier. In the narrow, windowless Jetway, the two last passengers followed right behind her, men lugging clear plastic bags that sported the Duty Free Shop logo and were stuffed with cigarettes, whiskey, perfumes, and a variety of cheeses and sausages.

The significance of the moment billowed in Brooke's chest: She, an American, was arriving in Russia a mere twenty-one months after the collapse of communism. Like a pioneer, she'd get a taste of the sights, sounds, and flavors of a country few Americans had visited since the days of the czars. Even though she'd had a sense of "there" through her parents' Eastern European upbringing, she expected the experience awaiting her in Moscow would be unlike anything she'd ever had before. On Monday, when her company's new management had ordered her to take her unused vacation days, she'd called her friend Amanda Cheng to let her know that she had become available to join Amanda's women's mission. She would use her business skills to help Russian women vault over decades of stagnation.

At the sound of swooshing behind her, Brooke glanced back to see that the far end of the Jetway had detached from the airplane and was closing with a soft whine. Brooke hurried along, pushed to a faster pace by the two men at her heels, when a small, triumphant voice inside her burst out. *Russia, I'm returning on behalf of all my millions of nameless fellow Jews lost on your soil. You didn't destroy us, after all.* She lifted her head. *I'm here.*

This was a new Russia, Brooke reminded herself, different from the Russia that had experimented with its people's lives and minds. This new Russia was fighting for liberty, placing the individual's right to happiness over the collective's good, and as it struggled to free itself from bigotry, so should she. The negative, judgmental attitudes merely reflected her mother's prejudices.

Brooke was nearing the door separating the Jetway from the main terminal when a guard approached it from inside. His eyes hooded with boredom, a machine gun dangling from the strap across his chest, he unfastened a door stopper and swung the door shut, locking it, then turned to leave.

"Hey!" Brooke waved, rushing forward. "Wait!"

But the guard just tossed her a blank look through the glass, and walked away.

"I'm still here!" she called to his retreating back. She banged on the door.

"They have orders." The younger of the two men behind her

spoke in heavily accented English. He wore a rumpled blue suit with a wrinkled open-collar shirt. The older man shook his head of dandelion-fuzz hair and rested his shopping bags on the floor.

From outside rose the hum of a forklift and the thuds of luggage falling onto a conveyor belt. "Welcome to Russia," Brooke muttered. She adjusted her watch for the time zone. Seven o'clock in the morning was midnight yesterday in New York. She banged again on the glass door, but could see the empty corridor beyond. Amanda and the ten other women executives recruited for this Citizen Diplomat mission must have reached passport control. They would be worried.

The hair falling on Brooke's cheeks smelled of microwaved airplane food and recirculated air. She tucked a strand behind her ear and took a deep breath. Eventually, someone would let her out; no one got stuck at an airport terminal forever. She glanced at her companions. The two Russian men stood motionless, as if forbidden to even lean against the wall for support.

Brooke hated losing control, which had been happening all week. Last Friday afternoon she was called to an unscheduled staff meeting at which her investment firm's CEO cheerfully reported that they had been taken over. His faux optimism only made Brooke wonder how big a golden parachute the new owners must have opened for him. He was no doubt making a soft landing into a pile of several million dollars. She left the meeting in a daze and ran off to the synagogue for the start of Yom Kippur. In observance of the day her parents had never honored, she absented herself from her colleagues' frantic phone calls until Sunday.

The uncertainties she and her colleagues pondered on Sunday

were sealed Monday when the *Wall Street Journal* speculated that the takeover would probably result in a bloodbath for the current employees. That afternoon, Brooke and the other executives were told to take off two full weeks, a gambit to flush out fraud by keeping the staff away from their accounts so they could be examined unhampered.

Not even allowed to visit the office, Brooke would be absent when she most needed to impress the new management, when her clients would be introduced to new teams she had never met, leaving her out of the loop. Never before had she experienced the insecurity of a job suddenly in jeopardy. Her CEO, her mentor, had betrayed her.

But adding expertise on Russia's new economy would help her keep her hard-won executive position. Not only did Brooke have the opportunity to help Russian women on this trip but she could poke her nose into business ventures of this nation untangling itself from a seventy-year time warp. She would return to New York brimming with new ideas and investment opportunities. She might even refresh the Russian language that must be lying dormant in her grey cells; she had heard it often enough in her childhood when her mother and her mother's friends still spoke it among themselves.

This trip would be a win–win situation, Brooke had decided that Monday night.

On Tuesday, the mission's Russian host had arranged for Brooke's visa while Brooke splurged for gifts the group could provide the women they would be counseling. On Wednesday she had boarded the flight, and now, Thursday morning, here she was, stuck in the Moscow airport.

She faced the two Russian men and smiled. "Do you live in New York, or were you visiting?"

The older man's gaze fixed on her throat, then turned away.

Brooke touched the spot he'd looked at and felt her Star of David hanging on a chain. "What exactly are we waiting for?" she asked.

No response.

On the tarmac outside, the conveyor beeped the mutiny of a thousand crickets. Her suitcase was probably circling the carousel, all alone, the name tag flapping. She hoped it wouldn't be stolen while she was imprisoned here.

Brooke banged on the door again. "Hello? Anybody?"

When no one answered, she sat down on the floor and crossed her legs, glad that she'd worn her comfortable gabardine pants. So much for discovering Russia. As a little girl, she had loved exploring new places. Her mother became anxious whenever young Bertha Feldman—as Brooke was called until she unshackled herself from both her Diaspora name and her parents' tragic pasts—had ventured beyond their home. "The anti-Semites might get you," her mother would whisper, the limp from Nazi beatings preventing her from keeping up with her child's energy. "You never know where they are."

Well, now she had been caught off-guard by some Soviet-era treatment. Brooke regretted taking a row of three open seats at the back of the plane to try to sleep. In doing so, she'd been separated from the group and upon landing had to wait for the rush of passengers to subside.

A truck passed below the enclosed tube. The linoleum beneath Brooke got colder, and perspiration broke on her brow.

From her overnight bag she retrieved the folder with the articles her assistant had copied at the public library and had messengered to Brooke's building concierge since Brooke was banned from entering the office. At Brooke's request, the articles weren't about the standoff between President Yeltsin and his parliament heating up but about the new economy.

She wished she had chatted with her Frankfurt-based colleague Karl Hoffenbach about more than their corporate takeover and the minutiae of traveling to Moscow. She'd already heard in the United States plenty of news about Russia's present political strife: Nine days earlier, in his frustration at the opposition to new reforms he introduced, President Boris Yeltsin had dismissed the Communist-ridden parliament, even though it had been democratically elected. The representatives had barricaded themselves inside the building. Yeltsin responded by installing his army outside but hadn't yet given the final order to remove the parliamentarians by force. The notion that a president believed he could fire the people's representatives was so Soviet styled that it became the butt of late-night TV comedy shows in the United States. The State Department was less blasé about it—the danger of the return of a totalitarian regime was real—but hadn't issued a travel alert. Amanda had assured the group that visiting Americans weren't in any direct physical danger.

But what was the country's economic picture? Leafing through the stack of photocopied papers, Brooke stopped at a sealed brown envelope her concierge must have included in her mail. She turned it over and stared at the red "Personal and Confidential" stamp. The left-hand corner posted a Seattle return address, one Brooke didn't recognize.

The breakfast she had eaten on the plane lurched in Brooke's stomach like a rubber bullet. She dropped the envelope onto her knees and felt a cardboard inside, the kind used to protect a photograph.

*No. Don't think about it. Not now, if ever.* She tucked the envelope in a side pocket of her case, zipped it, and placed the folder of articles in the main compartment. She glanced at her two companions, who continued to stand quietly, heads bowed, unmoving, as though they had been taxidermied. No one was going to help her out of this pickle. With a creeping headache, Brooke rose and walked back forty feet to the gaping side service door.

Looking down, she registered the absence of a staircase to bridge the fifteen feet to the ground. The raised luggage conveyor belt was gone.

Over the racket of an airplane revving up, Brooke heard mechanics hammering in the yawning belly of the nearest plane. "Hey, there! Can you hear me? I'm stuck!" Only when she braced her arms, leaned far out and pretended to prepare to jump did one of them yell and gesture for her to step back, then put down his tools and walk into the terminal building below her.

A few minutes later, another armed guard appeared at the locked door, the lit tip of his cigarette cupped backward in the palm of his hand. Relieved, Brooke scrambled over. He examined her through the glass with piercing, coal-dark eyes, and then sucked, exhaled, and sucked again on his cigarette. He studied her a minute longer from top to bottom, then lazily un-locked the door.

"Come." His pronunciation rhymed with poem.

The two Russian men rushed past Brooke, heading in the direction marked with a suitcase. Brooke made to follow, but the guard stopped her.

"I'm going to the luggage area." She pointed at the sign.

The guard waved toward the opposite direction.

"What now?" she asked.

He jerked his head to the left and began to march.

This was all wrong. Should she follow or defy him? Either option was equally alarming. She turned her gold chain backward so its Star of David rested above her shoulder blades.

But this wasn't her mother's life. Representatives from the women's cooperatives she was to counsel were to meet her group. They'd come looking for her and would straighten out any misunderstanding. Reluctantly, Brooke followed the guard.

He led her into a windowless room where two uniformed men perched on desks were chatting, their heads shrouded in swirls of cigarette smoke. The guard uttered a quick sentence in Russian.

"This is. A huge. Miss-take. I must. Join. My. Group." Brooke enunciated each word. "Where. Is. The. Luggage. Area? *Valise?*"

One of the men puffed up his chest. The front of his jacket sported two rows of ribbons, and green insignias with gold lettering shone on his epaulettes. Slowly, deliberately, he stubbed out his cigarette in the ashtray.

He raised his head. He was handsome in a fierce, dark macho way, the kind of man some women found attractive and therefore made him believe he was irresistible. "You make trouble in airport." His thick, walrus-like mustache reminded Brooke of villains in Cold War spy movies.

The only way to beat his power game was not to seem intimidated. Brooke's height allowed her to meet his gaze, yet her voice quivered as she asked, "Why am I here?"

"What there?" His chin cocked toward her purse.

She squared her shoulders. "That's my handbag."

He reached for it. She recoiled. "Who are you? What's your title?"

"Customs. Open."

She smelled the cheap cologne of his assistant, who sported only a half-circle insignia with a single word in Cyrillic on his upper sleeve. He hitched up his pants toward his huge belly. The rolls of chin dangling over his starched collar trembled as he grabbed Brooke's baggage carrier, unleashed the bungee cord, slammed her case on his desk, and began to rummage through it. Her vitamin box, Swiss knife by Tiffany, sleeping mask, packet of Wet-Naps, and the flash cards Amanda had given her tumbled down to the floor. The first officer turned over her purse and emptied it on his desk.

The men's thick fingers searched the seams of her bags, tapped and squeezed their sides and unzipped each pocket. Body odor hung in the room like a cloud. Brooke breathed through her mouth. What if these men went so far as to demand a body search? The fat assistant clicked open her camera chamber and yanked at the film, exposing it. Luckily, she hadn't taken any photos yet. Her pulse drummed. Trying to sound cooperative, she asked, "What are you looking for?"

Holding her passport, the officer checked her date of birth, counted on his fingers, then raked her body with his eyes. "Thirty-eight?" He went on flipping through page after page of green, blue, and red stamps, viewing entry and exit marks. He inspected the two extra photos she had clipped to the back page on Hoffenbach's advice. She might need a visa from another country, he had said, if she needed to flee. Right now, she wished she had taken his first advice: to stay in New York.

"You travel much," the customs officer said.

"Business."

The officer chuckled, and his eyes again roamed the length of Brooke's body, this time more slowly.

Heat rose up her neck. "You haven't told me why I'm here." She should offer a bribe, she thought while he returned to reading each page in her passport. She was familiar with the voracious appetite for American dollars in countries under a totalitarian regime.

At last, the customs officer looked up. "*Joor-nal?*"

"No. *Nyet* journalist," Brooke said. "Business."

The corpulent assistant handed the officer her Sharp Wizard electronic organizer. The man put down the passport and examined the gadget. He jabbed at the switch with a finger sprouting dark hairs. The day's New York Stock Exchange quotes flashed on the screen along with a rotating world globe.

He gazed at it. "Spy?"

Brooke's mouth went dry. "Oh, no. Not spy. Not media, not politics." She forced herself to smile as she reached out and tapped some keys without dislodging the Wizard from the officer's grip. Pac-Man came charging across the screen. "Look!"

The officer burst out laughing. His front teeth were little blackened pins, like a charred picket fence. Pac-Man began swallowing his enemies. The officer slapped his knees and guffawed. "*Rossiya.*" He pointed at a little fish. "America. *Rossiya* eat America."

Anger rose in Brooke. They had nothing on her. She hadn't come to this country to be hassled. "No more. Now I go." She grabbed the organizer from his hand, punched the escape key, and Pac-Man disappeared. Without waiting for permission, she made a move toward her strewn belongings.

"No." The officer's attention was arrested by a folded packet of paper she was about to shove back into her purse. He put out his hand. "What this?"

"My itinerary." She tried to stabilize her breathing. "I'm here to teach business to Russian women—"

"Teach *Rossiya* women?" He smirked and said something in Russian. His colleague laughed. The guard by the door snickered.

Perspiration trickled down Brooke's spine. *Just let me go.* "I'm a guest of the Economic Authority—" She stopped. The name of the local powerful man Amanda had asked to arrange Brooke's visa on the shortest notice suddenly evaporated from her mind.

"And this?" To her horror, the customs officer held out the envelope from Seattle.

*Don't open the letter,* Brooke silently begged the officer, or God. It would be like introducing a deadly virus back into her life.

His pinky nail, grown to an inch long curve, snaked under the Scotch tape that double-secured the sealed edge.

Brooke couldn't bear to watch. She looked away and caught sight of his assistant thumbing through the money in her wallet. There were ten fifty-dollar bills there, she knew.

"Give that to me!" Reaching over, she grabbed the wallet out of his hand. "This is my money." Her panic switched to indignation.

With clenched teeth, she pulled out three bills and handed one to each man.

Tossing the envelope back onto his desk, the officer snatched the bill from his assistant's hand. "One hundred," he said to her.

Her elbow pressed against her money belt under her blouse. She had followed Hoffenbach's third piece of advice and brought an additional two thousand dollars in small denominations; travelers' checks couldn't be cashed in Russia.

"You keep the hundred. Fifty each for the others."

"*Nyet.*" He waved the money. "You make trouble in airport."

The bastard. She handed him two more bills and fastened her wallet, aware that he could confiscate all of it. With shaking hands she gathered up her things into her handbag on the desk. This time rather than stopping her, the assistant helped as he stuffed her black cashmere shawl back into her overnight case. He stopped to squeeze the roll of toilet paper in there, and she was surprised by the reverence with which he tucked in the loose edge.

Too near, she felt the heat of the first officer. She turned to find him gawking at her neck. His mustache quivered. "Beautiful America." A lascivious grin twisted his mouth. "Good woman, like *Rossiya,* but no meat." He pointed to an open door in the back. Through the doorway, Brooke could see a small window-less room. "Wait there," he said.

The blood pumped in her temples. If she entered that jail cell, she might never get out to tell what happened. She visualized the headline: *Female American Investment Adviser Disappears in Moscow Airport.*

The man put his hand on her shoulder, and his finger curled around a highlighted strand of hair. Brooke gasped and stepped back, but found herself trapped between him and the desk. "Take your hand off me," she hissed. "Don't you dare touch me!"

His finger traced a line on the bare skin of her neck, from her earlobe down to the thin gold chain. Adrenaline buzzed in her veins, and the points of the Star of David jabbed her shoulder blade.

The guard at the door, who'd been studying his dollar bills, tucked them into his breast pocket. With new eagerness, the assistant resumed stuffing her belongings into the travel case. As he did so, Brooke caught a glimpse of the green orientation folder Amanda had distributed.

"One moment." There was hysteria in her voice. She snatched the folder and pulled out the Economic Authority invitation, its letterhead written in embellished Cyrillic. "Look."

The officer did a double take. He said something to the other man and pointed at the bold and flowery signature. Typed below it was the name Nikolai Sidorov.

The two men craned their necks and peered at the document in awed silence.

The pounding in Brooke's ears crescendoed. "Give me my money back," she commanded, "or I'll tell Nikolai Sidorov."

To her surprise, they reached into their pockets and pulled

out the money. "Everything okay?" The officer's mouth twisted in embarrassment. "Okay?"

"*Nyet*. Not okay." She checked that her case was fully zipped and her passport tucked in her purse. She fastened the bungee cord. "I am leaving."

"Want toilet?" The officer asked. "Good toilet," he added, sounding conciliatory.

She glowered at him. Her bladder was pressing, but did he think she'd lock herself in one of his little rooms? She headed to the door. "I'm going now."

The guard accompanied her as they followed the signs to the passport control area. With hand gestures, he kept offering to roll her carrier, but Brooke held on to it. Still distrustful of the sudden turn of events, she marched on. She couldn't believe what had just happened, what could have happened. She felt the officer's finger tracing a line on her neck as if a jellyfish had stung her skin.

Who was her host, this Nikolai Sidorov? She caught the name again as the guard said it to the passport control officer, who stamped her visa with no further question.

Finally, Brooke was through into the vast luggage claim of the Moscow airport. Soldiers armed with automatic weapons glared at travelers as if supervising prisoners plotting escape. Brooke spotted Jenny, a walking showroom of her own fashion accessory business. The short, plump woman wore dangling earrings in primary colors and a matching oversize pin, waist-length necklace, and bangles. Twirling her necklace on her index finger, she smiled at an apple-cheeked, blue-eyed boy in military uniform.

Brooke started toward Jenny to warn her that these men were

not to be messed with, when Amanda bounded toward her. "Brooke, are you all right? Where have you been?"

*I could have been raped,* Brooke wanted to scream. She felt eyes piercing her back as if she were still being observed by the customs officers. The curious gazes of the ten other women in the group were upon her. Jenny let go of her soldier and sauntered over, full hips swaying. "You look like hell."

Amanda touched Brooke's cheek. Her Eurasian eyes narrowed. "What happened?"

Brooke choked the urge to fall into her friend's arms. There would be private time later to tell her story.

"Just a little red tape," she said.

## *Two*

A S SOME GROUP members waited for their luggage to be inspected by customs, Brooke struck up a conversation with the group's translator, a young woman named Svetlana who was also the manager of a recently privatized manufacturing cooperative.

Since Brooke had rejoined the women fifteen minutes earlier, the young Russian had been openly studying her clothes and shoes.

"What industry is your factory?" Brooke asked.

"Industry?"

"I mean, do you manufacture housewares, paper goods, or medical supplies?"

"Oh. We sew clothes." Crimson climbed up the young woman's rounded cheeks, as though merely speaking was a daring act.

"Fashion. Great." Brooke touched her arm and smiled. "We'll accomplish a lot in just a day or two. I promise."

Svetlana continued to study Brooke's clothes as if shopping

for them. The scrutiny, though innocent, made Brooke uneasy. "I'm very excited to be here," she added.

Twenty feet away, porters unloaded piles of huge equipment boxes labeled CBS and CNN, and a team of lethargic customs officers pried open each box, then examined and registered each piece of equipment on a clipboard. The American crew members protested that the standoff between Boris Yeltsin and his parliament would be over before the inspection was completed.

Watching them, the political clash became real for Brooke. It was nearby, not just news on TV. *Russia? A lion's den crawling with anti-Semites?* These would have been her mother's words—had Brooke informed her parents about this trip. Her mother would have been devastated by a sense of betrayal. Somewhere west of here was the Russian village where she had been born and from which her family had been forced out. Her mother's people had escaped west to Riga—then in Russia—and ultimately had been herded farther west, to a concentration death camp only her mother had survived.

Brooke pushed the thoughts away. She was American, a child of the land of freedom. While the Holocaust had been fed into her with every spoonful of rich food she was forced to swallow, forever owing to her parents' years of starvation, her psyche was detached from her parents' haunted pasts.

"Want to see a picture of my girl?" Svetlana drew Brooke's attention again. "Natasha. She's nine years old." The accent—with its extra *y* inserted in the vowels, *u* as a full "yu," and *l* rolling into "lyu"—was stronger than Brooke's mother's. Svetlana displayed the photo of a lovely, pale girl.

Would it be inappropriate to reciprocate with a photograph of her cat? "She's adorable," Brooke said, and busied herself by unzipping her suitcase and taking out a small Crayola box. "Here's something American kids like."

Svetlana tucked away the photo and extended both hands as though accepting a sacred offering. "This is very expensive."

"Is your daughter a good student?"

"She's very smart."

"Then she should have it." Brooke pressed the box into the Russian's palms. "Please."

"Thank you. Thank you so much."

"Your English is terrific." Brooke turned as a porter arrived with a large cart. His gestures as he instructed the women to load their luggage, making no effort to help them, made the situation comical. Brooke hauled her suitcase on. "Where did you learn it?"

"I studied to be an interpreter." Svetlana touched her coiffed, honey-colored hair. Her nails were bitten down to the quick. "But then they sent me to sew clothes for the navy."

The dissolution of young dreams, the absence of choices. Her tone soft, Brooke said, "Life under Soviet rule must have been so incredibly frustrating."

"It is still very hard." Svetlana sighed. "My friends at the cooperative made me a director because of my education, but I don't know what to do."

"We're here to show you. And you can teach me Russian." Brooke smiled again. Here was an intelligent young woman with whom she'd enjoy spending time. She checked her watch.

It was well past midnight in New York, and her body was or-dering her to go to bed, not to start another day. "Are we going to the hotel now?"

"After the welcome ceremony." Svetlana walked away into a group of a dozen Russian women dressed in colorful suits and dresses.

Ceremony? Jet lag made her eyes feel grainy. Brooke glanced wistfully at the terminal sliding glass doors, where a napkin of frosted sky gleamed outside.

The news crews continued to argue with indifferent Rus-sians. Brooke yawned.

Jenny placed her camera in Brooke's hands. "Look at those soldiers' cute butts. Take my picture." She posed next to a sol-dier whose back was turned, and fluffed up her red curls. "These *muzhiks* love Western women."

*Muzhiks?* Brooke's mother spoke of those low-class peasants that had turned on their Jewish neighbors. *Stop it,* Brooke told herself and took in the backside of neatly fitted khaki pants, a shiny black belt, and knee-high polished boots. *Nazis every-where,* she heard her mother say. No, she must stop these obses-sive thoughts. Brooke clicked the camera. History was what the word indicated—over. New times were here.

Amanda slid to her side. "I'd like to tie and gag Jenny," she whispered.

"She's colorful." Brooke snapped a second photo.

"You'd find something nice to say about Saddam Hussein."

Brooke watched Jenny saunter away toward another soldier. "Why did you invite her?"

"All the jewelry she's wearing? Women in Africa and Asia make them for her. She sets up home-manufacturing in all kinds of godforsaken villages. She shows these women how to use their artistic skills in designs that sell in the West."

"A great idea all around." Brooke rubbed the spot on her neck where the customs officer's finger had touched. "It's been a long night. When can we move on?"

"In just a minute—Here is—" Amanda stepped away to hug a stout *babushka* wearing sensible shoes and red plastic beads over a flowered jacket. "Everyone! Meet Dr. Olga Leonidovna Rozanova. A sociologist, but really a woman the Russian army should fear."

With an effusive sweep of her arms, Dr. Rozanova gestured to the group of Russian women to approach. Those were the representatives of the women's organizations, Brooke figured. Moments later, their hugs and the spicy smell of the pink carnations they handed each of the Americans melted away her desire to flee the airport.

"You came to us as sisters, seeking our guidance as you venture into this new, exciting world of entrepreneurship," Amanda said in an impromptu speech, delivered with uncharacteristic formality. "But we are the ones filled with awe at your courage, and we expect to renew our spirits in your boundless optimism."

As one after another the Russians launched into flowery greetings about the collective power of women and expressed their hope for future friendship between their nations, Brooke, who was still holding Jenny's camera, found herself the official photographer. She framed Dr. Rozanova's face and her beaming blue eyes, liking the way the woman seemed to have been born middle-aged. Something about Dr. Rozanova reminded Brooke of her own mother, although she couldn't pinpoint any obvious resemblance between the Russian's round body and sturdy stance and her mother's gaunt, self-deprived figure and furtive gestures. Perhaps it was the acquired resolve of the thin lips, a mouth confined by twin grooves of exiled sorrow.

A pale man by the name of Aleksandr was introduced as the group's escort in charge of travel arrangements. Unlike the gruff manners of the Russian men Brooke had seen in the past hour, Aleksandr's seemed hesitant. Wordlessly, he gestured for them to go outside.

At last. A gust of wind whipped at Brooke with a spray of drizzle that made the morning feel like December rather than the end of September. She let out the stale air trapped in her chest, and put on her raincoat, glad she had kept the wool lining buttoned in. "Where's our bus?" she asked the backs of a few women ahead of her.

"Holy shit," Jenny called out.

Brooke peered around Jenny. At the curb, two men pinned a third against the back door of a small, rusty bus. One of the assailants, a short man with a trimmed black beard and the raisin-dark eyes of a Cossack, waved a long knife.

Brooke tightened her coat around her. "Let's get the hell out of here," she whispered to Amanda. "Where's our bus?"

"This is it." Amanda said.

Dr. Rozanova walked into the midst of the fight and said

something in a commanding tone. The second assailant, a massive blond man with flat Slavic features, shoved her away. For a moment, Brooke feared the older woman might fall, but undaunted, Dr. Rozanova went on arguing. Brooke heard her say "America" several times.

"What's going on?" she asked Svetlana.

The young Russian was breathing hard. "This mafia gang controls the airport. No private cars or buses are allowed."

"How are people supposed to leave the airport?"

"Pay them."

Aleksandr motioned toward a road curving around the terminal building. "It's less than a kilometer to the back parking lot. No problem. Or pay what mafia charges for taxis."

The Cossack raised his sword and slashed the bus's right front tire. He turned to the group and announced in accented English, "You pay one hundred dollars, or I cut more tire."

"*Nyet.*" The momentarily released man, who Brooke realized must be the driver, lunged at him, but the Slav dug his elbow into the man's throat, pinning him again.

Brooke had had her fill of extortion for one morning. "Where's Nikolai Sidorov?" she asked aloud, hoping the name that had helped her out before would do so again.

No one seemed to hear her. Amanda's face was ashen. "We'll give the guy the money," she told Dr. Rozanova.

"No. It is a bad lesson."

"I know," Amanda responded, "but we must get going." She pulled out her wallet. The group's pool of funds earmarked for incidentals would be depleted fast, spent on bribes, Brooke thought, as she watched her friend handing out the bills.

"I apologize." Dr. Rozanova nodded her head sadly. "I am embarrassed for this inhospitable welcome."

"They'll sell us another tire in the parking lot." Aleksandr shrugged. "No problem."

"Who's 'they'?" Brooke asked him.

"The mafia," he said, and Brooke was surprised at the reverence in his voice.

"I'm so sorry," Svetlana mumbled. "The driver paid someone for permission to pick you up, but there are so many gangs, maybe one hundred. Not like in Italy."

"Let's go before it costs us even more." Brooke signaled the porter toward the curved road, and turned in that direction before he asked the group to push his cart, too.

In the parking lot behind the terminal building, the replacement tire was paid for with more of the group's funds. When Brooke finally boarded, she found the floor littered and the windows covered with a thick film of dust. She spread her coat on the seat right behind the driver, where she could stretch her legs. She wished she could lean her head on the window to sleep, but the filthy glass squelched her desire. Svetlana passed by with Dr. Rozanova, the two of them whispering in quick Russian.

The driver engaged the gearshift, which protested with a screech. The bus wound its way out among airplane hangars and warehouses seemingly on their last legs. Minutes later, it rolled along the open road. The white line dividing the two lanes of the highway was crooked, as though a drunken crew had fought over the brush as they painted. Brooke took in a huge expanse of barley fields and a forest of birch trees beyond them.

The Partisans. Her father had lived through freezing winters in such woods after he'd witnessed the massacre of his first wife and three children and before he'd been caught. For a split second Brooke had an image of Jews in tattered wool coats stumbling out of the tree line. She blinked to clear her head of the phantom vision.

She closed her eyes. What had she learned already to advise her clients about this survival-of-the-fittest capitalism? To stay away. Just a few weeks before, someone pitched her firm to buy the K.G.B. photo archives, complete with confiscated photographs taken by disenchanted citizens of tortured gulag prisoners. It was a trove of documentation of profound suffering, and for the electronic rights alone, her team engaged Bill Gates and Steven Spielberg in a bidding war. In her heart, Brooke didn't care whether Bill or Steve would win; she merely wanted to see this archive in safe hands, so that anxious relatives would finally learn the fate of their long-lost loved ones. But in the report Hoffenbach had sent to evaluate investments here he warned that when you bought something in Russia, it was unclear if it was the seller's to sell and therefore far from guaranteed that it would stay sold rather than be reclaimed by a previously deceived owner. Since the defunct legal system of the Communist regime was yet to be replaced, there were no laws on the books—and no courts to adjudicate disputes.

A lawless country, literally. A crack in the plastic armrest snagged Brooke's sleeve. She released it and tucked a corner of her coat under her elbow. Could she have handled the incident at the customs office differently? Remembering the men's odor, she brought the pink carnation to her nose. Its aroma smelled potent yet sweet, like the Russian well-wisher who had given it to her.

An immense housing project popped up on the landscape: stark, cheerless gigantic structures with scores of small windows stretching for miles. Laundry hung on tiny balconies was the only sign of life. Not a park, not a playground, not even a tree broke the monotony of the bleak concrete landscape. It pained Brooke to think that Svetlana or Dr. Rozanova might be living in such dreary buildings.

Soon, billboards in English lined the side of the road. Sony, BMW, Marlboro, IBM, Reebok, Coca-Cola, and Rolex alternated with dilapidated old houses whose formerly ornate facades of peeling blue or coral paint testified to the opulent past, before the czarist regime had been toppled. Moscow was the new frontier of the Wild West. It was the entry city into a vast land of eleven time zones, whose populations—reeling from seventy years of social engineering gone awry—were ready to consume everything modernity offered. Brooke decided that rather than hold on to her negative first impressions, she would keep an open mind. There must be great ways to reap profits here.

She dozed off thinking that the deep-pocket advertisers on the billboards might also be good targets for supporting Amanda's programs for women entrepreneurs. Brooke knew how to pitch those corporations.

"This is a fucking Hollywood movie," Jenny yelled, jolting Brooke awake.

The driver uttered what sounded like a curse. He jerked the gearshift and yanked the wheel to the right. A horrible screech cried the gears' defiance. The bus lurched to a stop on the curb, sending Brooke flying out of her seat. She hit her knee, then grabbed the nearest pole.

In front of a green, semicircular building with white stone trim, hundreds of people shouted, their fists pounding the air.

"What's going on?" Brooke asked Aleksandr, who sat across the aisle.

"These are the criminals. Demonstrating." Aleksandr zipped his leather jacket.

Svetlana moved to the front of the bus and peered out the driver's window. "This is Moscow's central train station." Her face was pale.

Aleksandr looked out again. "They're just talking about what's going on."

"You call that talking? Well, what is going on?" Brooke leaned forward. "What's Yeltsin trying to achieve?"

"Yeltsin is our hero of the 1991 coup." Svetlana wrung her hands together. "He climbed the tank in defiance of Gorbachev—"

Aleksandr interrupted her. "He will talk to the criminals in our White House. That's our Russian parliament."

Brooke tore open a Wet-Nap and wiped the dusty window. "Why are you calling them criminals? If they are your legal representatives, they can't be fired on Yeltsin's whim."

He shrugged. "*Normalno.*"

Dr. Rozanova came down the aisle and spoke to the driver. He restarted the engine and struggled with the gearshift, while she walked back.

Brooke sat back, massaging her bruised knee. "Svetlana, would you please ask the driver to turn on the radio?"

Svetlana reached over the driver and turned the dial, finding a station. As the driver freed the gearshift and rolled the bus into a U-turn, Svetlana cocked her ear, straining to hear.

"What does it say?" Brooke asked. "What's happening?"

Before Svetlana responded, Aleksandr said something sharp to her in Russian. Svetlana slunk back to her seat without looking at Brooke.

"We'll take a longer route to the hotel through quieter parts of the city." Aleksandr unzipped his leather jacket. "There's nothing to worry about."

"Sure." Brooke let her head fall back. "This is *normalno*."

# ❧ CHAPTER ❧

## *Three*

THE VAST LOBBY of Hotel Moscow was like no other Brooke had ever seen. Instead of carpeting, wood parquet, or marble flooring, linoleum in speckled eggshell hues gave the place an institutional appearance. High walls of intricate wrought iron crisscrossed the lobby, partitioning off the elevator bank, a darkened gift shop, and a deserted seating area with worn plastic benches suitable for a subway station. Two armed, gray-uniformed guards stood inside the hotel entrance, two more were planted on either side of an ornate gate leading to the reception area, and two others were stationed at the entrance to a back corridor shrouded in shadows. Guests could not move about the lobby without passing through checkpoints.

Would she be able to sleep the night in such a place? During Brooke's childhood, her mother's talk about Nazis banging on the door in the middle of the night had kept her awake, lying stiff and listening for hard footfalls.

Right now she needed a shower. The lobby's musty odor and

smell of disinfectant stuck to her skin. But for half an hour, the group still waited with their suitcases, talking in hushed voices.

Finally Aleksandr approached, waving cards and keys. "The registration manager has assigned two to a room," he declared. "I'll read who goes where."

"We've paid in advance for single rooms," Amanda told him. "Your travel agency made the arrangements. Twenty-five dollars a night per room."

His face dropped. "The manager here decides," he mumbled.

"The reception manager?" Brooke's sympathy for Aleksandr turned into annoyance. "Don't worry. Amanda, shall we take care of it?"

"But the manager said you're not allowed to switch. You can't! Don't get him upset." Aleksandr looked miserably at his watch. "The chef is waiting for me. Yes? I can't be late."

"The *kitchen* chef?" Brooke asked.

"He's important, you know. . . ."

Amanda placed a hand on Brooke's arm. "Welcome to Soviet hospitality."

Brooke felt she'd been dropped into a hall of funhouse mirrors. "I don't get it. This is not a third world country."

"Will you be my roommate? Just like on our safari trip."

"Promise you won't wake me up at dawn with your chanting and exercises."

"Yoga is good for your soul. Time you give it a try."

"Seeking solace in my belly button?" Brooke lifted her suitcase. "I'd rather talk to a shrink." Of course, she wouldn't see a therapist, but she envied Amanda and others like her who embraced New Age spiritualism. And yet, Yom Kippur services had failed to give her such solace. The prayers were filled with so much fawning, self-flagellation, and fear of God's fiery wrath that she had left devoid of the uplifting spirituality she had come seeking. Where was the gracious God from whom her mother expected an apology for what He'd done to His people? A God to be trusted?

After ushering the rest of the group to the three elevators, Amanda distributed several five-dollar bills among the six guards. They accepted them without the crack of a grateful smile or even stiff words of thanks.

Brooke dragged her suitcase and Amanda's into the first elevator that came down and held the door open. As soon as Amanda entered, it swished shut, almost chopping off Brooke's hand.

"Is five bucks the standard bribe?" she asked Amanda. "And what does it get us?"

"It ensures our safety."

Or would it make the guards greedy? Brooke's eyes stung from fatigue.

On the ninth floor, an old woman with a frayed flowery apron tied around her barrel-shaped middle blocked their way, glaring. Twin gray braids circled her head like a crown. A TV blared in the room behind her.

"This is the floor matron." Amanda nudged Brooke. "Got one of your lipsticks?"

Brooke withdrew a prepacked Ziploc bag. The woman accepted it with an unsmiling nod and disappeared back into her room.

Amanda led Brooke a few doors farther down the hall and fumbled with the skeleton key in the door. "In most Russian hotels this *dezhurnayia* is in charge of the room key and keeps a record of your comings and goings." She pushed open the door and walked in.

Two cots were set against facing walls. A tattered lace curtain framed a large window. The mirror over the desk was blotchy, and the colored pattern in the carpet had faded into a dull brown. The 1950s-style armoire and the desk with its lopsided drawer were scratched and stained, as though generations of vodka-drinking officials had partied there.

Brooke took off her shoes and stretched out on one of the cots. It squeaked, and she could feel the wooden board underneath the five-inch foam mattress. "When do we get to meet our venerated host, Nikolai Sidorov?"

"Aleksandr will let us know."

"After he checks with the kitchen chef, of course." An image of the littered, broken-down bus flitted through Brooke's mind. "Look, Amanda, I can tough it out if needed. But I've been invited to enough countries, and even the poorest ones know how to treat a guest. What kind of hospitality is this? First we get that pile of junk called a bus, and now this place is creepy. It feels more like an asylum than a hotel." She took a deep breath. "Let's take care of ourselves, starting by moving to better accommodations."

Amanda pinned up her hair and grabbed a bath towel from her open suitcase. The list of necessities she had given the group included good towels, insecticide, and flashlights. "This hotel is in Lenin Hills. It's a residential area. With the parliament spat, Sidorov felt we'd be safer away from downtown."

Brooke sat up. One of the bed's legs wobbled. "The armed

standoff in front of the parliament is far more serious than 'a spat.' It's a civil war about to erupt." She changed her mind about sharing the tale of her brush with the customs officers. "Who is this Sidorov, anyway?"

"He heads the Economic Authority and he's in Yeltsin's close circle of fiscal advisers. The press touts him as an example of the new breed of Russians."

"Corrupt?"

"He's considered a leader in market economy." Amanda went into the bathroom.

Rain spattered the windows, cutting off the outside world. Brooke lay down. Her glance swept the ceiling, then the corners where the stained and bubbled wallpaper ended. In the twilight of dozing off to sleep on top of the bedspread, she wondered whether she was being watched by a hidden camera.

It wasn't yet noontime when she woke up to Amanda stretching, inhaling, and exhaling like a pneumatic door as she moved from plank pose to cobra. Brooke swung her feet off the bed. It creaked, but stayed up. She undressed and stuffed her feet into a pair of slippers. "That was a good nap," she announced.

Amanda moved to downward-facing dog. "Join me?" she grunted, her head down.

"A shower will help me face Russia."

When Brooke turned on the light in the bathroom, half a dozen cockroaches skittered over the sink, and an equal number scrambled into hiding on the floor. The small, round toilet seat did not cover the rim of the oblong bowl. There was no shower stall, but water, presumably from Amanda's shower, glistened on the walls.

It took Brooke some exploring to discover at the sink a clunky lever that diverted the water from the faucet to a side hose with a portable showerhead. The floor drain underneath the sink collected the waste water. She hung her towel on the hook outside the door, noticing that Amanda had left the toilet paper there also, and stood in front of the sink. Holding the sprayer high, she let the water cascade over her.

She smelled her own fruity shampoo, glad to be rid of the last of the airport's scents. She began to hum "I Will Survive," then moved her limbs, swiveling in a dance while the water splashed on the walls and ceiling. *I will survive,* she thought, feeling alive as the words of the song cleansed her. She danced some more, singing, and thought she heard Amanda joining her from the room.

When Brooke had scrubbed the past fifteen hours off her skin and out of her hair, she turned off the faucet, swept the errant water with her feet toward the drain, and toweled dry. She walked back into the room and retrieved her hair blower, the 220-watt one she kept for certain countries, and found the outlet in the opposite wall, too far from the mirror.

"I see that you are managing," Amanda said during a pause in a sun salutation.

"What could be more exotic than camping in Moscow?" Brooke laughed as she fanned her hair. Time to start anew in this country. In fact, as she dressed in a tweed wool suit, she realized how much she was looking forward to seeing Svetlana's factory and making things happen for that lovely young Russian.

## ❧ CHAPTER ❧
## *Four*

THE BUS STOPPED in a neighborhood of residential buildings interspersed with warehouses. Brooke peered at a decrepit concrete building that seemed to have been left unfinished during Stalin's days. There was no visible main entrance, and the yard was packed mud, punctuated by black oil spills.

"The Gorbachevskaya Street Factory," said Svetlana in a voice that flipped between bravery and self-consciousness. "We have lunch ready." She added shyly, "The British call it 'dinner,' but you call it 'lunch,' right?"

"You know more than I do." Brooke gave her a large smile. "Will Nikolai Sidorov join us?"

"Oh, no." Svetlana swallowed. "He is too important."

Brooke pushed aside her bafflement and lifted the tote in which she'd brought Ziploc bags, each prepacked with a lipstick, a vial of aspirin, and a collection of Western hotel amenities. Amanda had told Brooke that it was the baggies themselves that

Russian women would cherish the most. They would recycle them until they fell apart.

Brooke stepped off the bus. In front of her gaped the loading dock, a high cavernous hole in the structure's facade. Jenny's diminutive nose crinkled. "I smell piss," she said, holding on to Brooke's elbow, her steps tiny and measured lest her four-inch heels catch in the crack of rickety stones.

The group followed Svetlana along a grimy wall toward a gray metal door fixed in the side of the building, and soon entered a small factory cafeteria.

A long U-shaped table covered with faded oilcloth took up most of the floor space. The kitchen staff, wearing frayed yet freshly pressed bib aprons, stood behind a chest-high counter, smiling and nodding. Four other women in identical plaid skirts but different colorful cardigans waited by the door with welcoming smiles. Svetlana introduced them as the factory supervisors, and within moments, Brooke found herself in a round of hugs.

Jenny distributed large "Attitude Is Everything" buttons, and asked Svetlana to translate the words for her. Jenny tried to repeat the Russian, bringing the staff to laugh at her pronunciation.

"I'm having fun," Jenny said, then mumbled, still smiling into the Russians' faces. "Jesus, look at their teeth. Green, brown, gray, yellow, gold—"

"Shhhh." Amanda glared at her. "Some may understand English."

Brooke sat down at the table. The rancid air and the sticky oilcloth bore testimony to the thousands of past meals served there. Under the scrutiny of her hostesses, Brooke ignored the tiny gnats flying about and picked up a miniature hard-boiled-egg sandwich smeared with a dollop of fish egg roe. It was something her mother would have served to guests. Brooke put it in her mouth, chewed, swallowed, and picked up another. "Good." She smiled at the servers and was rewarded with even broader smiles. Frank wonder showed in their expressions as they stared at the Americans. Brooke had encountered such adulation when visiting distant villages in southeast Asia, but had never expected to see it in Russia. After all, this was a developed country, with strong industry and science. The roles women played here in both professions and politics often surpassed those in most Western countries.

Svetlana stood at the head of the table. Not a single strand escaped her coiffed hair, and her green eyes sparkled with the importance of the moment. Brooke admired how seriously she took this responsibility and, to give Svetlana her full attention, declined to hide behind Amanda's video camera. "Your visit symbolizes the new peace between our people." Svetlana's tone sounded portentously grave, Soviet-like, as if meant for eavesdropping ears. "Women have the special compassion to put old grievances aside and find the common denominator of the many things we share, to be friends."

Amanda stood and raised a glass. "It's *our* privilege, and we hope that one day you'll visit us."

More speeches followed, delivered with ceremonial flair by each of the supervisors and then by a male official whose role as district local administrator for internal affairs remained unclear. He poured small glasses of vodka and offered them to each of the Americans, but not to Svetlana or her colleagues.

Brooke tried to pass, but Svetlana whispered to her that she must accept it.

"You are the sirens singing in the flowery meadow," the man said, and Svetlana translated. He raised the glass on the back of his hand and tipped its contents into his mouth. Brooke just let the vodka wet her lower lip and felt its heat.

Finally the group trooped up an unlit, narrow metal staircase to the second floor.

Crude swipes of trowels were imprinted in the bare concrete floor on which dozens of sewing machines occupied a quarter of the huge loft. Exposed light bulbs poured a yellow glow on long worktables. Two dozen seamstresses scrambled to their feet and beamed at the guests.

"For years, millions of Soviet women labored in these factories for meager salaries," Svetlana announced, sounding again as if reading from a script. "Now, privatization handed us the factories and gave us a chance to become their owners."

Next to each "new owner" rested a stack of white cotton pieces. The finished products, looking like giant girls' panties, lay piled by size on another long table where Svetlana led the group next. More underwear gleamed in white from clusters of open boxes.

"Before privatization we manufactured these for the navy." Svetlana touched her hair. "They gave us the fabric, placed the orders, and bought the finished product. Now that we're on our own, we buy the fabric and manufacture the same underwear, but we don't know where to sell them. Can you help us export them to America?"

Jenny picked up one and examined it. "Is this a *man's* brief?

No fly, no front reinforcement, no slack to hold the precious Russian navy balls. You see?" She passed samples around. "The elastic is sewn on each side separately. Cheap."

A small man with bottle-thick glasses entered the room and stood plastered against the wall. A pocket protector protruded from his shirt and black rubber bands held up his sleeves. Svetlana motioned him away, and he glided out through the door.

"Who do you think he is?" Brooke whispered to Amanda.

Svetlana overheard her. "The economist."

"Isn't he the one working on pricing?"

"His job is in the back office," Svetlana replied pointedly. "Only a manager gets to talk to important guests."

Brooke let it pass. "Who besides the navy wears these briefs in Russia?"

"All men wear underwear, even in America, don't they?" Svetlana's brow showed her bewilderment.

"Here's a business problem right up your alley," Amanda told Brooke.

Dim midday light dripped through the soot-covered windows on three sides of the loft. Brooke settled at the nearest worktable and pulled out a yellow legal pad and a pen. "Svetlana, there's a whole bunch of issues we can discuss."

"We'll go ahead and check the leatherwear department two more floors up." Amanda motioned to the others, and they followed a supervisor. The sound of their shoes hitting the metal steps echoed in the hollow stairwell.

Jenny, who had broken away from the group, was roaming the production line, chatting with the seamstresses with dramatic hand animation as she inspected their work. Brooke watched her. If only the woman could curb her tongue.

She turned to Svetlana. "In America we first research the demand in the marketplace for a specific product design and usage, and also assess the competition. What are the features of their products? How do their products sell? What do consumers want—and how much are they willing to pay? We study all of that *before* we manufacture."

Svetlana's eyes narrowed in concentration. "That's the economist's job. I'm the director."

"You're the director of the *whole* factory. You are not only the production manager, right? In the new system, which we call 'market economy,' you must learn every aspect of the business." Brooke smiled as she wrote down a list of her points. "That's what managers in America do. Costs and pricing, too, are crucial."

Svetlana bit her lower lip. "Numbers and money? I wasn't very good at it in school." Then her face brightened. "But if that's what I must do to become a capitalist, I'll learn."

"You'll be a great capitalist," Brooke said. "Let's start with the most important elements: product, and the flow of money, in and out." She would explain distribution later. "Jenny will discuss product design with you. It must meet European or U.S. standards. For the revenues, let's talk to the economist. Together we'll go over costs and evaluate the pricing strategies so you, the director, can participate in the decisions—"

A woman's sudden scream reverberated up the stairwell and into the work loft. Blood surged in Brooke's chest. Shouts and angry male voices followed. Svetlana's porcelain skin turned ashy pale. Her eyes widened as furious shouts became louder, closer.

The economist, his glasses askew at the tip of his nose, stumbled into the room. His shirt was hanging out of his pants, and his hand clutched his side as blood spread under his fingers.

Three thugs in bright red-and-green jogging suits and Nike sneakers burst through the door behind him. Their faces looked flushed, their foreheads shiny with sweat, their eyes fierce.

Svetlana jumped to her feet and gripped the nearest pillar, her lips moving in silent discourse. Brooke sprang to the deep end of the loft, where Jenny stood rooted to her spot. Brooke grabbed her, and together they skittered to the farthest wall, away from the thugs but also too far from the door to escape.

The economist stumbled forward, then regained his footing. One of the ruffians with shoulders so massive that his big head seemed to be attached to them without the benefit of a neck, shoved him. "*Chort!*"

The economist fell down. Brooke heard the bang as his head hit the hard concrete floor. *Nazis.* That's how they must have smashed the heads of her father's three children while he watched. Brooke imagined him lying wounded on the ground as the economist did now. He must have looked dead or the Nazis would have shot him.

Pressed against the wall, she felt his helplessness. Minute details crowded into her awareness: screws on the sewing machines, the rough lumber of the worktables, the rust of the support steel columns, the sagging electric wires overhead. She must flee. But how? To where?

Another thug, with a Slavic face and porkchop sideburns, dragged a woman into the loft. Brooke recognized the blue-and-brown plaid skirt of a factory supervisor she had hugged in the cafeteria. The woman clutched at the doorframe. "*Yob tvoyu mat,*" the man cursed, kicking at her. A spasm ran through her, then she crumpled to the floor, listless.

Before her mind could stop her, Brooke's body sprang into action. "Hey." She stepped forward. "Stop it!"

Jenny pulled her back, reaching up to clasp a hand over Brooke's mouth. "Are you nuts?" She wheeled Brooke around. "Don't even think of it."

Brooke struggled to get free, then stopped. Jenny was right.

Svetlana seemed to have found her voice. Her palms gathered in supplication, she called out something to the third gang member barreling toward her, who looked like a rooster with his red pomaded hair. Her tone was a cross between an argument and a plea.

Brooke saw the neckless man wave a can of gasoline and douse his path with splashes of liquid. Her skin prickled. Her gaze darted between him, Svetlana, and the seamstresses clustered behind the farthest support pillars. It would take only one match to turn all of them into live torches. Beside her, clutching at her arm, Jenny started to whimper.

Svetlana cried out in Russian, her lips trembling. Brooke's knees buckled. "We must get help," she whispered to Jenny.

"*Pizda.*" The rooster man was so close, Brooke could count the freckles that covered his pinkish skin. He had taken off his jacket, and his arm, tufted with red fuzz, bulged from under a Hard Rock Cafe T-shirt.

"Americans." Svetlana held up her hands in surrender, then added something in Russian.

Rooster glanced at Brooke and Jenny, but moved on to Svetlana. Without warning, he punched her jaw, upward and back. She stumbled and fell against a steel column, but she recovered her breath and continued to plead as she held her jaw.

The smell of gasoline filled Brooke's nostrils. She pulled Jenny along the wall toward the door. The cinder block's jagged roughness caught at the threads of her tweed suit jacket. At the far end of the workroom, the Slav porkchop lifted and hurled sewing machines and smashed chairs. Rooster shifted his attention from Svetlana as he joined his friends in destroying the place. The neckless thug poured gasoline on the finished piles of navy briefs.

Svetlana slid along the wall toward Brooke, stealthy as an alley cat. Brooke's body shook as she and Jenny continued to edge their way along. *Thirty more feet to the door.*

But when they were almost at the door, a thought flashed through Brooke's head. How could she flee, a coward, and leave the other women to fend for themselves? She struggled to free herself from Jenny's clutches, but Jenny shoved her toward the door with surprising strength. "Don't you dare."

Jenny was right. What could she do? She'd better get help, Brooke decided just as Svetlana reached them, grabbed her other arm, and pulled her into the dark stairwell. Brooke threw a last glance at the hoodlums. They were hurling chairs at the windows. Glass shattered.

"Call the police," Brooke cried out.

Jenny crossed herself, pulled off her pumps, and sprinted

with unexpected agility down the stairs. Following her cue, Brooke yanked off her shoes, pressed them to her chest, and ran. "Amanda!" she screamed upward into the stairwell. At least the hoodlums hadn't lit a match yet. Once they did, they'd run down right behind them, through the only stairwell here. Her friend and the rest of the group would be trapped in a burning building. "Amanda!"

A gust of cold air swept over Brooke as she, Jenny, and Svetlana fled to a back office. After a quick exchange with more trembling workers who huddled there, Svetlana reported that someone had run over to fetch their protection gang.

"The rest of our group is upstairs," Brooke yelled as she sprinted to the exit. "Clear everyone out of the building before the men set the place on fire!"

## ❦ CHAPTER ❦

## *Five*

THE BUS DRIVER had kept the door open. His radio was playing Michael Jackson's "Black or White." Aleksandr, seated in the first row to the driver's right, chatted with him.

Brooke set one foot on the bus step. "Did you see them?" she called to Aleksandr, hearing her own hysteria. "Did you hear what's going on?" At the sound of her shout, a flock of ravens perched on the high concrete wall screeched and took off.

Aleksandr fidgeted. "It's none of our business."

"We almost got killed! The building might catch fire with the rest of our group trapped there."

He looked at her blankly.

She hoisted herself up the second step and brought her face inches from his. Her tongue felt thick, and her lips were parched. "Aleksandr, a man was stabbed. A woman may be dead. They're going to burn the place down. Get the police. Now!"

"Who?" Aleksandr clutched his leather manila case to his chest. "I don't have the number."

"You don't know the number for the police?"

"There's no phone here anyway, and it's almost four o'clock."

"*So?*"

"The police go home."

A chair burst through the second floor window, crashing by the bus. The ravens rose into the air again.

Workers poured out of the building. Jenny pushed past Brooke and plopped into a seat, sobbing. To Brooke's relief, Amanda came running out of another corner of the building, the rest of the group close at her heels. Amanda counted the women entering the bus. "What in God's name has happened?" she asked Brooke.

The shaking would not leave Brooke's body. "They're going to burn the place. I saw them punch Svetlana, stab the economist, and maybe kill another woman." She swallowed. "Didn't you hear it?"

"We were two floors up on the other end of the building—"

Brooke cut her off. "Maybe there's a cop at a street corner."

Without replying, Amanda took off in the direction of the gate, but turned around as soon as she rounded the bus. "The alley is blocked!" she yelled from her spot.

Brooke stepped behind the bus and saw a dark blue Mercedes parked across the passageway. "You're not going anywhere alone," she said to Amanda.

"The group is my responsibility." Amanda's brow crinkled as she tried to assess the situation. "I must get you all out of here." She turned and started ushering the agitated women into the bus.

Brooke got on the first step again and called out to Aleksandr. "Get up, get off the bus, and go to a neighbor, find a phone, and call for help. Now."

His hands moved in a gesture of powerlessness. "If the factory didn't make arrangements with the police or with a private group, it can't get protection."

Brooke stared at him.

"Things must be done *po blatu*," he added. "Through connections."

At a single uniform yelp from the women on the bus, Brooke's head snapped around. The thugs raced out of the building and jumped into their Mercedes. The engine revved up and the car jerked forward, then fishtailed through the gate.

"Brooke, get in and let's go," Amanda said to her.

But Brooke's glance took in the building and she saw Svetlana emerge, her face puffy, holding her jaw. She hurried toward Svetlana.

"Tell Amanda you should better leave. . . . I apologize," Svetlana said, panting. "This is bad hospitality—" She broke into a sob. Brooke pulled her close, the sweet perfume mingled with perspiration. Svetlana was almost a head shorter. Brooke stroked her back. She wished someone would comfort her, too.

"Brooke," Amanda called out.

On the front seat of the bus Jenny was crossing herself. Brooke hesitated, still stroking Svetlana's back. She had seen enough of Russia. She knew what to advise her clients about investing in a country where even in its largest city the police went home by four o'clock—and whose phone number was unlisted. Hoffenbach's report about the budding violence in Russia mentioned that mafia gangs sprouted on every street, every neighborhood, every industry. Brooke hadn't fathomed the extent of that, hadn't imagined a head-on collision with its ugly face.

She must leave. Now. Yet, how could she drive away from these women? How had the Holocaust righteous done it? Those non-Jews who had rescued people from torture and death had risked not only their own lives, but also the lives of their entire families—to save even one Jew. Brooke had been powerless during the attack, but now the danger was over. Or was it? The "protecting" gang might still show up.

"Amanda, I'm going back in." Not waiting for her friend's response, Brooke snapped her fingers to get Jenny's attention. "Take care of Svetlana."

Once inside the building, Brooke dashed up the stairs two at a time, Amanda and some others at her heels. In the second floor loft, the fetid smell of sweat, gasoline, and blood hung in the air. The economist, the supervisor, and another seamstress lay on the ground, crumpled white cotton fabric tucked under their heads. A few women surrounded each of the injured. One pressed a wad of cotton against the economist's bleeding abdomen wound. Wearing only one shoe, another worker hobbled about as though trying to figure out where she was. "*Slozhno,*" she wept. "*Slozhno.*"

*Slozhno.* The hair on Brooke's arms stood. Her mother had used that word. It meant "complicated, exhausting," and whenever her mother uttered it, little Bertha had felt powerless to ease her suffering.

Brooke caught the woman's hands to stop her pacing. "Are you okay?"

As though awakened, the woman startled.

"Telephone. Taxi. Hospital." Brooke gave the woman a few single dollars and pointed toward the injured.

Amanda knelt next to the gray-haired woman on the floor and took her pulse, then began mouth-to-mouth resuscitation.

Brooke scanned the devastated factory, the broken sewing machines, and the damaged rolls of raw material. All that cotton could have been cut in new designs that better served the market. In Brooke's years as an investment manager, she had devised funding for river dams in China and had worked with experts to build a desalination plant in Saudi Arabia. But this? Nothing had prepared her for the reality of the Russian women's business environment.

She breathed in gasoline fumes and stared at the broken windows. She couldn't muster a single spiritual, comforting thought. She had been delusional, thinking she could fix any of this. In her head, Brooke could hear her mother's horrified reaction if she found out her only child had joined a mission to help the hated Russians, of all people.

Brooke sagged against the rough cinder block wall and covered her face.

When she looked up again, the flock of ravens circled above the fence, made a sudden dip, then flapped upward again, screeching.

## ❧ CHAPTER ❧

### *Six*

URING THE HOUR-LONG drive to the hotel through traffic, gloom settled in the bus like smoke. Even Jenny, suffering from what she called the heebie-jeebies, was quiet. Brooke tightened her coat and sank deeper into her seat. She didn't realize how thirsty she was until Amanda, seated next to her, twisted the cap off an Evian bottle, and offered it to her. Brooke took a big gulp, then another. The lump in her throat remained lodged.

*I'm alive.* The gruesome fifteen-minute event was only one brief scene from the nightmare her parents had experienced day after day, month after month, year after year. No wonder their well of emotions had dried up.

Brooke turned to Amanda. "The mobsters saw the bus. They knew we were there. Why didn't they put off their attack until a more opportune time?"

Amanda shook her head. "I didn't see when it happened, but

I saw the aftermath. It's horrible. I'd never expected anything like this."

"There are no laws and no police here," Brooke said. "What if the mobsters want to get rid of the witnesses?"

Amanda gave her a strange look.

"We need security," Brooke pushed on. "Aleksandr saw these guys enter the building but he didn't even come looking for us. Can we replace him, get another escort?"

"I'll certainly put in a request. And also ask for protection."

"We need a small army."

"The escort from EuroTours is assigned by the Economic Authority. Security is a different story. Obviously, I can't just hire people off the street." Amanda sighed. "As soon as we get to the hotel, I will contact the American Embassy, see what they suggest."

"May I help? I can make phone calls."

"You've been through a lot. Let me take care of things. But we could both use a good cup of tea. Will you please ask the *dezhurnayia* to fill our thermos with hot water from her samovar?"

The driver turned on the radio again, and Gloria Estefan sang "Coming Out of the Dark." Brooke looked out the window, her body tuned to the rhythm of the wheels, their syncopated sound broken by the untuned clanking of rusty parts. The streets seemed cold even when filled with people, the pedestrians' gaits lethargic. Other than an occasional aluminum and glass kiosk, there was no sign of commerce on the boulevards. The buildings, even the magnificent ones, had no storefront windows, cafés, or restaurants. How long would a change take—if democracy won?

Springs jutted out of Brooke's seat cushion. She shifted her body to ease her contact points, but could still feel their jabbing. The month before, she had helped Prince Jamal of Morocco buy a Rolls-Royce at an auction. What was she doing on this clanking bus—and in this dammed country?

Words from Svetlana's welcome speech crossed her head. "Women have the special compassion to put old grievances aside and find the common denominator of the many things we share, to be friends." Tears sprouted into Brooke's eyes as she recalled hugging Svetlana. There had been more hugs today—the well-wishers at the airport, the cafeteria workers, the seamstresses at the factory—than she had received from her own mother over a lifetime. She had connected with these women whose language she didn't speak and whose wretched lives she barely comprehended. She had been inspired by their valiant hope. If the past of her parents' generation had come and gone before she was born, now she was staring at an alternate future for these Russian women, a future beyond the current obstacles they faced. Their desperate present shook her, but she had in abundance what they needed to change it: knowledge.

The dusty, mildewed air in the bus mingled with the aroma of discarded carnations. Brooke struggled with the window's latch until the glass panel slid down a notch. She sank back in her seat and sipped water. She must remember that she had come here to gather information, to exploit the trip in order to boost her prospects of keeping her job—not to get herself raped, beaten, or burned to death. How could she risk her life for the people who had persecuted her family? She touched her Star of David, hidden under her buttoned blouse. Helping people in despair was a Jewish value, the rabbi had said just last week. That was what defined her Judaism, not the Holocaust.

The bus rumbled through a densely inhabited area with wide streets that were strangely almost devoid of people, as if this were a deserted Hollywood set. No patch of grass brightened the exposed dirt, no benches welcomed pedestrians to rest along the boulevards, no stores beckoned shoppers. Brooke wanted to pierce through the massive buildings, right into people's kitchens, to understand this strange, complicated city whose fierce cruelty still contained a genuine vein of warmth.

BACK AT HER hotel room, Brooke changed into an oversize T-shirt. All her joints ached from the earlier surge of adrenalin. After retrieving hot water from the floor matron, she made tea for Amanda and herself, sat at the desk, and pulled out her yellow pad to write a fax to her parents. As much as she hated telling them where she was, worse would be her vanishing in this vast country without a word. Her father, at least, should know her whereabouts. Maybe he'd keep it from her mother.

"Writing to the office?" Amanda asked.

Brooke shook her head. Normally she would. The partners of her firm were men who had once mentored her; later, as she gained their trust and appreciation, their professional lives merged with their social lives. She attended Fourth of July barbecues at their homes, often the only single woman. Sometimes the hosting wife invited a nephew or a young neighbor, but beyond several dates, nothing ever came out of these matchmaking efforts. When it came to emotional intimacy, Brooke forever felt herself floating in a bubble of Holocaust second-generation syndrome.

Now, with the recent buyout, she could see that her office had given her a false sense of family, not unlike her parents' sad home, not unlike the bosom of her Berkeley commune of her college days: All were transient.

"How do I fax from here?" she asked Amanda.

"Aleksandr can bring them to his office tomorrow, while we're at the conference."

"Before or after he's fired?"

"Brooke, you've been witness to a horrific scene today. I'm sorry about it. Luckily none of us got hurt. Let's try to muster positive thoughts." Amanda rooted in her suitcase, and brought out a purple candle. She placed it on the edge of the desk.

"What's this for?"

"A scented candle. For healing."

Brooke rose and went to the window, but could see nothing. Darkness had fallen on Moscow early, suddenly, skipping the twilight stage, surprising her with its finality. She turned back to the room. "Will a candle heal the economist stabbed in his side? Or that woman you gave CPR to? Or Svetlana's jaw? What kind of powers do you attribute to a man-made candle—lit or not?"

"It gives me peace." Amanda struck a matchbook. "Why don't you give it a try?"

This was what Brooke's mother had railed against all her life: How, while members of their tribe had been slaughtered, Americans—Jews and non-Jews alike—were silent, inactive. Later, as the horrors came to public attention, Americans preferred first to ignore them, then turned them into clichés. In war films you couldn't feel how cold it was, her mother said, how the sewer where Jews hid stunk, how Nazi bands' music echoed in hungry stomachs, or how the odor of the incinerators where Jews burned stayed on the skin.

"Living in New York City, I too prefer to think that we've put cruelty and bigotry behind us," Brooke said. "When that 'We Are the World' song came along, I too nurtured the delusion that the world is one large global community. Today, I stared evil in the eyes."

"What do you think I'm doing here in Russia, organizing this mission?" Amanda asked. "I just don't show my compassion with your intensity."

Brooke clammed up and stepped to the bed. Lifting the covers, she peeked at the linens, then lay down. Frayed from years of repeated washing, the cotton sheets felt surprisingly welcoming. "Sorry to dump on you. I'm tired."

Sitting cross-legged on a towel she'd spread on the carpet, Amanda said, "Here's a lovely thought to fall asleep to. You have an admirer."

"Not Aleksandr, I hope."

Amanda smiled. Her face was at a level with Brooke's eyes.

"Nikolai Sidorov?"

"Not quite."

"An American?"

"Yup."

Brooke groaned. "Now I have to wait nine days until we return to meet him."

"How do you feel about the domestic package—a husband and kids in the suburbs?"

Brooke stared at the spider-like cracks in the ceiling. "It would be nice to have someone to snuggle with. But it may be too late for children." She shifted her gaze back to Amanda. "Are you trying to tell me something?"

"Just wondering. It wouldn't work for me. I can't be tied down."

"Some freedoms are overrated." Brooke closed her eyes again. Her experience of freedom at the commune at Berkeley had been exhilarating while it lasted; she would never have traded the love she had found there. Except that, like most loves, it had its price.

AMANDA'S VOICE BROKE through Brooke's sleep. "Wake up. You're late for dinner."

"No dinner. Thanks." Brooke turned to face the wall, pulling the covers over her head.

"Listen, I spoke with the commercial attaché at the embassy. He suggests we leave even though there's no State Department alert. He just wants to get rid of the headache we're already causing him. I had to relay the message to everyone, but no way am I canceling tomorrow's conference." She paused. "You're staying, right?"

"Of course."

"Thanks. Well, the commercial attaché has sent someone over. He's downstairs. Hurry up."

Amanda walked out. Brooke pushed herself off the bed and found her slippers. The lone electric bulb dangling from the ceiling wire illuminated the room in wan yellow light. In the mirror, her high cheeks looked bony over the hollows beneath them, her lips sleep-puffed. She rinsed her face, but there was no time to reapply makeup. She brushed her hair into a ponytail, curling the ends on her fingers for a finishing touch.

Dinner at the hotel should be an informal affair. As Brooke pulled a pair of jeans and a sweater out of her suitcase, something kept flitting at her consciousness like a moth stubbornly hitting its powdery wings against a glass window. *The unread letter from Seattle.* The long-ago tangy whiff of sage came to her nostrils, a scent that always accompanied the memories of the months she had spent at the commune . . . and what happened later.

She hauled her carrier bag onto the bed and searched for the envelope. Growing frantic, she unzipped every pocket and slipped her hand into each. Nothing. She turned the bag over and shook it empty.

Realization blasted through her head. In her mind's eye she could see the letter tossed on the customs officer's desk. The corpulent assistant had gathered her belongings only from his table, while Brooke was distracted by the predatory officer and eager to flee the room. She had failed to double-check his paper-strewn desk.

Those men had her letter. They would have a laugh. She hoped they wouldn't recognize her in the photograph. Brooke collapsed into a chair and sat there for long minutes, letting her anxiety come to rest. Perhaps losing the letter was meant to be. Some secrets should stay buried, until they disintegrated like a corpse in a grave.

## ❧ CHAPTER ❧

## *Eight*

S VETLANA WALKED THE few blocks from the subway station down deserted streets, alert to all sights and sounds in the boulevard. In this older section of town, darkness lurked in hidden doorways, broken fences, scraggly shrubs, and debris-filled alleyways.

The familiar fears of unchanging days, of hopelessness, and an inescapable destiny descended on her. The terror she'd experienced at Gorbachevskaya Street Factory—and the pulsating pain in her jaw—had transformed into a dread of Nikolai Sidorov. He'd hold her responsible for ruining the Americans' first day. Somehow he'd even blame her for the disaster, as if she could have prevented any of it. And her dreams for her cooperative's success had been trashed today under the thugs' feet as irreparably as the sewing machines. How could they work without equipment?

Behind Svetlana, the corner street light gave off a faint halo, but the two lampposts in the center of the block remained dark.

Their light bulbs had been stolen two years before, when Communist control had ended.

Keeping to the drier edges of the rutted pavement, she trudged around glistening mud puddles while glancing about her. Lately, talks of muggings and rapes had accelerated. Quickening her pace, she tried to push away the images of the wounded Pavel Borisovich and her battered workers. She touched the new "Attitude Is Everything" button on her lapel. It was easy for the American women to have a good attitude; they had everything. For them, life was to be enjoyed rather than endured.

Dr. Olga Leonidovna Rozanova, herself Russian, also possessed that positive outlook. Svetlana had been almost as excited about meeting the revered sociologist today as she was about the Americans. Just recently she had discovered that Dr. Rozanova had been the author of the underground newsletter "Women's True Voice," the *samizdat* that had given her so much hope during the Soviet days, scaffolding her spirit when she despaired with trying to envision a better future for Natasha.

Svetlana clutched her handbag, feeling its bulging contents. So many gifts. The hard candies and gums she would dole out to Natasha over the next year. The Snickers and Three Musketeers she would trade in the street for months of eggs and sausages. And Brooke had given her the most beautiful scarf she'd ever owned, a silk print. It would be a betrayal to sell it, yet the money it could fetch might pay for coal for the whole upcoming winter.

She stopped in front of the three-story building, feeling her skull contract. The facade, originally painted in peach, sported decades-old dark patches of mold. In places where the paint peeled off, lighter patches of ancient plaster showed even in the wan light.

Back to the hell of the communal apartment. If only she could turn around, this very moment, and flee the five-room apartment in which five families lived—fifteen people sharing one toilet, one shower, and one small kitchen. The curse of Russian life. The walls that trapped them all for life in a web of intimacy and hatred—of smells and sounds so familiar, yet so utterly detestable—spoke only of old grievances and gripes yet to come.

Only the thought of her Natasha, waiting for her, made Svetlana push open the creaking stairway door. Again the light bulb was missing. She wound her way up, knowing in the dark how to avoid the broken stairs. Like the rest of the building, the staircase hadn't been repaired in the seventy years since this once grandiose Stalin-era mansion had been converted into an anthill of rooms.

When Svetlana entered the room she shared with Natasha, the girl squealed and flung her stuffed rabbit aside. Her eyes searched for Svetlana's *avoska,* the string basket in which she carried provisions. "What did you bring to eat?"

"With the Americans here, I didn't have time to stand in lines." Svetlana planted kisses on her daughter's forehead and cheeks. It hurt her jaw to pucker her lips; she hoped it wasn't broken. Feigning cheerfulness, she said, "You'll have macaroni tonight." The candy would be a surprise.

"I hate macaroni."

"I'll add white cheese." Svetlana didn't blame Natasha. The grayish pasta, made of rotted wheat, tasted foul unless laced with sugar, which she could no longer afford. Sometimes,

Lyalya, a pretty twenty-one-year old student who lived with her mother across the hall, paid her for English and German lessons with groceries; the young woman's mother, a physician, received them as payment from patients.

Svetlana stepped next to the one bed in the room, removed the broomstick that held the hip-high refrigerator door closed, and crouched in front of it. She used a rag to scrape off ice that had formed on the exposed cooling pipe inside the refrigerator, and pressed it to her jaw. Natasha hung on her back while Svetlana peeked at the meager contents. "I'll also add honey," Svetlana said. "And we have potatoes from yesterday, and two eggs. I'll boil both so you can take one to school tomorrow."

"An egg?" Natasha's eyes widened with anticipation. "*Vkusno*! Yummy."

Someone tapped on the door, and without waiting for an invitation, opened it. Lyalya entered, dancing a jaunty jig. Svetlana gasped.

"What do you think?" Lyalya pirouetted. She was wearing a stunning, foreign-made, red Lycra dress that ended two centimeters below her crotch. It was topped with a matching jacket with a dozen gold-shimmering zippers. Her long legs, encased in fishnet stockings and tucked into black patent-leather high heels, completed the look of a pricey call girl. "I've joined an escort service," she chanted, and waved a hand in front of Svetlana's stunned face. "Earth to Svetlana?" she said in English, an expression they had picked up from an American magazine.

Svetlana swallowed. "Are you out of your mind?"

Lyalya's brown eyes twinkled through their heavy makeup. "I'll meet so many interesting people. Foreigners."

"But what will you have to do?" Svetlana whispered. She twitched her brows to warn of Natasha's presence.

"Oh, that?" Lyalya swung her hips and laughed. "Foreign men aren't bad, not like the disgusting Russians. The girls I've met have a great time; they go to restaurants, bars, and clubs." She giggled. "Have you ever been to a restaurant?"

"Once, for a wedding."

"I'll go every night and earn more money in one week—in one evening—than you'll make in a year in that miserable factory."

"But think of your future," Svetlana murmured, wrapping her arms around Natasha, who stood gawking at Lyalya.

"My future? Like my mother's? It's a new era. I can study for years and be a stupid doctor or I can have it better now."

Svetlana let go of Natasha and grabbed Lyalya's arms with both her hands. "There's a terrible price to pay for the road you're choosing. You can still change your mind before—before you catch some horrible disease. There's a new one, AIDS—" She searched her mind for ideas. "Remember when you wanted to be a journalist? Now you can apply again."

"Are you kidding? I'm still a Jewess. The university hasn't changed its policy or quota." Lyalya's voice mimicked an official's authoritative baritone. " 'Jews are involved in international conspiracy; they can't be trusted to work with foreigners.' " She pranced behind the laundry hung on a line across the bedroom, and her finger flicked Svetlana's pink underwear, their crotch patched. "I'll rent Mama a whole apartment. I want her out of this hell hole."

"We'll talk more later. I must make Natasha's dinner." Svetlana patted strands of her girl's fair hair.

Swaying her hips, Lyalya walked out, blowing them a kiss.

Svetlana gave her daughter a gentle nudge. "Go to the kitchen and put the pots on to boil. Then come right back." She began straightening the room while cocking her ear for the feared shuffling sounds of Zoya, the old woman who shared a room with a married daughter's family.

A commotion erupted a few seconds before Natasha burst in, her face convulsed with sobs. "Zoya slapped me and shoved me out of the kitchen."

"Baba Yaga, the witch." Svetlana rushed down the long corridor and burst into the kitchen. "I've warned you not to touch my child!" she yelled at Zoya.

"Your brat's always in my way," Zoya said over her shoulder. Her cooking utensils were scattered over every centimeter of surface. Potato peels flew about from under her quick flicks. "And now you're in my way."

"Everyone is in everyone's way," Svetlana shouted. "You won't get me to move out by hitting my daughter, you hear?" She clenched her fists and waved them in the woman's face.

Zoya shrugged, but her smiling, toothless, wrinkled mouth revealed that she was resolute in her effort to claim Svetlana's room. Since Zoya's daughter had had a baby, their one room was simply too small for three generations.

All Svetlana could do was go back to her room and wait for Zoya to leave the kitchen.

"I'm hungry," Natasha whined.

In her wash basin, Svetlana rinsed the two slices of salami and cheese she had managed to save from the cafeteria. The rest of the wasted leftover food—pieces of chicken, something none of the workers had been able to purchase in months—had to be thrown away after the hoodlums had urinated on them.

While Natasha was occupied with the unexpected delicacies, Svetlana stepped to the communal phone in the corridor to call the injured workers' families, and then her friend Katerina to thank her for lending her the leather coat so that she could look elegant when meeting the Americans. She was relieved that the coat hadn't been ruined in the attack.

Katerina gushed with questions. How did each of the Americans style her hair? Who wore the most elegant clothes? What did they say about the leather coat? Who had the most expensive shoes? Who was the most feminine?

"You should see their teeth," Svetlana said.

"Their teeth?"

Svetlana giggled in spite of the pain in her jaw. Teeth were something people had, then, in time, lost. If they had money, they ordered a gold front tooth, so everyone would know they could afford it. "Like in the magazines, Katerina. They're not made of plastic as we thought. They are real, and so white."

"All their teeth?"

"At least their front ones. Brooke has the best teeth. Tops and bottoms. She's also the bravest one." Even if Svetlana could speak about the attack—which she certainly couldn't over the phone—she would never admit how she had been too scared to go back into the factory. But Brooke had. And Jenny had hugged Svetlana, and the two of them had wept together, crossing themselves. "I've made a friend. Jenny Alfredo. She's full of fire. And her clothes—so many colors—you'd love them."

Katerina giggled. "What color shoes did she wear?"

"Striped shoes decorated with cherries." Svetlana smiled into the phone. "She gave away pins that say, 'Attitude Is Everything.' I got you one, too."

Zoya emerged from the kitchen, carrying her plates and pots. "In the Soviet days the government took care of its elderly citizens," she muttered.

The narrow hall barely left space for the Baba Yaga to pass by Svetlana without scalding her with her pots. Svetlana flattened herself against the wall, sending her nemesis a warning look. "I must go," she told Katerina and hung up. As soon as Zoya closed the door to her room, Svetlana rushed to the kitchen. As she had dreaded, the old woman had left her potato and carrot peels strewn about and not bothered to wipe up the spills of oil and dishwater on the floor.

"Clean up after yourself, witch," Svetlana muttered, wishing she were bolder and could raise her voice. The newspapers reported people who, desperate for extra rooms, murdered their neighbors. Zoya, on a warpath for her own survival, was capable of anything. After school each day, Natasha was home alone for hours; none of her friends had enough space in their single, crowded room for a visiting playmate. Their mothers, too, worked late or spent hours on food lines.

Her hands shaking with frustration, Svetlana lit two out of the four burners on the stove; a third burner that hadn't worked for years had been fixed by one of the neighbors, who now claimed it as exclusively his. She filled her pots with water that trickled from the rusted faucet, and placed them on to boil. While she scoured the chipped enamel sink, Natasha came in and wrapped her arms around Svetlana's hips. Through misty eyes, Svetlana smiled down at her. Natasha's emerald eyes, so like her own, seemed huge in her thin face, and her skin looked sallow, almost translucent. The freckles across the bridge of her nose had darkened since the school kitchen had closed months ago; the meals on which Svetlana had always relied to feed her daughter were no longer being served.

"One day we'll have our own kitchen," Svetlana said. "And plenty of food."

"When I grow up, I want to be just like Lyalya."

"No, you don't."

"Oh, yes, I do."

"You'll study law. Russia needs lawyers now. It's a good profession."

"When I grow up, I'll do what I want to do." Natasha stamped her foot. "You've said that's why we have *demokratia*."

Svetlana laughed and kissed her child's head. Her beautiful daughter possessed the spirit that had been beaten out of Svetlana herself.

Natasha whined, "Why is it taking so long? I'm hungry."

"Winter's coming." Svetlana tapped the dials on the stove as if to pump more gas. The flames were weaker than before. "Public Resources must have lowered the gas supply because people are using their kitchen stoves for warmth."

The potatoes in the larger pot would take more than an hour, but when the water boiled in the smaller pot, she could double-use it to save time. First, she would put in the two eggs. When they were done, she would reuse the same hot water for the macaroni. Then she'd save that carbohydrate-soaked water. Tomorrow, she'd fashion a meal from it by adding flour. With the apples she had picked in the park last weekend, she could make pancakes.

Also tomorrow she'd carry her tin container. After dining with the Americans, she could collect leftovers, even if it would be humiliating to reveal her poverty. Pride became irrelevant in the face of her child's hunger.

"Watch the pots while I straighten up our room," she told Natasha. "And scream if Zoya shows up."

The chamber pot under the bed was full, and the napkin covering it failed to hold back the pungent smell. For fear of Zoya, Natasha used the chamber pot during the hours her mother was away. Svetlana carried it to the communal toilet, but when she tried to empty it, she found the bowl clogged with excrement. Nostrils burning, she picked up the bucket ready for such eventualities, filled it with water from the small sink, and poured it into the toilet bowl. Using a plunger, she repeated the process, alternately holding her breath and breathing through her mouth. Who had not only caused this problem, but then added to its sorry state? More than once, Svetlana had suggested to the other tenants that together they could buy detergents and disinfect the place. But the bickering had rendered futile all attempts at scheduling cleaning duties.

"Mama!" She opened the stall door to her daughter's shriek. Natasha fell into her arms, bawling. "Zoya—" Through her hiccups, the girl was unable to speak. Svetlana sprinted back to the kitchen. Behind her, the click of Zoya's door was followed by the clank of a heavy bolt.

Her pots on the stove were finally boiling, the bubbles sputtering. The three small potatoes danced. No. There were four, and one was not a potato. Something small and dark bounced up and floated to the surface. Svetlana scooped it up, and a yelp of disgust erupted from her throat. A dead mouse. She flung it on the floor. Was anything beyond the Baba Yaga? It dawned on Svetlana why she had almost broken a tooth last week on a piece of wood in her soup.

She ran to Zoya's door and banged. "You move out. Go see if you can find two rooms anywhere," she shrieked. Her scream turned into a sob of frustration. Nausea twisted her stomach at the thought that she'd have to wash the precious potatoes.

She couldn't stop crying even as Natasha hugged her. She cried also for Lyalya, for the price the intelligent young woman was willing to pay to get out of this dump, for the role model Lyalya presented to the impressionable Natasha.

Svetlana's sadness did not lift after she had rinsed the mouse hair off the potatoes and boiled them again, or later as she sat in her room across the tiny table from Natasha, watching her eat the salvaged meal she couldn't afford to throw away, and still later when she checked her daughter's homework. She rewarded Natasha with Brooke's crayons and vicariously shared her child's awe of the candy, but the sadness wrapped her with tight fists.

Finally, she gave Natasha a sponge bath, pulled down the small mattress she kept leaning against the wall during the day, spread the sheet and blanket over it, and tucked Natasha in. Sitting at the corner of the cot and feeling the soft, dry cheek against her own, Svetlana sang Natasha's favorite German lullaby.

*Guten Abend, gut' Nacht,*
*Mit Röslein bedacht,*
*Mit Näglein besteckt,*
*Schlupf unter die Deck.*

The song over, Svetlana said to the sleeping girl. "I'm going to the bathroom. Be right back."

She locked her door behind her and knocked on Lyalya's mother's door. A few minutes later, she yelped in pain as her neighbor-doctor reset her jaw. "It's not broken. You're lucky," the woman said, and placed an ice cube inside Svetlana's mouth. "Salt rinse will help, too."

Back in her room, Svetlana locked her door for the night, turned off the lights, and crawled under the covers. The old man who lived with his wife and her sister in the room to Svetlana's left prepared for bed with his triple ritual of a cough, a fart, and the trumpet-like blowing of his nose. She stared at the old-fashioned ceiling, four meters high. Shadows from the single tall, arched window cast odd shapes across it. Blue light from a passing car stuttered on the broken moldings on the opposite wall, momentarily projecting illumination on the sleeping Natasha.

Her tongue massaging the inside of her jaw, Svetlana placed her arms under her head and listened to the music produced by the violinist on her other side. Soon, neighbors' angry shouts would cut it short, but this music was the one bit of noise Svetlana never minded. She sighed and closed her eyes, allowing her body to sink into the softness of the featherbed, her only luxurious possession, her wedding gift from her mother. How different her life would have been had she, after graduation fourteen years ago, been allowed to become a translator. But because she had been gang raped, the tribunal of the Communist school judged her to be of loose morals, and she was disqualified from working for the foreign ministry. Instead, she was sent to the factory to be reeducated in proletariat values. It had been only last year, when the cooperative was privatized, that her education finally gave her an advantage. But language school had never taught her the secrets of commerce—and certainly not of capitalism.

Perhaps some sewing machines could be repaired and more fabric bought. Whatever she could learn this week from Dr. Rozanova, and especially from the Americans, might give Natasha a brighter future. Surely there must be better dreams for a young Russian than becoming a call girl like Lyalya.

D R. ROZANOVA HADN'T been to Hotel Moscow since back in the 1970s when she had come to speak at a Young Socialist Women's conference. She had been delighted that morning at the airport when Amanda invited her to visit at the hotel, but timed herself to arrive after dinner in order not to seem greedy for an expensive hotel meal. It was now nine o'clock, and she felt her way up the stairs of Hotel Moscow and banged on the glass door.

A guard unlocked it. "Your internal passport," he said gruffly. His colleague stood a few feet away, staring at a wall with vacant eyes.

Whatever changes the country trudged through, rudeness was the one thing Olga could count on as a constant. "Soviet days are over; I don't need to identify myself to get into a hotel lobby." She shifted her weight. At the end of the long day, her legs ached. "I'm here to see the Americans."

"*Nichevo.* Whatever." The guard didn't move.

He expected a bribe, she knew. Like all employed Russians, guards kept their low-paying jobs for the off-the-books perks. "This is thievery of the first degree," Olga said, her tone belligerent. When he didn't respond, she unclasped the safety pin that attached her wallet to the lining of her purse. "No apple is free of worms," she mumbled. Cringing, she peeled off some rubles.

"Dollars," he demanded.

"How will I get dollars?" Her suit jacket felt too tight, even though she had bought it only twenty months earlier in celebration of the fall of the Soviet empire. "And you're to accompany me down to the dining hall. For all I know, the guards at the inside gate will stop me again."

Entering the dining hall located in the basement, she scanned the high-set ceiling and the tall windows that started six feet above ground. Their brocade curtains were tied with silk ropes. Even the expensive oak paneling had kept its polish in spite of the plummeting membership of Socialist organizations since *perestroika*. The policy of economic and governmental reform instituted by Mikhail Gorbachev in the mid-1980s had eliminated organizations' budgets for extravagant banquets.

The Americans had indeed finished dinner. The dirty dishes were being removed from the bleached, embroidered tablecloth, and strong fragrant coffee with white sugar—a special treat—was being served. After profuse words of welcome and hugs, Olga sat down and lit a Dukat.

A man with straight brown hair and rimless glasses sat at the end of the table. When making introductions, Amanda had mentioned that he had been sent by the American Embassy. Like an anthropologist studying a foreign tribe, Olga examined the first American man she had ever glimpsed in real life. With his set, square jaw not yet softened by loose skin, and with the self-possessiveness of a movie star, he looked as handsome and healthy as the men in the few Western magazines that had sneaked past censorship. Those men were so unlike Russian men, who aged at forty and died from alcoholism by age fifty-seven. Luckily, not her Viktor.

Olga listened in increasing horror as the women told the American man about the attack at the Gorbachevskaya Street Factory. Shocked and pained, Olga broke into their conversation. "I'm so sorry. I am embarrassed that twice today you've seen the hideous side of Russia."

"Neither one was your fault," Amanda said.

"But we're all accountable. The rampant crime has become our collective shame. It is disgraceful to expose to the world what our new freedom has unleashed: a feeding frenzy of corruption and violence." She sucked on her cigarette and blew a puff of smoke. "We were a society of good morals and high values. The moment we were let loose, we turned into vultures—or even worse, cannibals."

A lovely American woman ambled into the dining room, apparently late for dinner. She scanned the table for an empty seat and took the one next to Olga. The young woman's casual outfit, so unfeminine, surprised Olga. Pants were out of the question even for peasants, and only young women in Russia wore jeans, mostly prostitutes who could afford their high price. The woman's brown hair, highlighted with golden streaks, was pulled back in a ponytail without even the benefit of an ornate clip. No respectable Russian woman, especially a representative of her industry or country, would appear in public not wearing her finest clothes and showing off her jewelry. How else would everyone know that she could afford it? Olga watched the woman smile hellos to her friends around the table, exposing a beautiful set of teeth. All the Americans had healthy, white, straight teeth, so unlike the Russians. Yet no one had a front tooth adorned with gold as she did.

Olga noted that the American man fixed his gaze on this new arrival. However, the manner in which he looked at the young woman was open and friendly, unlike the lewd way in which Russian men examined females, their eyes raking women's bodies, their lecherous thoughts written on their smirking faces.

"I'm Brooke Fielding." The girl extended a hand to Olga.

Olga shook the extended hand, then held it longer. "How old are you?"

Brooke's eyebrows rose, and she burst out laughing. "Russians are so direct."

"You're too young to be a businesswoman."

"I am thirty-eight." Brooke didn't ask for Olga's age in return. "We met at the airport this morning. You may not remember because my face was hidden by a camera. I took photographs."

Olga couldn't help compare Brooke's youthful thirty-eight against her own aged forty-eight. America was so generous with her women, while Russia was parsimoniousness with hers.

A waiter brought a pot of strong fragrant coffee. Brooke signaled to him that she needed a cup. He ignored her. Mustering her most commanding tone, Olga spoke to him in Russian, but he snubbed her too.

After two more failed attempts to get attention, Brooke got up and walked to the door leading to the kitchen. Three waiters congregated outside it, smoking. When Brooke returned with a clean cup, Olga watched the men eyeing the slim, lithe figure.

Olga poured her coffee. "Sorry for not getting you the cup myself, but they are unionized." When she saw the American's confused expression she added, "They're prohibited from giving it to someone who is not a paying guest."

"I know all about unions," Brooke replied, but Olga doubted she really did. One had to live in Russia to experience its unions' impact on every minute human interaction. The job description of each occupation was so detailed that no employee could be faulted for sticking to cumbersome procedures, while in fact it guaranteed lack of courtesy. The regulation meant to control theft of hotel property now prevented her from getting a cup.

The conversation around the table turned to democracy and what could be expected in the new Russia.

"We have a very educated population with more women engineers and physicians than any other country," Olga said, seizing the opportunity to reclaim a sliver of her beloved Russia's pride. "Once we have the right tools, a real leap forward will surely follow."

Brooke nodded. "The rug has been pulled out from under this country with no preparation," she said. "The legal system collapsed with nothing to replace it. And the goals of the new economy have been defined, but not the means by which to reach them."

Olga noticed that Brooke's short, manicured nails sported

clear polish instead of the expected shade of red or magenta a Russian woman—especially a successful one—would apply. "Not enough reason to collapse into chaos," she said, and squashed her cigarette in a saucer.

"It will take strong leadership—and time—to draft a working legal system," Brooke said, "and then to establish effective enforcement of it."

"What about God's law and human law? What about respecting others' rights? What kind of new society are we building here? Yeltsin's new machinations have brought only distrust in his leadership. He's inciting a civil war!" Olga's indignation rose as she picked up her coffee cup, splashing some coffee. "I'm all for progress—especially when it includes making room for our women's development. New horizons have opened to our nation, and women will march toward them."

Brooke touched her sleeve. "That's why we're here. To help them in business."

*Business.* The new English word had a sweet taste. Olga rolled it on her tongue. Other new foreign words she marveled at, recently adopted into Russian, were *entrepreneur* and *marketing*. She asked Brooke, "What exactly is 'business'?"

Brooke looked at her for a long moment as if assessing whether Olga was serious or just ignorant. "Business is creating a product or service that people need or can use. Then you develop the infrastructure to market and distribute it, and make a profit at the end of the sale."

"What do you do?" Olga asked the young, unassuming woman who knew so much. "Are you a professor?"

"I'm an investment manager at a private firm that manages people's money."

"A whole company just to manage people's money? Must be very rich clients."

Brooke smiled, and Olga registered that the Americans smiled even when there was no reason to. Russians were born with a scowl on their faces.

"There are specializations for each business aspect," Brooke said. "I advise clients how to invest their funds or manage their assets. Often, I coach them when we examine businesses in which they consider investing, and sometimes I counsel the management of a venture in which my clients have on-going interests." She paused. "Am I boring you?"

"Go on, please. It's very interesting."

"Well, my work gives me a broad view of things, from business plans and the evaluation of financial projections for best- and worst-case scenarios, to analysis of marketing programs and the examination of distribution options."

"Fascinating. I've never read anything about it. I should find a book about capitalism."

"I can mail you some in English when I get back."

"Of course in English. We would have nothing in Russian." State enterprises, the only ones Olga was familiar with, abhorred the word *profit* as the ultimate symbol of corrupt capitalism. The black market, in which so many of her fellow Russians engaged, was beyond contempt. Yet, her wheeler-dealer compatriots must know a lot more about business than she did. "Will you teach it all tomorrow at Amanda's conference?"

"We'll cover only the entrepreneurial versions of the basics—small-scale research, pricing, advertising, accounting, customer service. In my workshop tomorrow I'll explain the selling process and how to focus on the consumer's needs—"

Olga cut her off. "You are contradicting yourself. If a business's goal is profit, by definition it is selfish, focused on its own interest, not the good of the public, or as you say, 'the consumer.' "

"These terms are not mutually exclusive." Brooke's tone was soft. "A business that cares about customer satisfaction, that is attuned to changes in mood or consumption, that takes care of problems when they arise stands to profit more in the long run."

The long run. Who had the luxury of a "long run" when no one knew what to expect at the end of the day? "Do American children learn all this in school?"

Brooke shook her head. "Not directly, but even young children are encouraged to open a lemonade stand."

"What's that?"

"A kid fills a pitcher with sliced lemon, sugar, and water; gets a stack of disposable cups, and places a table outside the house. She posts a sign, asking passersby to buy a glass of her lemonade for a few cents. The child learns to approach people and to try to sell."

"And that's how American children earn a living?"

Brooke broke off a piece of bread left on the table. "They only get their first lesson of supply and demand. Maybe no one buys the drink because she has priced it too high. Or there's not enough foot traffic on that street. The child learns that she needs to be creative to attract customers."

"Maybe no one is thirsty."

"That's also a lesson in assessing consumers' needs. Children who sell lemonade learn that it's best to set up their operations during the hot days of summer."

"So up and down the boulevards of Manhattan there are lemonade stands with children fighting each other to sell their drinks?"

Brooke laughed. "Lemonade stands are usually found in the suburbs, and each child does it for just a few days. Even if the kid makes no money, the only cost is a pitcher of lemonade."

"What kind of a lesson is that?"

"A lesson in business thinking." Brooke paused. "In seventh grade, I signed up for an investment class. Each student received a theoretical sum of money. We researched companies' stock offerings, we studied their products and operations, and then we invested in the companies we chose. We followed each company's progress or decline, sold some stocks and bought others, and by the end of the project some of us made a profit, others lost. On paper, of course, but it was fascinating."

"*Capitalism* was always a dirty word here. Can it really corrupt the soul?"

"How? My soul is not corrupted, I hope. In fact, my mother is an accountant. As a teenager, I helped in the office, did some clients' bookkeeping to earn my allowance. I grew up thinking figures and creative accounting."

" 'Creative accounting.' Isn't that an oxymoron?"

Brooke laughed. "You'd think so, right? It's using tax loopholes, deferring profits, burying income under legitimate expenses, investing employees' pension funds."

For a while, neither spoke as Olga mulled over the new concepts. There was so much to learn. "I'm glad you can see past the inexperience of the director of the Gorbachevskaya Street Factory and help her," she finally said.

"Svetlana. I felt her hope."

"Hope can't be a business concept. It can't be measured."

"It's intangible, but hope is an important ingredient in making things happen. It's the fuel that feeds motivation."

"There are many cooperatives like the Gorbachevskaya Street Factory. They all must learn to manage their ventures."

"Given what we've seen today, our consulting is hardly enough. What you're facing here is not only a matter of 'managing a venture.' "

Brooke was soft-spoken, Olga noticed. She didn't shout when expressing an opinion, not even employing the authoritative voice a knowledgeable Russian would assume when lecturing. Yet, she sounded sincere. And she knew her subject.

"Do you really want to help?" Olga glanced about to check where a bug might have been planted. The chandelier was too high for an effective microphone, but one must be built into the table. No institute catering to unions, the public, or foreigners was free from eavesdropping.

"Of course," Brooke replied.

Without fully getting up, Olga dragged her chair away from the table and turned her head away from its electronic ears. She motioned for Brooke to do the same. "A wave of terror is spreading over businesses in the Moscow region. Women's cooperatives, like Svetlana's, are being targeted."

"Targeted?" Brooke opened her palms in question. "Only *women's* businesses?"

Olga sighed. "Reports cross my desk every week. All businesses are fair game for one mafia gang or another, but women's ventures are being more brutally intimidated and exploited. Maybe they can't afford to buy better protection. Or maybe they're an easier target for the mafia. I'm not sure. All I've figured out is that as soon as a women-owned factory shows promise, someone begins to extort protection money. Even after they pay, violent goons show up, destroy the place, and break the workers' spirits—if not bodies."

"But why? How can they benefit if the venture can no longer pay them protection money?"

"Someone 'buys' the ruined cooperative for a hundred rubles."

"The mafia can't buy a business at a fire-sale price and then run it without friends in high places," Brooke said.

"That's what worries me. A fish begins to stink from the head."

"If the authorities are either powerless or won't cooperate, what can be done?" Brooke cocked her head as she looked at Olga. "If *you* were to dream of a solution, what would it be?"

"Our people are unused to dreaming, but many of us are nostalgic for simple living. I remember the Russia of my youth." Olga's voice warmed up. This was a chance to share the grandeur of her country, rather than criticizing it to a foreigner. "The countryside with its deep forests and bubbling springs, folk songs, and dancing on summer nights." Olga reached for her cigarette packet again, but detected Brooke almost impercepti-bly pulling back. "Don't American women smoke?" she asked.

Brooke shrugged. "There's a strong trend not to start—or to quit."

Everyone Olga knew smoked even if their cigarettes were made of seaweed. She dropped her hand.

"You have a beautiful artistic heritage that I'm sure will be preserved as you move ahead," Brooke went on, as if to bridge the awkward moment. "Pushkin, Dostoevsky, Tchaikovsky, and the Bolshoi Ballet."

"Those are our national treasures." Olga hoped that her lis-tener wouldn't bring up the Stalin years, that iron-fisted Bolshe-vik rule that starved millions of Russians and executed hundreds of thousands of them. "There's no reason we should lose them with democracy. So, if I dared to dream, I would incorporate the pride in our strong values and the cultural history with a demo-cratic, free future." Olga raised her chin. "When the dust settles, we will survive. Women will strive. The cooperatives must make it. They must."

"I agree that economic independence is the key to all the others, political or personal." Brooke's hand chopped the air. "But the extortion problem is the first that must be solved."

The American man left his spot at the head of the table and pulled over a chair. "Dr. Rozanova, may I?" He straddled the chair, facing Olga.

"Remind me of your name, please."

"Judd Kornblum." He extended his hand, and after she shook it, he smiled at Brooke. "We've already met." When a confused expression traversed Brooke's face, he added, "You're with

Norton, Hills, and Bridwell, right? I lectured about Latin America for some of your clients." His smile broadened. "Or was my presentation so unimpressive that you've forgotten?"

"Oh, yes. Of course. Sorry. It's hard to place someone in such a different context."

"Are you scouting the land for diamonds in the rough?"

"This is a vacation of sorts."

"Last I looked, the Bahamas were the leisure destination of choice."

Brooke laughed a beautiful throaty laughter, as relaxed as only an American woman might allow herself to be. Or a woman under the admiring gaze of a man she was attracted to. The flirting annoyed Olga. She had little patience for nonsense when so much needed to be accomplished.

"I'd like to hear your take on what the group saw today," the man said to Olga. The lenses of his spectacles were so clear they seemed nonexistent.

Olga considered him for a moment. He was from the American Embassy. No government employee could be trusted. One had to be careful when speaking in front of someone who might be a mole. "A tragedy," she responded.

"It's not an isolated incident, I hear." Kornblum scratched his chin, where a dark evening stubble showed. "The mafia can be as murderous as Stalin's rule. Seventy years of suppression are being replaced by another era of terror."

"I've just said that something must be done for ventures that are victims of extortion," Brooke responded, seemingly oblivious to Olga's cautionary approach.

"What do you have in mind?" Kornblum asked her.

Brooke turned to Olga. "You need a grassroots movement of citizens fed up with the mafia. As pervasive as the mafia is, can it face hundreds of thousands of people coming together?"

Olga regarded her, then raised her arms in mock protest. She liked the young woman's daring spirit. "Women of Russia, unite! But we've done that already—until recently, when we lost our guaranteed seats in the Duma. That's our congress."

Brooke pressed on. "Do you have any suspicion of who's behind the intimidation?"

"If criminals wore white caps, they'd look like a flock of sheep. Right?" Olga sighed. "How can one begin to find out who's behind something like this?"

"Well, who benefits?" Brooke tossed a glance at Kornblum as if sharing with him this particular thought, then looked back at Olga. "Who buys the collectives for 'a hundred rubles' as you've said, once they're almost ruined?"

Olga's fingers twisted her necklace so the two chipped beads wouldn't show. "The newspapers say it's the bankers. They are the most dishonest people in the new economy."

"How is that?"

Olga shrugged. It was safe to quote what she'd read in the government-sponsored newspaper, *Izvestia*. "They launder money, give 'loans' from government subsidies to their cronies, and embezzle funds from state and commercial accounts. That's what we always said was 'corrupt' capitalism."

"That's a Soviet version of capitalism," Kornblum said. "Self-fulfilling prophecy."

Brooke cut in. "Anyway, in this case, you need to find out which specific banks these cooperatives have been dependent on. It's that simple." Her eyes shone with intensity. "That's the thread you should follow."

"Right into the path of the crooks?" Kornblum's eyebrows rose behind his rimless glasses. "Then what?"

"If I am to help Svetlana, someone must get to the root of the problem." Brooke tucked back an errant strand of hair that had escaped her ponytail. "In the worst-case scenario, Svetlana will know who the enemy is. At best, knowing will help her develop a strategy to deal with it."

Of course corruption lay with some bureaucrat—and one with mob connections. Olga could have guessed it herself, except she hadn't. But Brooke, who understood the business process, just pinpointed the third corner of the triangle: the specific bankers that worked with the women's ventures. "In Russia, information is dangerous," Olga said quietly.

## ❧ CHAPTER ❧

## *Ten*

FEELING INVISIBLE EYES piercing her from the ceiling and walls, Brooke walked up the flight of broad steps out of the dining room, pretending ease. She had stayed behind to munch on the one piece of buttered bread and three cucumber slices the waiter had salvaged from the chef's tight hold in exchange for a five-dollar bill. But the delay had left her alone in the company of two shabby-looking men with brooms who focused on sweeping the floor of the vast dining hall just around her feet. Once again, lagging behind had left her exposed.

She reached the lobby floor still hungry. Her mother, scarred by wartime starvation and forever distrustful of the surety of her next meal, squirreled food away in her purse, pushing it on her little Bertha at all hours. When Brooke reached puberty, she had shut her mouth and became anorexic before the term was widely known. It had given her a measure of control, even as she floated about in a starved haze, in a weightless body. Now she wished she had packed cans of tuna, a box of matzos, and the granola bars she often carried when traveling to third world countries. She hadn't thought of Russia in such terms. Amanda had a bag of dried fruit, though, which she would no doubt share.

Yet Brooke wasn't ready to go to her room and decided to test the boundaries of her freedom to move about the lobby. As she ambled past the two sets of guards standing at the inside gates she held up her hand-written pass and was relieved that they let her through. Would the next guards stop her from venturing outside?

She stopped before the double glass doors of the front entrance and, adopting a stiff, commanding body language, scowled at the guards until one of them unlocked the door. Stepping out with no intention of going anywhere, she stood motionless on the top landing to breathe in crisp air fragrant with damp leaves. It was dark. No need to waste precious Russian light bulbs outdoors. This late in the evening, Moscow felt like any other city. Brooke's eyes adjusted to the darkness, and she noticed trees dotting the sidewalks. The huge residential buildings across the wide road seemed peaceful, the crumbling plaster on their facades concealed in darkness. Only the glow from hundreds of small golden lit windows in each mammoth building hinted at life gathering itself for the night.

She caught a movement at the bottom of the stairs. Half-hidden by the front post, Judd Kornblum was leaning against it, his hands tucked into his pants pockets and his legs crossed at the ankles. Although he didn't turn his head when Brooke walked down the last of the few steps, a slight shift in his position told her that he sensed her presence. In the light spilling from the doors behind them, his jaw tightened and rippled a vein at his temple.

"Are you all right?" she asked.

"I would have killed the bastards."

"Who?"

"I can't get over what happened at the factory today."

A chill zipped through her. Half an hour before, in Dr. Rozanova's presence, he had sounded insouciant. "For a security guy, you seem quite agitated. Isn't this routine here?"

His wrist gestured a dismissal. "I am not security. I'm here on business."

"Business?"

He shrugged. "You can raid this country and come up with incredible loot. I'm looking at proposals for nickel mines in the Urals, fishing rights in the Caspian Sea, and production of agricultural machinery in places whose names end with *akhstan*."

"That's interesting, but it's not what I meant. Why did the embassy send you here tonight?"

"Oh, that. I happened to be at a meeting with the commercial attaché at the embassy when Amanda called. He wanted you all to catch the first flight out in the morning. With the political situation about to blow up just a block away from the embassy, they don't need the additional responsibility of a group of women traipsing into all kinds of violent situations."

"I see," Brooke said, though she didn't. "How do you figure in this?"

"Amanda asked me to run a workshop tomorrow. She told me what a big deal it was for the Russian women who've registered; many have traveled huge distances to attend."

"You were quite pessimistic about the state of things just thirty minutes ago."

"Wanted to hear Dr. Rozanova's reaction." He paused. "And yours. Will you be leaving in the morning? A couple of women from your group are."

Brooke shook her head, then remembered that he couldn't see her, still standing slightly behind him. "Not yet. Don't tell me you're staying in this dump of a hotel out of free choice."

"Now I am."

Brooke shifted her weight. The group's security issue remained unresolved. And this guy, Judd, was as mysterious as the Russians. Why did he care about the conference? "When did Amanda ask you to present? I haven't seen your name on tomorrow's program."

"We were seated next to each other on the flight here. We talked all night. It had never occurred to me to consider the women's business perspective. I'm intrigued."

In the silence of the night, crickets trilled and an owl hooted. A sudden thought hit Brooke. Could Judd be the secret admirer Amanda had referred to? He had met her the year before, after all. On the flight to Moscow, he would have learned from Amanda that Brooke was on this Citizen Diplomat mission.

She examined his aquiline profile and the strong shoulders under the collared golf shirt. She could have been seated on his other side on the plane had she not caught that fretful sleep at the back.

"Would you like to take a walk?" He motioned with his head. "The river is four blocks behind here. There's a great panoramic view of the city."

Her eyes tried to pierce the darkness down the road. *Nazis behind every tree.* She had put herself in enough unsafe situations for one day. "As you've pointed out, this place is dangerous. Thanks anyway. I'll take a rain check."

She had taken one step up the stairs when he spoke again. "May I ask you a question?"

"Depends on the answer."

"Where did you disappear to at Sheremetyevo Airport this morning?"

His pronunciation of the airport's name sounded impeccably accent free. "Do you speak Russian?" Brooke asked.

"As much as your average American." He unfolded his legs and turned to face her. "So where were you?"

"How do you know about that?"

"Like I said, I was on your flight. I had to leave the airport just when Amanda became frantic about you."

Brooke wasn't up to reliving the airport ordeal; she had put it behind her. "Oh, I got my first taste of Russia; was shaken down for some bucks at customs." Standing one step above him put her at eye level, so she smiled directly at his face. "But I learned from that not to separate from the group, which is why I'm not taking a walk with a stranger in the dark."

"Fair enough."

"Good night."

"I'll come in, too."

At the sight of their passes, one of the bored guards let them in, then relocked the door behind them. Brooke and Judd rode the elevator without speaking, the tiny space enclosing them in intimacy. Too fast, too soon. Brooke turned to face the panel of buttons.

The ninth floor corridor smelled faintly of damp wool, cheap cologne, and fried food. Garbled Russian spilled from the TV through the open door of the *dezhurnayia*'s room, followed by canned laughter. The silhouettes of half a dozen men hovered in the far end of the long corridor, the red tips of their cigarettes glowing in the dim light.

Brooke motioned toward the men. "What's going on?"

"Johns waiting for the call girls." Judd walked her the few steps to her room door and waited as she fumbled with her large skeleton key, inserting and pulling and inserting again until it fit in the keyhole. "You'll be all right."

"I plan to move us to another hotel tomorrow." She stood by the open door, finding it hard to step in and close it.

"Not a bad idea. Not simple, though." He lifted her hand and brushed his lips against it. The gesture touched her in its unlikely Old-World courtliness. "Good night, Brooke."

She knew from the way her name rolled off his tongue that he had toyed with it, had said it over and over in his head. She extracted her hand from his fingers. "Good night, Judd," she replied, her tone soft, her heart singing.

AMANDA WAS CURLED up in her cot, face to the wall. She had lit another scented candle, and its faint glow in the dark room reminded Brooke of its meaning. Healing. She regretted being bitchy about it. Careful not to make any noise, she changed into her nightgown, then rooted in Amanda's backpack and found the bag of dried fruit. She took it to the bathroom, where she settled on the covered toilet, tore open the cellophane, and limited herself to one piece each of apple, pear, apricot, and peach. She drank bottled water, then brushed her teeth.

Before crawling into bed, she beamed her flashlight under the blanket for any errant cockroaches. Spotting none, she stretched out on the sheets and looked at the candle, now gutted into its own wax. She ordered herself to clear her head of all thoughts and to focus on a spot behind her navel, Amanda's Zen style. She wasn't going to think about the Gorbachevskaya Street Factory. Or worry about Nazis breaking down the door in the middle of the night. Or fret about the lost envelope and the burden of its costly secret.

And she especially was not going to think about Judd Kornblum.

# DAY TWO

*Friday, October 1, 1993*

THE SCREAMS THAT woke Olga came at the wrong time of night and from the wrong wall. Usually it was their neighbor to the right who brutalized his wife in the evenings until the vodka knocked him out. The charcoal-gray stripes breaking through the shutters meant it was predawn. And instead of the slamming of a body against the shared wall and the cries of a woman's pleading, the screams sounded like the prolonged bellow of a tortured animal.

She nudged her husband. "Viktor, wake up."

He grunted, but didn't move.

A far but distinct shriek pierced the wall, jerking Olga to full consciousness. Angry male voices, garbled like the sound from a public announcement system, came from the left.

"Did you hear that?" She pinched Viktor's arm. Of course he heard. Their building, a *Khrushchoby,* Khrushchev's slum, had thin prefabricated walls and single-pane glass windows that obstructed neither sound nor temperature.

Viktor turned onto his stomach. "It's none of our business."

She coughed, switched on the night lamp, and forced her legs off the bed. Her stiff, aching joints warned her of a coming harsh winter. She pushed herself up off the mattress, shivering. The building cooperative would not begin turning on the heat for another month, and then only for one hour in the morning and two in the evening.

Olga's feet skimmed the floor in search of her slippers. Another scream rang out. She ran to the kitchen barefoot. Through the window from which she chatted with her neighbors, she had a view of the wing perpendicular to hers. With horror, she distinguished the screams as coming from her friend Vera's apartment, one floor below her and diagonally across. In Vera's lit communal kitchen, Olga saw the lower halves of three pairs of legs, two in jogging suits and American sneakers, and a woman's bare feet below the edges of the baby-blue nightgown.

Her friend leaped closer to the window. A rip down the middle of her nightgown exposed her olive-skinned breasts and stomach.

Olga's trembling fingers struggled with the window latch. As soon as she released it, one of the men waved a steam iron at Vera. A scream traveled up Olga's throat, but she slammed her hand against her mouth as comprehension ripped through her. The mafia! No mistaking their tactics. Thank God she hadn't turned on the light.

"You didn't sign the papers," the man shouted. "We'll teach you a lesson, so all the dumb bitches will know we're serious."

"I will! I will sign anything!" Vera cried. "Please don't hurt me."

Olga ran back to the bedroom and shook her husband. "Viktor! Get up! They're torturing Vera."

Viktor leaned on one elbow and flipped on his reading lamp. His face, sleep puffed, drooped from its own weight, and a tuft of silver hair sprouted from his scalp. "Shhhh. Come back to bed."

"Get up," she whispered. "We must go over there!"

"Don't be crazy."

She stubbed her toe on the door frame running back to the kitchen, and to her spot at the window. One of the men now held Vera in a vise hold. With one hand he twisted and wrenched her waist-length dark hair, locking her head backward, while his other hand pinned her arms, arching her naked torso as a third man materialized, grabbed a handful of Vera's luscious hair, and hacked at it with scissors. Vera kicked at him as her tresses, too thick, resisted. He yanked harder, causing her body to jerk. Clumps of hair fell to the floor.

"No!" Vera struggled to twist away.

The man brandishing the iron reached down toward her middle, and the hot iron hissed, branding flesh. Olga smelled the sickening sweetness of charred skin, then realized it must be in her imagination; Vera's apartment was too far away for the smell to waft over. A fit of coughing seized her. She collapsed into a chair and dropped her face into her hands.

What could she, an old woman, do? Yet, how could she sit by idly?

Viktor stumbled in just as the refrigerator compressor kicked on with a thud, jolting Olga before it settled into a steady hum that muted the voices across the way. Tears of fury and helplessness rolled down Olga's cheeks. She pushed herself away from the table and marched back to the bedroom.

"You are not going anywhere." Viktor followed, grabbed her arm, and forced her to sit down on the bed. His hand rifled blindly through the clutter on the night table for the pack of Dukat. Finding it, he offered it to her. She ignored him, stood up again, and yanked open the armoire door. He pressed himself between her and the closet. "Don't even think of it."

"How can I not?" Reaching around him, she sifted through her clothes.

"If you interrupt them, they might take Vera with them, and then you'll never see her again. Or, they might take you, a witness." He lit a cigarette and put it between her lips. "Anyway, they've already done what they wanted to do to her."

Olga's body shook. In staccato drags, she drew hard on the cigarette. The K.G.B. era, with its free rein of torture and cruelty, was supposed to be over. She stared blankly at the wallpaper. The once delicate yellow roses sported water stains in meandering shapes of islands and continents. How she despised being unable to do something—anything—for her friend.

"It's cold. Cover up." Viktor held up her robe. The bright pink of thirty years before had long acquired a grayish hue.

The cigarette burned her fingertips. She crushed the smoldering end and went back to the armoire. All her clothes hung neatly layered on only two hangers; Viktor needed a strong wire to finish the third he'd been fashioning from a piece of cedar. Olga freed her brown skirt and flowered blouse from the tangle of loops and sleeves and got dressed. Since climbing up the five floors back to the apartment would be too much, she dressed for the day in her good sweater under a blazer.

"Olga Leonidovna, I know you." Viktor's fingers gathered the stretched-open fly of his striped pajamas and rearranged the fabric to cover himself, as if she cared if he looked dignified. "You think you can fight the whole Russian mafia single-handedly."

"Not single-handedly, but with all of Russia's women behind me." Olga thought of what that young American, Brooke, had said about people uniting.

"We're almost fifty, too old for new struggles." Viktor sat on the bed and hung his head. "You've done your share with your *samizdat*."

"You knew about the newsletter?"

"The K.G.B. interrogated me, too."

"I didn't tell you, for your own protection."

He shrugged.

Olga felt the blood slamming in her temples. "I'm going to Vera. Her mother's there. They might kill the old woman—if watching them torture her child didn't kill her first."

"Wait." Viktor made a move to get up. "Don't go yet. Olga, what can you do for Vera? What can anyone do about anything in this forsaken country?" The weary sweep of his arm encompassed the world outside.

"You expect me to sit by when Vera, and women like her, are being driven out of their businesses by torture?" Olga glanced at the photograph on her night table, where, even in the dim light, the blond hair of her granddaughter shone like hers had when she was young. "Russia has been given a second chance. I want a better future for Galina."

Short puffs of smoke swirled over Viktor's head in the lamplight before dissolving into the shadows. "She's Mikhail's responsibility, not yours." His tone was tired. "You raised him to be a good, modern man."

"A man nevertheless, and men don't make the world a better place."

"And women can without our help?" He leaned forward, and his pajama top strained over his protruding belly. His skin was the color of an eggshell. "Get it into your head. You can change nothing. Nothing."

He was wrong. Her *samizdat* had given women hope, even if it brought no change. He was right, though, that they were all worse off now, after the fall of communism, having lost their quota in the parliament along with the safety net of services guaranteed by laws, laws that were now wiped out. Outrageously, Yeltsin's new directive was to give all available jobs to men. As the old saying went, "It is easier for the donkey when a woman gets off the cart."

Olga stepped to the door, thinking of her conversation with Brooke. It did not matter that Brooke didn't understand Russia and had no idea what was not possible here. The confidence Brooke exuded and her professional stature proved that women could gain rights and be successful in the business world.

Back in the kitchen, she peered out the window. A man in a jogging suit stood by Vera's kitchen window, smoking. Olga couldn't see his face. There was no sign of Vera or her mother. Olga's heart pounded. Wait, she told herself. Viktor was right that rushing in would only get her or Vera—or both—into trouble.

Bile climbed up her throat. She walked to the bathroom to rinse her mouth with baking soda, and steadied herself at the sink. Cold water trickled from the faucet. In the mirror, blue irises peeked at her through the delicate folds of weary eyes. She probed the faint web of infinitesimal lines crisscrossing her cheeks.

Still shaking, Olga returned to the kitchen and opened the box of diced tea leaves saved for special occasions. Measuring a spoonful, she folded it into a torn piece of newspaper, and wrapped two spoonfuls of sugar in another newspaper piece.

She peered again through the window. All seemed quiet at Vera's apartment. The men must have left.

As Olga descended the five flights of stairs, her knees rebelled with stabs of pain. It was a relief to walk through the foyer even as the stench of urine and rotting potatoes caused her to gag. Exiting her building, she followed the well-trodden mud path to the street. After last night's rain, the concrete slabs were covered in mud, and the galoshes protecting her shoes made squishing sounds as she crossed the long block.

Rounding the corner, she was whipped by a gust of wind, almost knocking her off balance. She tightened the wool scarf around her head and neck. The coming winter would be long and harsh.

In the adjacent wing of the building, Vera's stairwell gaped, its door long stolen. Along the concrete wall in the building's foyer, Olga's fingers groped for the timed light switch. She tried to climb fast; in one minute, the light would run out.

An eerie silence shrouded the stairwell. Olga stopped on each landing to catch her breath, to wait out the last seconds of the timed light switch and press it again. Her joints screamed, but she hated to use her small cache of aspirin. Viktor had bought it at an inflated price from a colleague at the Academy of Sciences who had returned from a conference abroad, and she had been saving it for the long winter months, or for emergencies; a wrapped tablet for Vera now hid in her pocket. Olga felt eyes peering at her from behind the peepholes of the dozens of doors on each floor. The neighbors must have heard everything, must have watched the men bounding up, then later thumping down the stairs. No one could have missed the Mercedes that must have parked out front, the mark of a mafia gang.

Vera's mother fell into Olga's arms with deep, rasping sobs. Olga hugged the old woman, then stepped inside the cubicle that was their home. Vera's groans—guttural, tortured, animal-like—filled the room. She lay in the only bed, her long, thin abdomen naked except for soaked rags, and her heavy dark hair, cropped at odd angles like a logged forest, sticking out unevenly around her face. The sour smells of sweat and burned flesh saturated the air.

Olga bit her lower lip. Rage filled her: rage at what Russia was doing to her people, at what it permitted to be done to her people. Rage at herself for her own helplessness. "I brought you a *tabletka* of aspirin." She propped up Vera's head and made her swallow the pill with water.

"I used all our butter for her burn." The old woman pointed at the soaked rags.

"Ice is much better. See if you can get some." Few refrigerators came with freezers. Olga handed her the tea and sugar. "Can you also make her *mannaya kasha*?" Boiling semolina would occupy the old woman and give her a way to help her daughter.

Vera's mother shuffled out of the room. Olga sat at the edge of the bed. Vera moaned. "It hurts so much."

"I'm so sorry. So sorry." Olga brushed aside sweat-soaked wisps of hair that clung to Vera's forehead. "Shhhhhhh. Shhhh-hhh." She sat quietly, stroking the chopped hair, waiting for the pill to take whatever effect it could offer. Vera needed morphine, not an aspirin.

Vera fingered Olga's plastic beads. "Why are you dressed up?"

"I have a meeting with my boss, Chestikov, about the Tuesday symposium with the American women." She stopped. "I'll tell you another time."

"Tell me now. It'll take my mind off everything. Are the Americans exploited by their capitalist bosses?"

"Some are the bosses. And they seem happy." Olga heard the wonder in her own voice as she uttered the words. "And they are not even aware of it. They think they know how good things are for them, but they can't really, because they have no idea how bad things can be."

Vera shook her head and groaned. "No Russian woman is happy."

"Aren't we sometimes happy in very small ways? We find fresh mushrooms in the forest and we're happy. We see a friend, and we're happy. A young woman buys a pair of jeans, and for three years she can be happy just looking at them. But it's true: We're not life happy."

Vera lay silent for a short while. "It hurt so much. You know important people. Can you find a doctor?"

Olga cradled her friend's hand. "As soon as morning comes, I'll get someone I know. She doesn't have a phone." There was no question of taking Vera to a hospital. With no personal connections, she would be denied treatment.

"They came on payday and confiscated the payroll." Vera's lips were dry and cracked. "Just stole all our cash."

"You don't have to talk now."

"I want to, in case I die."

Olga touched Vera's lips with a water-soaked sponge. "You will not die; it may just feel like it now." Nevertheless, she knew that without antibiotics, infection of the exposed flesh might get into Vera's bloodstream and brain.

"They knew exactly how much money we had withdrawn, as if they had a direct phone line to the bank."

"They probably do." Olga dipped the sponge into the bowl of water and mopped her friend's forehead. "Shhhh. Try to get some sleep."

"I'm scared." Vera wept. "I can't keep up with their 'protection.' They want us to produce weird, useless stuff: Pots with no handles. Who can cook in them? They've dropped papers at the office, pressing me to turn the Cooperative of Metal Works over to them."

"Bad times are not forever. Russia will be a great country again. Just be strong." Olga caressed her friend's chopped hair. Russia had been a nation of decent people, of desperate people who, like the proverbial cows cursed with short horns, had long ceased to cope. Olga knew she had reached a decision. In her role as deputy director of the Institute for Social Research, she had the cover. But she lacked capitalistic savvy to untangle the complicated schemes that were destroying their new Russia. She must ask Brooke for help. "I'll try to find out exactly who's behind this." She patted Vera's forearm.

Vera touched her chopped hair, then quickly withdrew her hand. "Sure. You'll take on the mafia gangs, the corrupt bankers, and the police—all at the same time."

"Not 'take on.' Only learn the identity of the enemy. Knowledge is power."

A convulsion shook Vera's body. She groaned. "Before you can do anything with the knowledge, you'll be dead."

"You cannot die before your death," Olga quoted. Yes, she could die for a better Russia for her granddaughter, and it would be worth it.

Brooke entered the dining room, waved to the women at the breakfast table, and stopped by Aleksandr, who was speaking with a waiter. Although he had clearly seen her, he was in no hurry to give her his attention. She waited patiently until finally the waiter walked away, and Aleksandr turned to her.

"There's no English-speaking channel on TV, and the radio in the room is AM, in Russian." She smiled. "We need access to the news. Amanda said you'd bring the English newspaper."

Aleksandr shook his head. "Too dangerous to go downtown."

"How dangerous? What's the news about the standoff in the parliament?"

"It's getting better."

"But it's dangerous, you've just said." Brooke tried to hold his watery gaze. "Can you give me more details?"

He consulted a folded Russian newspaper and translated as

he read, his voice robotic. "The Russian Orthodox Church mediated, and the parties have reached an agreement. Electricity, heating, and telephone services will be restored to the parliament building."

"Sounds like a government press release. Where can we find a source for inside views? Actual opinions and analysis?"

He shrugged and turned to the group table.

"Look, Aleksandr," Brooke said, trying to control her annoyance. "There's a serious military confrontation going on. We may be caught up in it. We need information."

"I must collect the cost of breakfast." He played with the zipper of his leather jacket, then announced to the women at the table, "Seven dollars each."

"Just charge it to the room." Amanda waved her hand. Attired in a red suit for the first conference, she looked radiant.

"You pay when you eat," Aleksandr said.

Brooke sat down and eyed the sample of a salted fish, one-sixth of a hard-boiled egg swimming in mayonnaise, and four peas circling something lost inside fried batter. It was her mother's kind of cooking, and Brooke would have liked it if it weren't too heavy for this time of day. "Can we at least order what we want to eat?" she asked Aleksandr.

"The hotel economist has directives for the portions of the food, but EuroTours negotiated a very good deal for your group." He pointed at the prepared plates. For the first time since Brooke had met him, he sounded enthusiastic. "In each *zakuska* you get three pieces of cucumber instead of two. You see? And the compote has plums, apples, *and* apricots. It's planned for lunch, but we got it for your breakfast. And the kitchen is frying eggs for you. A whole one for each—no sharing. And real butter. You see? Fresh. It's included in the price."

"We appreciate it," Brooke said, giving up. Her mother, too, revered butter. She could never bring herself to share that particular wartime-rare commodity with strangers. The few times Brooke's friends ate over she had served margarine instead.

Brooke stabbed her fork into a slice of cucumber. When she looked up, she saw Svetlana standing behind Aleksandr and listening as he argued with Amanda. Other than a large red crescent below her eye, no residue of the previous afternoon marred her jaw. Her blue suit had been repaired and pressed, and her hair coiffed and sprayed back into full obedience. Brooke couldn't help but admire the young woman's fortitude. She motioned to the chair beside her, and Svetlana sat down.

"How are you feeling?" Brooke touched the back of Svetlana's hand.

Instead of spreading her cloth napkin, Svetlana's fingers wrung it. "You'll eat everything, yes? It takes six years of training to become a chef. It would be disrespectful to him if you don't eat."

"Okay." Feeling queasy, Brooke scooped a fried pea. She couldn't help recalling doing the same throughout her childhood, eating to satisfy someone else's need.

Forcing down the pea, she racked her brain about whom she could ask about a better hotel. Amanda's idea of staying in a Russian hotel to narrow the perception of the socioeconomic gap between the Americans and the factory managers they came to counsel had been a good idea in theory, but reality proved far less enchanting. When Brooke had mentioned it again that morning, Amanda had been too busy with the coming day's issues to tackle another problem, and asked Brooke to be a good sport and bear it for now. Doggedly, Brooke had checked the phone booth in the lobby, although she couldn't have read a directory if she had found one. Using hand gestures with the nearest sentry, she learned that Moscow had no phone directory. Hoffenbach had stayed at the luxurious Kempinski Hotel, which she was certain group members employed by nonprofit organizations, including Amanda, could ill afford. "Svetlana, do you know of another hotel, a bit better, but not too fancy?"

"This is the first hotel I've seen from the inside. Maybe ask Aleksandr?"

Brooke gave out a thin smile. Aleksandr and EuroTours had selected this Soviet-style dump. Judd, who seemed familiar with Moscow, last night had brushed off the idea of finding another hotel as not being simple. Why would finding a good hotel in Moscow be such an insurmountable task? When she saw Judd again, she'd probe further.

Sipping tea—the alternative, coffee, had the same transparency—Brooke felt Svetlana watching her. She turned her head and saw the Russian's eyes glued to the Star of David.

Brooke smiled at her. "Like the cross you have," she said, indicating the thin gold chain on Svetlana's neck.

"You're a Jewess?"

"Jewish. Yes." Brooke's hand swept the group at the table. "Some of us here are Jews." She smiled again, disliking the disapproving look in Svetlana's eyes. "Is there a problem?"

Svetlana's diagonal gesture with her head, a cross between a nod and a negative shake, was her answer. Brooke let it slide, but resisted the urge to hide the necklace.

Aleksandr took out a leather-bound notepad and chewed on a pencil, calculating. "I take your order for dinner now," he told the group.

"You mean lunch?" Amanda flipped her sheet of dark hair. "We'll be at the conference."

"Dinner. At seven o'clock. But you order and pay now."

Amanda pushed her chair back from the table and stood up. "We need to talk." She strode away. He followed.

Svetlana poured herself coffee, then squeezed in a slice of lemon. "Very Russian. Want to taste it?" She offered her cup.

"Not right now. Thanks."

Svetlana shrugged. "American women exercise every day, right?"

Brooke laughed. "Hardly."

"No, it's true. I read it in magazines." Svetlana nodded her head for emphasis. "Western women know how to lose weight, know how to get rid of a bad man. They dance in a club every night, they dine out all the time, they have time to read books and even to sit in the sun."

"Maybe one of those things or the other. Not everything." Brooke poked at her food. "I work long days, late into the evening."

"Don't you earn enough to work less?"

"My job requires me to put in many hours and travel overseas. If I wanted to work fewer hours, I'd have to find another profession."

"Then you must be very unhappy." Svetlana's eyes traveled

down from Brooke's face to her aubergine-colored skirt-suit, lingered on the flower-studded brooch, then continued down to Brooke's black pumps. She grinned shyly. "You're a very elegant Jewess. Very feminine, even if they force you to work hard—"

"No one's forcing me. I enjoy what I do; it gives me satisfaction. It might have been different if I had a husband and children. But in my free time, I try to do one of the things you mentioned— take a walk, go out to dinner with a friend, or read a book."

"You go dancing?"

"Sometimes at weddings. Do you like dancing?"

"Not possible here." Svetlana shook her head from side to side. "Here what matters is having enough food to eat and finding a good pair of boots for winter."

Brooke picked up her fork again.

"My neighbor is Jewish," Svetlana ventured. "But a good woman. She's a doctor. Her daughter—I like her a lot—can't get into university because she's Jewish."

"I'm sorry to hear that," Brooke replied, understanding Svetlana's offering of an olive branch, yet making another faux pas.

Amanda returned to the table from her chat with Aleksandr and sat down. Her lips were tight.

Svetlana leaned toward her. "Order them to finish their meal. Nikolai Sidorov's feelings as a host will be hurt if they don't."

"Sidorov?" Brooke tossed a glance at Amanda. "An economic adviser to President Yeltsin will find out that I left two peas on my plate? How?"

"In the report the chef submits." Svetlana looked at Amanda. "Surely the group must obey its leader."

"I can't order them to eat," Amanda said.

"We're not used to eating so much in the morning." Brooke kept her tone conciliatory.

"You eat porridge? Or maybe tomorrow Aleksandr will order you kasha in cream?"

"No, thanks. Really." Brooke put down her fork. "Tell me about yourself. You studied to be a translator, you said."

"English and German. But I never spoke with an American before. This past year I sometimes saw American men in the street. Never a woman. All my life I was told you're our enemy, but now we meet, and you're so nice."

Maybe Svetlana would realize at the same time that Jews, too, were nice. Brooke smiled. "I enjoy meeting you all." At her elementary school, only the country or the regime had been presented as enemies, not individual Russians. "How did you improve your conversational English without ever meeting foreigners?" she asked. "You're incredibly talented."

Svetlana blushed. "I listen to Radio Free Europe, repeat the words, and write down in a notebook all the new idioms. Russians always fantasize about traveling. I collect tea bags from all over the world. Sometimes only the wrappings, because they have little pictures of the places they come from."

"I have some tea bags, but they're not that fancy."

"I'd like a novel, if you've brought any—" Svetlana stopped as a young Russian man wearing a blue-and-white Dodgers jacket sauntered into the room. Given his neat, cropped light brown hair and pleasant features, Brooke assumed he was a hotel staffer about to get into his uniform. She registered a waiter elbowing one of his colleague, gesturing with his head as the new arrival circled the group, intently scrutinizing the women.

His second circle, though, was tighter, like a tiger closing on its prey. When he leaned on the back of Amanda's chair in a possessive gesture, a siren wailed in Brooke's head. Amanda, bending forward and talking, her silver bangles jingling, appeared unaware of his nearness behind her. "Amanda," Brooke called out.

At that instant, the man lunged forward and grabbed Amanda's arm.

Amanda jumped to her feet, knocking over her chair. "Let go of me!" she shouted.

He stood still. He didn't reach for her satchel that now lay at his feet, nor did he try to wrestle her. He stood completely still, his gaze fixed on her face. His composed expression didn't even look insane.

In the midst of women yelping with surprise, utensils dropping on china plates, glasses rolling off the table and crashing on the floor, and chairs tumbling backward, Brooke bolted out of her seat. She sprinted toward Amanda. To her horror, as if in slow motion, the man's other hand reached toward her friend's fingers. "Stop!" Brooke yelled, afraid he'd break them.

But then, with the gentlest touch, the man caressed Amanda's fingers. The expression on his face turned to awe.

Brooke seized his arm and yanked. His muscles felt as hard as iron. "Do something," she called to the waiters, who were watching the scene like spectators at a vodka-drinking contest. "Get the guards!" she yelled to Svetlana.

"It's not their job," Svetlana replied in a voice that sounded as if it came from far away.

"Well, get someone! Now!" Brooke repeated, still trying—and failing—to drag the man away.

Out of nowhere, the tip of a shoe hit the Russian's wrist close to Amanda's arm, and in a split second Judd flipped the Russian over onto his back. Rising on his elbows to a half-sitting position, the Russian scuttled backward, staring at Judd with fear. He tossed one last look at Amanda, then scrambled to his feet and disappeared into the darkness of the corridor. Judd did not pursue him.

"Jesus!" Amanda collapsed into a chair and rubbed her arm.

"What in the world was that all about? And what's the matter with the staff here?" Brooke picked up a chair to move it out of the way and glowered at the waiters who still lounged against the doorframe. "I guess it's not in their unionized employment description to help." She looked at Judd. His face revealed nothing. "Nice job."

His nod was imperceptible. He smiled and walked in the direction of the washroom.

"What was that guy trying to do?" Bewilderment etched Amanda's face. "He didn't go for my money or my bracelets."

Jenny came close, her delighted smile framed by a red bow on top of her hair and a pair of saucer-size earrings. "He only wanted to touch you," she chirped. "I knew it! Russian men are obsessed with American women. Wow, Amanda. You'll feed his sexual fantasies for a long time."

"This is ridiculous." Brooke picked up another overturned chair and sat down.

"Amanda's Asian look adds a dash of the exotic." Jenny cocked her head toward the corridor. "He *was* cute."

"He *attacked* Amanda," Brooke said pointedly. "There's nothing cute about it."

Amanda took a sip of coffee. She closed her eyes in what Brooke thought was a moment of recapturing her serenity.

Svetlana returned alone, biting a nail. "The security guards are in charge only of allowing guests into the building, not handling problems."

Brooke tossed her hair back. "Well, they allowed this one problem in." Noticing that Amanda had opened her eyes, Brooke whispered to her, "Didn't you pay them to look out for our safety?"

"Mostly not to hassle us, or they'd check us every time we cross the lobby."

"What was that talk you had with Aleksandr?" Brooke asked. "Are we switching hotels?"

Amanda sipped more coffee. "He'll check things out with his boss."

"Do you mean we need someone's approval as to where we stay?"

Amanda shook her head.

"Well, who's in charge of firing Aleksandr? He's been totally incompetent."

"He works for EuroTours, not for me." Amanda rotated her wrist in full circles. "He means well. In the Soviet tradition, he believes he's protecting us from unpleasant information."

Brooke examined the red mark on Amanda's arm. "Can you just tell me how we go about getting security, and I'll take care of it?"

Amanda let out a little chuckle. "I've never known you to lose your cool like this."

"If you had been alone, that guy would have raped you."

"But it didn't happen, right? So please calm down and let me go on with what will be a very busy day."

Brooke shut her mouth. Amanda was an idealist who waltzed through life sprinkling the world with her do-good dust. Brooke would have to look into matters herself.

The maitre d' appeared in the doorway of the kitchen, wiping his palms on the sides of his jacket. He peered around the dining room with a scowl on his face and mumbled something to the waiters, who sniggered and disappeared into the kitchen. A few minutes later, they reappeared with fresh plates of food. Brooke wondered how, given the economist's tight rationing, they had these extra plates ready.

Judd reentered the dining hall. His hair was damp and patted down. His tailored blue suit caused Brooke to wonder how she had missed noticing him back when he presented at her firm. He walked straight toward the now-vacant seat on Brooke's other side and grinned. "How are we this morning?"

Conscious of Amanda's presence, Brooke asked in an even voice, "Is there another hotel you'd recommend?"

"Not at twenty-five dollars a night. Any European hotel in Moscow costs three hundred or more. There's nothing in between."

Amanda broke in. "I checked on my scouting trip in July." Her hand swept to encompass the other women. "There's no way we can shell out almost three grand each for a nine-day visit."

How much did it cost not to get raped in this hotel? Brooke watched the two women who had decided to leave after yesterday's attack as they gathered their travel bags, said their good-byes, and walked out with Aleksandr. Their departure played havoc with Amanda's conference plans, and Brooke hadn't wanted to disappoint her friend by leaving too. But perhaps she should. Maybe tomorrow.

Yes. If she was unable to get an informed escort and a body-guard, that would be the wisest move. She wanted to ask Judd about that, too, but with Amanda at her side, she didn't want to sound like a pest.

"Have you tried the kefir?" Judd asked Brooke. "It's made of goat's milk rather than cow's. It's quite light and tasty."

"Do they serve it at ninja school?"

He smiled, and she reached for the glass of what looked like thick milk.

"Judd, yogurt will keep you vigorous," Jenny chirped from diagonally across the table.

He didn't even acknowledge the comment.

Jenny pushed her plate aside and leaned forward, breasts rest-ing on the table, causing her cleavage to rise. Her grin revealed a string of tiny teeth like a pearl necklace. "You doubly need it if you're married."

"Jenny, pipe down." Amanda frowned.

Married? It hadn't occurred to Brooke to fish for that infor-mation. So much for her new admirer. Of course, as Jenny did, she should have assumed any man in her age bracket was mar-ried. This breakfast was turning into a soap opera.

Brooke rose and pushed herself from the table. "I'll meet you all in the lobby in fifteen minutes."

ENTERING THE BUS, she breezed down the aisle, passing Judd in the front seat she had occupied the day before. Jenny could have him.

She settled toward the back, and on the empty seat next to her she placed a bag Amanda had entrusted to her. Filled with vials of leftover prescription drugs the group had brought from their medicine cabinets at home, it carried antibiotics, cortisone cream, and cough medicine—all rare commodities in Moscow, her friend had explained, and nonexistent elsewhere. Brooke had also bought dozens of vials of ibuprofen and aspirin, which, Amanda said, the average Russian had no access to.

Aleksandr settled across the aisle. Brooke took out her map of Moscow and motioned to him to look at it. As he bent over the map, looking perplexed, she grilled him until she figured out where they were heading and the travel route there. She wished the driver would not bypass the center of town so she could see what was going on with the showdown between the parliament and Yeltsin from the safety of the bus. Later, after her Frankfurt office opened, she would call Hoffenbach and get the names of his colleagues here. Any contact might come in handy. And when Sidorov finally showed up at the conference today, she would speak with him directly rather than rely on Amanda's, Svetlana's, or Aleksandr's mediation.

At one intersection, *Hustler* and cheap porno magazines, wrapped in cellophane and held in place by clothespins, hung on a rope stretched in front of a kiosk. Brooke averted her eyes, but visualized the photographer's studio: a basement shop with a stage set of a bedroom framed by drop cloths. Were the women who posed exploited or did they freely sell the commodity of beauty they had been blessed to possess?

"I was in America last summer with my wife and daughter. Miami," Aleksandr interrupted her thoughts. From his leather case, he produced a small album with snapshots of supermarket aisles and close-ups of price stickers with dollar signs. "The food displays—they were the best thing." He sighed.

Brooke tilted her head toward Aleksandr, giving him her full attention. "Did you like the beaches?"

"Everyone drives a fancy car," he said, and continued to flip through more photos of supermarket aisles. When he replaced the album in his folder, he said, "I have a Zhiguli car and a dacha, that's a country home, yes? If I get gasoline I drive my family out for the weekend."

"You can't always get gasoline?"

"Two days on line."

"You sleep in the car at night while waiting in the queue?"

"I pay someone to move the car along the line, then come back when it's my turn. For the trip to the United States, I was in line at the bank for six months to buy American dollars. First I came once a month, then once a week, then twice a day—two hours in the morning and two in the afternoon, yes? You have to be there when they call your name or you lose your spot."

Brooke took a moment to digest the information. "Right this moment, are you on line at the gas station for the weekend?"

He looked at his watch, a brushed aluminum Rolex—or a good knock-off. "Since five o'clock this morning."

Brooke wished he had invested a fraction of this effort to buy them the English-language newspaper. As the bus rumbled on, she kept her eyes toward the window, watching the lumbering pedestrians, overdressed in coats too heavy even for the morning chill. On street corners, soldiers with Kalashnikovs strapped across their chests puffed on cigarettes.

This was not the face of democracy. She lowered the grimy window pane and clicked her camera. As she captured images of soldiers stopping pedestrians to check their papers, she became conscious that she was photographing her parents' prewar experiences, when they could taste the threat hanging in the air. Her mother's sister, Bertha, was no longer around; she had died in a pogrom a decade earlier while she and Brooke's mother tried to hide in a large oak tree. Bertha lost her footing on the first branch and fell, and Brooke's mother watched helplessly from the thickness above as her sister was raped by five local men they had known all their lives. When the men were done, they beat Bertha to death. After that, the family fled to Riga, but that, too, wasn't far enough.

Brooke could smell that Russia was on the brink of a civil war. She should tear herself from her promises and leave.

## ❧ CHAPTER ❧

## *Thirteen*

D RIVING TO HER office, Olga was raging about Vera's torture when, two miles from the Institute for Social Research, her "tin-can on wheels" Lada was rear-ended by
a massive Volga. Olga's head whipped backward, but her hands
gripped the steering wheel and steadied the car before it could
skid into a ditch. The male Volga driver passed her, shouting and
giving her the finger. By the time she'd rolled down her window
to shout back, he was gone, leaving her seething. One more man
who believed that women had no business on the road.

She revved the engine and pulled once again into the traffic.
She'd be damned if she let anyone take away her freedom to move
about; she had worked hard for decades to reach the administrative ranking that entitled her to a government car.

At her office, she hung her coat in the armoire, rubbed her sore
neck, and plugged in her samovar. The muted buzz of gossip and
unanswered ringing phones droned in the background. As in all
Soviet institutions, most employees considered their jobs *sidyet,*

sitting at one's chair without being productive. Olga locked her door, then sat down at her desk with a cup of fragrant tea.

As deputy director of the institute she was granted a spacious office, larger than her apartment and converted from two rooms whose triple doors had been removed. Her furniture was a mismatched collection: her boss's former wooden desk and a pair of swivel guest chairs, worn but comfortable, sat in front of three bookcases—one made of teak, the others of metal—all filled with ring binders, boxed research material, and volumes of academic reviews. In the adjacent room, two upholstered armchairs covered with woven colorful quilts and a coffee table with an imitation lace tablecloth created a cozy seating area.

Olga flipped through new reports in her in-box: A recent survey found that 75 percent of schoolgirls aspired to become prostitutes, while a second survey found no basis in fact to support these figures. Another stated that the average life expectancy of the Russian male had dropped, yet again, to fifty-seven years, due to heavy alcohol use. After arranging the material for later reflection, she unlocked her desk drawer and pulled out a file containing newspaper clippings detailing stories of the intimidation of businesses and of violence against bank employees.

The terrorizing of women's enterprises was a police matter, no doubt, but there was also no question that the police were in on it. Olga lit a Dukat and leaned back, staring at a two-page news photo spread. Some crime syndicates had become so smug that photographs of their leaders, "The New Capitalists," who were the privileged courtiers of Czar Boris Yeltsin, made headlines. These mafia dons were shown attending the ballet and the opera, often with beautiful young women—most likely not their wives—hanging on their arms.

Olga sucked on her cigarette. Brooke had thought each violent intimidation was initiated by someone who stood to profit from the acquisition of a particular factory. It made sense. Could it be the same one person with an umbrella operation?

"Democracy or Kleptocracy?" Olga scribbled the heading of the report she would produce once she had gathered the facts. She looked at the title as pain contracted her abdomen and her nostrils recalled Vera's singed skin. The doctor Olga had fetched at dawn told them that she had seen worse mafia tortures.

Olga balled the title page of her report and set it on fire in her oversize ashtray. There would be time to put it all in writing. Letting out smoke, she stared up at the milky-yellow ceiling, where the paint had chipped to form an octopus, its tentacles spread out in all directions. Investigating this problem was overwhelming. Brooke's idea was to follow the money, but for that, Olga needed access to documents.

Should she start by driving to the agency that registered business ownerships? The bureaucratic maze would be too complicated to get straight answers—and certainly not on the spot. No "public records" were open to the public. She could use her contacts to reach someone high up, but everyone was either on the take or on the make. Her initiative would be reported immediately to whoever didn't wish the information revealed.

There was only one place to start: the original forms to transfer ownership, which Vera had refused to sign. They were at Vera's office in Metal Works 456.

Olga ground out her cigarette, unplugged the samovar,

and grabbed her coat and wool scarf. Walking down the corridor, she almost collided with a teacart rounding the corner. The two-tiered silver tray on it indicated that her boss, Arkady Ilyich Chestikov, again expected visitors, and lunch had been sent from Chez Philippe, the first French restaurant just opened in Moscow. The son of an *apparatchik,* a high-ranking party member, Arkady was the director of the institute, although he had no academic or scientific qualifications. Since Olga had not been invited to his luncheon, the visitors' business must be unrelated to the institute's core social research issues. Her boss was up to no good.

"Dr. Rozanova!" Arkady's secretary motioned to her with long, crimson-colored nails. The young woman, decked out in a red leather bodysuit, her black-rimmed glasses tucked into scrunched blond curls, flicked a mascaraed glance at the key ring dangling from Olga's index finger. "Arkady Ilyich wants to see you."

Olga suppressed a sigh and stepped in.

The oak paneling was new. The executive green leather chair seemed to give the diminutive Arkady added height. His huge mouth on his small face, his eyes set far apart, and his bald forehead slanting backward made him look like a toad perched on a lily pad.

"Arkady Ilyich, are you sitting on the holy Bible again?"

He laughed but did not remove the book as he had done before, showing her a new level of disrespect. Olga settled into the plush guest chair. From the adjoining seating room came the clinking sounds of dishes being set for lunch. The buttery, smooth aroma of chicken Kiev made her mouth water.

"You've met the Americans?" Arkady asked.

"Yes."

"A bunch of dykes, I'm sure. Our women have enough problems without corrupting their brains with new ideas."

"Women make up eighty percent of our unemployed. They're starting businesses in order to survive. Female entrepreneurship is the hottest trend in Western economies," Olga retorted. What was really on her boss's mind?

The secretary returned, teetering on stiletto heels and carrying a sterling silver teapot. She placed a plate of little almond cakes and a silver pot of marmalade in front of Olga and poured a cup of jasmine tea. Olga watched with growing suspicion as the young woman heaped four spoonfuls of white, sparkling sugar into the china cup.

"For your Tuesday symposium with the Americans, here's a list of people who should address the audience." Arkady handed her a typed sheet.

"Now you're bringing this up? The program was set weeks ago." Olga put down her cup and glanced at the dozen names on the page, drumming her fingers. "These bureaucrats have no working knowledge of modern market economy, which is the whole point of this symposium."

Arkady puffed up his chest. "Fit them in." He picked up a letter and held it between his stubby thumb and forefinger. The cuffs of his white dress shirt sported hand-embroidered initials. "We have an invitation to participate in the International Convention on Social Changes in Tokyo."

So, this was his agenda for the impromptu meeting. Yet again, he wanted to hijack her place on a trip abroad. Olga stopped drumming her fingers and closed them into a fist. She sat back, but couldn't control the frustration that erupted in a groan. She had so anticipated going to Tokyo. She needed the exchange of knowledge with like-minded fellow professionals, to gain new insights into research methods and up-to-date issues in capitalistic economies.

"You're not a scientist," she said, suppressing the tone of her fury. "In the past two years you went to the conferences in Paris and Buenos Aires that *I* was invited to—"

"Just prepare the reports, surveys, what have you," Arkady cut her off. "I'll read them aloud."

"You won't be able to field questions from the audience." Her anger soared like a swarm of bees. Had nothing changed? Would idiot bureaucrats continue forever to represent Russia in such international forums? For decades, their ignorance had been the butt of jokes of the foreign academics. She rose to her feet. "Since I have no say about anything, I might as well get on my way."

"Please hand over the keys to your Zhiguli. We need to use it for institute affairs."

She gasped. She might as well have been hit by a train. "You can't do that! You've already taken my shopping privileges and my vacation allowance." She stopped before she said, *and have redistributed them to some of your party bigwigs.* Nevertheless, as the saying went, "Those who lived among wolves must learn to howl like wolves." She steadied her voice, but let it cut like a razor. "Arkady Ilyich, in my position at the institute—and my seniority as a government employee—I am entitled to these perks. They are not yours to terminate."

"Olga Leonidovna, if you don't watch yourself you'll end up

sweeping the streets for a living. These days Ph.D.s are exchanging their pens for mops and their podiums for pails."

Her mouth went dry. "And who will turn out important scientific data that gives this institute its prestige?"

He sipped his tea. "You know about Yeltsin's new directive. There are plenty of qualified unemployed *male* sociologists waiting for an opportunity."

Olga drew in her breath as a new, unfamiliar fear joined her pent-up frustration. Never before had Arkady's treatment of her been so dismissive. For fifteen years he "had ridden in her sleigh, joining in her song," as the saying went.

He extended his hand. "The keys."

Since everything left in the car could be stolen, she kept only one cigarette and matches in the glove compartment. She tossed the keys on the desk as tears gathered in her throat. The loss of this hard-won perk resonated in every fiber of her body. Wordlessly, she stuffed Arkady's list of speakers into her bag and walked out.

He would learn his lesson soon enough when she published her "Democracy or Kleptocracy?" paper. With the exposure of what surely would point an accusing finger at his party's cronies, they would take away more from him than just the keys to his car.

# *Fourteen*

THE GRANDIOSE CONFERENCE facility must have been converted from a czar-era mansion. Brooke and the other nine American women followed Svetlana up a flight of broad steps flanked by Corinthian columns into a baroque-style ballroom turned lecture hall.

"Ready to show them how to become capitalists?" Amanda whispered.

Brooke squeezed her elbow, relieved that the tension between them had thawed.

With the group's entrance, a wave of excitement spread through the crowd. Brooke took in the bright eyes scrutinizing them and realized that simply by the confidence she and her colleagues projected, they were instant role models.

Svetlana, her own status elevated by the Americans' importance, beamed throughout first the introductions of local executives Amanda had invited from Kodak, Estée Lauder, and Adidas and then the welcome speeches by representatives of women's organizations.

"With the new world order, a woman's voice will no longer be a lonely violin but part of an orchestra made up of all the women of the world," began one of the well-wishers. Brooke snapped photographs of the attendees' rapturous faces.

Jenny stood up. "Attitude is everything," she cut in, in an impromptu response speech. She pointed at the collar necklace she wore, a beautifully studded strip with beads and rhinestones. "I manufacture these dog collars in Kenya. Three thousand pet stores and major chains in America already sell them. I will tell you how you can use your artistic talent to manufacture products you can export to America. The important thing to remember is that your work must be of high quality. I see around me a lot of shitty stuff that can't be sold." She turned to the interpreter. "Make sure you tell them 'shitty,' because if they don't face this fact they are wasting their time."

Amanda and the Russians continued with more eloquent speeches, and then the crowd rose amid a clutter of chairs scraping the floor. Brooke noticed that quite a few women accepted Jenny's "Attitude Is Everything" buttons and followed her into a classroom.

Brooke stepped into the adjacent room to conduct her two-hour marketing workshop. There was business-to-business marketing and there was business-to-consumer marketing, she explained, and drew a vertical line on the blackboard. She asked each attendee to describe her venture in two sentences, then asked the interpreter to enter them in Russian in either of two columns. "Now write down each of the features of your product or service, and the benefit attached to this particular feature," she said, raising a pen. "For example, the feature of this pen is that it has a rubber cushion near its tip. The benefit of this particular feature is the easy grip when writing."

She then elicited from the attendees a list of advertising and promotional options, adding ones they hadn't considered, such as creating brochures and postcards. The attendees chuckled at the idea of mailing out anything. One raised her hand. "Nobody does that here," she said.

"Of course nobody has done that—because you've had no history of selling practices," Brooke said. Furtive back-alley commerce didn't count. "Good marketing is also about originality. Being the first in your industry or community to do something gives you an advantage. Success lies with innovation, with coming up with fresh ways of approaching consumers."

"It's embarrassing to ask for business," said an attendee. "It's like begging."

"It's no different from when you apply for a job. You point out your relevant attributes, because you are the product you're promoting." As soon as she said that, Brooke realized that most likely, none of these women had gone out on job interviews; each had been assigned a position by some central office, sight unseen. Searching for a more uplifting idea, she thought of the ease with which Amanda had been able to place phone calls from their room. "We haven't even discussed selling by telephone. Your phone service is one thing here that I've noticed works well. Take advantage of it. We call it telemarketing."

There was silence.

"What have I missed?" she asked the interpreter.

"The phones work well only because the government needs to eavesdrop," the woman whispered.

"Well, the government agents can listen in on your sales pitches. They'll be so convinced they'll become customers, too," Brooke replied.

More silent stares. But there was no time to dwell on the point; there was a lot more to cover, starting with marketing strategy. Some products, such as bread, had a frequent, repeated need, and therefore could take a small profit on each of many transactions; other products, such as a sofa, had a rare need and therefore required a higher profit margin on each sale.

Encouraged by the revived interest of her audience, Brooke warmed up again. "After you figure out the strategy best suited for your product or service, write down the promotion ideas that are most likely to reach your target market. This will be the draft of your campaign plan. But before launching it, why don't you check with each other whether you've covered your bases? Meet or call each other to discuss your projects, share your ideas."

The chill that swept away the energy in the room felt as if a Siberian breeze had blown though. "We are all strangers here," a woman who ran a language school said in English.

"We call it networking," Brooke clarified. "You all live in different cities, right? You offer different products and services, and so you are not competing with one another for the same customers." When she saw heads nodding, she went on, "Networking creates support groups among a range of business owners." She pointed at two women, one who ran a ladder factory, and another who manufactured chairs, in cities six hundred miles apart. "Each of you may learn something new that works well and you can share with each other."

"You want me to tell my secrets to a stranger?" asked Ladders.

"Why would I help someone I've never met?" asked Chairs.

"Both of you end up with more information when you exchange experiences. Let's say you've found a good printer for your brochure. You share the source with the other person in your network. She, in turn, may have found a source for lumber she can't use—"

"We give the printer more work, and he will only raise the price. And if she buys more from the lumberyard, they may stop stocking the lumber I need," Ladders said. "I wouldn't even tell my own sister a business secret unless she pays me for the information."

Brooke realized that in a city that had never published a phone book, one's Rolodex equivalent had become a cherished commodity. It meant survival in a country where merely knowing where a product suddenly appeared in a store was a secret to be sold. Under a regime that glorified children turning in their parents to the authorities, Russians had been conditioned into deep distrust. They were unprepared for a world that held random kindness in high regard. They had become adept at navigating the system without ever negotiating between individuals.

Brooke wished she had more time to run exercises. But her two hours—cut in half by pauses for the translation of each paragraph she uttered—were over. "In time you will see that cooperation is the route for strength," she said to the room as it was emptying.

Nevertheless, she told herself, the women had learned a lot. She glanced at her watch and walked out to the main hall. She asked two of the organizers about Sidorov, but no one had seen him. One gestured to show that Sidorov might be eating; perhaps their host would join them all at lunch. Brooke glanced at her watch. She had planned to contact EuroTours, the American Embassy, and her Frankfurt office; she must reach them before they all closed for the weekend, just in case she didn't get to see Sidorov.

In search of a phone, Brooke walked into the administration office at the end of the corridor. Boxes of printed conference materials surrounded three secretaries. On a table were some of the various prescription drugs the Americans had brought. Three women were arguing over a bottle.

"May I use your phone?" Brooke asked the nearest secretary. "*Telephone?*"

"*Nyet* telephone."

Brooke glanced at the desks. There were no phones.

In a show of goodwill, one secretary called over an interpreter. "The planning of this district did not include telephone cables," the interpreter explained. "Now, anyone who wants a telephone buys a very long pole, puts it up, imports a cable, strings to the next district and finds someone to import the instrument from abroad. Then maybe the phone company will hook it up and give it a number."

"What about a pay phone? On the street?"

"I'll take you to the next district. I saw people lined up at a pay phone there." The secretary waved in some direction.

"*Spasiba*. Thanks." If she was lucky, Brooke might also stumble upon a kiosk selling an English newspaper. She put on her coat and followed the woman outside.

They had barely made it past the conference building when two gleaming Rolls-Royces sped toward them, sirens screaming and lights flashing. The cars were followed by BMWs and open Jeeps filled with muscular, armed guards.

The secretary pulled Brooke into a nook between two baroque pillars. "*Mafia.*" She shook her head in what looked like a cross between sorrow and wonder, and pointed to a peach-colored, twelve-foot-high wall across the street with barbed-wire twisted across its top. A wired telephone pole peeked over the wall.

At the nearest street junction, two policemen stopped traffic and directed all vehicles to the curb so the convoy could pass through. A minute later, an electric gate opened in the wall across the street, and tires screeching, the fleet disappeared inside. Six gunmen with cropped hair, wearing dark suits and ties, sprinted out of the last Jeep and took their posts outside the compound, automatic weapons at the ready.

"*Krysha,*" the secretary remarked.

Brooke pressed her back against the pillar, her hands clasped tight. In Hoffenbach's report, which she had believed to be an exaggeration, he had highlighted *krysha,* the private-security units that had taken over police duties. If their firm were to do business here, Hoffenbach had written, they'd need to hire trained gunmen.

The guards' eyes scanned the tops of the buildings around them, their guns pointing at one rooftop, then another. Two of them strode away, muttering into walkie-talkies and peering into doorways. One of the men looked at Brooke and the secretary.

Brooke flinched. Again, she had separated from the group, made herself vulnerable. She should have asked Judd for help this morning in spite of Amanda's request that she cool down.

Now, rather than try to find a phone—where the waiting line could be hours long—she should just go to the embassy.

"Taxi?" she asked the secretary.

The woman waved to the policeman in the corner, and he flagged down a passenger car. The driver made a quick U-turn and came to a stop. He rolled down the window and inspected Brooke from the bottom up, stopping at her chest.

"*Nyet taxi?*" Brooke asked the secretary.

"*Nyet taxi,*" the secretary repeated. "*Auto.*"

Brooke bit her lip. The secretary would return to her office, and Brooke would be stuck in a private car with a man whose scrutiny made her skin prickle, in a city whose street signs she couldn't read.

"American Embassy?" she asked the man.

He nodded vigorously.

Dare she get in the car, having no sense of direction or knowledge where in this vast city the embassy was located? "Hot dog stand?" she asked him. "Hot. Dog. Stand?"

He nodded again.

So he had no idea where she wanted to go. Where would he be taking her? No more risks. With regret, Brooke waved her finger in a gesture of no. What she had believed to be a temporary situation—Hotel Moscow and no bodyguards—would become permanent, at least for the weekend. And Aleksandr would continue to be ineffective, due either to ineptness or to his false assumption that he was protecting them.

Well, she'd speak to Sidorov himself at lunch. "Let's get back in," Brooke said to the secretary, and started toward to building.

I THOUGHT SIDOROV WOULD be here." Brooke gestured with
her chin toward the head lunch table. She was even prepared
to down a glass of vodka with him just to get him to cooperate with her.

"He's not here," Svetlana replied.

"When will we meet him?"

"Aleksandr knows. He's in charge of the itinerary. Today I'm
only an interpreter."

Aleksandr, who had gone to his office to drop off their faxes,
had never returned. As far as Brooke knew, he was checking on
his gasoline line.

After a meal of a pickle and a chicken wing dwarfed by a
mound of dry mashed potatoes, Brooke sat at her assigned
consultation table by the wall of a large hall. Across from her,
women displayed arts and crafts for sale. With an interpreter at
her side, Brooke counseled Irina, a timid Russian with anxious

black eyes who wanted to partner with an American company to start a tampon factory. Except that she had no experience in the production process or knowledge of the distribution system. She also had no contacts to set up the physical, financial, or administrative sides of the venture.

"What are you bringing to the table?" Brooke asked, then rephrased for easier translation. "What are you offering?"

"Give me the name of an American company, and I will tell them we need a tampon factory," the interpreter repeated Irina's words. "They pay me for telling them."

Brooke explained that coming up with a good idea was indeed a seed for a business venture, but not enough; Irina needed a broader understanding of the steps in the long road ahead. She suggested Irina attend some of the business workshops.

The woman broke into sobs. "What am I supposed to do? There are no jobs; I can't feed my children!" She rummaged through her bag and produced an unglazed clay ashtray that looked like something Brooke had made in kindergarten. "Would you buy this? Only fifty rubles." She pressed the ashtray forward. "Please. It will pay for half a loaf of bread."

Brooke found her wallet, bought the ashtray, and added one of her bagged gifts. "Please go to the workshop," she repeated, her tone soft. Pained, she watched Irina's dejected back retreat through the door. Irina could have been her mother, her aunt, or any powerless, despondent and suffering Jew seeking help that was not forthcoming.

"That was kind of you," she heard and turned to see Olga. Brooke kissed her on both cheeks, and the Russian reciprocated. "I came to watch and get ready for my Institute for Social Research symposium next week," Olga said. "That will be more academic, though. No workshops like here."

"Either way, prepare the attendees for disappointment. Business is not a quick money maker, certainly not in the beginning." Brooke motioned with her head in the direction in which Irina had departed. "And teach me how to handle such desperation. It's heartbreaking."

Olga sighed. "*Novostroika,* the new system, takes the heaviest toll on our women. Social safety nets have been removed. Children are sick, go hungry, and mothers are helpless. Just when women need their jobs the most, they lose them. Our men were always inept, drunk, or absent from their families."

"The propaganda cranked out to the West showed Russian women building bridges and driving tractors."

Olga let out a wry laugh. "For you it might have seemed like liberation, but for us, it was servitude. We were nothing more than cheap skilled labor. We could learn anything and everything, and then do the work. Yet, where did it take us? When communism collapsed, we were invited to the banquet, but at the end they offered us only the crumbs." She shook her head. "How would American women react if your president Bill Clinton told you that in the new world you should go back to being mothers and wives, and then passed a directive to offer all government jobs to men?"

"His wife would give him a piece of her mind." Brooke's finger traced the coarse, uneven rim of Irina's ashtray. She tried to fit it in her handbag, but it was heavy and bulky. She withdrew from her handbag a tiny blue package that unfolded into a briefcase-size nylon bag she used in her travels, and placed the ashtray in it.

Olga looked around at the busy hall with its consultation tables at one end and merchandise, shoppers, and vendors at the other. "Let's find a quiet place to talk."

"In thirty minutes I'll be giving a lecture about retail versus wholesale."

"What's that?"

Maybe Olga didn't know the English words. While walking, Brooke explained, "Store is retail, selling directly to the final consumer. But where does the store get its merchandise? Often through a wholesaler who maintains a large warehouse of related products and sells them to stores."

In the corridor, Brooke spotted the sign to the bathroom. But Olga told her to rethink using it. "Another one of our national disgraces."

"The state of toilets in Russia is not your personal responsibility."

"They're a sign of our failure to embrace individual accountability." Olga began to climb the stairs, her breathing labored. "We don't even place expectations upon ourselves."

Collapsed beams, piles of discarded files, and water-sogged books littered the stairs and the second-floor ballroom. The pressure on Brooke's bladder sent her in search of another working toilet. After scouting several rooms full of broken furniture, she found a stall that showed signs of having been discovered before by many users, but never by a cleaning crew.

A few minutes later she joined Olga at a window seat under an arched wood panel and a canopy of tattered brocade.

"Tell me about yourself," Olga said. "About your family."

Brooke touched the thin gold chain, whose Star of David rested on her back. Where could she start? How much could she tell? Brooke had always whitewashed her family's history. Growing up, she had learned that Americans understood immigrants, but Holocaust survivors posed an oddity, their history incomprehensible. And divulging to Olga that her mother had been born in Russia and fled to Ukraine would instantly reveal her Jewish identity, as in the 1930s and 1940s mostly Jews had left—forced out. As much as she trusted Olga, this was a country with a bloody history of pogroms against Jews.

"My mother was almost forty when she had me. I'm too different from her for us to be close. I am more like my father." Maybe her mother had once been an outgoing, curious, adventure-seeking woman; Brooke had never been able to peel away the layers of despondency and loss that had changed her so profoundly.

"Has there been love in your family?"

Brooke sat back. "Maybe not between my parents, but they protected me fiercely. They gave me everything materialistic they didn't have in their earlier years. Even if I didn't want it, they wanted me to want it." Brooke pushed away the memories of her torturous years at the piano. Although her father never put a record on the player, he insisted that Bertha stick to piano lessons; his three dead children had shown great musical promise, inherited from their mother. "Intellectually, my mother never got to bloom to her full potential. She was unable to go to medical school, but later became an accountant. My father bought and sold real estate. He was very quiet." Except for his bursts of inconsolable crying at holiday tables. An image flashed through

Brooke's head of herself, at age four, sitting on her father's knees and learning to read numbers from the blue tattoo on his arm. Afterward, he'd often made games out of adding and subtracting numbers.

Olga nodded, as though digesting the information. "I thought American families were happy, given the freedoms you have—and money. But of course, that's a naive generalization."

"Like everything else, one begins to take the good things for granted. Anyway, we're not a typical American family."

"Is there such a thing as a typical family?"

Brooke smiled. In her mind, a typical family was one in which laughter replaced melancholy. One where going on picnics and vacations created new shared memories rather than the obsessive regurgitation of old and haunting tragedies of the past. One where there were grandparents, aunts, uncles, cousins, and siblings—and they even had feuds. Her family couldn't have feuds with the dead.

Young Bertha liked to go to friends' homes after school. In normal homes, girls carped to their parents about pimples or unfair tests. They threw temper tantrums to demand a new blouse or to lift a curfew. They could rebel and even disobey. Bertha had to block all childhood wants and teenage angst; boyfriend troubles were inconsequential to watching your loved ones being shot into a mass grave, and exasperating teachers could never compete with remembered Nazi guards.

Olga was watching her, waiting.

Brooke said, "I was an excellent student. I wanted to give my grades as a gift to my parents. It was one thing I could do well and easily make them proud."

Olga nodded, then spoke, her voice gravelly from smoking. "I've thought about our conversation regarding the mafia. You are right, of course. Our women need to take action. 'Even nightingales can't live on fairy tales.'" The sweetness of her blue eyes contrasted with the twin lines that descended along the sides of her nose to her jaw, pulling her mouth into an expression of resolve, like Brooke's mother's. "Everything we'll talk about is completely confidential?" Olga added.

"Of course."

Olga pulled out her cigarette packet and lit one. "Last night you mentioned identifying the enemy. I've begun what you might call a citizen's quest." To Brooke's raised eyebrows, Olga said, "I'm a sociologist, always researching one trend or another. It's not unusual for me to look at the rise in a trend—or in a specific type of crime. But I have no experience in business, to which these acts of terror are related." A swell of pain crossed her face. "My friend Vera was attacked at home early this morning. Her factory had been subjected to extortion, so she switched banks, thinking the old one had given the mafia the information. However, the extortion continued without interruption. The mafia knew—that same day—which bank her factory now used."

"What kind of financial institutions were here before the fall of communism?"

"Then and now, workers are paid mostly in cash. There were some government banks where we could keep a savings book or pay for utilities, but we couldn't write checks against our money as you do in the West." Olga waved a hand impatiently. "The new banks are a different breed altogether. They're private—

and they are nests of corruption. *They* finance our government, which tells you who's running things now."

"Where do these banks get the money? Who prints it for them, if not the government?"

Olga opened her palms in gestures of befuddlement.

"They must use foreign currency, then," Brooke said.

Olga shook her head. "I'm like a person who plants a tree with its roots upward."

"If the source of the problem were one specific bank," Brooke went on, "the extortion would have stopped once your friend transferred her business account. At least for a while. Which banks are mentioned in the reports?"

"There are so many new ones. Every self-respecting gangster opens a bank." Olga blew the smoke away from Brooke, but it still stung her eyes. "Are you saying that the extortion is the bank managers' doing?"

"Not the bank manager, but whoever *selects* this bank or that and assigns it to the venture. It comes from above the banks or the bankers. It was not your friend Vera—the customer—who selected the bank, right?"

"True."

Rays of sunlight filtered through swirling smoke and dancing dust heated up the little alcove. Brooke unbuttoned her jacket. "The mafia gang clearly had inside information. And since we're seeing a pattern—the same timing, the same intimidation process—it is possible that it is one particular mafia group that instigates it. However, that would require the mafia group, as an umbrella, to recruit several bank managers as its minions. It makes no sense."

"It does to me," Olga said. The feathered ash perched on her cigarette, about to drop. Brooke withdrew Irina's ashtray from her nylon bag and placed it next to Olga as the Russian continued, "The mafia collects heavy dossiers on bankers and blackmails them into opening their books. Ninety bank employees were murdered this past year alone.

"Ninety?" Hoffenbach had mentioned a couple of assassinations. But ninety murdered?

"Oh, yes. The newspapers are filled with such killing stories."

"There you are, then. You've found your answer. It could be one specific mafia group pulling the strings behind the different banks."

"I found the answer? 'Even a blind horse can pull a cart if he's being led.' You did." Olga paused. "Now what?"

Brooke rose to her feet, accidentally knocking the ashtray to the floor. It cracked into four pieces. She stared at them. This poorly made knickknack consisted of the four basic ingredients of the universe, of life: earth, water, air, and fire. Back to basics.

"Follow the money." She gathered up the pieces. "Find out who stands to profit from the acquisition of these women-owned factories. The money trail will lead you there."

"Money trail." Olga enunciated the words. "I've never heard this phrase. I need your help in this."

"Me? I don't know this country or the language." Besides the glaring fact that she was being asked to investigate business crime, she was certainly not staying the full nine days of Amanda's citizen's mission.

"You have experience with money trail. With accounting—creative or otherwise."

The pull of the need tugged at Brooke. Also, such an investigation would involve a steep learning curve about the Russian fiscal economy. It would give her great material for her article, which in turn would enhance her credibility with her new bosses. She wasn't a great writer, but the firm's public relations consultants would edit and then place the piece at a leading business publication, enhancing her reputation all around.

Most important, Brooke thought as Olga's eyes, expecting, pleading, continued to bore into hers, how could she refuse?

# ❧ CHAPTER ❧

## *Sixteen*

OLGA DETESTED THE thought of what public transportation would entail. Sure enough, the first bus that stopped was so packed, some passengers stood on the stairs, blocking the door from opening. Only two people got off, elbowing their exit through the mass of angry, cursing riders who wouldn't make way lest they lose their spots. Olga could not squeeze in.

The next bus arrived on the heels of the first, but this time she was shoved aside by younger, more aggressive commuters who scrambled up before the impatient driver shut the door. When the third bus finally arrived, Olga was fuming at the injustice of it all. She pushed others to hold her place at the head of the line and climbed the two steps into a hot, sweaty fog of sour breath and coats smelling of naphthalene.

She clutched the leather strap above, swaying with each turn, hoping she wouldn't fall with a sudden stop. Within twenty minutes, her calves ached, and her feet swelled and throbbed inside her shoes. If it weren't for the *zhaba,* the toad, she would have her car.

It started to drizzle. Perfect. She had left her galoshes at the office.

Metal dust and noxious chemical fumes welcomed Olga into Vera Sergeevna's pots and pans factory. Entering the dilapidated building, she shook the raindrops off her kerchief and coat. A grating, high-pitched whine from the cutting and polishing machines broke through the thin walls, *bsssssszzzzzzz, bsssssszzzzzzz* like a thousand pieces of chalk scratching at blackboards. It made Olga's skin prickle. She could never get used to working in a place like this, with the noise, the smell of machine oil, and the air polluted with metal dust. Yet, if she lost her job at the institute, she would be grateful to scrub the one toilet at this plant, shared by over two hundred workers.

Neither the matron at the front cubicle next to the hissing samovar, nor the few idle workers passing in the corridor stopped to inquire of her purpose here. As the joke went, "I pretend to work and you pretend to pay me." Not only did they not care, but years of being expected to be their brothers' keepers—and their resentment of this role—had taught everyone to mind their own business.

In Vera's office, her friend's framed photograph stood on a corner of an organized desk. Olga examined the handsome woman in her early thirties, whose beautiful cheekbones and dark complexion suggested a north Asian ancestry. Olga's eyes misted at the sight of the luxuriant braid streaming down over Vera's right shoulder. Long after the burn had healed and her hair grew back, her friend's soul would remain scarred.

Olga opened the top desk drawer and found a stapled stack of papers with the letterhead of the Institute of External Market Resources. When was such an institute created? She'd never heard of it. What did the title mean? Yet a quick scan told her this was the very document she searched for. How easy! She had her first lead.

In the din of the machinery she could barely think. She stuffed the papers in her handbag and left. The daylight was melting away, and she was far from home, with no car to take her there.

A T FOUR O'CLOCK the merchants who had displayed their wares in the conference exhibition hall packed up. Through the tall windows, Svetlana watched the rays of the setting sun painting wispy clouds in coral-colored swirls. A string quartet played at the back of the lecture hall, a touch of culture in honor of the guests, but to her regret, few seemed to pay attention to the musicians. The crowd, like hens eager to flee their coop, was dispersing quickly. With street crimes increasing in direct ratio to the dwindling police patrol and with parliament sympathizers flooding the downtown area while the military suddenly popped up everywhere, Moscow had become more dangerous than ever.

Nevertheless, at least forty attendees still lingered, waiting for a second round of door-prize drawings. This door-prize concept still escaped Svetlana's grasp. She had obliged when Amanda asked her to distribute the small, red numbered tickets, but told Amanda it was wrong to give anyone something she hadn't earned. Amanda only laughed, which made Svetlana even more perplexed. How could Americans think of something so unfair? Not only were the drawn gifts of unequal value but there weren't enough for everyone. Some people received nothing. Wasn't democracy supposed to mean true social justice?

Irina, who should have been ashamed of her oily hair and unfeminine dandruff, looked full of energy for the game. Of course, she must have cheated in the first round. How else, with only one ticket, could she have won both a hair clip and a bottle of cough syrup? Eyeing a boxful of yet-to-be-raffled-off goodies, she now tried to coax Svetlana into dispensing one more ticket. When Svetlana refused, Irina went on to say she had another business idea to discuss with Brooke and needed an interpreter.

"I am not at *your* service," Svetlana responded, her tone haughty.

When Irina pushed her way toward Brooke, Svetlana rushed behind her. Brooke seemed to have an inexhaustible supply of Ziploc bags with precious surprises, and Svetlana wanted to protect her.

"She's only trying to exploit you for another gift," Svetlana told Brooke. "She says she has a new idea, but don't believe her."

"Let's hear it," Brooke said, smiling at Irina.

Svetlana fumed, but had no choice but translate. "My brother, he works for a garage," Irina explained. "When he's drunk, I go instead and jump-start cars. Russian cars are bad. They stall all the time. So I make jump-start cables and sell one every time I help someone. Next time they don't call garage. My brother is mad, but I make money."

"You know how to make jumper cables?" Brooke asked.

"If I can get black and red cables and those big—" Irina made a clamping motion.

It irked Svetlana that Brooke took Irina's hands in hers with obvious delight. "Write me a list of the steps you must take to manufacture a large quantity," Brooke said with enthusiasm. "Ask around and find out where to buy the raw materials you need—and research their costs. Calculate what you need now and the quantities you will need a year from now. Find out how much these jumper cables cost in the open market." She waited until Svetlana translated. "Figure out a facility where you can work. Maybe rent a small warehouse? Talk to people who may want to invest with you or give you loans."

"What people?" Irina asked.

"Friends, neighbors, family," Brooke said as if it was self-evident that anyone had money to spare—or that money had any value from one day to the next. Svetlana wanted to explain this to the American, but Brooke was too excited as she pointed at the packet of class notes in Irina's hands. "Write a business plan. Think where else you can sell your jumper cables, not only through your brother's garage calls. Then telephone me at Hotel Moscow. We'll talk more. Okay?"

Svetlana wished she could come up with an idea that would make Brooke similarly thrilled, but none came to mind. No wonder she couldn't even manage her cooperative.

As soon as the Americans climbed onto their bus and she waved them good-bye, Svetlana hurried to the Economic Authority building, a fifteen-minute subway ride. It was past work hours, and she was scared of the purpose of the meeting.

When Sidorov had called Svetlana at home early that morning, she told him she must first fetch the accounting books from the factory, but he'd said not to bother. Already a bad omen. She was behind, yet again, in repaying the loan the factory had received thanks to the Economic Authority's recommendation. What could she possibly say in her defense? That she had to pay protection money before all else? That she had paid the wrong gang, clearly, because it had failed to show up and fight off the attackers? Sidorov had already insisted that the Economic Authority couldn't tolerate her delinquency just because she claimed to have paid the mafia. Now her factory lay in ruins.

Svetlana clutched the workbook she had received at the conference. It would be hard to write a marketing plan, but she was determined to somehow do it. Brooke had said it was necessary for the cooperative's success. She said that Sidorov would respect her vision if he could see how she planned to handle the factory's recovery.

Before entering his office, Svetlana stopped in the washroom, where she rinsed her face and quickly applied makeup. When Svetlana had complimented Brooke for the rust-color shade of her lipstick, the American insisted that she accept the tube. And Jenny had given her the green eye shadow "to match your eyes," she had said, and added a mascara.

But Sidorov's wrath still scared her. Examining the effect of the makeup in the mirror, Svetlana thought that Brooke would never let a man intimidate her—and neither would Jenny. She squared her shoulders and walked the short corridor into Sidorov's office.

To her astonishment, he smiled. "I plan to join the sexy Americans for dinner tonight."

"I . . . tonight?" She wished she sounded more intelligent. "They have tickets to the circus."

He hooked one thick, rough-skinned finger into the soft hollow under her chin, forcing her head up, his face much too close. She avoided looking into the waxen blue eyes that scowled from under tufted brows and focused instead on the few hairs at the tip of his bulbous nose. The smell of vodka hung heavy on his breath.

"Are you having a good time?" he asked.

She tried to nod, but the movement caused his finger to dig deeper into her chin.

"What were the Americans doing at the Gorbachevskaya Street Factory yesterday?"

A worm wriggled in her stomach. "It was on their itinerary! I was to meet them at the airport and later bring them there for lunch—"

Sidorov let go of her head and walked backward to his desk. His gaze assessed her body from top to bottom. "I see you got the idea." He perched on the desk's edge, and his finger beckoned her.

She didn't like the gesture. Fear snaked its way up her throat, yet how could she not approach? Her factory and its workers depended on this man's goodwill. "What idea?" Taking tentative steps, she crossed the Persian rug.

His loosened his tie, then flattened down the imaginary hair on his bald pate. "You gussied up for me, yes?"

She gulped. She had only meant to show confidence, like the elegant Americans.

"Tell me, do you know what it means, 'Do not cut the bough you're sitting on?' " Without taking his eyes off her, he pushed off from the desk, and in a few large steps walked over to the door. He turned the key in the lock, then returned to his spot close to her. Too close.

"Nikolai Antonovich—"

He cupped her breast. His fingers found her nipple and squeezed hard. Dark patches swayed behind her eyes. "No, please. . . . "

His voice, heavy and smooth as cream, cut her off. "Come now. Be a good sport and turn around. I want you to sit on the bough." He laughed at his own joke.

"Oh, uh, no. . . . "

"You've been a bad girl. You took our guests to where they were not supposed to be."

"I— I didn't! You'd told me to. Because I speak English, you said!"

His fingers pawed her other breast. "Don't you want to continue working with the Economic Authority?"

Natasha. How would I feed her? And what about all the workers? Each of the women—her friends—had children at home, or sick mothers to take care of. And what about the Americans? If Sidorov removed her from this assignment, her dream to learn from them would shatter.

"Turn around and lift your skirt." His hand still gripping her breast, Sidorov brought his other to his collar under his double chin and released the top button.

She stared at his moving fingers, "No. Please . . . Nikolai Antonovich—"

His brows raised quizzically. She could tell he thought her stupid for making such a fuss. He swiveled her body around. She clutched the desk as he lifted her skirt and tugged at her underwear over the garter belt.

Her palms pressed the cold, smooth mahogany. She grasped the corners and squeezed hard, staring at her whitening knuckles, wanting them to hurt. He fumbled behind her, and the fabric of his pants brushed against the bare skin of her thighs. The sound of the opening zipper made her jump, but his hand on her hip pinned her in place.

"This rump is made for fucking." His hand caressed her right buttock. "A good-size shit basket."

Stinging tears blinded her as his fingers searched her opening, pushing her forward. Her head tipped downward, and her necklace with the tiny gold cross dangled near her face. She grabbed it in her mouth and sucked on it, tracing its hard edges with her tongue. Wordless prayers formed around the cross.

"You see why you shouldn't cut the bough?" Sidorov shoved himself into her.

Svetlana felt her mouth twist in a silent scream, and the cross fell out. She'd always been terrified of an attack by strangers, in dark woods and deserted stairwells, not in well-lit offices. But this was different. She had seen Sidorov's photograph in the newspaper with President Yeltsin. He was a powerful man. You couldn't fight someone like him.

*Natasha. God help me, but I have to. For you, for us, for my friends at the factory.*

Sidorov's breath came in short gasps. "All you bitches want a real man."

Loud drums beat in Svetlana's head. She willed her soul to turn to ice, as she had done with the gang and later, with her husband when he had forced sex on her between beatings. She told herself that like in marriage, it wasn't a rape if the man was the boss. Sidorov had such rights. He had power, and this was what powerful men did.

"Show appreciation," Sidorov huffed from behind. His hands on her hips commanded her to gyrate in widening circles. "Or I'll remember you didn't want to sit on the bough."

A metallic taste filled Svetlana's mouth as he climaxed with a shudder and a low moan. Crying openly, she bent down to pull up her frumpy cotton underwear that lay in a small heap at her ankles.

"Stop making such a big deal. I did you a favor." Sidorov opened his desk drawer and pulled out a roll of toilet paper. He cleaned himself and, aiming like it was a basketball, tossed the crumpled tissue into the wastebasket. He passed Svetlana the roll and she wiped herself, still trembling, tears streaming down her face.

He opened another desk drawer and withdrew a Hershey bar. "Here." His tone was almost kind. "For your kid. Next time I'll get you pantyhose."

Next time? She forced her hand to take the chocolate. She should throw it away as soon as she got out of there. But how could she not give it to Natasha? Or sell it?

She turned to leave and felt a slap on her buttocks. At the door, blinded by tears, she fumbled with the lock.

"Svetlana," he called to her. "You be good, and I'll arrange for another business loan."

Another loan? If she weren't so distraught, so eager to escape, she would have told him that the factory couldn't pay the interest on the few loans already stolen right at the bank lobby by gangsters. She would have begged Sidorov to help erase those loans, not add to the factory's debt. But the door was now open, and she couldn't begin to speak.

In the bathroom, she inspected herself in the mirror over the sink. Since there was no soap, she used her handkerchief to violently wipe away the green eye shadow and the brown smears of mascara. Red patches appeared where she rubbed her skin too hard. So much for using makeup; it was all her fault for giving Sidorov the wrong impression. She hadn't fought him; she'd even gyrated a bit, helping him along so the ordeal would be over. It wasn't rape if it was her fault.

A woman of loose morals, the committee had once decreed. That's what she was, for life.

Her fingers yanked at her curls, ruining the rigid set of hairspray. She pulled the tendrils in all directions until they stuck out and gave her the look of the madwoman she now was. She scrubbed away Sidorov's stickiness, swiping at the back of her thighs with her panties. Again. More. Harder. Anything to undo the imprint of his flesh.

She wanted to run away, to jump out of her skin. She couldn't face going home; she couldn't face Zoya and her harassment, nor could she ever face Natasha without breaking down. Yet, there was no other place to go. Nowhere in all of Moscow to hide.

Outside the washroom window, an oppressive blanket of inky

sky had descended over the city. Svetlana folded the leather coat Katerina had loaned her, straightened its sleeves and lapel, and placed it in her string bag. Never again would she attempt to look elegant. It attracted the wrong kind of attention. She stepped out to the street, into the familiar darkness, permeated with the stagnant smell of the city.

## ❧ CHAPTER ❧

## *Eighteen*

BACK FROM THE conference, Brooke looked around the lobby of Hotel Moscow and felt the claustrophobic environment tightening around her. She pulled out her camera and aimed it toward the forever-closed and dark gift shop.

With uncharacteristic speed, two guards were upon her. "*Nyet!*"

"Okay." Why fight it? In a few minutes she would be upstairs, call the embassy, and catch whoever was on duty. They must work after hours; it was the American Embassy, not the Russian. She put away the camera, chiding herself for her impetuousness. The guards could have yanked out the film and exposed it to light. The photos she had taken at the conference would have been lost.

Heading to the elevator, she remembered that her passport was still at the reception desk, where Aleksandr had deposited it upon their arrival the day before. In all European cities she'd visited, passports were returned after registration had been completed. Brooke swiveled on her heel and headed to the reception area.

Behind the desk, a young woman with a small face and a huge hairdo was absorbed in a book. She didn't raise her head as Brooke waited.

"*Dobriy dyen,* good day."

No response.

"Passport, *pazhalusta,* please," Brooke finally said, using the words of politeness that had come back to her. "Fielding."

Without looking up, the girl scribbled something on a piece of paper, slid it toward Brooke, and continued reading.

"Ten dollars? What for?"

"Government," the girl replied in English without looking up.

"You don't understand. I just want my passport back. I'm not checking out."

The girl tapped her red fingernail on the written note, not bothering to repeat herself.

Brooke felt Amanda joining her. "I don't believe it," Brooke mumbled.

"Let Aleksandr get all our passports," Amanda said. More women, now off the bus, gathered behind them.

Not wishing to dampen the exhilaration of the day by arguing with Amanda, Brooke stepped back to the lobby. It took fifteen minutes before Aleksandr lumbered over, a stack of blue passports in his hands. He opened his mouth as if to speak, and closed it.

"May I have mine, please?" Brooke asked him.

"Well, the front desk, they were insulted."

A muscle in Brooke's back twitched. "What's that supposed to mean?"

His face turned crimson. "You argued with them. They must be treated with respect."

"Respect?" She bristled. "That clerk was rude, yet she has the audacity to complain that I asked for a clarification about some phony tax?"

"She was insulted."

"Too bad!" Brooke yanked the passports from his fingers, found hers, and distributed the rest to the other women.

"You should give her a gift," Aleksandr said to her back.

She pivoted on her heel to face him. "So that's what this is all about? You're accusing me of insulting the clerk only to milk me to tip her? Has it occurred to you that you're insulting *me*? And where is my room key? Did you get it at the same time you got the passport, or should I pay someone for it?"

"Take it easy." Amanda went to retrieve their keys.

Arguing with Aleksandr had the effect of a dog barking at a lamppost. Brooke plopped down on a vinyl-upholstered bench, and dropped her face into her hands. Her fingertips pressed on her tired eyeballs. Last year, in a Taiwanese factory, the director had demonstrated the pressure points his Chinese employees massaged after long hours of stringing fine electric wires. Now she must retrieve her key, get to her room—and to the phone. She would do the rest of the group a favor by arranging bodyguards. Maybe she would also call Delta Air Lines to find out their schedule for the coming days, as she needed to keep her options open.

"Having fun?"

Even before raising her head, Brooke knew by the whiff of cinnamon-and-wood aftershave who it was. She looked up, certain he could see the flush sweeping her face. "You look bright-eyed and bushy-tailed. Don't you ever get tired?"

Judd's laughter revealed a set of straight, square teeth. "I'm the product of postwar starving Eastern European immigrants fattening up their kids with good nutrition."

She stared at him. Was he, too, a child of survivors? She had never been able to speak about her second-generation experience with an adult who had actually shared it. Holocaust survivors were assumed to have been damaged by exposure to hunger, abuse, loss, cold, degradation, and death. What kind of life could they make for their children? Once, a son of her parents' friends pointed at a lampshade. "Meet my uncle," he said, and Bertha, age eight, burst out laughing, immediately getting it: The Nazis had made lampshades out of Jewish skin. The following day, she tried the joke on a playdate. The girl didn't understand, and the next day she declared in school that Bertha was a liar who made up horrible stories. Afterward, Bertha didn't tell anyone that the Nazis had also made soap out of Jewish fat.

Brooke swallowed and let a moment pass. "How was your day?" she asked. "I didn't see you at lunch."

He smiled. "I was busy at private sessions, and I've picked up some business ideas. A meat-processing plant, a cellular-phone company, chains of laundromats, an equipment leasing venture—"

"Are you joining the government privatization feast? If I were you, I'd invest in cement. I've never seen so much construction in concrete." She flipped back her hair. His presence suddenly made her feel recharged. "But then again, a deal gone sour might end up with you inside a mixer."

He laughed.

Just then Brooke caught sight of Svetlana arguing with the sentries at the entrance. Her hair, which had been neat after a full day at the conference, now stuck out in clumps. Red scratches ran down her cheeks, and her eyes were swollen.

Brooke rushed over and waved her in past the guards. "It's okay," she told them. She put her arm around Svetlana's shoulders. Stifling her shock, she whispered, "Have the hoodlums come back?"

Svetlana wouldn't meet her eyes. "No."

"What then?"

"Uh, it's personal." Svetlana's hand fondled the "Attitude Is Everything" button, and she glanced suspiciously toward Judd as he approached.

"You look like you could use a shot of vodka." He snapped his fingers like he had just remembered something, and walked away.

"Would you like to speak in private?" Brooke checked her watch. Only forty-five minutes before the group was to leave for the circus, and she still had to make those phone calls. "Let's get some fresh air."

"*Nichevo*, never mind."

"Please. Something happened to you."

Svetlana shook her head, then her face crumpled.

Brooke tightened her arm around the heaving shoulders and pulled Svetlana outside.

At the line of trees, there were two flagstones. Brooke sat down, motioning to Svetlana. "Can you tell me now?"

Svetlana made a visible effort to control her weeping. She shook her head.

Brooke took a Wet-Nap out of her purse, tore it open, and dabbed the red marks on the Russian's face. "It helps to talk," she said in a soft voice.

"We don't talk about these things." Svetlana pulled away, found a cloth handkerchief in her vinyl handbag, and swiped at her tears.

"Please, I may be able to help. At least let me try—"

"I don't want foreigners to laugh at our misfortune."

"Laugh? Did I laugh yesterday? Let me tell you something. Each of the women in our group has taken vacation time off her job and most paid from their own pockets to be here."

"How much?"

Brooke recalled the women in her workshop who didn't understand helping others. "Twenty-five hundred dollars."

"Two thousand, five hundred dollars? Each of you?"

"Some, like Amanda, are funded by an organization. I am not."

"But why would you pay so much to come here?" Svetlana's face clouded. "It's because you're Jewish."

"What's that got to do with anything?"

"Jews are greedy. Maybe you want to steal our ventures?"

Brooke jumped to her feet. "Come on, Svetlana, you know better." Czars toppled, religions disappeared, villages were erased by pogroms, regimes revolutionized, but like a deadly virus, anti-Semitism was immune to change. "What about the women in the group who aren't Jewish? What's their motivation?"

"But why would *you* come here?" Svetlana repeated.

Brooke sat down again. "Who's going to help women around the globe? Not men, for sure. Not the mafia." She hesitated, realizing that volunteerism on such a scale was more foreign to Svetlana than Mars. Svetlana could more readily grasp the anti-Semitism she'd heard all her life than the notion of extending kindness toward strangers. "Only women who've made it can understand—maybe Jews even more so, because of our history of suffering. Jews believe in helping; doing good is one of the foundations of our religion." She took a deep breath. "So maybe you should trust me, like you trust your neighbor, that doctor you told me about."

Svetlana nodded slowly. "Yes. I admire you for going back into the factory yesterday. It was dangerous."

"Can you now tell me what happened this evening?"

"No."

"Then how about what happened before yesterday's incident? What led up to it?"

Svetlana bit her lip. "Okay. I will tell."

It had started three months earlier. After confirming that the Gorbachevskaya Street Factory could turn out a profit from orders placed for its leather outerwear in the coming season, the Economic Authority guaranteed a loan for the purchase of hides.

The morning the money cleared in the bank account, the thugs appeared. They wore suits. They were polite. They asked the economist to accompany them to the bank and withdraw the money. He had to comply. He gave them the money right there, so it wasn't a robbery.

"It's still a robbery even if done in full daylight by polite people," Brooke said. "Was it the bank manager or a lower-level clerk who collaborated with them?"

Svetlana shrugged, a gesture of resignation that contained all the contradictions and tribulations of life in Russia. "What's the difference? Someone at the bank had given them the information."

"If it was a clerk, you could have complained to the manager."

"Complain?" Svetlana spit out words. "Only stupid people complain. Nothing would be done anyway. Only trouble."

Of course, Brooke thought. With no expectation of justice, Russians sought to circumvent problems on their own. Like an industrious ant, Svetlana diligently blazed a new trail each day. "Go on." She reached out for Svetlana's hand, hoping to uncover the circumstances of Svetlana's disheveled appearance. "What happened next?"

"The following weeks, whenever there was money in the bank account, the men returned to demand it. But we needed the funds for our payroll and to purchase raw materials. And now we had to pay interest for a loan that we never saw, on money that was taken away before it left the bank lobby." Svetlana shrugged. "After two months, my request to change banks was approved."

Follow the money. It worked every time. "What do you mean by 'request to change banks?' Whose permission did you have to obtain?"

Svetlana examined her worn black shoes. "A business can work only with a bank that invites it. You can't choose. We filed a request with the Economic Authority, and they found a bank that would invite us to service our business."

"What happened after you switched banks?"

"Same." Svetlana's lips quivered. "The morning the account cleared."

Judd appeared with a pint-size vodka bottle. He unscrewed the top and handed it to Svetlana, tossing Brooke a glance of understanding. She watched him stride away back to the hotel. His lithe figure radiated confidence.

Svetlana sipped the vodka.

"How have you been paying your bills if no money stays in your account?" Brooke asked.

Two old women carrying large brooms began sweeping crushed cigarettes butts from the circular driveway in front of the hotel. Svetlana eyed them.

"We—the workers—sell our vouchers," she finally said.

"What vouchers?"

Svetlana's hand shielded the side of her mouth as if she was concerned that the cleaning women were listening. "The shares in government properties all Russian citizens received when communism ended. Many people lost their savings because of inflation. These vouchers are the only thing they have left."

"The employees sell their shares in order to keep the business afloat?" Brooke sighed. "You won't own your business much longer if you sell your rights to it. That's what selling means."

"What choice do we have? The government gives us no money. We haven't paid our workers in three months. We've been issuing *veksels*, I.O.U.s, but they trade those for half their value for food. We're just trying to survive!" Svetlana finished the vodka. "We're just trying to survive," she repeated.

Sadness crept over Brooke. Survival was the best these women hoped for. "The hoodlums have taken all the money they could get. What more do they want?" she asked, wondering if they'd been the ones to attack Svetlana again in the past hour.

Svetlana's gaze followed the two old women moving away with their brooms. "Why do you want to know so much?"

"I'm trying to find out who's behind the intimidation of small cooperatives like yours. Maybe we'll be able to stop this."

"Stop the mafia?" Svetlana raised her eyebrows. "You're a foreigner. You're naive. No one can stop them."

"It's not my idea. There are Russians who think it's possible."

Again, tears welled up in Svetlana's eyes. "You want to know what they want? They want us to pretend we transferred ownership but received nothing for it!"

Whoever was behind this scheme still had an interest in the factory after it had been sucked dry and ransacked. Where was the value?

"We'll talk more after I give it some thought." Then an idea hit Brooke. "How far is your home?"

"Why?"

"I want you to take your daughter to the circus. Use my ticket. I know Amanda has one for you, too. Go home and get Natasha." What was it like to see the world through her child's eyes? Brooke rooted in her bag and pulled out a ten-dollar bill. "Take a taxi, have the driver wait while you get her, and have him drive you to the arena. You'll just make it in time."

Svetlana took the money. "For my daughter, I cannot refuse. Thank you so much!"

"It will do you both good." Brooke rose to her feet. Once, after Brooke's father demanded that his wife pretend to have fun for their daughter's sake, her mother took her to the Barnum &

Bailey Circus. Bertha's begging for cotton candy, though, had met a wall. Cotton candy wasn't food, her mother said, producing instead a tomato-and-cheese sandwich and a banana softened into brown. Bertha wanted to scream and demand cotton candy, but that wasn't behavior she could inflict on a mother who had suffered so much. Pretending to eat the soggy sandwich, she had stared, envious, at the children around her. Their fluffy pink concoction looked as if plucked from sweet clouds in the sky.

Svetlana sniffled, but there was alacrity in her step as she got up.

"I've just thought of something else." Brooke stopped Svetlana with a touch on her arm. "Is there a way to get hold of your file at the Economic Authority?"

Svetlana stared at her. "I don't mean to be disrespectful. You have a good heart, even if it is Jewish. But you know nothing of what you're talking about." She waved down a passing car that braked with a screech. Turning back at the car door, Svetlana repeated, "Thank you very, very much."

Brooke watched her drive away, forcing herself to ignore Svetlana's naive anti-Semitism, at least for now, and focus on the problem. Who was right—Svetlana or Olga? One had faced the mafia's wrath, the other had access to resources of information Brooke couldn't begin to fathom.

Brooke climbed up the front stairs of Hotel Moscow to call the embassy and the airline. While she waited for the elevator, Judd approached. "What was that all about?" he asked.

She waved her hand in dismissal. "Svetlana's got problems." The elevator door opened and they stepped into it together.

"Aren't you going to the circus?" he asked.

n. "I just gave her my ticket."

"Let's have dinner this evening," he suggested.

Heat coursed in her. In a voice as gentle as she could muster, she asked, "How would your wife feel about that?"

Something dimmed in his eyes. "You're right to ask." He looked away, then back at her. "It's complicated."

She noticed with regret the hazel speckles of his eyes behind the glasses. "It's not a multiple-choice question. Either you are married or not. Sleeping on the living-room couch doesn't constitute marital separation."

"Fair enough."

But as she stepped out of the elevator at her floor, he held the door. "Will you let me explain at dinner?" When she nodded, he let go of the door and stayed behind to take the elevator back down two flights.

## CHAPTER

## *Nineteen*

**T**HERE WAS NO one of authority to come to the phone at the embassy. No, her passport hadn't been lost or stolen. No, this wasn't a medical emergency either. No, she wasn't in physical danger right this moment, but needed advice regarding security. Brooke left a message for someone to call her back. No, she wouldn't be by the phone all day tomorrow, but please try her later that night or early in the morning. Hanging up in frustration, she thought of the moment in New York when she had decided to travel to Moscow and could now laugh at herself. How the significance of coming here in these historic times had burst into kaleidoscopic colors in her romantic head. She had anticipated watching history unfold, but not this kind of history. Svetlana's sentence *The Economic Authority selected the banks* had made this history real.

Brooke needed to watch herself from being carried away too easily by fantasy. Ditto with Judd. If she weren't careful, she might be swept into feelings she would be unable to rein in; she couldn't afford more personal mistakes.

She had been fourteen when she changed her name from Bertha to Brooke. But the name change failed to free her from the sorrow that hung around her family. At seventeen, when applying for a scholarship at Berkeley, she changed her last name from Feldman to Fielding. She had not revealed to her parents that she hadn't applied to any universities in the east, and as she planned to flee across the country she forced her heart to ignore their stunned reaction, to harden herself against the pain she was causing them. She had to save herself.

Her classes left her stimulated and the new music spouting out of transistors everywhere was thrilling. But the best part was the big, old Victorian house on Allston Way that she moved into within a few months. There, she found a home. Instead of regarding their house as a booby trap of loss and pain, those people created a family life full of hugs and words of love.

The commune consisted of hippies fired up by antiwar protests. While staying around school longer than intended, they clung to their alternative way of life as their new utopia. For the first time, Brooke's lacerating loneliness eased. These people, who believed in the goodness of the planet and its inhabitants, had chosen her. They loved her for who she was, unlike her parents, who had viewed her only as a stand-in for all their lost relatives. In the spirit of fair-mindedness, her new friends accepted with good humor the business-major teenager who had landed in their midst, even as she seemed indifferent to talks about war. Besides, she was the only one who could balance the commune checkbook—or cared to.

Snug inside this cocoon of affection, Brooke prized their commitment to love, to each other and to their mutual happiness. At night, they slept cuddled together like puppies, in clusters of three or four, with sprigs of sage grown in their garden spread around their mattresses. Suddenly Brooke had a huge family to replace all the siblings and cousins that she could never have.

Her euphoria ended without notice when the house lease came up for renewal. The landlord, who had watched the neighborhood replacing the free love of the sixties with middle-class families of the seventies, wanted to refurbish and sell. As though suddenly awakened from a protracted adolescence, the commune members rolled up their futons, removed their beads, cut their long hair, and unrolled their diplomas. They wrote their first résumés and went on job interviews. Within two weeks, they had scattered in all directions, the pledges of commitment an embarrassment, the words of love outgrown. The sage garden was left to wilt.

Brooke was left alone again, with no idea which of the five men in the commune—the tall Swede, the stout Japanese, the black hunk, the Jewish Marxist, or the blue-eyed Texan—had left behind the one sperm that impregnated her fertile egg.

BROOKE AND JUDD stepped outside the hotel into the cool, clear evening. He paid the guard at the door to stop a car. Before entering it, he presented the driver with a note in Cyrillic with the address.

When the driver nodded, Judd put his hand on the small of Brooke's back while he opened the back door with the other.

The feel of his hand, so assured, so intimate, sent a dangerous swell of warmth through her. "Ready for a home-cooked Russian meal?"

She laughed as she slid into the car. "I'm ready for anything better than fried chicken that has been run over by a tank." She would only bear Hotel Moscow's food through the weekend, then she'd see. When she had called Delta Air Lines, she learned that there was a daily flight at five P.M. to Frankfurt, but only twice a week nonstop to New York. The flights weren't full. Her options were open. All she had waiting at home this weekend was her cat Sushi, cared for by the superintendent's wife.

Judd slid in behind her. Just as he was about to shut the door, Jenny materialized. "I'm coming with you," she called out and grabbed the door handle, pulling it open.

Brooke was taken aback. "Didn't you go to the circus?"

"All those gymnasts were trained for the Olympics. I can see them better on TV."

Judd seesawed his eyebrows toward Brooke in warning and mouthed, "No way."

Brooke leaned over. "I'm sorry, Jenny."

"Where are you going?"

"We're off." Judd yanked the door shut, leaving Jenny at the curb, her mouth puckered in a pout. The driver pulled away before Brooke could hear Jenny's retort.

She laid a hand on the left side of her chest. "Did we have to be so rude?"

"You weren't. I was—and she was even more."

"She's misguided. Or craves attention."

"More like missing a chromosome."

"The Russians admire her. And she has a good sense of the craft market."

"Your good breeding is taking you too far on this one. Do you take care of every person who suffers from low self-esteem? She has too much *chutzpah*, that's all."

Remembering how Jenny had cornered Judd in the dining room, Brooke said no more.

No outside sign indicated that a restaurant was housed in the building where they stopped. They entered a gap in the wall with no door, took a lit flight of steps to the basement, and Judd rang a doorbell. A matron with cheeks like ripe peaches and a huge bosom opened the door and greeted them with a broad smile.

With only a few tables well spaced in the front room and a ten-inch-wide stenciled strip of red roses running along the ceiling and door frames, the place felt cozy, like someone's dining room. Paintings of the Russian countryside depicted bales of hay, gushing springs, log cabins, plowing oxen, and fields of snow edged by tall forests—Olga's nostalgic description of the Russia she loved.

Fleshy wings hung from the matron's bare arms as she reached out to hug Judd and addressed him in Russian.

He shook his head. "English?"

The woman seemed perplexed. She peered up at his face again and spoke again in Russian.

"She thinks she knows you," Brooke observed.

Judd said again, "Do you speak English?"

The matron shrugged and called over a strapping youth with pale blue eyes identical to hers.

"Please." The young man bowed from his waist and led them to a table.

A few moments later, he placed a small jar of caviar with silver dollar–size blinis in front of them and popped open a Champagne bottle they hadn't ordered.

"Thanks. We're starving." Judd flashed him a smile. "What do you have?"

"I bring food Mama cooked."

A Gypsy couple in colorful costumes and handkerchief headdresses swooped over, their long nails clacking against their string and percussion instruments. The woman broke into a dance, and the fake coins strung into her black curls jiggled to her singing.

"To new friendship." Judd touched his glass to Brooke's.

She smiled. "To Moscow?"

"To a new friendship that begins in Moscow."

She clinked her glass to his. "And to Russia quickly catching up with the rest of civilization."

"Wow, you're down on this country."

"I'm confused. It is a place of extremes. And our Jewish people's bloody history here is yet another layer I haven't begun to deal with." There. She'd opened the subject a crack.

Just as Judd was about to speak, three suit-clad teenagers, one of them sporting the fuzz of a mustache, entered the restaurant. They wore giant gold-and-diamond pins, finger-thick gold chains, and heavy rings. A watch winked from under one of the sleeves. The bling of mafia saplings.

Brooke shifted her gaze back to Judd. "To be fair, I love the women I've gotten to know, and I'm enormously impressed with the ones I've counseled today. They have so much to catch up on, yet the odds are stacked against them." She bit into a caviar-covered blini. "I advised a marketing director for a ladder company about exporting her products. But guess what? Russian ladders are a joke in Poland and Romania, a synonym for products deemed unsafe. The steps are known to fall off."

"Along with the unlucky user who happens to be climbing them?"

She smiled. "They need to understand quality control as the basis of market economy, where there is open competition. They can't just unload inferior or defective products and expect a second order—"

"Here, let me." Judd interrupted, and reached over to touch Brooke's nose. He turned his finger to show a black caviar egg stuck to it, then placed it on his tongue. "It tastes better now."

She laughed and sipped her Champagne. It tasted both earthy and heavenly. "In poking around business ventures here, have you dealt with the Economic Authority?" she asked. "What do you know about the privatization process?"

"I believe that after the fall of communism, the Economic Authority issued the original sets of ownership vouchers as part of the privatization of industries. It's now helping these ventures by channeling financing through its Finance Division. Without steady revenues, most need operating cash flow to get started. The Economic Authority arranges for bank loans to newly privatized businesses. Why do you ask?"

That's it! Brooke sat back. She could feel the taste of victory in her mouth. All Olga needed to do now was to get hold of the ventures' files. "I'm still waiting to meet my host, Nikolai Sidorov. Have you heard anything about him?"

"He's a close adviser to Yeltsin, Russia's reformation meister."

Sidorov might be ignorant of the corruption at one of his divisions, right under his nose. Or he might not, Brooke thought.

The son-waiter served the food. He pointed at the names of the dishes printed on a card: "*Okroshka,* cold soup with a base of beer." He set the bowl in front of Brooke, then placed *pelmeni,* meat dumpling, in front of Judd and put *kotleta po pozharsky,* chicken cutlets, on the table for both of them. He also served several small dishes, rattling off names that Brooke could no longer follow. Without asking, he set down tiny glasses and poured vodka into them.

"No, thanks," Brooke told him.

"In Russia, drink vodka," he replied.

"Shall we give it a try?" Judd placed his glass on the back of his hand, and, as she had seen the official do at the Gorbachevskaya Street Factory, tipped it toward his mouth.

She tried to emulate his movement, but her glass tilted precariously. She caught it with her other hand before it spilled. "I should sign up for your ninja school to learn Russian survival tricks."

When he just smiled, she took a spoonful of her soup. "It's delicious." She took another spoonful, then looked up to see Judd examining her. Heat rose up her neck. "Is there another caviar egg on my nose?"

"No."

She pushed away the soup and leaned back. "Okay then. It's your turn to speak."

In the brief silence that followed, Judd drummed his fingers to the slow, melancholic song the Gypsy man was singing. A whiff of bay leaves from a passing dish reached Brooke.

"First I have a confession to make," Judd said finally. "I never planned to stay at Hotel Moscow. After meeting Amanda on the plane, my only involvement with your mission was to give a couple of seminars." He paused. "But when I learned what happened on your first day and overheard the U.S. commercial attaché insist that you all leave, I decided that it wouldn't be a bad idea to hang around the group. So here I am, a macho man, taking it upon myself to provide some male presence, unasked."

"That is very gallant of you. It has already come in handy."

He tilted his head. "No hard feelings?"

"About your risking a knife stuck in your ribs?"

Although her Champagne glass was still half full, he refilled it. When he put down the bottle in its ice bucket, she noticed the soft fuzz peeking from under his shirt cuff.

"The fact that you were in the group helped my decision." He looked into her eyes. "After meeting you last year, I read about your projects in your firm's annual report. Quite impressive."

Brooke raised her eyebrows in surprise. "They don't list them by executives' names."

"It wasn't difficult to connect the dots. The desalination plant in Saudi Arabia that supports a girls' boarding school; the railroad system in Liberia that scheduled visits of nurses to villages with no medical care."

She smiled. "Guilty as charged."

"Isn't the royal prince of Morocco your client?" When she

nodded he said, "Then he must have been the one to agree to install hundreds of water pumps."

"Otherwise women carry water twice daily from distant wells. You should try it once."

"So," Judd went on, "I'm glad that you've finally noticed me."

The words sent a tingle down her spine. The musicians moved to the next room, but their melodious chords carried over sentiments of love and hope.

"I don't notice married men," she replied quietly.

He opened his mouth, closed it, then shook his head. "I wish I could tell you that I am not married. However, for what it's worth, the situation is about to change. We're going through divorce mediation. I am aware, too, that I sound like a cliché."

Brooke played with the stem of her glass. "We choose our comfort zone when it comes to relationships. That's where people tend to stay." Or to get stuck.

"Is that the case with you?"

"I carry my own baggage." She paused. "We're discussing your situation. There's a huge leap between talking and final divorce."

Her parents had neither talked nor mediated. They just existed in the no-man's land of their marriage, their incompatibility too wide to bridge. They had met at a displaced persons camp, where, besides some Yiddish, they didn't even share a common language—he spoke Czech while she spoke Russian. The Holocaust bound them together as they crawled out from the ashes.

If originally the unquenched instinct to cling to life motivated them to cleave to each other, once they settled, they didn't share a vision of what that life meant. Her father was extravagant. He wanted to achieve business success to "show the *goyim*." He delighted in accumulating possessions to make up for deprivation and enjoyed showering them on those around him. When he moved the family from a dingy Brooklyn apartment into a suburban home in Long Island—and later, against his wife's wishes, bought a nicer home in the same town—Brooke's guilt-ridden, self-punishing mother chose to move into the closet-size maid's room off the kitchen, where she could live the Spartan life she felt she deserved for having stayed alive.

Yet even after Brooke fled their constant bickering and moved to California, they hung on. Her mother would never have sought happiness, but what about her father? No doubt his inability to go through more upheaval and pain had fused with habit and kept him married to a woman with whom he shared nothing.

"I would have waited a few months before finding an excuse to bump into you in New York," Judd said, bringing Brooke back from her musing. When she said nothing, he took a deep breath. "I have two boys. I don't want them to feel short-changed like I did, with my father's attention diverted elsewhere."

"Aren't you embarking on just the same path?"

"That's not what happened." Judd shook his head. "My father wasn't your ordinary Lothario. Look, I wasn't planning to turn this into a sappy confession about my childhood, so I'll stop."

"I'm sorry. I want to hear it." Brooke was caught off guard by the sudden tears misting her vision. "I'm also second generation."

"Wow." He gazed at her as if trying to peel off the layers this statement encompassed. "I had no idea."

"Yes, wow."

"Technically, I'm third generation, but in practicality I'm

second." He finished his drink. "My mother died when I was only five. Her parents took over my upbringing. My father traveled for business and divided his week between our home in New Jersey and his trips to Chicago. When I was about to leave for Vietnam, he told me that he'd been remarried for years, in Chicago, and had fathered and raised two more children. His rationale for hiding it seemed quite noble: Since my grandmother had become my mother, he was afraid to devastate my young soul—or their wounded ones—by snatching me away. But I wished that, at some point, he had told me about his new family and given me a choice. His motivation to hide his marriage probably had to do with the fact that my grandparents had lost all their relatives, but later were blessed with one beloved daughter who then died. He pretended for their sakes to have remained faithful to her memory."

Brooke's throat contracted. "Your father sounds like a man who had a lot of love to give."

"That's not how I saw it." Judd's eyes reddened behind his glasses. "I was torn. I loved my grandparents very much, but they had never assimilated, and I felt cheated for not growing up with my half brother and half sister in their normal family. I envied children growing up in American families, with young parents."

"I, too, envied 'normal' families. The *goyim,* especially, had cocktails. I adored the sound of a blender buzz, of clinking ice, and of parents chatting over their cool glasses. The only liquor in my house was one bottle of Sabra someone had brought them from Israel."

He smiled. "In my case, knowing nothing of my father's full

life, I missed getting to know the real man. In the end, while I was in Vietnam, his heart caved under the pressure."

"He must have loved your grandparents. He could have had an orderly life: A wife and all three kids in one household in Chicago. No weekly commute. No heart attack at the end."

"My grandparents were the only winners in this scheme, and I was the loser, growing up with their Holocaust *mishegas*." Judd looked down at his fingers and frowned. "Back to now: The thought of inflicting on my boys the kind of upheaval from which my father shielded me paralyzed me for too long. Finally it became clear that witnessing a venomous marriage was worse. My wife and I called it quits and started mediation to finalize things."

"I should be delighted, but I'm not." Brooke played with her fork. "The timing of this is poor. I don't date anyone who must hide my existence."

"For now, all I want is for you to know that you're special." He reached across the table and covered her hand with his. "This is special."

She only had to turn her palm up and curve her fingers to meet his dry, warm touch. Instead, she mustered all her willpower to extricate her hand and fastened her fingers around the stem of her Champagne glass. Then, realizing her tight grip might break it, she loosened her hold.

For a while, neither of them spoke. Finally she said, "Judd, these past twenty-four hours have been intense, but being away from one's natural habitat distorts things, plays tricks with one's perspective."

He raised an eyebrow and smiled. "We've gotten a gut feeling about each other. We've experienced some unpleasant events and some highs. Wouldn't you say that's worth at least three New York dates?"

How she wished she were younger, willing to bet all her emotional marbles. An image of the lost envelope flashed through her mind. Such recklessness—borne out of neediness—had once damaged her almost beyond repair. She pushed the rest of her food away. "I've seen divorces drag out for years, even when the two parties supposedly wished it to end. I am too vulnerable, not nearly as strong as I seem. There can't be any 'us' until you are truly, legally available."

The candle flame flickered and half drowned in the liquid wax. Only its tip still glowed. She couldn't see Judd's eyes in the shadows of his glasses.

"I'm sorry. It was presumptuous of me." He pulled back his hand from the table. "I apologize if I made you uncomfortable."

She wouldn't look at him.

"Let's order dessert." He waved to the waiter, but his hand stopped. As did the music.

In the sudden silence, Brooke turned her head. Four young men stood at the entrance, more burly looking than the three who were seated, and a few years older. Attired in lilac and burgundy striped suits, they planted their legs apart, their fingers hooked into their belt loops cowboy style. Their open jackets revealed chromed handguns.

Brooke and Judd exchanged a look. As soon as the four strutted past their table, they jumped to their feet. Judd slapped a fifty-dollar bill on a plate, and the two of them rushed out.

# DAY THREE

*Saturday, October 2, 1993*

## ❧ CHAPTER ❧

## *Twenty*

A RUSSIAN LADA CHUGGED up to the hotel entrance, its windshield dappled with crushed insects and its exhaust pipe burping a puff of gray fumes. Brooke, who was checking to see if the tour bus had arrived for the day's planned sightseeing, was surprised to see Irina struggling to get out. At the same time, a dark-haired woman emerged from the passenger door. When Irina pointed at Brooke, the woman said in English that she had come to translate.

"My deep apologies for late. Much chaos downtown," she said.

"You are not late because we had no appointment," Brooke replied. She had been looking forward to this morning's tour; finally she would get to see Red Square bordered by St. Basil's Cathedral, Lenin's Mausoleum, the Kremlin, and GUM, the state department store. If the bus hadn't been an hour late, Irina and her interpreter would have made the trip for naught. Luckily, also because of the bus's tardiness, Brooke had been in her room when a messenger delivered a flowery handwritten note from Olga, inviting her to dinner at Olga's home. The day was getting short on both ends. "I have only ten minutes," Brooke now told the translator.

"Thank you," Irina said. Her hair was washed and clipped up with what Brooke recognized as one of the conference's door prizes, and her olive skin was brightened by her alert eyes.

Brooke led the two women inside the hotel lobby. In no mood to hassle with the front desk over the use of the locked conference room, she walked downstairs to the dining room. There, the maitre d' tried to shoo her away, but she tossed a five-dollar bill on the table. "Coffee, bread, and marmalade, *spasiba*."

On a sheet torn from a school notebook, Irina had scribbled the steps needed to launch her jumper-cable business. The list was a far cry from the detailed business plan Brooke would have liked to see from an enterprise in a stable economy, complete with cash-flow charts and monthly expenses and revenues as well as five-year projections and alternate pricing strategies. Given Russia's current four-digit inflation rate, no economist could have developed such projections. Nevertheless, Brooke felt her excitement mounting; Irina was using the business thinking she'd acquired just yesterday. She had found hope.

Irina explained that she would manufacture the products in her apartment with raw materials her brother would obtain. "There's an army base twenty kilometers out of town. My brother's friend serves there, and he'll sell us cables and clamps, even the red paint for one clamp in each pair."

"Your brother can buy military surplus?"

"They're just army supplies. The soldiers sell them because

they don't get paid their salaries," the translator said. "The officers allow it, or the soldiers would leave."

Brooke scratched her head. "Stealing military inventory is not a sound business idea." Yet, she realized, in a country that had never developed manufacturing outside the government's heavy industry, supplies were simply unavailable anywhere. "How many will you produce and how do you plan to sell them?"

As Irina detailed her plan, it became apparent that she wouldn't take a bank loan even if one were available. "If I do, I'll be listed as an enterprise," she explained. "The mafia will be at my doorstep before I get home."

"You're doing great, thinking about all aspects of the venture."

"So you'll give me the money?"

"Me?"

"You said you wanted to help."

"And I did. Look at what you've already pulled together—"

"Talking is not money. No money, no help."

Brooke winced. "Teaching is help."

Irina began to weep. "I need to pay for the cables. I'll pay you back. I swear."

Brooke threw her hands up. "Lending money is not an option; we didn't come here to finance businesses." She regretted sounding as cold-hearted as any banker. Perhaps, long-term, she should consider establishing a fund to finance these women's ventures; most would require very little to put them on their feet. Yet even if she created a fund, how could it support Irina's purchasing pilfered military supplies? The world was wringing its hands in fear of deadly Russian weapons appearing in the hands of criminal gangs and Russian nuclear warheads finding their way to terrorist nations. How could she support a project—as small as it was—based on the corruption of army officers or the desperation of soldiers?

"You're my only hope!" Tears laced with mascara streaked down Irina's cheeks as Brooke ushered the two women upstairs to the hotel lobby. "Please!" She grabbed Brooke's hand and tried kissing it.

Irina's emotional drama grated on Brooke's nerves; she already knew that Irina's M.O. was to use every arrow in her quiver to try to break down Brooke's resolve. She kept walking toward the door, speaking in her kindest voice. "Your intensity will serve you well when you run your business." She craned her neck to check past the sentries, but there was no sign of the bus. She willed it to materialize. "Now I must get on with my day."

"But you have another meeting," the interpreter said.

"I do?"

"With a very powerful man. He wants to see you at his office."

Brooke halted. "Now, at ten-thirty on a Saturday morning?" For a split second she hoped it might be Sidorov at last. But he surely would have approached her through Svetlana or Aleksandr.

"His driver is waiting outside," the woman said, her tone urgent.

Brooke would have laughed if the idea wasn't beyond absurd. The business cards she had given out liberally at the conference were now circulating in Moscow, as contact with an American corporate executive had become a tradable commodity. The interpreter probably was receiving a commission for bringing Brooke over. "Thank you, but I've made other plans."

"This businessman, he has a very big business deal for your firm," the interpreter pressed.

Brooke didn't ask for details; she didn't want to show even the slightest interest. "No, thank you." She turned to leave.

The interpreter grabbed her arm to turn Brooke toward her and went on speaking. The more the Russian insisted—never revealing any specific information that might persuade Brooke—the more she confirmed Brooke's suspicion of her vested interest in the meeting. No way would Brooke enter a car and be driven to some unknown destination for the self-interest of someone's obscure agenda.

"What's his name?" Brooke heard Judd's voice behind her, and turned to see him in a sweat suit, a terry-cloth band across his forehead holding back perspiration. He still panted from his jog.

"Konstantin Tkachev," the woman replied. "A very important man."

Judd smiled at Brooke. "What do you say we go together?"

"What?"

As the driver bypassed the barricaded downtown streets, Brooke took in the armed militiamen clustered at major intersections. In the large boulevards where merchants opened their kiosks to display products from Revlon, Marlboro, and Chivas Regal as well as Mickey Mouse sweatshirts, people walked their dogs, seemingly impervious to the military presence.

Wary that the driver might understand English, Brooke whispered to Judd, "Remind me again why we're here?"

"I listen to everything and keep my options open." He shrugged. "You never know who might come up with what. I've heard that this character is well plugged into the military."

"You're an incorrigible capitalist, as Olga would say."

The limousine stopped in front of a modern office building—the first plush one Brooke had seen since her arrival—and they were ushered by two suited, silent bodyguards into a lobby paneled in chrome and mirrors, with a huge black slab mounted as a sculpture. Two more bodyguards bookended them in the elevator.

In the office anteroom, the contemporary Scandinavian furniture looked as though it had been lifted from a showroom. An abstract collage on the wall enhanced the unlived-in quality, and not a piece of paper cluttered the surface of the desk behind which sat a beautiful redhead wearing false eyelashes and sporting generous cleavage.

The redhead showed Brooke and Judd into a conference room with a polished oak table that could seat thirty people. A bodyguard was planted against the back wall, his muscular arms crossed over a barrel chest. A burly man wearing a suit jacket but no tie slouched in a center chair along the conference table. The top two buttons of his shirt were undone and revealed the edge of an undershirt and a gold chain as thick as Brooke's pinkie. On his fingers twinkled two heavy gold rings, one studded with a five-karat diamond. The smile that teased his lips failed to reach his liquid eyes.

"Welcome into my empire." The man Brooke assumed was Tkachev rose and smiled broadly at Judd. He gave Judd a vigorous handshake and handed him a business card.

Brooke watched with amusement as he ignored her; he must think that she had brought her boss along. "I'm glad you can meet my colleague, Judd Kornblum," she said pointedly.

"Hello." Her host gave her a cursory once-over, ending with a slight nod. She would have gotten his attention, Brooke thought, had she appeared in a miniskirt, spiked pumps, and a tight red sweater.

The moment they sat down, Tkachev said to Judd, "You must agree fifty–fifty."

"Excuse me?" Brooke asked.

"Fifty–fifty for the business."

"What business?" Brooke asked.

The Russian's gaze remained on Judd as if he had been the invited guest. "What business I'm going to tell you about."

"Ninety–ten," Judd replied, amusement in his voice.

The Russian shook his head. "No business then."

Judd suppressed a chuckle. "What's the business?"

Brooke stood up. "Well, this was fun. If your driver would please take us back—"

Tkachev cut her off. "I'll tell you what. You came all this way so I will be *large* and tell you what business." He motioned for her to sit down.

Brooke remained standing. "I'm listening."

"You buy ten airplanes," Tkachev said, again speaking to Judd, who was still sitting. "We start domestic airline."

"Ten airplanes," Brooke repeated.

"First year. And you put four million dollars in bank." The Russian continued to speak to Judd. "Second year, you buy ten more airplanes—"

"I buy twenty airplanes and put up four million dollars?" A shade of a smile played on Judd's face. "And you buy twenty more airplanes and put up four million dollars more?"

"We don't buy airplanes. We manage airline."

"Where would these airplanes be flying to?" Brooke asked.

Tkachev made a broad sweep of his hand. "All over Russia."

Now Judd stood up, too. "Thanks, but I don't see what's in it for us—"

"Wait. Sit down." The Russian motioned with his head. The driver-bodyguard opened a panel in the wall, retrieved a tray with vodka and small glasses and placed it in front of them. "We drink to business."

Judd remained standing. "We'd better get going."

"No. We have a good idea. The government will pay."

"How does the government figure into this?" Brooke sat down, her curiosity piqued. This was material for her article.

"Your four million, government matches with special low-interest loan for airline. Only twenty-six percent. Yes? We put it in the bank and get big interest, maybe three hundred percent. We make maybe eleven million dollars, put it in *offshorsky* bank. We pay you consultation fee. Yes?"

"Consultation fee? What happened to the fifty–fifty deal?"

"Airline is fifty–fifty."

"Oh, the airplanes. I forgot," Judd said. "Do they fly in the meantime?"

"We will own Russia's national airline."

"Sounds like a Groucho Marx routine," Brooke murmured.

"You American make jokes." Tkachev shot her a warning look. "We are serious businessmen. You are our American partner or government don't give us money."

Brooke rose to her feet again and extended her hand to Tkachev. "It's not for my firm. Nice meeting you."

Tkachev circled the table as they made for the door and gave Judd's back a hearty slap. "Fifty–fifty?"

"Maybe ninety–ten."

Anger knotted the Russian's eyebrows into one black line, like electrical tape. "We shake hands on it now or no business."

"No deal, then." Judd smiled, reaching for the door handle. "Any nukes?"

The man's eyes narrowed as he surveyed him. "Maybe."

"That's a yes."

"I only trust a partner."

"Oh, well. If you come across anything good in that department, please let me know." Judd steered Brooke toward the anteroom.

There were no bodyguards in the elevator; probably Brooke and Judd had passed security clearance. She would have entered the elevator laughing at Tkachev's offer had it not been for the hidden cameras she was certain were trained on them. She whispered to Judd, "You blew your chance of being an airline tycoon."

"A steal for only four million dollars."

"What's with the nukes? You can't be serious."

"Contacts here are convoluted, interlocking. It was a test to find out who I'm dealing with."

The answer didn't satisfy her. It would never have occurred to her to ask about nuclear weapons. But Judd had obviously recognized Tkachev's name when the interpreter mentioned it. The Wild West had attracted many unsavory opportunists, and she had just learned how no one in power in Russia "bought" anything. This privatization orgy was nothing but the biggest transfer of government-owned rights to a few robber barons since the European nations had carved up Africa.

The driver, in dark aviator glasses and a black leather jacket, was waiting outside and held the limousine door open for them. Once Brooke and Judd were in, he pointed to the teakwood bar in the center of the car, where cut crystal glasses and a decanter of vodka shimmered on a silver tray.

Brooke stared out the window, feeling Judd's presence at the far end of the same seat. Nukes? There was no free market in Russia, or it was free indeed but the only "market" was the competition among the vultures descending on it both from the inside and the outside. How did Judd fit into this, and what had really brought him to Russia in the first place?

## ❧ CHAPTER ❧

## *Twenty-two*

ATURDAY WAS THE day her parents expected her to visit—or at least expected to hear from her if she were either working on the weekend or traveling. With the time difference, it was dawn in New York, but they were early risers and would soon be staring at the phone, willing it to ring. Yesterday, her father would have received her fax in his office. She hadn't asked him not to tell her mother, leaving it to him to decide whether to hurt her.

"EuroTours forgot to book a tour bus," Amanda told Brooke upon her return to their room. "But they're sending one now." She went downstairs to wait for it.

Brooke placed a request with the international operator and waited for the call back. Through the window she could see only some distant buildings. Somewhere, hundreds of kilometers west in Riga, Latvia, her mother had spent her pubescent years.

Brooke recalled first becoming aware of her mother's "otherness" on a summer Saturday, when her mother came to pick her up from dance class. All the other mothers picking up their daughters wore shorts or Capris in pastel colors. Her much-older mother looked out of place in a dark, flowery cotton dress that hung below her knees. And not only was her hair not high-lighted, teased, or coiffed, it was steely gray and pulled back into a severe bun. Her mother looked more than just ancient; she looked embarrassingly foreign, a stranger Brooke wanted noth-ing to do with.

Glancing at the phone, waiting for its ring, remorse and fond-ness filled Brooke. She wished she hadn't been so judgmental of her mother's shortcomings, so acutely alert to what was lacking in their home life. From the vantage point of maturity, Brooke could see that her mother was a brilliant woman whose educa-tion had been cut short, whose life had been thrown out of orbit. In spite of the hurdles, her mother managed to pave her own professional path in a new land, in a new language she studied obsessively. Starting as a bookkeeper, she eventually majored in accounting, and by the time Brooke was a teenager, her mother had learned to drive and had opened her own accounting office. The same frugal, exacting, opinionated, and unforgiving nature that made her difficult for Brooke to bear were perfectly suited for this career.

It was only in the bosom of her family that her mother's aus-tere and tormented soul snuffed out any moments of joy. Bertha had been merely five years old, still living in their tiny Brooklyn apartment, when one night she overheard her father begging her mother to "just try once in a while." Her mother had responded, "My dead relatives don't get a 'once in a while.' They are dead. And so am I—or I should be."

Brooke sighed. When the phone finally rang, she dreaded what she had to say. "Mom? How are you?" she asked in a cheerful tone.

"No better than expected. Not worse either. Where are you?"

Brooke gulped air. "In Moscow."

Thunderous silence, then, "What do you want with those anti-Semites?"

Brooke's father had picked up the other extension. "She's probably there on business."

Business reasons might be acceptable to her mother, as had been Brooke's visits to her firm's Frankfurt office; profiting from the Germans was the little that Jews could do in return for the horrors they had suffered. "You can call it that," Brooke said.

"Meaning what? Are you there on business or not?" her mother demanded.

"What else would send her to that cursed country?" her father replied. "She needs to know all the international machinations."

"Can't she exclude the one country that killed my whole family?"

Brooke held the phone away from her ear, letting their bickering take its course. A couple of exchanges later, when the two of them ran out of steam, she asked, "So how is the weather in New York?"

"Weather, *shmether*. Who cares? It's raining, all right? Now can you explain why you went to Russia, of all places?"

"Actually, Mom, I came here to take a look at the new economy. But I got involved in helping women make sense of it. They know nothing about business. They are like five-year-olds when it comes to finances or marketing—"

"Helping? You're there for charity? Of all places on earth, you chose to help our enemies?"

Brooke bit her lip, holding back the retort that, perhaps by showing them benevolence, they'd no longer be enemies. Such liberal ideas had never taken root in her mother's thinking. "It came by chance. All the executives at the office were told by the new management to take two weeks off. That new banking practice was applied to us." Brooke shifted the receiver to her other ear. "Amanda already had this mission set up so I just joined—"

"Why not just stick a knife in my back?"

"Martha, leave her alone," her father said. "She's a grown woman."

"Grown? And where did she grow up, you tell me? What kind of home did she need to grow up in in order to know that she owes it to her dead grandparents, aunts, and uncles not to go out of her way to help these murderers?"

Pulling the phone cord, Brooke stepped to the window. When had her mother's enemies ceased to be her enemies? At what time in the process of purging herself of her parents' past had she leaped over the clear separation of "us" versus "them"? She sat down on her cot, the enormity of her betrayal filling her. She had been insensitive to her mother's psyche, to her own family heritage.

"Next she'll be helping the murderers of your children in Prague," her mother told her father. "Will you defend her then? Maybe you'll send a donation?"

"Bertha, there are other miserable places around the globe," her father said feebly.

"Yes," her mother said. "India. Lots of unhappy people

there—and they never had pogroms. You can find poverty there, even leprosy. But get out of Russia!"

"Go to Israel, and do *tzedakah* for our own people," her father said.

Brooke dropped her head into her hands as she clutched the phone to her ear. Her heart pounded with the old pain, the wound her parents had carved in the center of her being. They had assigned her one job—to remember—and she had willfully ignored it. "Mom, I just arrived two days ago," she said. "I've made promises—"

"Why do you care about the feelings of some Russians more than you care about the feelings of your family? Why can't you do the simple thing and maintain respect—" Her mother's indignant voice suddenly pinched and choked.

*Dead people did not have feelings,* Brooke thought.

"Brooke," her father took over the conversation, using the name he'd never grown comfortable with. "Do they know you are Jewish?"

"It rarely comes up." Brooke shifted the chain so the Star of David returned to rest in the front. Instinctively, she had turned it when Irina arrived, wanting to keep her Jewishness out of the picture.

Her mother sobbed into the phone.

"Okay, Mom. I've been considering not staying for the whole program—"

"Today," her mother cut her off. "Get out of there today. Please. Remember—"

"I remember! You never let me forget!" Brooke screamed, then sobered. "Sorry. I'm sorry. I didn't mean to hurt you." She replaced the receiver in the old-fashioned cradle, feeling drained and ashamed of her outburst.

She could fly to Frankfurt; it would be a good opportunity to discuss the new office landscape with Hoffenbach. Also, she could use visiting his office as an excuse to tell Amanda that although she, too, was deserting the group, she would explore the launching of a micro-lending fund here. Yet, how could she manage such a project without setting foot in Russia again? Anti-Semitism wouldn't be eradicated here in the coming decades. No, there was nothing for Brooke here. She'd be better off investing her energy helping Israeli women and making her parents happy in the process.

She called Delta and booked a flight for the next day, Sunday. Then she left a message at Hoffenbach's office because she didn't have his home number.

## ❧ CHAPTER ❧

## *Twenty-three*

THE MORNING WAS bright and warm, and Olga was filled with anticipation for the evening. Who would have ever believed that one day she'd host an American guest in her own home? In the outdoor market, on rickety tables constructed of wood planks, autumn colors played in the piles of yellow squash, brown potatoes in open burlap sacks, mud-covered carrots, and mounds of purple beets. Every few meters, Olga examined a bottle of oil, a wheel of cheese, or a crock of butter produced in the farmers' kitchens.

The chicken merchant beckoned her, pointing at four emaciated fowl hanging from a post over his head. The state of the chicken reflected the economic problems of Russia, Olga thought: the leaner the times, the scrawnier the chicken.

"How much?" She poked her finger at the clammy, yellowish skin.

He unhooked one from the post and held it up in both palms, like an offering. "Three thousand rubles."

"That's a week's salary! Thievery!" She sniffed the chicken front and back for signs of decay. "Two thousand." She pointed at the smudges of feathers left. "Burn them and clean the insides."

"Twenty-five hundred."

"Twenty-two hundred. And let me check the inner organs before you wrap them. Don't break the liver or the spleen."

"Do you think this is America?" In quick, short slices, his knife cleaved the chicken's center. "Twenty-three hundred."

"We should only have it as good as in America." She lit a Dukat. "In America citizens have shopping centers and supermarkets. Do you know they have stores with dozens of washing machines where you can do your wash and then put them in other machines that dry your clothes while you wait?" She punctuated her words with a wave of her cigarette. "In America, every woman has electric appliances to do her kitchen work—to peel, chop, or mix. You can't begin to imagine what they have in America. Have you heard of an electric *toothbrush*?"

"They're too lazy to brush their own teeth that they need a machine for that?" The merchant's knife gutted out the chicken's innards and laid them on a newspaper for her to examine. "Americans are stupid. They order things by mail! Can you imagine not inspecting the merchandise before they send it to you? What do you do when they dump on you all the ruined or broken items? And anyway, anybody can steal from the package before you even get it."

Olga nodded. "You may be right about that. But think of the other things that make life easy: freezers with prepared frozen meals, ready to eat, and canned vegetables of the best quality, not rotten stuff like here." She would ask Brooke what they did with the bad fruits and vegetables, if they didn't slip them onto consumers' plates.

She scrutinized the chicken's liver and heart for color, and the guts for feed, then watched as the merchant dangled the chicken over a candle to burn off the remaining feathers. "Throw away the head, but I'll use the stomach, neck, and the knuckles in my soup." She would cook the iron-rich liver over the open flame of her stove. It would be a delicacy for Galina.

"In America, chicken is bought already cleaned, cut up, and wrapped." The merchant rolled the purchase into a newspaper. "Even seasoned. Ha! A sure way to hide an old chicken that died of disease."

As she tucked her purchase into her string bag, Olga thought that tonight she'd ask Brooke how American housewives knew how to select a chicken if it came preseasoned and wrapped.

There would be other questions, such as how to proceed with her investigation. She hoped it would be *their* investigation. Olga couldn't do it alone, not without the American's financial savvy. She had no idea how to follow "the money trail."

An hour and a half later, Olga's legs throbbed from walking on the uneven, muddy paths of the market. The strings of her three bags, filled with onions, beets, carrots, parsley, squash, turnips, cucumbers, and radishes, strained her shoulder muscles. For her guest tonight, she had splurged on herring and cheese, and had even bought three eggs. Her favorite meat merchant had been in the market, and she bought sausage, almost certain he didn't make it out of old horse meat.

She took the subway to Baumansky market, thirty minutes away, where she bought fresh oranges for Galina to keep away the flu—Olga's daughter-in-law was busy with both a job and university classes. Olga wanted to help the young mother become a modern woman, the kind Russia needed.

At the flower stand, she bought fresh red carnations for her table. When she returned home, she would send Viktor to the dairy factory for milk and butter, and then have him stop at the baker. Let him stand on line for an hour in each place. Her husband might be an *intelligent,* but when it came to housework, he was as lazy as any other man. Right now, while her stiffening joints cried out for a day of rest, he was home, reading a book and listening to classical music. When would she get to stay in bed for the day and read a good novel?

The sun grew hotter as Olga, still wearing her wool coat, trekked the four blocks from the subway. She felt dizzy. She missed her little Zhiguli, as old and unreliable as it had been. Damn the toad. She removed her scarf and stuffed it into her coat pocket. Her bags became heavier with each step.

She heard the pounding of feet before someone elbowed her hard. Strong hands knocked her to the ground. The bags were ripped from her hands, almost tearing off her arms.

It was so fast. Lying face down, she felt the grating taste of dirt in her mouth. She spat, but her saliva was mixed with mud and drooled down her lip. She lifted her head and a sharp pain pierced her temples as she saw three strapping youths fleeing with her bags. She recognized one of the boys; he had been a good son who used to sit with his mother in the park. How had he turned into a no-goodnik, a thief? And right in his own neighborhood! Didn't he care about the shame he brought upon his mother?

Olga propped herself up on one elbow in the caked mud. Inch by inch, she pushed herself up to a sitting position. She checked her limbs and rubbed her scraped, throbbing knees. To her left, a lonely turnip was all that remained of her stolen bags. Gone was her food for the week. Three hours of shopping and hard-earned money wasted.

The bouquet of carnations lay strewn about, stems broken.

She was tired. A sense of loss, of injustice, of powerlessness, washed over her. As if through an outer pair of eyes, she saw herself, a lonely *babushka* in a heavy coat, scruffy-looking and sitting in the dust, unable even to pull herself up.

Her hands covered her face as silent sobs heaved her chest, broke, and choked in her throat. How she wished she could cry. Cry for all the boys whose mothers had taught them good values but who learned bad things because they had to. Cry for Mother Russia, where her granddaughter would grow up.

Still, she held back many unshed tears. They hardened into anger.

# *Twenty-four*

THE DOORBELL AWOKE Olga from a rare nap, but when she tried to get up, a groan escaped her throat, so foreign to her ears that for a split second she wondered if someone else was in her bedroom. Pain pierced her right knee. She removed the ice pack and found the knee swollen. The rest of her body throbbed, as if the adrenaline that had rushed through her during her fall had pooled in her bones. "The last thing I need right now," she muttered. Then she remembered that she had telephoned Svetlana to come over.

She called out to Viktor to open the door, but he hadn't returned from his shopping. The attack had forced him to go out to replace some of the stolen groceries. They couldn't afford all of it, and anyway, by noon there wasn't much left in the market. Canceling the dinner invitation to Brooke, though, was out of the question. When Viktor returned, two neighbor friends would come over and help her cook whatever he'd managed to buy.

Olga squeezed her feet into her slippers and drew herself up to go to the door. A few minutes later, as Olga climbed back into bed, Svetlana pulled a chair over and sat down on its edge.

Olga fumbled for her pack of Dukat, then thought better of it. She sipped water with a *tabletka* from Brooke's precious gift of Tylenol. "Thank you for coming," she told the young woman.

Svetlana lowered her head. "I'm honored that Dr. Leonidovna Rozanova has invited me." She spoke in the deferential third person address, the form used for a figure of authority. "I used to read her *samizdat*. Once I retyped it and distributed eight carbon copies."

"You did good. That was the only way to get the word out then."

Svetlana tipped her head respectfully.

"You were brave then," Olga said, "and I've heard that you were brave at the Gorbachevskaya Street Factory the other day."

Red blotched Svetlana's round cheeks. "What choice did I have? All my comrades were there. And I had the American guests to worry about."

Was Svetlana suited for the crusade Olga had in mind? She touched the young woman's arm. "Things have changed. *Samizdat* days are over. Those were words, now we're ready for action. There are things we can do to help improve women's lives. Your cooperative is not the only one attacked. With Brooke's help, I may find out who is behind these acts of terror. We must stop the mafia."

"Brooke—uh—" Svetlana swallowed hard. "She's here now, but soon she will be gone."

"She's an outsider with the courage to get involved."

Svetlana wound the straps of her handbag around her fingers.

"She went back to the factory after the attack. She can be brave, but, Dr. Rozanova, I have a daughter."

" 'Make yourself into a sheep, and you'll meet a wolf nearby.' Don't you see that your daughter is all the more reason? Help make Russia a better place for her, just as I'm doing for my granddaughter."

A tremor took hold of Svetlana's chin. "I can't take chances. I am all she has."

Olga straightened up in bed, feeling the ache in every joint. "You are not as helpless as you think. We women are not as powerless as we make ourselves believe." She squeezed Svetlana's fingers. "I believe that the scheme originated at the Economic Authority."

Svetlana recoiled as if slapped. "The director, Sidorov, is—"

"What?"

Svetlana's pale face turned crimson. "He's—uh, very influential."

The fear powerful men instilled in others was part of their game. Olga let out a cough that cleared her throat. "You must have been to the Finance Division on your cooperative business. Can you think of ways to get some of the files?"

Svetlana looked down at the twisted straps of her handbag. Her eyes filled with tears. "I can't."

Olga pressed on, her voice softer. "How do you feel about democracy?"

"It makes me very happy."

"What about democracy for men only? We'll lose our place unless we claim it. Misogyny is rampant—in the street, at home, in offices and factories. In the Duma we no longer have the one-third minimum quota to represent our interests. The laws that guaranteed our rights have been wiped out. Your daughter's school meal? Gone. Svetlana, we are being defeated in a battle we hadn't been prepared to fight."

"It's difficult to fight. It's so unfeminine."

Olga waved her hand impatiently. "Feminine! What idealistic nonsense! The curse we inflict on ourselves. How self-defeating it is to always judge everything we do with an external, critical eye? Whether it's the way we discuss a painting or the voice in which we tell our child a story, we obsess over whether we sound and act feminine. Don't you see that our own attitude hands the power to men? That it makes them our masters more than any official policy could ever do?" She adjusted the ice pack on her swollen knee. "From women who won't leave an abusive husband because self-sacrifice is a feminine virtue, to those who won't learn to drive because driving is unfeminine! We're the losers."

Svetlana's eyes were wide, glued to Olga's face.

Olga laughed caustically. "I'm being *unfeminine* myself preaching like this. Our greatest tragedy is that women who are born leaders are beaten down—by men and women alike—if they try to run for political office just because it is considered unfeminine to be in a position of authority."

"Dr. Rozanova should run for political office."

Olga lit a Dukat and took her time to suck in its aroma. "I very well might." She let the smoke out of her nostrils and watched the plumes rise. "You cannot break through a wall with only your forehead. Someone out there must listen to us. We want a true democracy and a life without fear for our bodies, for our rights, for our children, isn't that so? That's why we all must act." She waved the cigarette to emphasize her words. "It's now or never."

Svetlana dabbed at her eyes with the corner of her handkerchief.

"Will you help?" Olga held out a list of ventures she had prepared—Vera's, the Gorbachevskaya Street Factory, and a couple of other cooperatives whose stories she had found in the newspapers.

"My friend Katerina works for Sidorov. She says he is, uh, dangerous."

"I'm sure he is. Can you ask her to obtain the files for these companies?"

Svetlana nodded, then shook her head. "I'm too scared. She will be even more."

"Take it." Olga pressed the piece of paper into her palm. "Think hard, and you'll change your mind."

T HE MAN WHO came to fetch Brooke before dusk introduced himself as Viktor Rozanov, Olga's husband. A
stocky man, his weighted-down features made him look
like a harmless bulldog. With his unruly, thin gray hair and tie-
less shirt unbuttoned under a rumpled suit jacket, it seemed as
though he couldn't decide whether to wake up from a nap or go
take one.

"I came early, in case there are roadblocks." He opened the
passenger door of a small Lada. The interior, though old and
steeped in cigarette smoke, was clean. "I borrowed it from a
friend. I apologize that it's not elegant."

"It's fine. Thanks for picking me up." Brooke slid inside.
"Were there any roadblocks on your way?"

He shrugged. "Most traffic is being diverted away from the
White House."

"Would it be possible to drive by and see it?" Today, when the
group finally set out sightseeing, they had been dropped off in a

park where they were told it was much safer. As beautiful as the park had been, Brooke was disappointed. This had been her last chance to see the city.

Viktor chuckled. "Now I know why Olga likes you."

Fifteen minutes later, he slowed the car down. "Novoarbatsky Bridge." He pointed with one hand as he deftly turned the wheel with the other.

Under the glare of stadium-like lights posted at intervals, tanks surrounded the massive white parliament, their barrels aimed at its many windows. Behind the tanks, armored trucks lined up and hundreds of police troopers crouched, watching the building where, Brooke knew, political representatives from all over Russia and from the many Republics still under its control had barricaded themselves.

"Our White House," Viktor said. "Parliament, not your president's home. The revolutionaries, they give us a bad name." He corkscrewed his finger near his temple. "They are violent and crazy. Communists, Fascists, anti-Semites. But one thing they're right about: We all want Western-style democracy, not Yeltsin's anarchy. He's an idiot. Nothing but a drunk, blundering fool. We love our country, and we want our self-respect back."

As the Lada inched its way through the meandering crowd, Brooke spotted hats with their fur earflaps tied upward over sober faces with vacant eyes. Something sluggish, resigned in the people's aimless wandering indicated that they weren't surprised by yet another leader's dramatic show of force.

Viktor slalomed through the crowd at the next intersection, which was flooded with armed soldiers who seemed oblivious to both cars and people. He boldly continued toward the outer ring of troopers who had their guns at the ready.

"Could we stop for a minute?" Brooke asked.

When Viktor did, she opened her door and got out, but stayed behind the open door as a shield, ready to duck if necessary. She viewed the scene. There was something bizarre about it, and it took her a few moments to grasp that the disconnect came from the loud men's choir of the Soviet-era Red Army Band blaring through the speakers. "Music?" She leaned in toward Viktor. "Why music?"

He rolled down the window to listen. "When the music is on, the deputies can't shout out their slogans." He let out a nicotine-coated laugh. "Yeltsin, *musika*—parliament, no propaganda," he said as if he were quoting some news bulletin.

In a break between songs, two young men in camouflage fatigues emerged from the huge glass door of the parliament building, carrying bullhorns. Exuberantly, they shouted what sounded like slogans, then broke into their repertoire of military songs.

"Communists." Viktor flicked away the stub of his still-lit cigarette. "*Re'aktzionyer.*"

The police, through thundering bullhorns, responded, shouting demands. "They want the deputies to surrender. Give up their guns," Viktor volunteered, then added, "Get back in the car."

Brooke didn't move. The loud piped music resumed, interrupting the rebels with Yeltsin's repertoire. The musical competition between the military and the parliament would have been amusing if the situation weren't so dire. If Yeltsin lost, communism would return—and with it the possible renewal of the Cold War. This time, nuclear weapons would be controlled by hot-headed civilians who had tasted freedom from a totalitarian regime.

Brooke pointed to a cluster of people who watched the building. They shouted occasionally, but the music drowned out their voices "What about them? They think it's safe here."

"Foreigners. From the Republics. Many come to Moscow now. They are dangerous."

"Dangerous how?"

"Crazy. Unpredictable. Foreigners."

Brooke examined the crowd. With more than a hundred nationalities within the redefined borders of Russia, how could anyone tell who was foreign? Some of the people in the crowd had the light Slavic coloring and broad, flat features; others appeared more Cossack-like, with dark hair, olive skin, and intense eyes. Even from a distance Brooke could discern Asian nationalities with Mongolian and Chinese features. Some people were large, others of slight build. And where did the Jews fall among them? Their features were as diverse as the cultures and people among whom they lived.

"Look. Yeltsin militia." Viktor pointed up at a modern glass skyscraper to the far right of the White House. "All he knows is confrontation, not compromise."

Still holding her door as a shield, Brooke peered high into the darkened rooms of the building that towered over the parliament. Silhouettes showed through the shattered glass, the shadows of snipers with their guns pointing at targets below. Even straight at her, it seemed.

Brooke reentered the car and slammed the door, and Viktor resumed driving.

When they passed by a corrugated fence, Brooke saw two large Stars of David sprayed haphazardly. "Why are those here?" she asked.

"The anti-Semites. They blame the Zionists for stirring it all up."

The skin on her arms contracted. "How are the Jews involved?"

Viktor shrugged. "They are not. But it's always like this."

Brooke slid down in her seat, apprehension filling her. World War II happened, millions of Russians perished in Stalin's gulags, many others were killed by the Nazis, communism collapsed, yet the former Soviet hatred of her mother's powerless minority people remained unchanged.

The car passed more graffiti, this time a Cyrillic word with one of the letters drawn as a Jewish star. Brooke pointed at it. "What does it say?"

"It's Yeltsin's name. The letter *L* in the middle means that he's a traitor because of his Jewish connections."

Brooke felt a chill climbing up her body. As history had shown, graffiti on walls could be merely a few steps away from genocide. Her mother was right: What had made her forget everything she had known? She was glad she was leaving this horrible place.

She pulled out her Star of David and rested its shiny face over her stretch-knit shirt, then shifted the knot of her small silk scarf to the side so it wouldn't block it.

"WHAT HAPPENED TO you?" Brooke asked as she followed Olga into the living room. Olga was limping, obviously in pain. "Have you been to a doctor?"

"Not important." Olga waved her hand in dismissal.

"You should take it easy."

"I'll rest in my grave."

"Thank you for inviting me." Brooke handed her a small package in which she had wrapped a pair of her own pearl earrings.

"I cannot accept this," Olga said, upon opening it.

"Please. I have an almost identical pair in New York."

"How is that? Do all American women have two of every piece of jewelry?"

"I thought I'd left mine at a hotel, bought a second pair, then found the first pair in my toiletry kit." Brooke smiled. "It will give me great pleasure to see you wear them."

Viktor wiped his hands on a kitchen towel before placing a record on a Grundig record player the size of a suitcase. A Mozart symphony filled the small room.

Brooke looked around her. An oil painting of a flower vase, a watercolor of a Russian winter landscape, and a Renoir print of a girl brushing her hair hung above the upright piano and the couch. A lighting fixture with a shade made of scarlet velvet with a gold fringe hung over the coffee table and illuminated plates of food in a medley of textures. The scent of carnations in a vase mixed with the smell of cigarette smoke and the aromas of cooking.

In response to Viktor's inviting gesture, Brooke eased into a chair upholstered in brocade. "It's so lovely here."

"We have an old proverb: 'Don't judge a home by its appearance, but by the warmth of its welcome.' " Olga handed her a tiny liqueur glass. "Ours is not as elegant as in America, but it's good for Russia."

"It's a true *intelligentsia* salon." *Intelligentsia* was a word Brooke's mother still used to describe a class of people she admired, defined by cultural rather than economic superiority. Brooke pointed at the dark wood bookshelf stretching along the entire wall. Many of the books were bound in brown or burgundy, their titles embossed in gold. "What are the subjects?"

"History, fiction, biographies, philosophy. Some poetry. These books are our most precious possession." Still sitting, Olga stroked the tomes' spines. Pride resonated in her voice. "For thirty years, Viktor and I hunted for books in back alleys and in the homes of unemployed *refuseniks*."

*Refuseniks*. Jews who had demanded the right to leave, but while being denied exit visas, lost their jobs and all attached benefits. "Were books unavailable?" Brooke asked. "Russians are so highly educated."

"If people wanted something, our government made sure to hold back its production. Scarcity makes citizens needy and vulnerable. It makes them dependent on the government's favoritism and selective hand-outs."

Viktor raised his glass in silent salute, and Brooke, imitating him and Olga, sipped from hers. The almond liqueur tasted delicious.

Olga pushed a plate of dumplings toward her. "These are stuffed with chopped lamb. Eat, eat."

"*Pirozhki,*" Brooke said, accepting the familiar food her mother adored. She took a bite. "Delicious!" Pointing at the old TV set, she said, "I hope you won't consider me rude, but is there an English-speaking station where I might hear some news?"

Viktor found the BBC, but the commentary was about domestic British topics.

"How about CNN?" Brooke asked.

He surfed the channels. CNN came on in Russian.

"Isn't it supposed to be in English?"

"You get the censored Russian version here. Only a couple of European hotels get direct broadcast."

"This must be the European version, in this time zone, but dubbed," Brooke said as she looked at the pictures of curiosity-seekers who ambled around the ring of police, barbed wire, and steel roadblocks. "In New York, in a report issued probably by Yeltsin's camp, it said that the parliament deputies wanted to keep their jobs only because they preferred to live in Moscow, in large luxurious apartments, with chauffeured cars and generous salaries."

"No! These are lies." Olga banged her fist on the arm of her chair. "They stay in the White House for the highest moral values of our country: law and order. They would not spit on the Constitution."

"Sorry," Brooke said. "I know it's a touchy subject."

"Only the lies are. But now you are here to learn firsthand."

Not for long. "Except no one tells me anything. I have been unable to get either English TV or newspapers."

Olga looked surprised. "The *Moscow Times* is in English."

"For two days our escort, Aleksandr, has been saying it's too dangerous to go downtown to get it, yet Viktor and I just drove through the thick of it."

"Danger is relative," Olga said, hooking her gaze into Brooke's eyes.

Brooke surreptitiously touched her Star of David. She wouldn't be around to help in the dangerous investigation and must let Olga know out of Viktor's earshot. "I need to speak with you—"

Olga raised her hand. "Now we eat. No topics that interfere with digestion."

Brooke felt as if she were deceiving Olga as, for the next hour, the Russian introduced her to homemade blinis, their golden surface spread with sour cream and sprinkled with black caviar, and cabbage soup thick with kohlrabi root and pieces of lamb, and flavored with plums and onions that were first fried in lard.

"You're an incredible cook. What a feast," Brooke said, thinking that this meal must have also cost a bundle of rubles. "How long did it take you?"

"The neighbors helped. We do that for one another." Olga pushed toward Brooke plates of pickled eggplants, sliced sausage, and sturgeon in cream. "Eat, eat. It can't possibly be healthy to be so thin."

Brooke laughed. "You sound like my mother." Imitating Viktor, she tore a piece of brown bread and dunked it into the remains of her soup, then wiped the bowl clean. She tasted the herring, the salty farmer's cheese, and the cucumbers marinated in vinegar. Finally, she patted her stomach. "No more."

Viktor spoke little during dinner in spite of Brooke's efforts to engage him in conversation about his work at the Academy of Sciences. He chewed slowly. Suddenly, as if awakened by a thought, he waved his fork in a warning gesture. "Be careful. They tap your phone and search your room while you're out. Commit even a minor violation, and they'll use it against you when it suits them."

Brooke looked at him. "Suits them? Who are 'they'?"

"Same as before. Officials have the same jobs, just new titles. The K.G.B. still operates, but under a new name." He shook his head and rose to clear the dishes.

"Let me help." Brooke grabbed some plates.

"He'll only stack them. It's rude to wash dishes while guests are still in the house," Olga said. She wobbled to the buffet, where a polished-brass samovar hissed, and poured hot water into tall, clear, tea glasses, each resting in a silver-handled holder, the kind Brooke's parents still used daily. "I inherited this samovar from my mother. Look." Olga pointed at several embossed seals.

"Seventeen eighty-eight?" Brooke studied the seal, its edges eroded from years of polishing. "Over two hundred years old."

"My mother got it from her grandmother." Olga's eyes were wistful. "This is how we pass on our Russian values. Mothers carry the traditions of home and family. By handing over the samovar, they make sure their daughters do so, too." She opened a door in the buffet below, took out a set of matryoshka nesting dolls, and presented it to Brooke. "I want you to have this. Another heirloom. We are all products of our mothers, and carry their joys and sorrows inside us."

"Yes." Brooke's throat contracted. "Don't we?"

The finely painted egg-shaped wooden doll of a maiden with

a long, blond braid was beautifully done. Unlike other matryoshka dolls Brooke had seen, hastily painted in broad brush
strokes in primary colors, this one was exquisitely detailed by a
fine artist. The outside figure carried a wooden pail in her right
hand. Behind her stretched a scene of meadows.

Brooke twisted open the doll. The figure nesting inside carried a loaf of bread, and the scene behind her was of a forest.
The next doll held a washboard, and the one after her, a crock of
cheese. "Oh, Olga. It's beautiful."

"I'm glad to give it to my new American friend. It represents
our women: delicate, survivors, curators of home and country. There isn't much we can do to reciprocate your generosity,
coming here to help us."

Brooke cringed. "Well, it's really a very short visit. I'm leaving
tomorrow."

"Not so soon!"

Just then the record ended, and Viktor returned from the
kitchen. He stepped to the piano and glanced at the open music
sheets. "Rimsky-Korsakov?" he asked Brooke. "Or Schubert?"

"Which of you plays?"

"Both of us." Olga lifted the top of the bench and searched the
music sheets. "*Fantaisie* for four hands?"

Moments later, buoyant, enchanted notes tumbled from the
couple's fingers. Brooke watched them, envious of their close relationship, their shared history and values.

And their talent. She couldn't help thinking of her own failure at mastering the piano. The long hours she practiced, hating
every moment of it, had stretched into years of frustration when
she tried to please her father. When one teacher despaired, her

father hired another; someone must be able to tease the music out of his tone-deaf Bertha.

At thirteen, along with puberty, Bertha became conscious that she wasn't merely a replacement for her father's lost children and her mother's dead family, that she was more than their entrusted carrier of memories. She was her own person! She stopped the piano lessons and changed her first name. She hadn't been aware yet that within a few years, at Berkeley, she would fail her parents on a grander scale.

Brooke was so carried away by her thoughts that only when Olga and Viktor played the finale of the piece did it bring her back to reality. She clapped. "Bravo. Bravo."

"You should come to our weekly musical evening." Olga turned around on the piano bench. "Viktor also plays the violin."

Brooke watched him walk to the bedroom. "A good husband and a friend," she said.

"Yes, and I don't beat up my woman," he called from the door with a twitch of a smile.

Brooke laughed at his unexpected humor.

Olga didn't join in. "That is one more of our national tragedies. Wife-beating is a shameful nonsecret. Women here are punching bags for their drunken, angry men. At least before *perestroika,* women who had their bones broken too frequently could complain to their husband's supervisor at the factory or appeal to the local party official. Now even those measures are gone."

Brooke picked up the matryoshka and opened the fifth doll. The figure held up a red apple. Behind her, a river tumbled over rocks. Brooke twisted the doll open to reveal the smallest wooden matryoshka, the size of an olive pit, who was waving a spoon. Behind her was the opening of a tunnel.

"We Russian women often must dig a tunnel with nothing but a spoon," Olga remarked. "I understood your message about the Economic Authority. I've taken steps already." She looked around as though concerned that Viktor might hear. "I asked Svetlana to get their files for me."

"Will she?" Brooke asked. The poor young woman had been through so much this week. Even without the shock, would she be up to the task?

"She has a friend who has access. But getting the files is merely the first step." Olga gave a rare smile. "I am thinking bigger."

Brooke studied her. "What are you planning?"

Olga broke into a cough that convulsed her body. When the attack stopped, she said, "It's time I run for a seat in parliament. If Yeltsin gets his way, he'll announce new elections in December. There's a lot that needs to be done for our women."

Brooke felt small next to this feisty woman. Her own challenges seemed insignificant and self-indulgent. She hugged Olga. "That's wonderful."

"I keep complaining about how women's interests are underrepresented in the Duma, our lower house of representatives. I'm determined to do something concrete. I have some supporters." She tapped on her cigarette packet. "As much as I disagree with Yeltsin's methods, I admit that he was right that more competent, educated, and democratic people should fill our parliament."

"Amen."

Olga lit a cigarette. "There's a lot you and I will be able to do if your hunch about the Economic Authority's correct."

Brooke winced. "I'll be leaving tomorrow."

"So you've said. But you were going to participate in my symposium on Tuesday!"

"I'm sorry." Brooke felt her face redden. "Life is calling me back."

Olga's eyebrows pressed together. "You can't leave yet. I'll need your help with the investigation."

"I'm so sorry to disappoint you." Guilt clutched Brooke's insides. "But we'll keep in touch—"

"How? By phone? We can't trust it." Olga scrambled back to her feet. "Come with me." She stepped into the kitchen and returned within a minute with a covered dish.

"Where to?"

But Olga was already in her tiny foyer, where she removed Brooke's coat as well as her own off the hook.

"Where are we going?" Brooke asked again.

"You'll see why Russia must join the twentieth century—or we go back to the eighteenth."

## ❧ CHAPTER ❧

## *Twenty-six*

THE APARTMENT BUILDING was quiet tonight. On Saturdays, some neighbors went visiting friends. Svetlana could steal private time in the communal bathroom. She needed to think. And she needed to cleanse herself from Sidorov's filth that had burrowed since yesterday under her skin like maggots.

She removed her oversize laundry tub, *vanna,* from its hook high on the wall and placed it on the old checkered linoleum. She would never bathe in the claw-foot tub, whose fifty-year-old yellowed enamel had chipped down to the black cast iron and was covered with layers of grime. She brought two pots of boiling water from the kitchen, poured them into the *vanna,* and then added as much warm water as she could get from the faucet.

"Attitude is everything," Jenny had said. Svetlana threw in petals from two wilted roses she had taken from the Hotel Moscow dining room, and lit two stubs of her remaining scented candles. When she turned off the one bare light bulb, the warped and moldy plaster on the walls disappeared into the shadows.

Slowly, she lowered herself into the water, savoring its feel against her skin. In the short *vanna* her legs crossed at the ankles, and her bent knees dropped to the sides. She leaned back and wriggled her toes as warmth crept up her body. Brooke had given her a soap bar. The name, Lux, was as delicious as it smelled, and Svetlana would save the satiny wrapper to scent her lingerie and sweaters drawer. She closed her eyes.

"Attitude is everything." Tonight, in her tub, she would think only happy thoughts, like an American woman. Not a single thought about Sidorov. She would think of Natasha, her girl who was smart and, despite the malnutrition, healthy. And, as she had told Dr. Rozanova, she was happy about democracy, even if it turned out to be different from what she had expected. But Dr. Rozanova wanted her to take part in making new dreams happen. What did she stand to gain? Saving her cooperative and the livelihood of the women who trusted her. What did she have to lose? Everything, including her life.

To fend off the chill in the air, Svetlana used a plastic bowl to splash water over her back and arms and leaned back again, leisurely cupping more warm water and pouring it over her shoulders and chest. Because of democracy, she had been given the chance to meet the Americans, and they turned out to be more wonderful than the magazines had written. Important women like Brooke and Jenny made her feel she was one of them. That, too, was democracy: Everyone was equal—more equal than under communism. Under communism, important people made sure that everyone knew they were above others by reducing the others to little ants.

Rubbing the soap over a Georgian loofah, soft from years of use, Svetlana created mounds of foam over her breasts and upper arms. The candlelight reflected in the iridescent bubbles. She lathered the tufts of hair under her arms and rinsed well. Ads in Western magazines advertised deodorant. She wasn't sure how that product did the job. Did one spray stop the body's production of perspiration? Everywhere, or just on the patch of skin that was sprayed? True, American women emitted no body odor. Interestingly, according to the magazines, American men, too, used deodorant after their daily gym exercises. A couple of times she had stood close to Judd Kornblum and sniffed surreptitiously. He smelled good.

What would it feel like to breathe in the aroma of a fresh, clean, masculine body? What would it feel like to have a handsome man hovering over her, lowering himself tenderly onto her, like she'd seen on TV's *Simple Maria*?

Was it only yesterday that Nikolai Sidorov had violated her? Last night she had scoured herself to remove the muck and had douched against a chance of pregnancy. Even as she scrubbed again now, the despicable, vile act still dwelled under her skin. But most businessmen behaved this way. That was the reason she hadn't applied for a job as a secretary, where she could use her language skills. All Help Wanted advertisements stated clearly what was expected: "Long legs. No inhibitions."

Maybe now that the factory was ruined and Sidorov held her responsible, she would have no choice. Lots of women got used to giving their bosses the personal attention they demanded.

No, Svetlana chided herself. Her thoughts were transgressing into a negative attitude. She should think of happy things, like this instant, treating herself to a luxurious bath with an American soap. Reaching down, she touched her raised mound, the curly, honey-colored hair stirring softly just below the surface of the water. The velvety folds flared, opening with hunger. Heat spread through her veins, mounting, surging. A tight knot contracted deep inside her, bearing downward, demanding relief.

Svetlana arched her back and stretched a rigid leg over the rim of the tub, opening herself, allowing deeper access, blood rushing to her nerve-endings, her breath coming in short gasps. Then time stopped and hung, motionless, waiting for her. Her insides quivered in sweet tremors.

She barely caught her breath when Sidorov's face popped out of the shadows behind the candles and hung in the air, leering at her.

The banging on the door made her climb out of the tub. She was no closer to deciding what to do about Dr. Rozanova's request.

On the other side of the door, Zoya grunted and rattled the handle. Any moment, the latch installed after previous locks had been broken would dislodge.

"Just a minute!" Svetlana called. She dropped her weekly laundry into the *vanna*. The warm water, seeped with the remnant of the soap's fragrance, was too precious to waste.

## ❧ CHAPTER ❧

## *Twenty-seven*

I WAS PLANNING TO visit my friend, Vera, after you left," Olga told Brooke as they trekked around the block, Olga carrying her covered plate of delicacies. "But I know how blessed she'll feel to meet you."

Holding onto Olga's elbow to steady her, Brooke fixed the beam of her flashlight at the partially paved sidewalk. The night had turned cold. As Olga described Vera's encounter with the mafia, Brooke's skin tightened, and dread crawled to her scalp.

Still, she was unprepared for the sight of the woman in bed, her abdomen exposed. Vera's burned flesh glistened like raw meat. Brooke fought to keep her face composed, but the pain she felt was physical. She became conscious of every stitch of her own clothing: her bra was too tight over her rib cage, the waistband of her pantyhose cut into her skin, her scarf choked her.

Her fists closed, nails digging into her palm. The word *beating* had been repeated so often when Bertha was younger that it had lost its visual effect. Now, it blasted in its full meaning. This was what torture looked like. This was a version of what her parents had endured. In a split second, her mind's eye conjured a Nazi guard beating her mother with a stick—a senseless, brutal thrashing that had left her mother limping for the rest of her life. Brooke saw her father being hung with his arms tied backward until he fainted, the reason for the surgeries on his shoulders over the years. This was why her mother had always railed about Americans' naïveté, about their shutting themselves off from the truth while seeking hedonistic pleasures in moronic TV entertainment. They watched *Fiddler on the Roof* and thought they knew what a pogrom was.

Vera's mother pulled a hand-knit blanket over her daughter's knees to create a tent. Vera's dark eyes, burning with fever, were intelligent, and although her chopped hair stood out in clumps, Brooke could see that this long-limbed woman was beautiful.

Less than three feet separated the bed pushed against the left wall and the built-in cabinet and bookcase on the right wall. A jutting shelf served as a table, wide enough for one chair. Vera's mother gestured to Brooke to sit, then shuffled out of the tiny room. Brooke remained standing, but found no spot to rest her eyes lest it be perceived as a critical stare.

"They put up the wall to divide the room when Vera's brother got married," Olga said by way of explanation. "Then he got a job elsewhere and sold his space rather than give it back to his mother."

At the orientation before leaving New York, Amanda had talked about the abhorrent living conditions of most Russians, but Brooke had anticipated a modest dwelling like her family's first apartment in Brooklyn—three tiny yet functional rooms, not this wretched crowding. Vera was a factory director, and, judging by the number of books on the shelves, an educated woman.

Vera moaned. Olga crouched next to her and uncovered the plate. With her fingers, she fed Vera a small dumpling. "She speaks a little English," she told Brooke. "She'll understand what you say."

Vera nodded, swallowed, and moaned again.

Brooke couldn't dislodge a sound. "I'm so sorry about what happened," she finally managed to say, her voice tinged with tears. Then the dam broke. She was stunned by her own burst of crying. "So sorry," she murmured and turned her head away, embarrassed. She wasn't the victim here.

"Honor to meet you," Vera croaked.

Brooke buried her face in her hands, crying.

Olga patted her back.

"Sorry." Brooke stepped away. She must compose herself. What would these valiant women think of the spoiled New Yorker?

"You never imagined that teaching our women business skills would mean literally watching them fight for their lives," Olga said, handing Brooke her handkerchief.

"I truly apologize." Brooke sniffed, but unable to control herself, she went on crying. "Just let me get some fresh air. I'll be right back," she managed to say. With such a display, surely Olga would think her emotionally unstable. Brooke had never before had a public meltdown. When at age four she had tried a temper tantrum, her mother said that having endured the Nazis, she could stand up to a child's fit. After that, Bertha cried only when she was alone.

Brooke made her way out to the broken sidewalk, where her bottled-up grief surged, heaved, and finally subsided into hiccups. She wiped her eyes and looked around at the darkened buildings. Had the Russians, and then the Ukrainians, followed by the Nazis, not destroyed her mother's family, her mother would still be here, living like this. Her mother's siblings probably would still be alive. Her mother would have been a whole person, not the mourning shell she had become. She would have married a Jewish man whom she loved, and Brooke would have been born in the Soviet Union. She could have been Vera or Svetlana or Irina. Or, if more fortunate, Olga. Instead, by several twists of fate and a parade of unbearable miseries, Brooke had become the recipient of the rarest of commodity— luck. She had been lucky to be born in the United States of America.

This was her debt. She had always known that she had been put on earth to rectify the world's atrocities; she had been born with the responsibility of redressing all the injustices her parents—and by extension, all humanity—suffered. This was how one repaid luck.

Back in Vera's apartment, Brooke rinsed her face in the communal kitchen sink. "I will explain later," she told Olga as she handed her back the damp handkerchief, wondering whether she had ruined the fine embroidery, but not knowing what to do about it.

She stood next to Vera's bed and took the woman's hand. "Again, I apologize."

Vera attempted a weak smile. "Olga say you know everything business. That you earn million dollars."

Brooke smiled, her eyes misting again. "Not even close."

Olga chuckled. "Americans don't talk about income. Russians always do."

"Maybe Russians are right," Brooke said. Her New York friends discussed their sex lives but never their money.

"Maybe you explain things," Vera said. Her voice turned weaker, like a week radio signal, and she switched to Russian.

Olga translated. "I—meaning Vera—I am the director of a factory for pots and pans. Not good stuff, everyday quality, Russian level." Both women let out chortles. "I can't make sense of what the new owners want. They order us to cast nickel into the bottom of our cheapest pans. What for? Or make copper bowls without finish. Their edges are so sharp you could cut your fingers, but they don't let us polish them to make them safe. For export, they say. Western cooks don't mind cutting their fingers?"

Nickel? Copper? The picture became instantly clear. "They know exactly what they're doing," Brooke said. She sat down in the chair Vera's mother had vacated. "The cost of raw metals in Russia is way below the European cartel price, but the European Common Market can't allow Russia to create unbeatable competition. Metals from Russia must be sold at the higher Common Market prices." She bent toward the injured woman. "Therefore the nickel and copper are cast into anything, in whichever shape, because Russia is allowed to export to Europe finished products at any price it chooses."

"So what do they do with our pots?"

Brooke hesitated. All of Vera's employees' hard work was purposeless. Yet the woman had suffered too much to be denied the truth. "Since Russian raw material is worth a lot more in Europe's open market than the finished product, once your pots and bowls reach their destination, they are probably melted down. The nickel and copper are then sold at a huge profit. The money, in foreign denominations, is probably tucked away in an offshore bank account."

"*Offshorsky.* We've already adopted the word." Olga shook her head.

Brooke sat back. A new apprehension filled her head. "These smugglers are not fools. They know what they're doing," she told Olga. "Vera's up against an international crime cartel whose business practices must be as sophisticated as Coca-Cola and IBM put together."

As THEY TRAMPED their way back, Brooke's mouth tasted metallic. Frogs burped somewhere in the darkness. When the women rounded the corner, wind whipped down at them from the open fields to the north. Brooke removed her cashmere shawl and placed it over Olga's coat. "Keep it."

Olga fingered the fine wool. "It's too elegant. You've given me an expensive gift already. I can't take this—"

Brooke tucked her hands in her coat pockets for warmth. "You've given me a far more precious gift."

"What's that?"

Emotions rippled through Brooke, too complex to define. How could she begin to explain that seeing the misfortune and courage with which Russian women faced life finally made her grasp the magnitude of her parents' survival?

As though she'd read her mind, Olga's cold fingers laced into

Brooke's. "Only our stories are different. Not what they represent to us."

"My story is still different from most Americans'." Brooke bit her lower lip. "My mother was born in Russia. She is Jewish. Her sister was murdered in a pogrom. Afterward, the family escaped to Riga, but later ended up in a concentration camp. She survived, but her entire family was murdered before and during the war." She continued to speak as they reached the shelter of Olga's stairwell, where they stood in darkness. "In my childhood, the Holocaust was always present by the void of what was gone. I grew up without grandparents, aunts, uncles, or cousins. My parents were too old and too beaten to produce more than one child, so I had no living siblings, only the ghosts of three murdered ones. I was given an impossible legacy of responsibility, one I tried to escape my entire life."

"What sort of responsibility?"

"To never forget."

"I am so sorry to hear about your family tragedies." Olga lit a cigarette, and Brooke tried to read her face in the flicker of the lighter. Olga's brows were squeezed together. "We were horrible to our Jews. For centuries we stored up deadly hatred against them. Our priests gave us permission to rob them, to ridicule them, to beat them, to kill them—all under the premise of vindicating their killing our Jesus. Where was the goodness and compassion and Christian charity the priests were also telling us about? Shamelessly, we were the oppressors and the persecutors of the Jews in our midst."

Brooke felt the hair rising on her arms. She had never imagined she'd be facing one of "them," and certainly not one who confessed. "You say 'we,' yet you distance yourself from it—"

Olga cut her off. "It's our collective guilt—and it should be our collective shame—except that it is not." She sucked on her cigarette. "Even under communism we let minorities thrive and maintain their cultural identity, but we continued to persecute your people. We closed their synagogues and shut down their newspapers. Yet, when the Jews wanted to leave, we forbade it. We only tightened the noose on their necks."

Was Olga asking for Brooke's forgiveness? It wasn't hers to give. "How much of it have you witnessed yourself?" Brooke asked.

"I grew up with it. I am guilty both collectively and personally. My family was friends with our Jewish neighbors. I had liked Mrs. Horvitz's cooking. She was kind to me. I was only three or four years old when, one night, I heard a lot of shouting outside and noise of banging and breaking glass. Then my mother brought in down-feather quilts, and I saw from the window my older brothers lead the Horvitzes' cow and horse to our barn. I asked where the Horvitzes went without their horse, and was told they ran away by foot. In the morning, I received the wool coat of their daughter, who was a few years older than me. All winter I worried about her being cold somewhere, but then I too, forgot." Olga pressed the light switch, as if wanting Brooke to take a full measure of her culpability. "With alterations, the coat served me for years." She tapped her cigarette, and the feathered ashes fell to the floor. "When the war ended, Mr. Horvitz came back to town—alone. A neighbor who had worked for him had taken over his home and business. He stabbed Mr. Horvitz with a pitch fork in front of my eyes."

Brooke couldn't find words and anyway wouldn't have been able to get them through the contracted passage of her throat.

Olga went on, "I was older then and was both ashamed and horrified. My parents told me that the Horvitzes weren't worth getting upset about, but I couldn't get them out of my mind. I knew that my parents were wrong, and this knowledge was my first awakening into adulthood and independent thinking. I understood that it wasn't just hate. It was greed, even envy. I never saw a Jew again until I went to university, and even there, we were jealous of them because they were so smart that if our academic institutions hadn't limited their enrollment, there would have been too many Jewish students and then Jewish professors churning out Jewish graduates that would qualify for the best jobs. Universities that were supposed to be the temple of knowledge, open thinking, and academic achievement were scared of the Jews' intellectual powers."

When Brooke said nothing, Olga sighed. "So you see, I was complicit, if not active, in horrific acts against your people. Maybe today a more clever Jewish woman would have been director of the Institute of Social Research. Perhaps I've benefited from the vengeance we unleashed upon our Jews with more than just a coat."

"Your honesty alone must redeem you," Brooke managed to say. But who was she to forgive transgressions committed against others?

"Redeemed in whose eyes? The Lord? Our priests told us that He punished His Chosen People for killing His son, Jesus."

Olga drew in a rough breath. "Just so you know, I don't believe the priests—most of them are greedy and corrupt—but I believe in the Lord, and I still don't understand why He let down your people."

"You sound like my mother. She won't talk to Him until He asks the Jews for forgiveness." Brooke swallowed. "Thank you for admitting all that. It takes courage."

"It takes courage to flaunt your being a Jewess. No one in Russia would wear that." Olga pointed to the Star of David.

"It's because of my mother that I must go home." Olga's confession, the honesty of it, had both chipped at Brooke's resolve and reinforced it. She admired Olga even more than before, but also there was no doubt that she was in the wrong place.

Olga let out a plume of smoke from the side of her mouth. "I admire filial loyalty—our Soviet regime glorified children that turned in their parents; it broke the crucial bond of a core family in any healthy society. But I am deeply disappointed to see you leave. Look how easily you've just figured out the scheme with the nickel and copper. You have so much to teach us."

Brooke felt the pull. "I apologize for leaving you in the lurch." She bent a little to hug Olga. "Thank you."

Olga pulled back and punched the timed light switch. "We've said everything we can say. Viktor will drive you back to the hotel. Wait here. He'll come right down."

After Olga walked up, the light went out. Brooke did not punch the button again.

# DAY FOUR

*Sunday, October 3, 1993*

## *Twenty-eight*

BROOKE WOKE UP on her last day in Moscow to spokes of sun spraying through the window. In the morning light, her initial urge to help Olga investigate the mafia seemed like sheer lunacy. Vera had shown her their methods. Establishing a fund for women would be a much more reasonable way to help—if she could bring herself to defile the memory of her relatives.

She held the matryoshka and admired the delicate brush strokes. The symbolism of motherhood moving back through history, one the product of another, would forever remain with her. She wrapped her silk nightgown around it, then placed the one remaining piece of Irina's broken ashtray between two sweaters.

"Are you all packed?" Amanda asked, walking in from the bathroom. Her glance took in the suitcase still open on the bed. The collection of plastic bags and gifts of lipstick, aspirin, condoms, and music cassettes Brooke had brought was piled on the desk.

"I'm going down for breakfast," Brooke said. "The chef will probably have bagels and lox for us, and Aleksandr will have bought the Sunday *New York Times,* right?"

Amanda put her arms around Brooke. "I'm sorry to see you leave."

Brooke returned the hug, glad that their friendship would survive her departure. "I have till the afternoon to join your trip to the arts and crafts market."

In the dining room, Aleksandr was nursing a cup of coffee. Brooke stopped by his table. "What's the news today?"

"About what?"

"The parliament. Have you heard of the almost-war that's been going on there for over two weeks?"

Aleksandr shrugged. "Nothing's new, yes?"

"No news is good news." Jenny chirped from the next table, where she sat with two strange men.

"Are the roads to the airport clear?" Brooke asked Aleksandr.

"You shouldn't worry."

"Aleksandr." She forced her tone to remain pleasant this last time she must deal with him. "It's not for you to decide what I should or shouldn't worry about. It's your job to keep us informed."

Aleksandr blushed and pulled a newspaper clipping from the pocket of his leather jacket. As he did so, a wad of papers fell on the floor. Quickly, he bent to retrieve them, but Brooke stomped her foot on them.

"Hold it." She picked up the papers and stared at the top

one. "My faxes are here. You were supposed to drop them off at EuroTours on Friday."

Aleksandr stared at his shoes. "I didn't get to the office."

"Any reason you didn't tell us that in the forty-eight hours since then?" Brooke's father hadn't known before their phone conversation that she was here—nor was Hoffenbach made aware of her whereabouts. She studied the papers. Among them was a list of the group members' names in English and their respective room phone numbers. She was astonished to also recognize the numbers for her office phone in New York along with her unlisted home phone. On the margin next to her name was a note in Cyrillic. "What does it say?" she asked Aleksandr, pointing at the scribbles.

She hadn't noticed that Judd was standing behind her, looking over her shoulder, until she smelled his cinnamon-and-wood aftershave. "May I?" he asked. Gently, he extracted the list from her hand, folded it, and placed it in his pocket.

"It's mine!" Aleksandr protested. "This paper is mine."

"Not any more," Judd replied. He handed Brooke her faxes. "You want them?"

Unnerved by Aleksandr, baffled by Judd, Brooke took her faxes. Thankfully, she was about to go home. She stepped away and settled at a small table behind a paneled column. On her plate, the now-familiar measured quantities of sliced hard-boiled egg, cucumber, yellow cheese, beet, salami, pickled red cabbage, herring, and radish must have been set out last night and had since dried up. She poured herself kefir, preferring it to the alternatives, borscht or a "coffee-flavored drink" that looked and tasted like brown dishwater.

Judd took the chair across from her. Light streamed down through the tall windows. A ray of sunlight illuminated the gray of his eyes. His long fingers played with a piece of bread. His nails were filthy; even the creases of his skin seemed to have caked-in dirt.

"Have you been planting trees all night?" Brooke asked.

Unruffled, he sipped his kefir. "I spilled this goddamned liquid shoe polish all over the place. Lemon will clean it." He called over a waiter, and, using his pocket Russian dictionary, said, "*Leemon.*"

"What was the deal with that paper you confiscated from Aleksandr?"

"I didn't like the information he was gathering."

She sat back in her seat and crossed her arms. "So you read Russian."

"I'd rather everyone not know that."

She glanced at the tourist dictionary he'd just used with the waiter. She thought of their meeting with Tkachev, and of the restaurant, where Judd had pretended not to know the language—or the owner. It was easy to connect the dots. He had been raised by grandparents who never assimilated. She knew such families, and they spoke Russian at home. Judd was merely one of the gold rush opportunists, those who often blurred ethical lines when laws didn't exist—

She rose from the table, still hungry. "I hope that whatever brought you to Russia will pan out for you." She lifted a slice of brown rye bread to take along. "I'm leaving today. At five."

"I'll be in touch in a few months."

"I'd rather you didn't."

## ❧ CHAPTER ❧

## *Twenty-nine*

THANKS TO JENNY, the morning in Izmailovo art and craft market was one of the most exciting adventures Svetlana had ever had. Jenny's chatter, her quick eye for merchandise, her way with the vendors, and her brazen bargaining left Svetlana breathless.

"I'm glad you're hanging out with me." Jenny looped Svetlana's arm though hers. "Let the other interpreters take care of these tootsies."

Svetlana giggled, reveling in the feel of Jenny's plump arm, as though they were old school friends, equals. Jenny was the only plump woman among the Americans, but her voluptuousness was feminine, like that of a sexy Russian. Today she was striking in her turquoise kimono jacket, embroidered with cranes and water lilies, so unlike the all-black Amanda often wore, or Brooke's interchangeable pastel-colored shirts. If Svetlana had their money, she would dress like Jenny.

Jenny stopped in front of an artist's easel that displayed a painting of two fish in bright blues and aqua. Their dark eyes were thoughtful, human. "Aquarius. My sign." Jenny kissed the tips of her own fingers. "Ask him how much."

"Two hundred dollars. First price," Svetlana translated the artist's words, almost choking. Two hundred dollars was her entire yearly salary.

"Twenty," Jenny said.

"Twenty? You want me to tell him only twenty?"

"Didn't he say 'first price'?"

Of course, no one ever paid the price quoted. Svetlana always bargained, yet a counteroffer at 10 percent was insulting; she would have offered at least 50 percent. When Svetlana hesitated, Jenny said, "This is how supply and demand points meet. It's the fun part of selling, or business would be boring."

To Svetlana's astonishment, Jenny ended up buying the painting for only fifty dollars. While the artist wrapped it in newspaper, Jenny said, "This place reminds me of Little Italy. That's where I grew up, in New York City. Promise me that one day you'll come visit. It has the best food in the world outside of Italy." She looked around. "Can we grab a bite?"

Svetlana shook her head. "They don't sell food here."

"It's a market. There must be something. A snack bar, a kiosk—"

"We don't waste food by eating it fast, in the street."

"Oh, well. I'm dangerous when I'm hungry."

Svetlana giggled.

Jenny smacked her own forehead. "Whoopsy-do. I almost forgot. Have the artist sign the painting and print his full name on the back."

The artist shook his head. "It's not a good idea," Svetlana translated.

"Why? Artists should be proud to sign their work."

"An old Communist law. Art is the intellectual property of Russia, not to be exploited by the West. The artist can get into trouble."

"Russia has nothing better to do than chase after poor painters who try to make a living?" Shaking her head in disgust, Jenny resumed strolling, toting the painting by the string of its wrap. "I can't wait for the customs officer to stop me—" She halted mid-sentence and clutched Svetlana's arm. "Look at those!"

"What? Where?" All Svetlana could see were peasant blouses hanging from a bar on top of a stand. "These are just proletariat shirts. Not worth much."

"The embroidery! Look at the rich, colorful, dense patterns. Fabulous. What fine handiwork." Jenny pulled Svetlana over to the stand.

"Don't spend good money on them," Svetlana said. "They aren't made of silk or cut in a Western style that's hard to get. They're common, like potatoes."

"So what? It's the people's art. Notice the cross-stitching? How the red and black play off each other? The white on white? See how exact the workmanship is? It's exquisite." Jenny's fingers traced the stitches, the seams. "Beautiful things are part of everyday life. Art is part of life."

In the next hour, with Jenny's guidance, Svetlana understood for the first time the beauty of things that had always surrounded her: the intricate designs in the Persian rugs, the enchanting simplicity of painted ceramic plates, the nostalgia of war memorabilia, the spirituality of antique icons. Jenny's discerning eye stopped at a handsewn fur hat, an exotic stamp collection, a Chinese vase dating back before the 1917 Revolution—and she bought them all.

Jenny's verve lit a spark that had lain dormant in Svetlana. She felt inspired, pushed through the boundaries of her own skin. Then she remembered: Emulating Jenny had been a mistake. A painful recollection of Sidorov passed through her. Without warning, he was behind her. Her nipples stung from his pinch. Her insides recoiled from his flesh.

*Stop it! Attitude Is Everything,* Svetlana chided herself. She must force herself not think of him. She must ignore her fear of their next encounter.

"Hey, are you with me?" Jenny snapped her fingers in front of Svetlana's face. "Help me put these on."

A Communist official's hat rested on Jenny's rust-colored curls, the hammer-and-sickle emblem shining in red and gold. Svetlana helped wrap a hand-crocheted shawl around Jenny's satin jacket and pinned it with a miniature ceramic vegetable bouquet. Jenny grabbed a five-foot wooden staff with writhing snakes carved into it, her face shining with pleasure.

Svetlana thought they couldn't carry any more packages when Jenny asked her to negotiate for a magnificent life-size doll. The doll wore a straw hat strewn with rose petals and a beautiful white lace dress with pink ribbons. The merchant wanted ninety dollars, but Jenny concluded the bargain by paying thirty.

To Svetlana's amazement, Jenny handed her the doll. "For your daughter. What's her name?"

"Natasha, but—" Svetlana's heart leaped with excitement. "It's too . . . too much."

"Nonsense. Every girl should have a beautiful doll. As you say, 'it's feminine.' " She imitated Svetlana's accent.

Svetlana clutched the doll to her chest. "Thank you so much." But Jenny marched away, heels clicking, her staff punching the packed earth, her purchases banging against her legs. Svetlana hurried behind her, carrying more packages, still disbelieving this most extraordinary gift.

"Let's call it a day." Jenny adjusted the rope handle of a bundle containing a hand-knitted bedspread. "Too much schlepping."

The waiting bus was empty. The driver listened to a radio station that, strangely, broadcast Red Army Band songs instead of the American pop music Russians were now permitted to listen to. The music grated on Svetlana's nerves, reminding her of the heavy decision she must weigh. Should she proceed with Dr. Olga Rozanova's request to get the Economic Authority's files? Could she do it without Katerina's help? Svetlana regretted failing to invite her friend to join them today. Two hours in Jenny's company and Katerina might finally leave her brute of a husband—and be inspired to obtain the files.

Svetlana glanced at Jenny, who had removed her shoes and was massaging her toes. "I'd like to ask your advice," she finally said.

"Shoot."

"There's this situation. Uh—the attack at my factory."

"I'll never forget it as long as I live."

"Well, I was asked to help get information about it." Svetlana explained her predicament and her conversations with Brooke and Dr. Rozanova. "I might get caught. What would happen to my factory and to the workers? What would happen to my daughter?"

"Look." Jenny raised her finger and put it up against the sky, squinting her left eye. "With one finger you can block out the whole big mighty sun."

Something weightless rose in Svetlana's heart.

"Don't chicken out," Jenny continued. "Go for it. Do something important. Life is too short. Where d'you think I would have been with what little God has given me? A fatso nobody, like a zillion others. Never mind that I built a great business that has made me rich. I'm still ugly. But I act as if I am a goddess, so I feel beautiful." Jenny touched the "Attitude Is Everything" button on Svetlana's lapel. "Don't wait for life to happen. Make it happen."

Inside Svetlana, a small butterfly spread its wings.

## ❧ CHAPTER ❧
### *Thirty*

BROOKE HAD BEEN careful not to indulge in purchases that might not fit in her suitcase, but couldn't resist a small black-lacquered box, finely painted in minute detail. She fetched her luggage from the bus driver, checked that the lock hadn't been broken and the contents of her wheeled bag were undisturbed, then asked one of the interpreters to help her get an official taxi among the few parked at the entrance to the market. She would arrive at the airport well ahead of nightfall—and with two hours to kill before her five o'clock flight, enough spare time for any eventualities.

A half mile of dirt road led away from the market. By the time Brooke left, it was lined with people, each hawking a single possession: a bird cage, a hand-knit shawl, a steam iron, a box of imported crackers, a samovar, a book of crossword puzzles, a pair of women's shoes, a silver candlestick, a violin, a puppy. Shifting their weight from one foot to the other, these sellers were visibly tired, their eyes devoid of hope. Their pleas sounded desperate, urgent.

Driving past these destitute people, Brooke's indignation rose. Russia was a superpower, not a third world nation, but the government's ideologically driven economic policy, so misguided, had brought its people to their knees. Given its rich natural resources, this country could have done so much for its population, yet, indifferent to the deprivations of its masses, it had spent lavishly on a grand space program. Brooke rolled up the window and leaned back, emotionally drained.

She was jolted awake as the driver jerked to a stop. She heard shouting, the thunder of an enraged mob. Her eyes scanned the four-lane road. "What's going on?"

The driver said something in Russian. Brooke rooted in her bag for a city map and showed it to him. "Where are we?" His index fingernail pointed to a junction a block away from the Garden Ring Road, the center of the city.

Brooke looked up. Along the wide road, waving the red hammer-and-sickle flags of the defunct Soviet Union, swarms of men ran past marchers who carried the white, black, and gold czarist flags of extreme nationalists. Thousands of feet pounded. Placards bobbed up and down. Raised fists sliced the air in a show of power—or anger. Shouting rhythmic slogans, some people broke ranks, wielding clubs and iron staves, while others brandished Kalashnikov assault rifles. Rocks flew and smashed into kiosk windows, shattering glass. A vendor just ahead of Brooke's taxi cowered on the floor of his booth.

Panicked, spewing curses that Brooke actually recognized, the driver skidded into a U-turn and hit the curb, throwing her sideways on the seat. He tried again, then finally made it, driving in the wrong lane and swerving to avoid the oncoming traffic before the other drivers did the same.

This was insanity. In the mayhem, Brooke heard the rumble of heavy vehicles. An armored car veered into the road from a side street. Its wheels slammed against the corner of the curb. Two dozen men, eyes blazing, fists punching the air, hung from its windows; more stood on its steps and bumper, clinging desperately to the vehicle as it sped by Brooke's taxi.

Her driver trailed in their wake a hundred yards until orderly troopers wearing black shirts with swastikas goose-stepped into the center of the street, saluting with straightened arms as if lifted from a Hollywood set. *Neo-Nazis.* Brooke's blood pumped harder in her ears.

Her driver jerked the car sharply into a side street, only to face a swell of people waving farm tools. Caught between the colliding mobs, he zigzagged his way through another alley where men were piling up garbage pails, bed frames, and broken lumber to erect a barricade. The driver shot through them. Timber cracked and hit the windshield, and Brooke heard screaming and realized that the car had just injured people. Her knuckles turned white as she held on to a strap with one hand and the seat with the other. She must get to the airport, but they hadn't left the city yet.

Brooke craned her neck and saw demonstrators destroying kiosks. In the new wave of people, the taxi slowed to a crawl.

A banging on her other side made her jump. She turned to see a man wearing a photographer's vest, a badge of media credentials tangled with the straps of his two cameras. "American?" he mouthed. Hanging onto the taxi as it continued to crawl, he held up a name badge.

She recognized the name Peter Norcress. This was the journalist who had besmirched her client the Prince of Morocco. She cranked down the window two inches.

"May I get a ride?" he asked in American English. "I'm from the *Los Angeles Record.*"

Brooke recognized his narrow face from the photo on his column, the thinness of a marathon runner. She motioned the driver to stop and unlocked the door.

The journalist slid in and locked the door behind him. "Thank you, thank you, thank you," he said between breaths. His panting filled the taxi. "Norcress." He extended his hand for a shake. His palm was sticky.

"Fielding. I know who you are."

He laughed. "I hope you know only the good things." He eyed her. "What is an American fair maiden doing here?"

Brooke gestured with her chin outside. "What's going on?"

He wiped his forehead with his sleeve. "A revolution! At two o'clock, Yeltsin's opponents commandeered a truck and broke through police lines. Rutskoy, once Yeltsin's darling and now his arch enemy, called from the White House balcony for everyone to take to the streets. They stormed the mayor's office in Tverskaya Street."

Norcress spoke to the driver in Russian, and the driver continued to pull forward through the crowd. There were angry people whichever way Brooke looked, streaming in no particular direction. "Water?" She handed Norcress her water bottle, and he took a large gulp.

"So far, Yeltsin has ordered his troops to hold their fire," he continued. "Whether they'll obey him is yet to be seen."

"It only takes one soldier to disobey—or panic—and the shooting will begin," Brooke said. "I need to get out of here. I'm on my way to the airport. I don't want to miss my flight."

"The airport is shut down."

"Shut down?" The hair stood on Brooke's arms. She should have left yesterday. Or the day before. Her heart pounded hard as the provoked mob broke in a roar, and torches bobbed over the crowd. *Just get me out of here.* "Until when?"

"Who knows? And the State Department has issued a warning to Americans not to travel to Moscow."

"Too late, isn't it?" She scanned the street while the driver continued to move at a turtle's pace. People pounded on the car hood as they passed. A man pressed his face to the window, and his distorted features grimaced at Brooke. She recoiled and slid away from the window. Then a group of angry people surrounded the car and started rocking it.

Brooke slid down as much as the tight space allowed, and bent her head into her knees. The driver gunned the gas pedal and forced the mob to scatter.

In the next street she raised her head to look out. "How do I call the American Embassy?" she asked Norcress.

"By the time you find a working phone, you'd be better off just going there. It's not far, but you'll need to walk. It's right by the White House."

How could she walk through this wild mob? What would she do with her two pieces of luggage? Brooke crossed her arms, pressing them hard into her body. "What about an international phone call?"

"Cash-call. At the central post office—if it's open." Norcress gestured behind them. "Good luck!"

A huge blast tore the air, followed by more blasts. "Cannon. The army is firing its cannons," he said, his voice excited. "Action!"

Brooke covered her ears. She recalled the artillery she had seen surrounding the White House. A seismic shift of world power had begun—and she was caught in its epicenter. "It doesn't sound like a good idea to walk toward it," she said when the noise receded.

"No, although I should be out there." He craned his neck to look out the window. "Maybe not."

She followed his gaze. At the near corner, policemen held white shields and raised Kalashnikovs. Their presence offered no comfort—nor were they any deterrent to the roaring mob that continued to swarm in every which way. "I must get out of here," she said. "Is there an airport hotel?"

"Where were you staying until now?"

"I checked out of Hotel Moscow this morning."

"Isn't that in Lenin Hills? It's far from the action. Get your ass back there."

She dropped back into her seat. "I guess I have no choice."

Norcress gave the driver new instructions. The driver gunned the car again, cut across a street corner, slalomed the wrong way down a street, and finally found a less crowded avenue.

Brooke took in a big breath of relief. "I didn't think you were a war correspondent," she said to Norcress.

"Why is that?"

"When you crucified my client the Prince of Morocco, you seemed to have a bleeding heart. Not the right kind of temperament for war reporting."

He let out a short whistle. "He deserved every word I wrote. If he's your client, you must have seen the squalor his people live in right outside each of his twenty-three palaces, while he diverts his fortune to investments abroad."

He was right, of course. Although at Brooke's suggestion the prince had dug hundreds of wells that saved women hours of walking to fetch water, she had been powerless to change the abject poverty she had seen. She was glad Norcress hadn't seen the one hundred pure-bred horses living in a palatial barn, fifty decorated stalls on each side of a magnificent octagonal reception hall. The hall's dome was inlaid with mother-of-pearl and semiprecious stones, and the display of gifts given by dozens of heads of state included a larger-than-life, diamond-studded U.S. eagle. She never asked which president had given it.

When she said nothing, Norcress added, "My assignment is to look for the people's stories. How they manage change."

"Or don't." Brooke waved toward the world outside.

He fished in his vest for a business card, and handed it to her. "Just in case another one of your other clients has a better tale than that Moroccan dude."

They rode the rest of the way to Hotel Moscow in silence. He didn't let her pay when he dropped her off, saying he'd continue to his hotel. "I owe you one," he said.

"Two," she replied.

He raised her water bottle. "May I keep it? It will make three."

BACK AT THE hotel, Brooke could hardly believe that she could feel so safe in this shabby place. Again she submitted her passport at the reception desk, and a ten-dollar bill gave her the key to Amanda's room.

Although it was the weekend, she phoned and left a message at Hoffenbach's office. Should she call Olga to tell her about the forced change of plans? After all, they had said their good-byes. Brooke's need for information overcame her hesitation. She dialed Olga's number, surprised yet again at how easy it was to place a phone call in a hotel—and a city—where nothing else worked smoothly.

"The riots are spreading. Things have gotten out of control." Olga's voice was so loud, Brooke had to shift the receiver away from her ear. "Communists and nationalists are fighting in the streets. About ten thousand—" Olga's cough turned into a fit.

Viktor took the receiver from his wife. "We've heard that the rebels blasted through the door of the Ostankino television station. They fought the police inside. Yeltsin's troops opened fire. Shot everyone in sight." He sounded as agitated as his wife. "Half the armed staff in the parliament are registered fascists. Their leader, Zhirinovsky—"

Olga recovered enough to call out, "The man is a joke."

"Nobody took Mussolini and Hitler seriously until it was too late," Viktor said.

"What do they say on CNN?" Brooke asked.

"Wait. Viktor is turning to the channel," Olga said, back on the phone. After a moment, her voice dropped. "Nothing. Another economic crisis in Brazil. A soccer game in Hong Kong. Nothing."

In the background, Brooke heard Viktor call out.

"The Russian channel, it's all fuzzy," Olga said. "Now it's a blackout. Wait! Yegor Gaidar, the prime minister, is on!"

"The government recaptured the TV station?"

"It's another station." Suddenly Olga cried out. "Oh, no! He's telling Yeltsin's supporters to gather at the City Council and set up barricades. He's calling for a civil war!"

The brief history chapter in Brooke's guide book covered in one sentence the last civilian clashes during the 1917 Bolshevik revolution, when the czar had been overthrown. "Who exactly is fighting whom?" Brooke asked. "I saw demonstrators destroying kiosks. The owners were their own people!"

"Those kiosks sell capitalists' goods. They represent Yeltsin's free-market plans. All capitalistic economy has done so far is bring corruption out into the open."

Olga was silent for a while, probably watching the ongoing reports on TV. Finally she said, "*Uzhasno*. Terrible. These are terrible days for Russia. We've been humiliated and depersonalized for so long. All we wanted was our freedom, yet look how miserably we're managing it now that we have it."

Who had said that people received the rulers they deserved? Brooke could offer no words of comfort. This had nothing to do with her, she told herself. Her Russian chapter was closed. She wished she were at the airport now, just in case she could talk her way onto an oligarch's private plane.

## ❧ CHAPTER ❧

## *Thirty-one*

IN THE HOTEL dining hall, Nikolai Sidorov raised his glass of vodka. "Another toast! One more toast!" He winked at Amanda, seated next to him.

Jenny, seated farther down the table, adored the way Russians toasted, always with drinks, especially the male officials she'd seen. Russians knew how to have fun, so unlike boring American gatherings, where she was expected to hold back raucous laughter and to smile at stupid jokes.

She admired Sidorov's dexterity as, for the fifth or sixth time, he balanced the tiny glass on the back of his hand. "To beautiful American women—and real Russian men." With a swift movement of his wrist, he tipped the glass and downed the contents in one gulp.

Jenny picked at the chopped beets, black olives, and herring swimming in cream on her plate, but her eyes were on the only man in the room. She felt like a lizard sitting on a tree limb, waiting for a bug to stumble her way. It would, soon. The heady combination of attractive American women and vodka had erupted in perspiration on Sidorov's forehead. His eyelids were heavy, and his waxen-blue pupils glimmered in arousal.

Jenny glanced around the table at the other women. They were talking about the revolution, or uprising, or whatever it was Brooke claimed had started, but there was no sign of it here. Sidorov, in fact, seemed insouciantly jolly.

"We might be looking at another totalitarian regime, this time with nuclear power," Brooke whispered to Amanda. "But he's acting like he's partying in a brothel."

"C'mon, Brooke," Jenny shot. "You're upset that he hasn't hit on you."

Brooke rolled her eyes. "Jenny, it's been a long day."

Jenny would have died for that thick brunette hair curling at the shoulders, reflecting the light. "Admit it: Wouldn't you drop that big-time job of yours for the right rich, gorgeous man? Everyone has a price. You too."

Brooke pushed herself from the table and walked away, just as Jenny had hoped. She liked Brooke well enough, but right now Jenny wanted her out of the way. Until Sidorov stumbled her way, she would enjoy the garlicky sautéed meat that was now being served with steamed cabbage flavored with lard.

Sidorov rose to salute again and tried to wrap his arm around Amanda. She squirmed and disengaged from his hold. "To the new American–Russian friendship," he roared. He chugged the glass of vodka.

"To our host—and the boss!" Jenny called out, raising her glass. She emptied it down her throat although she had never taken to its taste.

Still standing, Sidorov threw a lascivious smile at her, finally noticing her. "In business, you women have so much more to offer than we do," he declared to the table. "You can always close a deal by using what nature gave you."

"I can assure you, Mr. Sidorov, that American women do not do business that way." Amanda slid from her seat to the chair Brooke had vacated.

"Russian women have no such inhibitions."

"In the United States, it's called sexual harassment, and it's a crime."

"Our women don't mind. Ask Svetlana Alitkina here." He looked around the room. "Where is she?"

"Curfew. We've sent her home," Brooke said from the door. She was holding Amanda's video camera and trained it on Sidorov.

"What are you doing?" he snapped.

"I assume you won't mind if we record you. Americans would be interested in your views."

"Put it down. Shut it off." Saliva gathered in the corners of his mouth.

Svetlana. Jenny thought about their conversation. Maybe she could help the little Russian woman. There was a time, long ago, when inside Jenny a Svetlana had resided—timid, afraid to taste life.

"I don't think we'll stay for coffee." Amanda rose from the table.

Everyone but Jenny finished eating in a rush. Cooling herself with a Chinese fan, Jenny threw Sidorov an inviting smile. He lumbered around and took the empty seat beside her. Still fanning herself, Jenny opened the top button of her silk blouse. As Sidorov had just said, in any successful transaction, a woman should put her best-selling point forward.

"You're a real woman." Sidorov assessed her cleavage with an appreciative gaze.

She lowered her eyelashes. The vodka was sending pleasant sensations throughout her body. "Only a real man would know. But I haven't met any here—until now, that is."

"You've been wasting your time in Moscow, then." He refilled her vodka glass, and she drank it in two gulps. How she loved Sidorov's deep, baritone voice as he said, "Nothing exciting, uh?"

"Not when I'm with women day and night. The most they want to do is play spies."

He burst out laughing. "And whom would the beautiful ladies spy for, the C.I.A.?"

"Well, maybe. Actually, I'd like to hear your advice about it." She stroked her neck, allowing her hand to disappear into her blouse. She could help Svetlana and herself at the same time. "We're looking for Russian terrorists."

Sidorov gave out a hearty chuckle. His eyes were glued to her rippling blouse. His nostrils flared. "What kind of terrorists do you expect to find?"

Jenny leaned closer, one of her breasts brushing his arm. "The kind we saw at the Gorbachevskaya Street Factory. Scared the living chibaberini out of me."

Sidorov sobered up. "Oh, yes. I've heard."

She raised her Champagne glass and licked its rim. His eyes followed her tongue. "We're talking to people," she added.

"Who's talking?" He bent forward, and she inhaled the masculine scent of cigarettes, vodka, and Armani aftershave.

She motioned with her head toward Brooke, who was about to go up the stairs leading to the lobby, then regretted diverting Sidorov's panting attention. To draw him back, she said, "It's too warm in here. Would you protect me if we went outside?"

Beads of perspiration trickled down his temples. He mopped them with a napkin. "Would you like to take a ride? I have a Rolls-Royce."

THE GUARDS NODDED deferentially as she and Sidorov passed through the lobby. Once they descended the steps to the street, he told his chauffeur to take a hike.

The joyride lasted three hundred feet, to the end of the empty parking lot, which was fine with Jenny. Sidorov could bestow this aphrodisiac of a car ride on his little Soviet girlfriends. If she cared one bird-poo about a Rolls-Royce, she could buy herself three.

At the edge of the lot, where a large oak tree blocked the glare of the only lamppost, Sidorov killed the engine and turned toward her.

This was going to be exciting. Jenny opened the door, slid out, and resettled in the back seat, motioning the Russian to join her.

He laughed, got out, and plopped himself down next to her. He pawed at her neck and breasts, slathering saliva all over her skin and blouse. His eagerness was contagious. She felt a low, deep rumble of gratification flare up at the bottom of her tummy.

She reached for his pants and unzipped his fly. Taking him out and covering him with her hands, she mumbled, "What a big boy. Better than any American man." She leaned over and took him in her mouth.

He groaned. "That's a real woman. Knows how to appreciate a good thing."

Her loose knit slacks slipped off easily. She led Sidorov's right hand toward her moist cavity, rocking over his manicured, thick fingers as they entered her. A few minutes later, she moved to straddle him. Her thighs felt luxurious, full and feminine as his hands squeezed them while he buried his face between her breasts. His muffled grunts of pleasure were music to her ears.

She directed a nipple into his mouth. "Suck on it, big man," she moaned. "Suck hard." She brought up the fingers of his right hand, still glistening from her moisture, to his nose. "American caviar."

Sidorov inhaled and groaned. His upward pumping grew faster.

"What a big man." Jenny slid up and down over him, meeting his pace.

He strained and, in three more quick thrusts, climaxed.

Triumphantly, she gyrated a few more seconds. Mission accomplished. Nothing was better than feeling that a man found her utterly irresistible.

HAVING FINALLY MET her host, Brooke was disillusioned and disgusted. The civil war that so troubled Olga and Viktor seemed to be just a backdrop for Sidorov's indulgence.

When the night clerk hesitated to return her passport—she hated not having it in her possession—she paid him ten dollars. Upstairs, she lay on her cot. Everyone had a price, Jenny had said. Brooke stared at the ceiling. Twenty years ago, she, too, had had her price.

Two weeks after leaving the hospital, no longer in the care of the kind strangers who had sheltered her for a month each in five different homes and then taken her baby away, Brooke vacillated between searing loneliness and feeling numb. She had been deposited at a truckers' motel room along Seattle's Rainier Avenue, where she alternated between sleep and crying. None of her recent benefactors visited her, and she ate nothing until the maid started bringing her sandwiches, apples, and Coke. Brooke almost broke down and called her parents, but being the designated caretaker of their hearts, she couldn't hurt them with a disappointment that topped all possible letdowns.

Returning to school was her only hope, her lifeline to sanity. However, having missed the spring semester, she had lost her scholarship.

The depression—a rock stuck in her heart—left her fuzzy, spent. Yet, in her moments of clarity, Brooke knew that her parents had survived much worse. She would endure this, and perhaps even find a future, if only she could pull herself together.

A week into her stay, the motel clerk informed her that her bill was no longer covered. She took the bus downtown, and the first employment agency she walked into sent her, as a summer temp, to the billing department of an entertainment magazine. She had no choice but to accept minimum wage pay, knowing it would be insufficient to pay tuition.

Her breasts were still full; her milk hadn't dried in spite of the shot and the pills she had received at the hospital. Her stomach, though, was already as flat as a virgin prairie. She was beautiful, a photographer at the magazine told her. With heavy makeup and a wig, no one would ever recognize her.

Four months later, when her nude photographs were published in *Penthouse,* her figure was back to its boyish self, and she was back in Berkeley. The money had replaced the lost scholarship. Her parents never learned of her betrayal, never had to face the disappointment.

For twenty years, Brooke had been on the lookout for those photographs, certain they would jump out of her past and bite her, reclaiming every penny she had received with a compound interest that would leave her life in bankruptcy. Five days ago, they had finally arrived—and then immediately been lost at the Moscow airport's customs office.

Fighting the depressing thought that she was being blackmailed, Brooke rose from her cot, grabbed her thermos, and set out to ask the floor matron to fill it with hot water. At the end of the corridor, several men hung about, waiting for their turn with the prostitutes. Brooke caught sight of two striking young women chatting outside their rooms, both dressed in lace, taking a smoking break.

A man emerged from the elevator and inspected her. Brooke quickened her steps. As usual, the floor matron's door was wide open, and the old woman sat across from a blaring TV, her elbows resting on her protruding belly. She turned her head toward Brooke. Rivulets of tears streamed down the creases of her face.

The pain in the hooded eyes startled Brooke. Silently, the woman pointed to the TV, which showed soldiers fleeing in all directions, chased by crowds brandishing clubs and farm tools. Bystanders hurled cobblestones at a group of soldiers, who fled into a building.

"*Uzhasno,*" the woman cried. "*Uzhasno.*" She shook her fist at the TV set, and began to sob, mumbling in Russian.

The sight of the defeated soldiers alarmed Brooke. If wild crowds were winning against a trained army, it could only lead to anarchy. "*Dah. Uzhasno,*" she said. The picture suddenly cut to a rectangle of storming snowflakes. The old woman rose to her feet, sniffling. Brooke wanted to retreat, but the woman yanked the thermos out of her hand. "*Keep-ya-tok.* Boiling water," she said, and filled it.

"*Spasiba*. Thanks." Brooke handed her a packet of gum and returned to her room. She had given the rest of her tea bags to Svetlana, but Amanda had left a used one in a plastic baggie. Brooke dropped it into the steaming thermos.

She searched her packed suitcase, took out Olga's nesting matryoshka, opened all six dolls, and lined them up on her night table. The carved wood was thin, the hollowed-out insides as smooth as little wombs.

When Amanda returned, both of them silently readied for bed. Brooke peeked under her blanket for cockroaches and, finding the bed uninvaded, crawled in. She fell into the long tunnel of sleep.

The first knocks on the door, a light rapping, became a part of a dream where she leaped and hopped in a tribal circle. There was some ancient, deep, and monotonous chanting, and a soothsayer disguised as Olga stood in the center, tapping her stick to the rhythm. The tapping became louder and more insistent. Jerked out of her sleep, Brooke bolted upright.

"Amanda? Brooke?"

"Judd?" Brooke jumped out of bed and opened the door, conscious of her thin negligee and bare feet. "What is it?"

Judd stepped into the small vestibule and closed the door behind him. In the light coming from the bathroom, there was something strange about him, but she was too self-conscious about her own state of undress to stare.

She brushed her hair from her face. The travel clock on her night table indicated it was two-thirty in the morning. "What's wrong?"

"The uprising is getting nasty, possibly dangerous."

"How bad?" Amanda asked from her bed. She rose to lean on her elbow.

"Yeltsin is finally responding, but the army is on Rutskoy's side. So Yeltsin's asked *civilians* to fight."

"That already happened, yesterday at five o'clock," Brooke said, recalling her conversation with Olga. "What's different?"

"Fifteen thousand people showed up and thousands more are flooding into the city—in addition to the many thousands that had poured in these past two weeks of standoff."

Cold sweat erupted on Brooke's back. "Civil war?"

"So far, the army says it's not their job to shoot Russian citizens, but that could change." Judd's tone was urgent. "Without the army, Yeltsin might not make it."

"We could wake up in the morning back in Communist Russia," Brooke said to Amanda. "I don't get it. Yeltsin's had weeks to prepare."

Amanda got up and stepped to the vestibule. "What are we supposed to do?"

Judd said, "I want the group packed and ready to leave. I don't want the bunch of you stuck here with no protection."

Brooke stared at him. "Where would we go? The airport is shut down."

"What about the embassy?" Amanda asked. "We are registered with them."

Judd shook his head. "Their compound is closed. I'm checking some possibilities, maybe move you all to a village outside of town."

"You sound like you're back in Vietnam." Brooke's eyes suddenly took in his clothes. He wore tattered pants held up by a rope, and the soles of his work shoes had separated. "Why are you dressed like a hobo?"

"I've been outside tonight and didn't want to attract attention."

"With the curfew on?" *Who was he?* Brooke hugged herself, hearing the distant roar of something heavy thundering down a hill. "Are those tanks?" she asked.

He nodded.

"If the army doesn't support Yeltsin, where are the tanks going?"

"We're caught in a goddamned war." He crossed the room and pushed the window open. Brooke heard the muffled rumble punctuated by the *rat-a-tat* of machine guns. The air smelled of gun powder and something orangey, like rotten garbage.

A cold breeze rushed in. Brooke threw open her suitcase, yanked out her robe and put it on. Whatever scheme Judd was concocting, he was the only one trying to help them. She began placing the matryoshka dolls one inside the other. How she wished she had Hoffenbach's home phone number. Although it was still the weekend, she hoped he had received either the message she'd left at his office or news of Moscow before heading to the airport to fetch her.

Judd closed the window and lifted the phone receiver. Brooke could hear the dial tone's flat shrill. "We may lose electricity soon." He hung up the phone and stepped to the door.

"What should we do?" Amanda asked.

"Stay tuned."

# DAY FIVE

*Monday, October 4, 1993*

### ❧ CHAPTER ❧

## *Thirty-three*

N O ADDITIONAL NEWS arrived. Amanda woke the rest of the group and asked them all to pack and be ready—and then catch sleep for the rest of the night in their clothes. They'd have to wait to leave until curfew was lifted. Brooke's memories of her harrowing journey through downtown Moscow still fresh in her mind, she was relieved not to have to brave wild masses or barricades in the dark of the night.

At seven, she placed a phone call to the embassy—just in case someone picked up—but there was no answer at the other end. Only a few members of the hotel staff could arrive this early, so the women settled in the seating area on the ninth floor, drinking tea and munching on their supplies of crackers and cookies. Brooke couldn't read the thin smile on Amanda's colorless lips, but her own eyes burned from lack of sleep.

Aleksandr had surprisingly managed to show up early, and so had the bus.

"Just check us out," Amanda told him. "We're ready."

"We can't check out until we settle the bill."

"It's long settled. We paid EuroTours in advance."

"I must talk to my boss first. The guards won't let you take out your suitcases until they get approval."

"Whose approval?" Amanda asked.

"Let's ditch the bags and get the hell out," Brooke said.

Before Aleksandr had a chance to protest, Jenny yelled from the floor matron's room, "Come quick! Everyone! CNN!"

On the screen, tanks rolled down the boulevards, scattering citizens. Clusters of people, huddled in winter coats, flattened themselves against walls as the heavy armor moved through. Alternate cameras zoomed in on units of militiamen and soldiers taking up positions in city squares and in front of office buildings whose super-size Soviet insignias indicated they belonged to the government.

Bile rose in Brooke's throat. Except for the color picture, she could be watching a World War II movie. In the corner of the screen showing the besieged parliament building appeared the bearded face of CNN's Wolf Blitzer, his words dubbed into Russian. Brooke searched for Aleksandr to translate, but he hadn't bothered to enter the room.

Judd, who had come up behind the group, said, "Looks like the army's negotiated with Yeltsin and has finally agreed to support him. Yeltsin's counterattack has already begun—"

"Can you read Blitzer's lips?" Jenny asked. "You're full of surprises."

Brooke said nothing. Judd's keeping secret his knowledge of Russian annoyed her.

"If the uprising is contained—" Amanda began.

"Yeltsin unleashing his army on civilians is hardly a comforting thought," Brooke said. "I'd rather hide in a remote village than be stuck in the city."

"We're far enough from downtown, so we're better off staying put," Amanda said.

"With tanks and lunatics all over the place, we may not be safe here," Brooke said, and looked at Judd for guidance.

Amanda glanced at a watch she had picked up at the craft market, a huge Russian-made contraption with a hammer-and-sickle emblem on its face. "Let's see how the next couple of hours develop. Our meetings must be canceled, so there's no place we need to be. Let's ride out the storm here."

"In the meantime, please get EuroTours to release us from this prison," Brooke said. "We can't be beholden to some mistake."

As the women filed out, murmuring, she slunk back to her room to think and evaluate the situation. Judd must have a way to get things done. What kind of people were his contacts here? What had been his purpose when he prowled the streets during the night? What village had he planned to take them to?

Olga's was the only voice of reason she knew in this city. She called her again.

A radio was blaring on the other end. "I saw the tanks on TV," Brooke said. "What's really going on?"

"*Disinformatsiya*. The old propaganda, all half-truths." Olga's voice plodded on as through sludge, and Brooke figured that Olga was starting her political campaign in case someone was eavesdropping. "When Gorbachev established *glasnost* in the late 1980s, it meant 'openness.' He promised to end these predigested slogans, these force-fed scripts. He promised freedom of expression, freedom of the press—and we began to believe it. Yet here we are, five years later. No democracy looks, sounds, or behaves like this—"

An explosion jolted Brooke. A louder *boom* followed. The glass in the window quaked, once, twice. "Did you hear that?" she called out to Olga.

"Hear what?" Olga paused as though listening, and then whispered, "Go with Svetlana and meet me later at my office."

It took Brooke's brain a few seconds to switch gears. *Go with Svetlana where? Go to the Economic Authority offices?* Bile arose again from her gut. "Today?"

"Just go in for twenty minutes, she'll translate for you, then you leave."

"Olga, I can't—"

"It's simple."

The line went dead.

## ❧ CHAPTER ❧

# *Thirty-four*

BROOKE SLID INTO the back seat of a private car Svetlana had hired as a taxi. As they headed out of Lenin Hills, all Brooke could discern from Svetlana's responses was that the cab wouldn't drive them to the Economic Authority building—only to the subway that would take them to the station nearest their destination.

They drove along the southern embankment road that followed the twisting Moskva River. Beyond it, hills curved up and away, nestling under a blanket of red and yellow trees as picturesque as upstate New York would be right now on the other side of the globe. Apprehension welled in Brooke. She told herself that Olga was right; she had the savvy to read the files, and if she was lucky, a brief glance accompanied by Svetlana's translation would give her all the cues. In and out in twenty minutes, she would offer some basic assistance to women working in Svetlana's or Vera's factory.

Only a few passengers were on the train when she got on with

Svetlana. When Brooke sat down the ridges of the window frame dug into her back.

The train swooshed through Moscow at full speed. "Hey! It didn't stop at the station!" Svetlana called out as the empty platform disappeared behind them.

All Brooke wanted was for the ordeal to be over, the uprising to be squelched, and the airport to reopen.

Fifteen minutes later, they managed to get off and take another train back. This time, they were delivered to the station they wanted. When the door opened, Brooke saw soldiers moving about the platform, their guns hanging from shoulder straps as they stopped random passengers and interrogated them. She clutched the train door until it began to close. Svetlana gave her a quizzical look, and Brooke stepped out.

A couple in front of them fumbled for their passports. Brooke touched Svetlana's elbow and, holding her chin high, strutted on. Svetlana imitated her, and the soldiers let them through.

As they emerged from the underground station, cannon fire shook the ground under Brooke's feet. Windows rattled in the building above her, echoing the booming explosions. Brooke covered her ears. This was indeed a war zone.

She pulled Svetlana back inside the entrance. "This is insane."

"Dr. Rozanova said—"

Brooke's heart pounded. She produced a notepad and map of Moscow. "In case we get separated, show me where we are and where we're going."

Svetlana traced with a bitten fingernail the ten blocks to the Economic Authority, and Brooke's blood ran cold. "The building is only a few hundred yards away from the White House!"

Svetlana dropped her head. "I know."

Did Olga know that? Brooke scanned the empty street. The military must have cleared the unruly mob she had seen the evening before. She glanced back into the long corridor of the subway and considered turning around.

It was too late, she realized. They were here. There might never be another chance to check the files. "Please write down in Cyrillic Dr. Rozanova's office address," she said, handing her notepad and pen to Svetlana.

Nearby, cannon shells exploded and the rapid fire of machine guns rattled the air. Svetlana handed the pad back to Brooke, who tucked it in her bag. Then she glanced right and left and stepped back into the street, incredulous at her own foolhardiness. Linking arms with Svetlana, Brooke whispered, "Don't lose me."

They scurried along, keeping close to the buildings. Brooke's heartbeat thumped loudly in her ears. Smoke hung in the air like the aftermath of a fireworks display, making her eyes and throat burn.

They darted across a wide street, and Brooke caught sight of the Novoarbatsky Bridge a hundred yards away. She had passed the bridge with Viktor some forty hours earlier. A few brave bystanders were still gathered on it. In the open space, the noise of the cannonade was deafening and dust thickened the air, but the people seemed untroubled as they watched the battle raging around the White House in front of them as if it were a sports competition.

Brooke quickened her pace, ignoring Svetlana's labored breathing. She let out a sigh of relief as they entered the unheated lobby of the Economic Authority just ahead of a nearby blast. A guard behind a desk clutched the edges of his coat against the cold. Brooke was prepared to give him a five-dollar bill, but the man only wiggled the end of a finger poked through a buttonhole, waving her and Svetlana in.

The hallway on the eleventh floor was deserted, the lights off, the doors closed on both sides. Wan light poured in from the uncovered window at the end. A thin carpet absorbed their footsteps. Neither woman spoke until Svetlana stopped in front of a door.

"This is the Finance Department," she whispered. "Where they approved my loans." She put her ear to the door. "My friend Katerina works on this floor."

A cannon shell exploded outside, its echo reverberating through the hallway. The window at the far end shattered, and glass flew toward them, some pieces landing just feet away.

"God Almighty." Trembling, Brooke pressed herself against the wall and shook her clothes to free whatever minute shards might have stuck to them. "You'll just read and translate for me the important page from each file and then we'll leave."

Svetlana turned the door knob, and Brooke hurried after her into a room lined with wooden filing cabinets, handwritten Cyrillic letters marking each drawer. She took out an Evian bottle, twisted open the top, and, after taking a sip, handed it to Svetlana. "Do you have the list?" she whispered.

"I memorized it, then destroyed it." Svetlana struggled with the latch of a drawer.

Another explosion boomed outside. When the windows stopped rattling, Brooke peeked out and realized that that side of the building overlooked the Moskva River. All she could see was a hanging stripe of smoke bifurcating the sky: crisp blue morning above, murky gray below.

Svetlana laid out four files on one of the desks. "Which one do you want me to translate?" Her voice quaked.

A huge explosion tore the air, shaking the windows. Brooke fell to her knees, then crawled under the desk. Plaster fell from the ceiling. Gunfire followed. Svetlana, crouching next to Brooke, reached for the files and put them on the floor. Brooke couldn't help but admire her tenacity. She looked dubiously at the files. Each was one to three inches thick. What had made Olga think it would take only twenty minutes? Of course, she realized, Olga had never seen a business folder. As educated as she was, the sociologist possessed not a shred of knowledge of the world of commerce.

"We can't go through them now," Brooke whispered. The *rat-a-tat* of machine gun fire sounded.

"We must do as we're told," Svetlana said.

"Not to get killed. I'm not staying." Brooke glanced at Svetlana's glum expression and compromised. "Let's take them and get out of here." She withdrew her folded nylon bag from her purse. "You'll return the files another time."

Svetlana's fingers fluttered near her throat. "We might get searched."

"You'll tell the soldiers that we're on a special assignment for Yeltsin," Brooke said, her heart hammering, and her patience wearing thin. She regretted her blind acceptance of Olga's assurance that this was simple. Simple? If she got caught, she might be charged as a spy and her government might be unable to save her; it had failed to release American hostages in Iran and Lebanon. Still, she stretched the bag open. "Put the files in."

Svetlana's lips were pale. "Nothing is right when the whole thing is wrong in the first place," she mumbled, dumping in the files. The weight strained the bag's straps.

Svetlana was right, of course. The whole scheme was insane from the get go. Heading toward the elevator, Brooke searched for words to keep the young Russian calm. Her own safety depended on it. "So far so good. It's great that you know the building."

"My friend wanted me to apply to work here. They hire people who know two foreign languages—" Svetlana stopped. An expression of horror settled on her face as she slammed her hand against her forehead. "*Bozhe moi,* my God." She leaned against the marbled wall. "I forgot!"

"Forgot what?"

"That place," Svetlana replied weakly. "Katerina told me about it— I must check—" She shook her head as though to clear it.

"Now? What place?"

"The eavesdropping center."

Unwillingly, Brooke followed Svetlana back down the hallway.

Svetlana opened a door. "You wait in Katerina's office."

Brooke stood gaping. All around the room, laid out on mismatched shelves, stands and small tables, were recycled marmalade jars, tin cans, and butter crocks holding large and small house plants in every shade of green. "This is incredible," she said.

"Katerina can't grow them at home. She has no window." Svetlana handed her a watering can. "Pretend you water the plants."

An American caught watering plants in the Economic Authority? "Hurry back, please." Brooke surveyed a sweet-potato vine that was so long it had been snaked up to the ceiling and was tied to the overhead light fixture, where it intertwined with other plants suspended from hooks to create a canopy of leaves. Spider plants and ferns hung in front of the window, while large ficus and elephant ears stood in the corners. Jade plants, aloes, cacti, and a midget palm completed the thick foliage.

Who was this Katerina who could create such a sanctuary of beauty in the midst of drabness? In what kind of hovel did she live if it didn't even have a window? Brooke rationed the water in the can to make it last, and pictured this unknown, spirited woman. Would a woman with such a soul turn on her Jewish neighbors?

The door swung open, and a young man in uniform barged in. His eyes assessed Brooke's clothes, and he glowered at her, then shot words in Russian.

Brooke's vision swam. She held the watering can over a plant, trying to act natural. "Do you speak English?" she asked.

Her words seemed to jolt him. "America? *Handzup,*" he said in a heavy Russian accent. "*Chia?*"

Whatever he meant, she shook her head vigorously. "No. No."

"*Russiya*—K.G.B. America—*Chia,*" he said.

*Chia?* C.I.A.! Dread spread down to Brooke's toes. "No *Chia.*" She shook her head again. "*Nyet.*"

A cannonade rattled the planters. The soldier drew a pistol

from his belt with his right hand, and brought out handcuffs with his left. "*Handzup,*" he said, cowboy-style.

"I'm okay." She suppressed the tremor creeping into her voice. "Okay. Look." She pointed at her purse on the desk. "Dollars?"

His eyes narrowed. The slight movement of his pistol indicated she could lift her bag.

She didn't count the wad of twenties in her wallet; just handed it to him and watched it disappear inside his pocket. She must catch Svetlana before she returned and walked right into this trap. Swallowing hard, Brooke moved toward the door and picked up her blue nylon bag. The files shouldn't be found in Katerina's office, implicating an innocent woman.

All the way down to the lobby, the soldier remained so close at Brooke's heels she could smell his sour sweat. In the empty lobby, he gave her shoulder a rough shove toward the exit door.

Stepping out, Brooke held herself from breaking into a run. The street was devoid of traffic. The cannon blasts were deafening. Brooke turned in the direction of the subway station. Sooner or later Svetlana would have to get there.

Her senses heightened by adrenaline, she began to retrace the ten-block route. She tried not to catch the eyes of the men who milled about by the bridge. Thirty feet ahead, a half-dozen teenagers frolicked, roughhousing and laughing through the din.

Suddenly Brooke was thrown to the ground. Her brain jiggled inside her skull. A huge boom followed a split second later, her teeth slammed together, and a sharp pain pierced her tongue. Her eardrums hurt as a shower of stone and thick dust fell on her. She tasted blood.

Echoes of the blast ricocheted around the high-rise buildings along with the sound of glass falling and then what sounded like a wall collapsing. It took willpower to wiggle her fingers and toes. She took inventory of her limbs. A helicopter rotor chugged in her ears, and she registered that the sound came from inside her head. A strong hand pressed her pulse, and she forced herself to scramble to all fours as a kaleidoscope of yellows and reds pulsated behind her eyes. Her tongue throbbed and her body felt like lead. Two arms in militia fatigue snaked from behind her, closed on her chest, and pulled her up. A voice behind her commanded something in Russian.

"I'm okay," Brooke tried to say, but it came out as a croak. The straps of the blue vinyl bag were still looped on her shoulder, and the bag's weight bore into her flesh. She staggered to her feet, and pulled the militiaman's arms apart, stepping away. She coughed out dust. "What the hell happened?" she asked, realizing a moment too late that she should have kept her mouth shut rather than speak English.

The soldier responded in gruff Russian.

Brooke scanned her surrounding, her brains swimming in confusion. A large hole gaped in the middle of the street in front of her. A teenager was writhing on the ground eight feet away, and it took Brooke a couple of seconds to digest that the detached leg with the sock and sneaker lying at her feet belonged to him. Horror spread through her, the street swayed, undulated, and she blinked twice, wondering whether she would faint and hit her head again.

The militiaman pushed her against a wall to steady her. Soldiers ran to the hole and hoisted out the bodies of two more boys.

"I'm okay," Brooke said. She forced her brain to focus. She

must get away fast. What if they inspected the vinyl bag? She had lost her courage; she would dump the files if she had to.

The teenagers' bodies were hoisted on stretchers. Another boy, seemingly unhurt, stood at a distance, screaming, his hands and face raised toward the sky. Brooke clutched the vinyl bag to her chest and inched away from the wall. Her mouth was filled with soil and blood. "I'm okay," she repeated, feeling her tongue swelling. She reached down for her purse, and nearly lost consciousness as she grasped it. The boy's detached limb was inches away from it. Tears spurted into her eyes.

The militiaman pointed at the newly made hole in the street. "*Bombe*. Kill America. Stupid bitch."

Brooke's body shook. The trembling underscored the pain in her mouth. She turned and ran, powered by primal panic, stumbling over debris, until her feet pounded flat pavement and the wind blew in her face. She didn't stop until she reached the subway. Inside the entrance she hesitated. Should she wait for Svetlana here, on top, or go down to the platform?

The adrenaline rush sent her down. Weak-kneed, she sank onto the first bench on the platform. She pulled a square of toilet paper from her purse and spat dust into it, then reached for a stick of cinnamon-flavored gum, her shaking hands barely able to unwrap the paper. When she slipped the gum into her mouth, the cinnamon stung her tongue, but numbed the throbbing. Chewing was too painful, so Brooke sucked on the gum to produce saliva. A minute later, the pain refocused as a sharp ice pick.

Setting the bag in her lap and her purse atop it, she waited. Now she felt her knees burning from scrapes beneath her pants, although the gabardine hadn't torn. Her neck, clammy with sweat, itched where pebbles had left small cuts. She tore open the wrapping of a Wet-Nap and cleaned herself as best as she could. Brownish-red stains appeared on the napkin after she dabbed her neck around the chain holding her Star of David.

She touched the gold amulet. She had never given it magic powers, but right now she could believe it had saved her life. She brought it to her lips to kiss it. A few more steps and that un-attached leg would have been hers. It could be her dead body being hoisted on a stretcher. Poor, poor boy. She fought back a wave of tears.

Stupid bitch indeed. Why hadn't it occurred to her, when she was ordered to take this time off, that she should go to the Carib-bean and spend them on a beach, stretching out in the sun and digging her toes in the warm sand?

Soldiers lurked on the opposite platform, and Brooke felt a momentary relief when a train slowed down and blocked them from her view. But the train did not stop. Brooke took a few deep breaths, trying to regain her faculties. Where was Svetlana? She looked around. The station was grand, with high, vaulted ceilings, the mahogany paneling punctuated by heroic bronze sculptures. From here, the shelling was barely audible.

A whiff of cigarette smoke—entirely different from gunpowder—reached her nostrils. Brooke turned her head and saw a lone soldier leaning against a column, his eyes narrowed on her. Between two farther columns framing a side corridor, a group of soldiers materialized, sending her long glances. What if they asked to see her passport?

A train pulled in and came to a stop. Brooke remained seated as passengers got off. The group of soldiers turned their attention to checking the new arrivals' documents. But the lone soldier's stare pierced the side of Brooke's head. She turned and saw him detaching himself from the column and sauntering toward her.

A bell rang. The train's doors huffed a pneumatic sound and began closing. Brooke jumped to her feet and sprinted inside just before the doors shut. Wherever this train was headed was surely preferable to staying put.

Twenty minutes later, when no passengers got on the train, she guessed that she was far enough from the city center. She exited the subway to an uncanny silence. The cannons were indeed far, replaced by a thumping headache. She hailed a passing car, and when it stopped, presented the driver with a ten-dollar bill and the Cyrillic note with Olga's address at the Institute for Social Research.

All she wanted was to get rid of the files and fly back home.

SVETLANA CHIDED HERSELF. How had she failed to think about the eavesdropping center, a holdover from the K.G.B. reign? Since receiving Dr. Rozanova's phone call early in the morning, she had been in a state of confusion. She had hoped the respected sociologist would release her from the dangerous scheme she had concocted with Brooke. Instead, Dr. Rozanova broke into the double-speak that had been used during Soviet days. "Today is *not* a good day to tackle a new project," she said, meaning the exact opposite. "Government offices are closed. No one wants to look at documents when so much is going on. Many downtown metro stations are closed; the trains just pass through them without stopping. I don't know why Smolenskaya station is open."

"No one can move about—"

"Don't you think it's a good thing roadblocks have been erected everywhere to prevent more help from reaching the rebels?" Dr. Rozanova went on in her double-speak.

Svetlana had leaned against the wall. If she refused, her life would remain unchanged. Yes, she had hated it when all her tomorrows looked the same as her yesterdays, but right now sameness seemed comforting. Jenny's idea "to go for it" meant little now that the riots had spread. And what would happen to Natasha if something befell her mother? She glanced through the open door at her daughter, sleeping next to Jenny's precious new doll. It was so large that it was unclear who was cuddling whom.

In the kitchen, Svetlana rushed through the preparations of *mannaya kasha,* the breakfast semolina gruel for Natasha. Her thoughts continued to swirl. Could there be a worse fate than to believe in nothing and aspire to nothing? Her life, always devoid of possibilities, had been presented with a challenge, with hope. She could be submissively pathetic like she'd always been, or daring like Brooke and Jenny.

She brought the pot into the room and placed it on the table, folding an old towel over it to keep the breakfast warm. She pulled her simple floral dress over her woolen undershirt. The dress was too summery for the cold fall weather, but she had nothing else presentable that the Americans hadn't seen. She kissed the sleeping Natasha's forehead, grabbed her blue cardigan, and tiptoed out again.

In the street, she stopped beside the aging oak, her heart pounding. If this was how it felt to be brave, it was the same as feeling terrified. Still, there was a difference: Her center, where forlornness and dejection had resided, had turned into a fist.

Now, in the corridor of the Economic Authority, her mission not half accomplished, she faced this new obstacle. Katerina had told her the eavesdropping center still operated twenty-four hours a day to cover all phone conversations of the Economic Authority's guests. Katerina had suggested that Svetlana could use her language skills for a job there, but the thought of losing her soul in the process of spying was more than Svetlana could stomach. At least at her factory her comrades believed in her, looked up to her with hope.

In the elevator, she jabbed the button for the top floor, the one marked "off-limits." A minute later, fighting nausea, she struggled to assume an authoritative air. Without knocking first, she pushed open the door and gasped at the sight of the large room stretching out before her. All but three of its many cubicles were unmanned. Three men wearing headsets faced panels of wires, plugs, and flickering yellow lights. One of them, a man in his fifties with thinning blond hair and a face ruddy with broken capillaries, raised his head, and Svetlana realized how foolish she had been not to think this whole thing through. She had no clue how the operation ran. How could the Economic Authority wire itself to all of Moscow? Didn't the phone company control the switches?

The realization hit Svetlana like a slap of wet canvas: The Economic Authority didn't need to be wired to all of Moscow—just to places where its guests stayed. Such as Hotel Moscow. "I'm here to check on the status of Sidorov's requests," she blurted.

"We're doing as instructed." The man adjusted his earphones, as though listening to something requiring his attention.

"Well, what's the status?"

"Who's asking?"

Svetlana swallowed hard. Giving her name would be like sticking her head in the oven and turning on the gas. "Zoya

Samoilva," she replied. Her witch of a neighbor deserved this. She held her breath. He might ask her to identify herself with her internal passport.

"You're working with Aleksandr Kusnetsov?" he asked.

*Aleksandr? What did he have to do with anything?* "Absolutely," she exclaimed.

"Listening in on Miss Fielding's phone has been no problem all along. We wired Dr. Rozanova's home this morning."

Svetlana's heart skipped. He could have picked up the sociologist's call to her apartment instructing her to come here! And, furthermore, if Sidorov could wire whomever he wished at such short notice, his *po blatu* at the phone company must be extraordinarily strong. "At what time this morning was Dr. Rozanova's line wired?" she asked.

"Before eight. Our men had to break curfew to be out early. Tell your boss that."

She managed to nod. "I'm sure he'll remember the favor." For all she knew, Sidorov had learned of her own part in the investigation. Something heaved into Svetlana's throat, then receded back into her stomach. She clamped her hand over her mouth. "I'm sorry," she mumbled through her fingers.

"Pregnant?" He leered and pointed. "Bathroom's on the left."

She vomited into a filthy sink, and retched again. But there was no time to waste; she must escape now. She washed her face and rinsed her mouth in a hurry. Her terror must have coagulated her blood, because an icy calm seized her. She would get Brooke where she had left her—and run as far as Siberia, if needed.

While she waited for the elevator, the sour taste still clung to her mouth. She decided to sacrifice one of her chocolate bars. Only one small bite, and then she would save the rest for Natasha.

But the chocolate was so good. It had been so long, she had forgotten the rich, sweet taste. She broke off a second section and placed it on her tongue. She put the rest in her bag, but soon opened it to bite one more piece. The end of the world was near; one chocolate bar would do no good.

The minutes it took to get back to the eleventh floor and down the hallway to Katerina's office were among the longest in her life. Inside Katerina's office, dangling leaves swayed as she burst into the room. But in the silence of the greenhouse, there was not one soul. Brooke was gone.

## ❧ CHAPTER ❧

## *Thirty-six*

THE CAR PULLED up in front of a large office building. The bright light of the sunny day pierced Brooke's eyes as she looked up. "Is this it?" she asked the driver, knowing he understood not a word.

The driver examined the note Svetlana had written, nodded vigorously, and handed it back to Brooke.

Apprehensive, she scanned the area. The single office building sat amid behemoth residential complexes, which stood on vast lots strewn with puddles and overgrown with dry weeds. Even the occasional poplar trees along the sidewalk were scraggly looking, dwarfed by the open space. Past the wide but desolate four-lane road, produce stands were almost bare, and there were no shoppers. In this quiet, forgotten neighborhood, the battle raging downtown seemed as improbable as a passing parade of jesters and flowered floats. Brooke scanned again the all-concrete office building and the large sign in Cyrillic on top. She recognized the four initials for the Institute of Social Research from the translated sheet announcing the symposium scheduled for the next day, Tuesday.

Her tongue throbbed, her temples pounded, her joints ached, and a muscle in her back spasmed. Glancing at her watch, she was surprised that it was only nine-thirty in the morning. She pushed herself out of the car, eager to see Olga. Hopefully Svetlana was somewhere safe.

A main entrance to the building was permanently boarded, but a single side door led into a narrow, concrete passage like a man-high foxhole. "The better to check you with, my dear," Brooke mumbled, and realized that her swollen tongue moved with difficulty. She watched the brick walls on either side of her as if any moment something might jump at her. She watched them so closely that she almost tripped over a metal bar fixed across the bottom, an inch above the floor. In the United States, consumers—people—had basic rights to safety. Tort law saw to it, she thought.

A narrow door at the end opened onto a modern, spacious lobby with a brown marble floor. A mosaic mural glorifying the working proletariat stretched across the length of the vast wall: Under a canopy of clear skies, workers toiled in fields, factories, mines, and ports—robust and healthy, smiling and proud.

A diminutive man sat in a booth set high and protected by iron bars, his face as dark and grooved as a walnut. He looked at Brooke's passport, turned it up and down and over, and leafed through the pages, mumbling with astonishment, "America, America, America," then waved her in.

As in the Economic Authority building, the fourteenth floor was devoid of business activity. Brooke found the bathroom by the stench and splashed water on her face and neck. She didn't trust the water to rinse her mouth even though her tongue throbbed. Outside the bathroom again, she dried her cheeks and neck with the edge of her shirt, powdered her face, and combed her hair.

One office door along the hallway was open, daylight streaming into the corridor. Cautiously, Brooke peeked inside. Olga stood facing the large window. She didn't turn when Brooke entered, but waved her in with her hand.

Brooke came up behind her. Olga's finger pointed at a spot in the distance where the city outline met the blue, indifferent sky. A gray feather of smoke burped upward in slow motion. With no wind to diffuse it, it curved gently into the sky and hung there for a while before melting away. Was that what neighbors of concentration camps had seen coming out of the incinerators? Had it seemed similarly unreal?

"They're shelling our parliament." Olga's raspy voice was choked. When she finally turned toward Brooke, there were tears in her eyes. She dropped into the chair by the window. "Enough! The price is too high."

Brooke stepped closer and squeezed Olga's shoulder.

"Who could have imagined it?" Olga turned to Brooke. "I didn't realize until I saw this how dangerous it was for you to go downtown. I'm so sorry. You hear about it on the radio, you see on TV, but you just don't know how bad it is. Are you all right?"

"More or less, but I've lost Svetlana."

"You're speaking funny."

"I bit my tongue badly. May I have some boiled water? I need to take a Tylenol."

Olga poured water from a jug, and Brooke downed two pills while watching the White House blacken on the far horizon as if in a silent movie. After the events of the last hour, she finally felt safe.

"Sit down. We'll have tea," Olga said.

Brooke sank into the faded green chair, surprisingly comfortable in spite of its uneven springs. While Olga busied herself in front of a white wooden chest, Brooke closed her eyes. She opened them a few minutes later to see the Russian filling china cups from the hissing samovar. Olga laid out the tea cups on a small table covered with lace.

"Our group has brought a carton of disposable cups and plates for tomorrow's symposium—if it takes place," Brooke said, speaking slowly so her speech wouldn't come out garbled. No need to mention again that if the symposium held, she might not be there if the airport opened. "I helped Amanda box up all the tea and coffee you'll need, plus a lot of cakes and cookies."

Olga handed her a cup. "A gift well appreciated, but we will not insult our guests by serving in plastic dishes. China is the only way."

"Aren't you expecting a hundred people? Do you have enough porcelain cups? And who'll wash everything?"

"The employees will donate theirs. Then we'll clean up. No problem." Olga lit a cigarette, inhaled deeply, and tapped the gray wisps from its tip into an ashtray. She sucked again, and her lungs responded with a long, violent cough. When she had recovered, she dabbed her bloodshot eyes with an embroidered muslin handkerchief.

"I can't help but comment that you should quit smoking," Brooke said.

Olga shrugged. With careful movements, she unwrapped a sugar cube, quartered it with her teeth, picked up a piece and motioned to Brooke to pick one too. Olga placed hers between her front teeth and, with pursed lips, sucked in a dainty sip from her cup. "That's the best way to drink tea." Her eyelids drooped as steam from her cup rose to her nostrils.

"That's how my mother still drinks her tea," Brooke said, dropping her sugar into the cup. She stirred it. "She also quarters the sugar cube and rations it." Savoring the moment was one tiny pleasure her mother permitted herself.

For a while, neither spoke. Exhausted, Brooke brought the tea to her lips, careful not to aggravate the pain in her tongue. She closed her eyes. Scenes of her life in New York flashed in her head: the ballet performances, Broadway shows, and gala concerts to which she treated clients; the invitations to opulent black-tie charity events that made the gossip columns. With all the comforts, had she or her clients ever enjoyed their tea the way Olga did?

Olga cleared her throat. Brooke peeked again at the horizon of downtown buildings. The burning White House's center now appeared like a gap between twin teeth. Brooke's near-death experience and its rush of adrenaline knitted itself into her body, and images of the boy writhing in the crater, his leg torn off, flashed in her head. But the worst was behind her now. Her tongue would heal, and a shower and an afternoon nap would revive her. But the boy, if he lived, would be crippled.

"You're so certain people will show up for the symposium tomorrow," Brooke said. "How will they get here? What if the fighting escalates?"

"They're coming from all over Russia. Many are already here. Others have been traveling for days."

"Are the trains running in all this chaos?"

"The fighting, as you see, is only in Moscow." Olga glanced at the White House and back. "Our women are so eager to meet American businesswomen; they can hardly believe it's happening. It's better than meeting our Olympian stars."

If history hadn't intervened, this American would be gone. Olga didn't say it, but the knowledge hovered between them like miasma.

"Let's get to work," Brooke said.

Olga locked the door and cleared her desk. A large black fly hurled itself against the window, bounced back, and circled the room only to hurl itself again against the glass.

Brooke yawned and scanned the ceiling. The paint was yellow and chipped, and the bare fluorescent lights glared.

"My office is not bugged," Olga said, but she nevertheless unplugged the phone and her computer. Her hand swept toward the ceiling. "If bugs had been put in, it would have left marks in the plaster."

Brooke removed the stack of files from the vinyl bag and placed them on the desk. "I hope you can make heads or tails of this." She rifled through a file. It was neatly partitioned with colored dividers labeled in Cyrillic and jammed with documents. "A lot of papers for such a new institution," she remarked.

Olga picked up another file. "The documents are organized chronologically within each category: Permits, Production, Purchasing, Orders, Shipments, Expenses." She leafed through the pages. "Lots of figures." She pushed it across the desk. "Your turn. Our numerals are the same as your Arabic ones."

Brooke peered at the file. Untangling a financial scheme required a forensic accountant; she had no experience investigating fraud, but she knew a lot more about accounting than Olga did. She sighed and pointed to the title of the thinnest file. "What does this say?"

"Factory number three hundred seventy-six. Manufactures soap and toothpaste."

"How many brands?"

Olga crinkled her forehead. "Brands?"

"How many different products in each line?"

"Just those two. Toothpaste and soap."

"No different types of each, such as toothpaste for children, toothpaste in large tubes and small tubes, in different flavors? Different names of toothpaste?"

"Just toothpaste, and the soap is a large, big cube." Olga's hands shaped themselves around an imaginary solid block. "Russian soap. Doesn't smell good, but we use it to wash everything: clothes, hair, dishes." She laughed. "Our national soap."

"The soap may be rough, but it sounds like it's a leading brand. That's huge," Brooke said. "Okay. Let's look first for the privatization certificate. When were the ownership shares issued, and to whom?"

Olga looked at the papers. "In January 1992, with privatization, ownership vouchers were distributed to each of the four hundred employees."

Olga went over the file page by page, briefly translating each. The fly left the window, circling and buzzing around their heads. Brooke threw her scarf over it, caught it, and then opened the door to the corridor to let it free.

Olga raised her head. "Why didn't you kill it?"

"It's harmless. Another one of God's creatures, don't you think?"

Olga chuckled. "No wonder Americans fight for human rights. You spare even the life of a fly."

"Probably my Jewish upbringing." Brooke resettled in her chair and yawned again. "Go on." The length of each form and the number of copies filed with various government agencies created a staggering amount of paperwork, much of it redundant.

"The Economic Authority arranged to open a bank account and also guaranteed the bank loans for the initial operating costs," Olga explained haltingly as she gathered the facts under Brooke's probing. "Then a request was filed to switch banks. Let me see. It was signed by the head of the Finance Division at the Economic Authority."

"Like in the Gorbachevskaya Street Factory and Vera's. We're moving along." Brooke craned her neck above the file. "Let's look for the ledger. It should have two to four columns of figures." But there was no page with columns. No accounting practices, Western or other. "Hmmm," Brooke said. "Since the factory has been doing business with one bank or another, there should be some sort of a bank statement. A monthly or a quarterly list of transactions. Something."

Olga shook her head as she flipped through a stack of yellow slips barely larger than theater tickets.

"What about those?" Brooke asked.

"Copies of transactions. Bank deposits and withdrawals."

"I'll have to reconstruct the financial history," Brooke said. Olga's cigarette smoke didn't help her headache, but Olga seemed to need it like air. On a lined sheet of paper, Brooke drew up columns for a hypothetical ledger and began to fill it in. "Dictate for me each bank deposit—from sales, from loans—and each withdrawal. Start with the dates."

Soon, her reconstructed ledger began to tell a story. Each deposit from a sale was followed by a cash withdrawal of the same amount, leaving no operational cash flow. The salaries that had been paid at the early stage of privatization had stopped months ago, and no other bills had been paid either.

Brooke tapped her pencil. "How does the factory buy raw materials? And what about gas and electricity? They can't keep running for so long without paying their electric bills."

"This may answer your question." Olga held up a three-page form. "This is a request the factory has filed, asking for the Economic Authority's permission to sell parcels of ownership certificates. The employees—now the owners—want to sell their shares. It says here that since the venture has failed to manage itself—"

"Failed? What's the factory's output? Let's go back to the previous documents. Can you find the output in '91, when the factory was still government owned?"

After a short review of the file, Olga dictated the 1991 number of tons shipped for each of the two products: twenty million tons of soap and seven million tons of toothpaste.

"It's safe to assume that production would show a marked upturn after privatization," Brooke explained. "That's the case when workers have a new incentive to succeed as owners." She examined her ledger, then waved it. "We already totaled the purchase orders in 1992. We can assume this was the minimal output because additional inventory may have been stored rather than shipped." She pointed to the next page. "You see? In 1992 they almost doubled the factory's output from 1991."

"Meaning what?"

"The factory did well—is doing well and producing more. No failure here, only financial shenanigans. More important, now with the government out of the picture, owners of a private venture shouldn't have to ask anyone's permission to sell their shares. And regardless, there is no need to; their factory should be making a profit."

Olga's lips squeezed into a hard line. Remnants of her pink lipstick bled into fine crinkles around them. "Now what? Have we reached a dead end?" She tapped her cigarette pack.

Brooke laid a hand over Olga's to stop her from pulling out yet another cigarette, and for a moment both stared at their hands, Brooke's manicured fingernails with their clear nail polish resting on Olga's ruddy, short fingers stained by nicotine. A wave of affection for the dauntless woman washed over Brooke. For an instant, in spite of her pounding headache and everything she had been through, she was glad she had been detained in Moscow.

"Let's search for another angle." Brooke sucked on her throb-bing tongue and contemplated the options. She glanced at her watch. There was no choice but to plow on. "The shipping orders. Let's compare them to the purchasing reports."

With Olga again sifting through the file, Brooke taped a page next to the one she was writing on and added a column of ship-ping orders. They matched the production. "No merchandise has left the factory unaccounted for."

"Meaning what?"

"The workers are not stealing. Someone else is," Brooke re-plied. She added another column. "Please find me an invoice for each of these shipments. They should correlate to the sales."

But the information had ceased to be available by the spring of 1992. Goods had been produced, ordered, and shipped, but no invoices had been recorded.

"Maybe the factory was paid by *veksels*," Olga said. "What do you call them?"

"IOUs. Svetlana has mentioned those."

Olga smiled her little sad smile. "One more double-system. Everybody now trades in them instead of currency. If the factory cashes them for half their value, it gets what you call cash flow."

Brooke shook her head. "In which case there should be in-voices, marked as paid." She sipped her tea. The sugar, which she never took in New York, revived her. "Who at the factory signed these shipping orders?"

"It's stamped by the Finance Division of the Economic Au-thority."

Brooke paused. "You can't mean someone from the Economic Authority hangs around the loading dock and signs paperwork?

There's no reason for it. The Economic Authority's supposed to be long out of the picture." She could almost hear the gears clicking into place. "It should not be involved in a factory's internal affairs—shipping or purchasing orders."

Olga drummed her fingers. "Meaning what?"

Brooke hesitated. "To whom were the ownership shares sold?"

"The Economic Authority."

"The Economic Authority's a government agency with only a service function. It doesn't own anything. Its job is to free the venture from its former dependence on the government; it certainly doesn't buy a cooperative that it helped to privatize." Brooke took in a deep breath. "Someone at the Economic Authority's behind it all."

"You're sure?"

Brooke looked at Olga until the Russian woman met her gaze. Olga held her own, the blue of her eyes challenging Brooke's stare.

Then Olga's face crumbled. "Of course I must believe it. This is what this country has been for much too long. Corrupt."

Brooke waited a moment, then picked up the file and leafed through the documents. Her headache lingered; she needed hours of sleep, but she was close to solving this puzzle. "Let's check the day the Economic Authority purchased the shares of the factory," she finally said. "Read me the signatures on each of the forms."

Olga scoured through a dozen forms. "This is an application to the External Market Resources—"

"What's that?"

"Some new agency with which all ownerships must register."

"Good. Who's signed it?"

"Sidorov— No—" Olga squinted. "It's strange. . . . It's not Nikolai Sidorov; it's a different name. See?" Olga flicked through the stapled papers. "It's someone named . . . Nadia Sidorova."

Nikolai Sidorov's wife? Mother? It didn't matter. Brooke grabbed Olga by the shoulders. "You've got it! Sidorov, the head of privatization of small businesses, robs them at gunpoint and then takes over."

"Sidorov is the new owner? How could he sabotage these ventures? How could he take these peoples' livelihood?" Shock was embedded in Olga's voice. "Maybe there's a mistake?"

"I don't think so," Brooke said softly. "You already know that the employees were persuaded to sell by violent means." She thought of the drunken, pompous man she had met. "I try not to attribute to malice what can be explained by incompetence, but this is too deliberate. No incompetence here. Just pure, cynical evil."

Olga pushed herself up, brushed the wrinkles out of her skirt, and paced around the room, still limping slightly. "Sidorov operates like a feudal lord."

"This is not a one-man operation—and I'm not referring to the thugs he hires to do his dirty work. He must have powerful connections. What do you call them?"

"*Po blatu?*"

"Yes, *po blatu*. Someone high up—must be in the Kremlin—assigned the Economic Authority to privatize small businesses in the Moscow region. That person must be enjoying the fruits of this looting, too."

Olga fell back into her chair. "The Communist legacy of corruption is so pervasive, it has made a mockery of democracy before it has started." She looked out the window. "They are shelling our parliament. Even if we get through today, we may never make it because of this." Her hand slammed the file shut, then she looked at Brooke. "Sidorov is the person in charge of your group's well-being."

Brooke nodded slowly. She was thinking the same. What had been his intentions in inviting them?

## ❧ CHAPTER ❧

## *Thirty-seven*

OLGA HAD STOPPED a private car for Brooke and given the owner instructions, but he wouldn't start driving unless Brooke first paid him his five-dollar fee. She had dozed off during the ride through eerily empty streets and now felt better and further relieved when, upon exiting the elevator at the ninth floor of Hotel Moscow, she saw Svetlana jump to her feet.

"You're here!" The Russian searched Brooke's face. "Are you all right? I didn't know what happened to you."

Brooke hugged her. "And I was worried about you, so we're even. Someone in uniform began to ask me questions, so I got out." She smiled and touched the blue vinyl bag, again filled with the files. Olga had photocopied some incriminating documents. "Mission completed. Olga and I have figured it all out—thanks to you."

A twitch dimpled Svetlana's chin. Her fingers wrung her sodden handkerchief. "It's not over."

Brooke grabbed her arm. "Let's go to my room."

Svetlana shook her head. "It's not safe," she whispered. "Sidorov—he wiretapped us— you, Dr. Rozanova, maybe me."

"Are you sure?"

Svetlana's head bobbed. Her words were barely audible; Brooke had to lower her head to catch them. "That's what I went to check. As of this morning, his people have been listening in on Dr. Rozanova's phone conversations. They may have listened to yours all along."

"Just me? What about the rest of my group?"

"I don't know." Svetlana sniffled. "I'm scared. You don't know him. He's cruel."

Brooke looked around. The mustard-colored set of couches making up the floor's sitting area, one elevator door to her left and two to her right, the men loitering at the end of the corridor, the TV's chitchat pouring out of the floor matron's open door a few feet away. They were familiar, yet something had shifted. She had turned from a hunter to being hunted.

She had missed both breakfast and lunch. She needed a meal, a shower, and a nap to clear her head. But there was no time; the ground was burning under her feet. She was an American entangled in industrial espionage.

There was no question of going to the central post office downtown—anyway, those government phones were surely wiretapped. "Please tell the *dezhurnayia* that the phone in my room is out of order and I must use hers," Brooke said, folding a five-dollar bill into Svetlana's palm. "Give her this."

While Svetlana walked into the *dezhurnayia*'s room, Brooke rushed to retrieve a can of tuna and a packet of crackers from Amanda's sizable stock.

A few moments later, she settled by the table in the *dezhur-nayia*'s room and waited for the hotel operator to connect her to the international switchboard. She opened the can of tuna and softened a cracker in cold tea so it wouldn't hurt her cut tongue.

The wait stretched on. The TV blared some soap opera, and the floor matron eyed her with a furrowed brow. Brooke didn't want to test the woman's reluctant hospitality by asking her to find the BBC or another English-speaking station.

She got up and paced the room. In the confusion of the day, she had failed to notice the sunshine, which now flooded through the lace curtains. She gestured to the matron and received her nod to open the window a crack, then listened to the choppers circling the city. The beating of their rotors intensified or waned with every shift in the wind.

She should be in Frankfurt now. Brooke closed her eyes and let the afternoon sun soak into her skin. Frightening old Soviet movie scenarios paraded through her mind. Any minute, Sidorov's long arms might seize her and her accomplices. She could be thrown in jail. Olga would be marched into the deep snow of Siberia, and Svetlana forced into a mental institution.

"Everything okay? Why are you here?" Brooke turned to see Amanda in the doorway, looking at her with curiosity.

Feigning nonchalance, Brooke put a moist cracker in her mouth. On TV, a couple was kissing. "Any news? I'm about to ask her to switch channels." Trying to enunciate and pretend it was the cracker that slurred her speech didn't work.

"What's with you?" Amanda asked. "Are you hurt?"

"I bit my tongue."

Amanda stared at Brooke's neck. "And what about these cuts?"

"I was efficient. Did it all at the same time. I tripped."

Amanda smoothed her sleek sheet of black hair. She let a moment pass, as if weighing the sum of Brooke's misfortune along with the oddity of her hanging out in the matron's room.

Brooke tossed a glance at the phone, wishing it to ring, wishing Amanda would leave. She couldn't reveal her trip downtown without spilling out the reason.

"We're getting cabin fever," Amanda said. "Aleksandr says we can all take a trip to Troista-Sergyeva Lavra. It's a monastery that's the ancient seat of the Orthodox Russian Church, about forty miles away in a town called Zagorsk." As though reading Brooke's mind, she added, "EuroTours got special permits to pass through roadblocks."

"How efficient of Aleksandr," Brooke said. Being on the move was a good idea. But Sidorov employed EuroTours, and this sudden switch in attention to the group's spirit seemed suspicious.

"Are you all right?" Amanda asked. "You don't look so hot."

"Nothing that a shower won't wash away." Brooke looked at her watch. It was one forty-five. "I'll see you in the room in a few minutes."

"No more than fifteen. Then we're off." Amanda flung her satchel over her shoulder and turned to leave. At the door, she almost collided with Svetlana. Next to her was Irina.

Brooke's glance traveled from one Russian to the other. "Did something happen?"

"Irina—she wants to know about that loan," Svetlana said. Her voice shook.

Had Russians never heard of appointments? "I'm sorry, but I am very busy now." Any moment, the matron might chase them all out, and Brooke would miss her phone call. "She was supposed to telephone if she wanted to speak with me, not just show up."

"Irina wants to know about the loan," Svetlana repeated.

"I've told her that I *do not* give out loans." Brooke was losing patience. "And I know of no financial institution that will approve a loan for a business that is founded on stealing military equipment."

"This is so unfair! Everybody steals!" Irina responded when Svetlana translated. "That's why men succeed. You can't have a business in Russia without stealing!"

"Smuggling, racketeering, and stealing are not 'business' the way we know it in the West," Brooke said, softening her voice. If every Russian businessman was a wheeler-dealer who hustled, swapped, or hawked stolen goods, why did she expect women to be any better? "I apologize, but I really don't have time right now."

She had half anticipated a spurt of tears or an attempt to sell yet another pitiful knickknack. Instead, Irina exchanged more words with Svetlana. Brooke heard the name "Marlboro" repeated three times. She glanced at the phone. *Please ring.*

The matron said something, and Svetlana responded, her tone placating. Her scowl deepening, the matron turned back to her TV.

"Irina has another idea," Svetlana said to Brooke. "I'm not

sure it's legitimate. Marlboro costs less in Moscow than in the Republics. Irina's brother can buy them here in large quantities and sell them there."

"Speculating is not illegal. But what's Irina's role in this? It sounds like it's her brother's business."

Irina shrugged. "If you give me the money, I'll drive with him in the truck. He's drunk most of the time, as I've told you."

"And I told you that I do not give out money." Brooke glanced again at her watch. *Would this goddamn phone never ring?* "I've come to Russia to teach business thinking, and that's the best gift I can give you. When you ask for financing, you should have a clear plan how you'll use it, who will be responsible for handling it, and when and how you intend to repay it." She paused. "And one word of advice. I suggest you leave your brother out of the picture. At best, pay him a commission." She handed Irina an unopened sleeve of crackers from her box, brushing off Svetlana's claim that Irina's visits had to do less with business than with getting gifts. If Irina traded them for bread, so be it.

The blessed ringing of the phone cut off Irina's *spasiba*. "Good-bye," Brooke said and, turning her back on Irina and Svetlana, lunged toward her lifeline.

The crackling sound on the other end was so loud, she had to hold the receiver away from her head. "Good God, Brooke! Where are you?" Hoffenbach's voice bellowed through the static. "You got stuck in the political putsch?"

"You got that right."

"Where are you staying?"

"Hotel Moscow."

"That Soviet flea bag? Union organizers stay there. Move to

Kempinsky, as fine a luxury German hotel as you'll find any-where—"

"It's too close to Red Square. Listen. I'm in kind of a pickle, and the American Embassy is closed."

Hoffenbach spoke to someone, then returned to her. "My secretary's calling the president of Lufthansa. When the upris-ing is suppressed and the airport reopens, you'll be on the first flight out."

"Great. Thanks." She spoke quickly. "Listen. I need a friendly Russian contact. Do you have some names? Who was the one who proposed the Russian deals in your reports?"

"The ones I wouldn't allow NHB to touch?" He chuckled, and Brooke heard a rustle of papers. "Two names. Have a pen and paper ready?"

"Go on."

"The first is an influential man. Plugged deeply into the gov-ernment, and is about to run for the seat of the mayor of Moscow. He's been trying to get us to invest with him for a long time, and he would definitely extend us favors. Nikolai Sidorov."

A cold wave washed through her.

Hoffenbach went on. "Do you remember when someone offered to sell us the K.G.B. photo archives? You liked the electronic-media possibilities. That was him."

"I see." She tapped her pen. Her drunken host's fingers were in every pot. The mayor of Moscow? He was far more conniving and astute than she had given him credit for even after glimpsing the scope of his operation.

"Here is Sidorov's number," Hoffenbach said.

"Thanks, but he's part of my problem."

"Sidorov is?"

"File this info away for another time." Hoffenbach might be the last Westerner to speak with her. "Any other contact here?"

Hoffenbach must have caught on as, without missing a beat, he replied, "Roman Belgorov. Used to head the Department of Economics at Moscow University. A year ago, with a couple of colleagues, he started his own consulting firm. Some major Western corporations have signed on as clients. He's a reliable chap. I'll get you the number."

"What makes him trustworthy?"

"He believes that the only way to move the Russian economy forward is to think long term and to build ventures with solid business strategies. He's not looking for a quick turnaround, which is one marker of corruption. "

"Okay. His home number?"

As Brooke wrote it down, Amanda peeked in. "The bus is leaving; we need daylight to see the place."

"I'll be down in a minute."

Amanda ducked away, and the matron motioned to Brooke to leave, too. Brooke spoke fast, giving Hoffenbach her room phone number. "Call me tonight. If you don't get me, start searching for me." If Sidorov was listening in—and now it turned out that he knew Hoffenbach—he'd know that Brooke was protected. He would know that if she disappeared, there would be a lead to him.

"Are you in physical danger?" Hoffenbach asked.

"I might be, other than from the uprising." Brooke took a

deep breath and forced a smile into her voice. "I can't wait to have a long talk over beer and frankfurters and sauerkraut in that pub of yours. I'll even join your sing-along."

"Brooke, what's going on?"

"I must go. Good-bye, and thanks!" Brooke hit the button in the cradle to disconnect the line. She handed another five-dollar bill to the matron and dialed Belgorov's number. When he answered on the first ring, she let out a sigh of relief. Introducing herself, she said, "I'm rushing out now, but need urgent advice. Where can we meet?"

"Any public place far away from downtown."

"I'm on my way to Zagorsk. Is it very far from where you are?"

He laughed. "I didn't mean *that* far. But yes, for a VP of Norton, Hills, and Bridwell, I will go there." He paused. "We now call the town Sergiyev Posad. There's a small museum building at the back of the monastery. I will meet you in front of it at two forty-five."

## ❧ CHAPTER ❧

## *Thirty-eight*

BROOKE ADJUSTED HER scarf to cover the abrasions on her neck. She had considered removing her Star of David as the chain irritated her skin, but it might have been the shield that had spared her life. Too preoccupied and tired for a social chat, she spread her coat across the seats at the back of the bus. She could see the tips of Judd's sneakers sticking out from the double seat up front, where he was tightly curled, asleep.

Only twice the bus stopped at checkpoints teeming with armored vehicles and soldiers brandishing automatic weapons. Each time, Brooke saw Aleksandr presenting his documents, and the bus was allowed to go through.

Soon, they pulled to the curb on a wide, unusually clean street. A regal line of cypress trees shadowed benches underneath, and the tree beds were planted with flowers, the first Brooke had seen since her arrival. The street opened to a square bordered by the whitewashed stone wall of a fortress. Above it rose magnificent gold-and-blue domes shaped like tulips.

Strolling into a large plaza, Brooke relaxed as she examined merchants' tables with displays of matryoshka dolls, ornate Easter eggs, and oversize wooden spoons—all painted with miniature scenes of Russia's proud past. For a fleeting moment, the present seemed like a bad dream.

The high wall surrounded a cluster of monastery buildings. At the gate, Brooke handed a packet of gum to an old woman who, in spite of the warmth of the day, had wrapped a gray, woolen scarf over her head and around her hunched shoulders. Profuse words of thanks poured out from her toothless mouth as she grabbed Brooke's sleeve and kissed it.

As the group headed into the monastery grounds, Brooke glanced at her watch. Fifteen minutes until her meeting with Belgorov. She fell back, half listening to the guide's talk as the group ambled along wide paths past priories and dining halls decorated with magnificent filigree carvings of leaves, birds, flowers, and cherubim. She turned alone into a cathedral. Its cool, high-vaulted ceiling enveloped her with a sense of peace and serenity, so incongruous with the cannonade in Moscow. A smell of burning wax hung about the place, biting and sacred.

Facing an exquisitely decorated gold altar, Brooke's stomach tightened. She could never visit a church without feeling the weariness of knowing that at such places of worship—as Olga had confirmed—priests, pastors, preachers, and ministers had been teaching their parishes that Jews killed Christ. From such places Soviet children had learned to taunt Jewish children; here Christians' hearts hardened as they were indoctrinated to view Jews as evil. It was in places like this that wild crowds decided to loot Jewish villages, defile girls and women, and kill babies. And the church forgave them time and again.

*I am a Jew, and I am proud of it,* she told the faces on the icons that loomed over her, glowing with gold and semiprecious stones. Their eyes seemed deceivingly compassionate. *Isn't it time to rid yourself of your prejudice and hatred of my people?* It occurred to Brooke that she had never given so much thought to how being a Jew defined her. Now she was certain she wouldn't have wanted to be anything else.

She dropped a coin in a box and lit a candle for the teenagers who had died that morning, boys whose only sin was recklessness. "May their souls rest in peace," she murmured, and considered adding the Jewish prayer for the dead, *"Baruch dayan emet,"* but held back. The words meant praising God's fair judgment no matter what. But taking young lives? She did not share that unfailing faith. Suddenly Brooke understood her mother, who couldn't forgive Him for what He had done to His people.

As she turned to leave, she recognized Judd's silhouette leaning against a large marble column, melting into it like one of the life-size sculptures scattered about. She walked past him without changing her pace.

He caught up with her outside. "Are you all right?" His voice had that rich-as-cream quality she had grown to like. He was freshly shaven and wore a short-sleeve shirt printed in small geometric designs, and a beige cotton sweater draped casually over his shoulders. No trace was left of the disheveled figure in her room before dawn.

"I feel great. Thanks."

He pointed at her neck. "What happened?"

She stopped to face him. "Look, Judd. I'm from the what-you-see-is-what-you-get school. And what I see, I don't like."

His face clouded. He stared at a point above her head. "There's a good explanation for everything. A dignified one, even." The words came out slowly, as though they were coins he held up to the light. "It's unfortunate that I'm not at liberty to talk about it."

"Take your time," she said. "You seem to have more than one situation that you need to process." She swiveled on her heel and walked away.

THE MUSEUM WAS a low and wide building that crouched at the back of a small flagstone plaza with a water fountain at its center. The whitewashed walls looked unadorned and timid, so unlike the wedding-cake opulence of the other buildings.

A man waited next to the fountain. He was in his early fifties, dressed in an Italian-cut suit and a pink silk tie, and his hair was slicked back from a graying widow's peak. In spite of his short stature, his dark mustache brooding over full lips gave him the look of a star from the silent movie era.

At Brooke's approach, he signaled to two sunglass-wearing men with square faces and TV-size chests, who stood forty feet apart on either side of him, their bulging arms angled away from their sides.

"Roman Belgorov," he said, and bent to kiss Brooke's hand. "You should not miss this museum. Small, but one of our best." The pride in his voice reminded her of Olga's when she spoke of "her Russia."

He handed ticket stubs to a uniformed attendant at the door and led Brooke into a vestibule. From an open trunk he pulled out felt booties, which they put on over their shoes to protect the ancient polished parquet floors. As they shuffled along a display of religious artifacts, she was too apprehensive to give them attention. "Explain to me what you do," she said.

"We represent Western clients in their dealings here and lobby our government to pass the necessary regulatory laws or mandate tax concessions to make the investments worthwhile both for them and for Russia's long-term future. But we categorically refuse to pay the *nomenklatura apparatchiks* to allow us access—be it for the rights to natural resources or for the purchasing of heavy industries."

Brooke's glance was fixed on the richest collection of tabernacles, censers, Gospel covers, pendants, chalices, and holy water basins she had ever seen. All were inlaid with thousands of semiprecious stones and millions of seed pearls.

"How successful are you brokering deals without bribing?" she asked.

A sad smile quirked his lips. "My partner, Yuri, disappeared six months ago on a trip to Georgia."

Her heart skipped a beat. "I'm so sorry."

They walked in silence through a display of jeweled crowns. "Do you have any dealings with the Economic Authority?" she finally asked.

He shook his head. "They're mandated to work only with small businesses, or ones with under one thousand employees. I deal with giant ones, or whole industries."

"Well, then." She gave him a brief description of Olga's investigation, the results she had glimpsed from the files, and her current predicament. "We started with a bang, wanting to stop the extortion of the women's cooperatives, and we're ending with a whimper—if we're lucky."

"You are a courageous woman to get involved—or a foolish one."

"Probably the latter." She took a deep breath. "But these local women couldn't have done it without me. All I want now is to save them and get out while I still can."

"Are you aware of the complex network Sidorov has developed, stretching outside our borders?"

"Outside Russia?"

They stopped in a hall with hammered-gold icons inlaid with diamonds and colorful precious stones.

"The Gorbachevskaya Street Factory, for instance," Belgorov said. "Forget about their men's briefs. You've said they do well with their leather outerwear. Here's a hypothetical scenario, but one that takes place here every day in one version or another." Belgorov gestured with both hands as he spoke. "Someone needs the leather coats to bribe the Iraqi Republican Guard, for instance."

Iraq? Brooke couldn't hide her mocking tone. "Leather coats in the desert?"

Belgorov smiled. "Inside their air-conditioned palaces, elite Iraqi women dress in high fashion. Along with vodka, furs, caviar, and bales of wool, the leatherwear may be shipped from Russia to Iran, which then trades these to Iraq for ammunition. In turn, Iraq sends oil to Russia."

"You've lost me on two counts. First, Russia sits on huge reserves of oil; it doesn't need to import it. Second, Iran and Iraq have been at war for years; they don't trade with each other—

especially not ammunition. Saddam Hussein has bombed Iran with poisonous gas."

"Nonetheless, commerce of all kinds is alive and well between them." He paused. "To answer your first point, Russia's oil production has fallen drastically this past year and a half, and what's produced is not used domestically. It is shipped to countries outside the Republics. In fact, Russia has cut off most of its former oil allocation to Belarus and Ukraine."

"How does oil from Iraq get to Russia? They don't even share a border. You can't smuggle oil in a suitcase."

"In tankers through Turkey."

"Turkey?" She scanned a mental map of the area.

"By land, and then through the Black Sea."

"Never mind the U.N. sanctions against Iraq?"

"The United States closes its eyes because the Kurds are the link between Iraq and Turkey, and the U.S. supports the Kurds. It hopes they will kill Saddam Hussein."

Brooke's head reeled. Whatever specialty she had planned to acquire in Russia for her job security, this lecture was one lesson she must memorize. "I have underestimated Sidorov's business savvy and his reach," she said. The scheme involving Vera's pots and pans now seemed simple compared with these elaborate machinations.

Belgorov went on strolling, his bodyguards trailing at a respectful distance. "Once the oil tankers get to Crimea, the oil is sold right at the port in Sevastopol—that's in Ukraine, at the southern tip of the Black Sea—or in Odessa, less than two hundred and fifty miles away from there. The smugglers need not bother to transport the oil inland. You should see the scene at the ports. There are so many ships docked that there's a ten-day wait at sea. The demand here for goods and raw materials is so huge that in addition to oil, dealers buy, sight unseen, full containers of whatever they can lay their hands on. They bribe the local authorities to allow their selected ships to dock at the top of the queue."

"They have no idea if the container is filled with toaster ovens or canned peaches?"

"Right. There's a huge market for everything. That's how your friend Svetlana's leather coats end up as oil, which is far more valuable."

"And your firm can circumvent such practices?"

"In the long run, it's the only way for a healthy economy. We're pushing for tough legislation and tough enforcement. Right now, without a conspiracy law—like your RICO laws in the States—no mob boss can be prosecuted." His shrug contained a note of resignation.

The room smelled of lemony wood polish and light mildew. Brooke chewed her lower lip. "Svetlana believes that we are in physical danger, having found Sidorov out."

"If I were you, I would not return to Moscow. I can drive you right now to friends an hour away from here. They'll get you to Odessa, where you can board the night train to Vienna."

She could desert her luggage in the hotel; her passport was in her money belt. She could leave Russia tonight, just as she had hoped. "You make going back to Moscow sound like suicide," she said.

Then it occurred to her: What if Hoffenbach had been wrong, and Belgorov was actually in Sidorov's service? What if Belgorov meant to scare her into becoming a willing kidnapping victim?

She stepped to the window. Across the plaza, her group followed the tour guide around a church and snapped photos of its ornamental facade. Then they stepped toward the museum, under the lowering afternoon sun. Bathed in the sun rays, Jenny's hair ignited in bright red and Amanda's skin shone like polished ivory. But Svetlana's flowery dress under an open jacket looked faded.

A new wave of guilt washed over Brooke. Would Sidorov's minions be waiting for Svetlana when she returned the files? Brooke would have suggested abandoning the files, but their disappearance would cause irrevocable harm to the four businesses, each employing hundreds of workers—the majority of whom were women, mothers of children. They would be the ones to bear the consequences of her cowardice.

Brooke took a deep breath. She must keep herself together, and her mind sharp. She must believe that Belgorov was an honest man; her fear was causing her to become suspicious, to unravel at the seams. Without turning away from the window, she said, "I can't just run away. I'm involved with two Russian women. I must first ensure their safety."

"How are you planning to do that?"

She shook her head. "I'm at a loss. And I have less time than I thought." With Olga's phone tapped, Brooke couldn't even warn her. She had never taken Olga's home address, and had no idea how to get there even if crossing the city were possible.

She kept her gaze on the group. Amanda was attempting to entice a response from Aleksandr, whose shoulders did all his talking in a series of shrugs. Judd was chatting with one of the women, his hands animated. He threw his head back in laughter.

Suddenly, behind the group, Brooke spotted two unfamiliar men in rumpled gray suits. "Am I being followed?" she whispered to Belgorov.

He looked out. "*My* tail. Right now it serves me well; the more they know of my daily access to foreigners, the less likely they are to meddle with Yuri, if he's still alive."

"Will this meeting hurt me in regard to Sidorov?"

Belgorov shook his head. "Stay visible as much as you can."

Through the window, she could see the group still waiting at the ticket line to the museum. "Then let's go out and let your tail get a full view of us talking," she said.

After dropping their felt booties into a trunk at the exit, they sat down on a stone bench under a row of cypresses. A squirrel scampered away, stopped, bobbed its head, and, gripping an acorn, turned to look at them.

"Do you have any suggestion how to save my two friends here?" Brooke asked.

Belgorov stroked his mustache. "Why not go the international media publicity route? That offers protection like no other."

"I don't see you using it for Yuri."

"When hundreds of bank tellers and innocent merchants have been shot this past year alone, one more Russian businessman's disappearance—well, who cares? But you're an American." He glanced around. "Our government and its cronies—the bankers and mafia dons—are becoming sensitive to global public opinion, especially since the International Monetary Fund has been asking some tough questions before handing out billions of dollars to save a fiscal policy that's out of control."

"By nightfall, Russia might not have a government, let alone a fiscal policy." Brooke gestured in what she assumed was the direction of Moscow. "Even if Yeltsin doesn't cave in, it's going to be difficult to grab headlines while cannons are firing at your parliament."

"The revolt is being squelched as we speak." He shook his head with sadness. "Although what can one expect from a militia whose tank commanders literally stopped at intersections to ask people for directions to the White House?"

"We say in the States that men never ask for directions." She picked at the scuffed knees of her pants. "Do you support Yeltsin?"

"We need him around until a better leader emerges. He shouldn't have started this mess, but now that he has, he'd better be careful with the casualties. Six Americans were wounded since yesterday, including four journalists."

In the soreness of her tongue, Brooke tasted earth and blood. She could have been the seventh.

Belgorov steepled his fingers in thought. "Do you have immediate access to major U.S. media?"

The media? The notion slammed in her head. Norcress owed her a favor. Three of them. "Where can I find a working phone for a domestic call?"

"Not in this town." He thought for a moment. "If it's in Moscow, you may write a note and I'll see that it is hand delivered."

She rooted in her purse and found Norcress's card. The phone number was in California and would do her no good. "He's stay-ing wherever the foreign press can be found." She checked her itinerary, then wrote a note, asking Norcress to come to Hotel Moscow that night or at least call. It was urgent.

She glanced over at the group. The women still dawdled by the ticket line, where Aleksandr was arguing with someone at the cashier's window. The pull of his contacts that had shooed him through city checkpoints ended with the cashier of a small, out-of-the way museum. Amanda waved at Brooke, and Brooke waved back. Judd turned to look. Brooke couldn't imagine what they thought of her sitting and talking to a Russian, with his twin bodyguards hovering about.

"Last question," she said to Belgorov. "If Sidorov is the Rus-sian Don Corleone you're describing, why did he sponsor a mis-sion of American women to come teach entrepreneurial skills?"

"I wouldn't be surprised if he thought little of the request when it was proposed to him." He paused, considering. "Or else he needs U.S. contacts and has been watching to see which of you could be recruited into his employ."

"Recruited? What could he possibly offer any of us?"

"*Recruit* in Soviet-speak means 'coerce,' 'blackmail.' Just like the K.G.B. used to recruit spies in the West, Sidorov will search for a weakness and then will exploit it."

An image of her lost envelope hit Brooke. She had been trying hard to focus on the immediate issues, but the lost letter—if it was indeed the blackmail letter she had always feared—would surely be followed by another soon after her return home, then by threatening phone calls. If her old photos got out, she would surely lose her job and her reputation would be forever destroyed.

The notion of a second extortion by a Russian mafia baron was too preposterous to let in.

Brooke decided that she had exhausted Belgorov's goodwill and insights. "Thank you for everything," she said, and he kissed her hand again.

Although wiser, she was no closer to solving her plight.

## ❧ CHAPTER ❧

# *Thirty-nine*

TRACER FIRE WHISTLED as it made a wide arc in the sky. Olga watched Viktor open the window. On the far horizon, helicopter floodlights still circled the city, although the distant barrage of cannon fire had stopped. A gunshot pierced the air, and was answered by two others. After that, silence fell on Moscow. The low, dark skies felt like a down blanket, but the layers of darkness receded where light seeped upward from the city skyline.

Viktor went to the liquor cabinet and took out the brandy he kept for special occasions. "The worst is over. Shall we celebrate?"

"Too soon." He needed to fortify himself, she knew. Her eyes were riveted to the TV set. "And too many comrades dead."

"Comrades? You call Rutskoy and his bunch of fascists 'comrades'?"

"They are still Russians. Each one of them. All three systems tried so far—czarism, communism, democracy—were seriously flawed," she said. "Each was a failed attempt at social engineering and all ended up as an unfortunate new version of Russian roulette."

He crouched in front of her and handed her a half-filled glass. "Stop torturing yourself about every political upheaval."

For a while, the only sounds in the room were those of the neighbors going through their evening routines. Pots clanked, chairs were dragged. No one was arguing tonight.

She tipped her glass and emptied it. She would wait to tell Viktor of her plans to run for the Duma after her symposium tomorrow, where she hoped to secure the support of leaders of women's organizations from farther regions. Thinking of tomorrow, she wondered what Brooke had in mind when she'd called earlier, asking her to arrive at the office early.

Absentmindedly, her hand ruffled Viktor's thinning hair. A long time ago, his head had been a tangle of dark, thick curls that she used to cut. Once she had taped a lock onto a piece of paper and kept it in the back of her closet until moths got to it.

"We're too old for another social system," he finally said. "Too old for battles."

An image of Brooke flitted through Olga's mind. In ten years, Brooke would still look beautiful. "In the West, forty-eight is young," Olga said. Between her fingers, dark blotches dotted Viktor's forehead and scalp. She had never noticed those before. Did she, too, have them? Her monthly flow had almost ceased. She doubted she could get pregnant.

Still kneeling in front of her, Viktor laid his head in her lap.

She leaned forward and ran her fingers across his back. He breathed in, then raised his mouth until it reached her breasts, burrowing his face as deeply as her tight sweater would allow.

Their breathing grew heavier. With a grunt, Viktor rose to his feet and extended his hand. Holding on to it, Olga pushed herself off the chair, fighting the pain in her knee, fighting the depressing thought that she was no longer the lovely petite blonde she had once been.

If she held firm to that younger image of herself, she could close her eyes and would again be hugging the young Viktor she had once so desired. They would be back at that barn at the edge of the forest, their bodies hot after hours of folk dancing, aroused from a long night of devouring each other with their eyes. Once again, he would lay her gently on the hay, release her small breasts from the embroidered blouse and lift her full cotton skirt. Her legs, slender and strong, would once again wrap around his muscular back, and her fingers would dig into his thick hair.

They weren't old. It was their country that had aged them. With a little encouragement, Viktor could still sink into her flesh, now more slowly, methodically, like the scientist he had become since those summer nights of their youth. They would move in unison, no longer the frantic groping and stripping, no longer the passion that had once made her scream into the night.

But they would love each other nevertheless. Even Russia could not take that away from them.

# DAY SIX

*Tuesday, October 5, 1993*

## ❧ CHAPTER ❧

# *Forty*

S HORTLY AFTER CURFEW had been lifted in the morning, Brooke headed to the Institute for Social Research "to have an early cup of coffee with Olga," she told Amanda, who would arrive with the rest of the group an hour later for the day's symposium. After Brooke tipped one of the sentries at the hotel entrance, he managed to get her a taxi within minutes.

She found Olga upstairs in her office, wetting a lock of hair with saliva and attempting to curl it. But the hair, too dry and brittle, sprang straight out again.

"I give up." Olga used a hairpin to keep the curl in place and turned to Brooke. Her blue eyes were bright.

Brooke hugged her. "Excited about the symposium?"

In contrast to her eyes, Olga's lips curved downward in a sad little smile. "The uprising isn't over yet." She pointed at the White House on the distant horizon. With the center charred, the formerly massive rectangular building looked like a two-tower structure. "The radio announced that repairs have already begun. Incredibly efficient, and a good theme for my opening speech: They'll whitewash the outside to symbolize the restoration of hope, but the scorched core of our parliament signifies the black void of lawlessness and corruption in our midst. It has sucked in everything that's good here."

Brooke noticed the unplugged ends of the phone and the computer wires. Being wary of wiretapping had become second nature here. She glanced at her watch. "Sit down. We have a major problem, but a possible solution." She relayed Svetlana's discovery at the Economic Authority eavesdropping center: Their phones were being tapped.

Against the burgundy color of Olga's tweed suit, the blood seemed to drain out of her face. The faint blue veins in her temples made the translucent skin look like marble.

"We were careful to say nothing specific over the phone, right?" Brooke asked.

Her voice wobbling, Olga replied, "This is Russia; suspicion is enough. That's how it was in the Communist days, that's how it is now. Who cares about evidence? Certainly not the mafia." She picked up her cigarette from the ashtray, puffed on it, then stubbed it out. "I feel like a fish in a glass bowl."

Brooke bit her lip. When Norcress had called last night, she promised him an exclusive scoop on a story with a combination of angst and local celebrity. "I said I may have a solution," she now said to Olga, and explained her plan. "If we get this journalist to publish Sidorov's story in the international media, it will not only expose the corruption, but it will also protect you by publicly naming him."

"In Russia, attention can only be bad for you."

"Publicity might be your best—and only—defense."

Olga looked at her, doubt in her eyes. "The new Russia is still Russia. The only difference is that in the new Russia the mafia is more efficient than the K.G.B. ever was."

"Do you have a better idea?"

Olga shook her head.

"Use Norcress's article to announce you are running for parliament," Brooke said, thinking of Belgorov's advice. "It will give you credibility, and the drama will draw more international attention to your plight."

"The more reason the mafia will have to try to eliminate me. Anyway, I'm not ready to make that announcement until I 'tie my shoelaces.' "

"We call it 'tie loose ends.' " Brooke smiled. "I would like to give the journalist the copies of the documents. He will need them to authenticate the story."

Olga unlocked a drawer, pulled out a folder, and laid it on her desk. "I've made another copy and hidden it with your ledger." She swiveled in her chair, turning her back to Brooke.

Even though the room was chilly, perspiration gathered at Brooke's temples. "I'll wait outside until Norcress arrives," she said to Olga's back.

Olga nodded without turning around. Her fingers drummed on the arm of her chair.

Outside in the corridor, Brooke paced, willing her panic to ease. A clock was ticking somewhere.

She heard the ring of the elevator bell, followed by the mechanical swish of the opening door. When Norcress stepped out, his thin face broadened into a smile as if they were old acquaintances. He wore the same multipocketed vest she had seen before, but instead of cameras he carried a canvas briefcase.

"Come," Brooke said. "I want you to meet Dr. Olga Leonidovna Rozanova. A sociologist. My partner in crime." She was placing Olga's and Svetlana's lives—and, ultimately, her own safety as well—in the hands of a complete stranger.

As they entered the office, Olga offered to make tea. Brooke shook her head. "Let's begin. We don't have much time."

"This trouble may finish me, but no one will be able to deny I was a good hostess," Olga replied. "Sit down."

Against the clink of Olga's china and the hiss of the samovar, Brooke asked Norcress, "Is the uprising truly contained?"

"It is, but not the mess. The thousands of parliament supporters who poured into the center of Moscow have dispersed all over the city, and now Yeltsin's militia is searching for them." He accepted the cup of tea from Olga, and said to her, "Your president never faces a confrontation he'd rather avoid." He turned back to Brooke. "Get this. He's issued a directive for Muscovites to report any sighting of 'foreigners' being sheltered by their neighbors."

"How Soviet. And how embarrassing," Olga muttered. "We're still in charge of each other's morals, spying on our neighbors and relatives."

"Is there still a threat of civil war?" Brooke asked.

"Civil-war-like clashes, for sure. Civilians continue to attack the military—and one another." He looked at her. "Better not get into trouble. The American Embassy is still closed."

"When is the airport opening?"

"Maybe later today. But you may need to shoot your way out through roadblocks to get out of the city."

Just yesterday, miraculously, Aleksandr's documents had let the group through the roadblocks. It suddenly occurred to Brooke that someone—Sidorov perhaps—might have wanted them out of the hotel in order to have access to her still-packed suitcase. Since last night, she had only retrieved whatever she needed without checking to see if anything had been disturbed.

Olga settled in her seat and unbuttoned her suit jacket. Her face, so pale earlier, was flushed. "Go ahead, Brooke. You tell him what's happening; my English is not so good."

Norcress's eyes scanned the office. "Is this place secure?"

Olga nodded. "For years, my work was too academic to warrant the expense of wiring me."

"What about your hotel?" Brooke asked Norcress. "Foreign correspondents must be watched closely."

"The Interior Ministry monitors us, for sure. But what do they do with the information? Since yesterday their militia has been too busy breaking up street brawls. Anyway, why shouldn't we, two Americans, speak?"

"Some Russians might care if they knew what I am about to tell you."

He placed his tape recorder on the small coffee table. "I'm ready if you are."

Brooke recounted Olga's investigation. She described the attack at the Gorbachevskaya Street Factory and explained how she had joined forces with Olga to follow the money trail, and that she'd retrieved four files.

"You went *alone* to the Economic Authority offices?"

Brooke tilted her head. "Let's assume I did, okay?"

"Sure. You read Russian, too. That's how you found your way around a local government office."

Brooke let out a thin smile and went on, skipping her near-death ordeal; Olga had enough to handle without feeling guilty for having put her in jeopardy. "What's important," Brooke continued, "is what we've learned. Nikolai Sidorov, an economic adviser to Yeltsin, is the man who has spearheaded the intimidation of the very same ventures he was supposed to help get on their feet."

"I like this story. A lot," Norcress said.

"There's more." Brooke took in a deep breath. "I've discovered that this man runs complex business shenanigans that penetrate deep into Iran, Iraq, and maybe other nations. And now he aspires to become the mayor of Moscow."

"The mayor of Moscow." Norcress whistled.

"And this same man is the host of our group. He's found out what we're up to, and now he's wiretapped us."

"Maybe he wiretapped you because of your contacts with foreigners," Norcress said to Olga.

"We've had visiting foreign academicians before, although no Americans." Olga's voice was raspier than usual. "There's a Russian saying, 'Don't dig a hole for somebody else lest you fall into it yourself.' And this is where we are now. In that hole."

"What tipped him off?" Norcress asked.

"I told no one," Brooke replied. "Neither Olga nor I, nor the director of the Gorbachevskaya Street Factory discussed any of it over the phone. Only the three of us knew."

"Nevertheless, there's been a leak." He leaned forward, elbows on knees. "Your danger is greater as long as you don't know how the information is getting out."

Olga lit another cigarette and blew the smoke away from them. "Will publishing your story help?"

Norcress made some notes. "I'll write the story. I will even ask my editor to distribute it through an international news service to reach a far wider audience than the *Los Angeles Record*."

"There's a 'but' hidden somewhere," Brooke said.

He turned to Olga. "Dr. Rozanova—"

"Olga is better."

"Olga, it will take me time to write the story, even if I spend the rest of today on it. I need to check many facts for complete accuracy."

"Here are copies of the most damning documents for you," Brooke said, and motioned to Olga to hand him the folder. "You read Russian, I assume," she added, recalling that he had talked to the taxi driver.

"How do I know that these are copies of the original documents from the Economic Authority?" Norcress's brows raised as he leafed through the papers.

"We're talking old Soviet Union," Brooke said. "Let's not get sources involved."

"I personally copied the original forms from the Economic Authority files, including the signature of Sidorov's wife or daughter for the transfer of ownership," Olga said.

"Okay for now. If there's a discrepancy when I cross-reference with other sources, I'll need to speak to whoever had direct access to the files."

"That's me," Brooke said. "I pulled them up from the file cabinets at the Finance Department."

He addressed Olga. "Dr. Rozanova, I hate to think that your life depends on my article getting published, and it may take more than one story to smoke out these mafia barons. In a paradoxical way, it might strengthen Sidorov; sometimes publicity—even damaging—enhances a head honcho's clout. Even if he leaves you alone, he might hurt your family." He paused. "But you know that, I'm sure."

Olga spoke through a cloud of smoke. "I'll leave first thing in the morning for my dacha and stay there until I see the results. Maybe my husband can take his vacation days. Either way, I'll have my granddaughter with me, but our son and his wife, they have jobs. They can't just disappear."

"They would if they were dead," Norcress said.

Olga dropped her face into her hands.

Brooke patted her shoulder. "I'm so sorry," she whispered.

"We say, 'If you offer to carry the basket, don't complain of the weight.' But it's unfair that I dragged you into it." Olga's words came muffled from between her fingers. "I've taken risks before, and lived."

"You should make your announcement," Brooke told her.

"I haven't yet secured the commitment of all key supporters."

"Am I missing something?" Norcress asked.

Olga nodded her assent to Brooke, who then said, "She's planning to run for a seat in the Duma on the women's platform ticket. Olga is well known and highly respected; she used to publish a *samizdat* with wide readership. Her chances are quite good."

A broad smile spread over Norcress's face. "Now that's a story."

Brooke straightened. "Olga, if, as Belgorov believes, publishing the story in the international media has the power to control Sidorov, what about the reverse?"

"The reverse?" Norcress asked.

"A simple blackmail," Brooke said. "Olga will negotiate with Sidorov not to run the story if he leaves her and her family alone."

Olga chortled. "So now I must trust the mafia to make a deal? No, never."

"Look," Brooke said. "Sidorov has political aspirations."

"Yes." Olga nodded pensively. "And he wouldn't want to lose his place in Yeltsin's inner circle."

Norcress tapped his foot. "What am I doing here, then? You're killing my story?"

He was right, of course. Brooke rose and went to the far window. It was preposterous of her; she had invited the journalist so he could write a story. "Editors sit on stories all the time. Especially human-interest stories."

"Of a corrupt, violent man gearing up to run for the mayoralty of Moscow and a woman who is a candidate for the Russian parliament?"

"Look, if the story doesn't get published, you can use the material for a deeper and broader investigative report into the political corruption here." Brooke thought of Roman Belgorov's partner. "I personally guarantee you another excellent lead."

"What kind?"

"Not yet."

"I know what you can give me." Locking his fingers behind

his head, Norcress tipped his chair back, then landed forward with a thud. "Who's that guy Judd Kornblum?"

Surprise hit Brooke like the snapping of a bent branch. "What?"

"You heard me. That Jewish dude who's using your group as a cover."

"What has given you the impression that he's operating anything, covert or otherwise?" Brooke asked.

Norcress's raised eyebrow gave her a you-know-I-can't-tell look.

"I haven't figured him out either." Brooke sighed, but she hoped that Judd would help her send Svetlana and her daughter to a safe place. "So, where do we stand on this?"

"You have a deal." Norcress turned to Olga. "I'll have the article ready tonight. You can start negotiating with Sidorov."

"When? My symposium is about to start."

"It's your life." He rose to his feet. "Call me at my hotel no later than tomorrow morning—even during the night—and let me know how to proceed." He pulled out a small black notebook. "Also, write down for me your full name and address."

After Olga scribbled it, Brooke asked for a copy for herself. While Olga wrote it for her, Brooke wrote down Belgorov's phone number in Norcress's book. The Russian had done as he had promised, and last night had delivered the note to Norcress, anonymously. "Here is your other lead. He has lots of good material."

"If we don't break this story, I may still want to do a profile on you when you announce your candidacy for the Duma," Norcress told Olga.

"Thanks, but that won't be necessary."

He laughed. "It's campaigning American-style." Norcress kissed Brooke's cheek. "Get the hell out of Moscow."

"I'll probably make it out tomorrow."

"If I were you, I'd be at the airport now, sitting on my suitcase to catch the first flight out when air traffic opens—even if it were to Kathmandu."

## ❧ CHAPTER ❧

## *Forty-one*

BROOKE CRANED HER neck to see whether Olga had returned to the auditorium. Where was she? The Russian had been summoned by an attendee during the coffee break, but that had been an hour ago. Perhaps she was consulting additional people about running for the Duma.

The auditorium on the ground floor of Olga's institute must have been refurbished in recent years. Brooke scanned the rows of custom-made oak tables equipped with built-in microphones, and the interpreters sitting behind a glass divider at the back of the room, speaking into the attendees' headsets. A giant tapestry in swirling yellow, orange, and red dominated the front wall, a rare abstract public decor with no Soviet theme.

The crowd's anguish over the war downtown thickened the air as people accustomed to sitting still so as not to draw attention fidgeted and whispered. Nevertheless, Olga had been right: They had shown up. Brooke plugged her headset into the portable transmitter, but quickly lost interest as the pathos-filled, canned speeches of the male representatives continued. The one hundred women who had traveled from distant places to this symposium deserved a lot more than what they were getting. The *apparatchiks* were wasting everyone's time. The event was nothing like the hands-on day of workshops Amanda had organized in which dozens of Irinas acquired new insights and skills, nor was there any speech of business substance that called for the American guests' response as originally planned.

Brooke glanced at her watch. Where was Olga?

Fifteen minutes later, she unplugged her earphones and walked out of the auditorium.

In the large foyer, artisans had set up tables to sell handmade dolls, jewelry, embroidered shirts, painted bowls, crocheted napkins, and mosaic pictures. As Brooke rushed through, none of the women met her gaze, and the gloom of the day lingered on their faces, more grave than the usual dour Russian expression. Looking around the lobby for a glimpse of Olga, Brooke made a mental note to buy a matryoshka doll later for the wife of her superintendent back in New York as thanks for watching Sushi.

The bathrooms on the ground floor were empty, but smelly. Olga wasn't there. Back in the foyer, a large wall clock struck the hour. In thirty minutes, according to the translated typed schedule, Olga would give the morning's closing remarks, and the program would break for lunch. Where was she? Clammy fingers of dread touched Brooke's skin. She hurried to the elevator, took it to the fourteenth floor, and marched down the corridor toward Olga's office.

A man's mocking laughter rushed adrenaline into her veins. She pushed the door open.

The combined odor of alcohol, vomit, and cigar smoke reminded her of a cheap pub. Nikolai Sidorov sat in Olga's desk chair, a cigar dangling from the corner of his mouth, ringlets of blue-gray smoke swirling lazily over his head. Unhurriedly, he raised his eyes to meet Brooke's stare. Brooke immediately broke eye contact. She scanned the room.

Between the two large windows stood a tall, broad young man in a colorful jogging suit. Olga was slumped like a puppet in one of the upholstered chairs, her legs splayed. Her right arm almost touched the floor, and her chin had dropped onto her high bosom. Clumps of her hair stood up as though electrified.

Brooke started toward her, shouting, "What have you done to her?"

The bodyguard blocked her way.

"She's drunk," Sidorov said. "Go back to where you came from."

Brooke tried to step around the bodyguard, but his pointed index finger almost punctured her collarbone.

"I'm not going anywhere until I know what's wrong with Dr. Rozanova."

"You know us Russians." Sidorov smirked. "She's had too much vodka."

A bottle of brown liquid sat on the desk. Brooke recognized the Cyrillic letters for vodka. But vodka was clear. . . . "What have you forced down her throat?"

Sidorov puffed on his cigar. The bodyguard stepped closer to Brooke until his broad chest touched her face. It felt like an iron gate.

"Get away from me," she growled through clenched teeth. "Who do you think you are?"

Sidorov said something in Russian, and the man clomped back to his spot by the wall.

"She's been drinking and talking." Slowly, Sidorov laid his cigar in the ashtray. "But since you're here, there are a couple of things you can clarify for me."

Olga's skin was sickly gray. She moaned. Brooke moved toward her, but Sidorov's voice stopped her.

"You'd better 'spill the beans,' as you say in America, or you'll be very thirsty, too." He chuckled. "That Chinese girl who leads your group—"

"Amanda Cheng is an American."

"A liar, like all of you. Did she really think I'd believe that each of you would pay from her own pocket to come teach business to our *women*?" He shook his head in pity. "Americans think Russians are stupid."

The turn in the conversation startled Brooke. "I don't follow you."

"Who sent you? Your government? The C.I.A.? Your boyfriends?"

"Aren't you the host who invited us?"

"Don't play with me." He banged the table with his fist. "Some women's organization came asking for you. Dykes, all of them. Who selected each of you? Answer me! I want to know about the conspiracy behind all this."

"I see." She was on familiar grounds again. "Women can't help other women unless there's some conspiracy? Whether you understand it or not, volunteerism is an American ideal." She walked toward Olga. This time the bodyguard didn't stop her.

"American ideal is dollars."

Brooke ignored him and gently touched the Russian woman's clammy cheek. "Olga?"

Olga's hooded eyes opened to reveal unfocused irises. With effort, they came to rest on Brooke. In a split moment of clarity, an understanding passed between them. The two of them were in this together, undeterred.

Sidorov spoke behind Brooke's back. "Either she talks or you talk, or our little friend Svetlana will. But you are the best person to tell me the name of the client you're snooping around for."

Brooke rose from her crouching position. "You're wrong. There's no such client."

"Well, let's find out." His finger beckoned the bodyguard who picked up the bottle and approached Olga. "She's still thirsty."

"Don't you touch her!"

From behind the desk, Sidorov brought up a vodka bottle—this one filled with clear liquid—and two tiny glasses. Unhurriedly, he filled them, slid one toward Brooke, and placed the other on the back of his hand. Brooke made no move to take the glass. As she had seen him do at dinner a couple of nights before, Sidorov tipped the glass to his mouth and gulped the contents. "To Russian–American friendship." Then, slowly, deliberately, he pulled an envelope from his inside pocket. "What will the new management at NHB think about this?"

Brooke's scalp tightened with shock. She recognized the envelope. That goddamned letter from Seattle, lost at customs.

Her nude photos. She felt as vulnerable as if she were standing unclothed in front of him.

Sidorov stretched forward as if to hand it to her. "Here."

She stepped forward and reached for the envelope, but he quickly withdrew it. His raucous laugh, guttural, insolent, was punctuated by snorting. Her cheeks burned.

"Come and get it." He waved the envelope. The expression of pleasure on his face was like Sushi's when toying with a bug.

Brooke's mouth felt full of ashes. She crossed her arms. "What do you want?"

"Now we're talking." He wiped his eyes, then refilled his glass. "First, tell me what you've been sniffing around for in Moscow. Second, you could help our business interests in New York. You know, some financial transactions you could handle for us."

"Laundering your money? You're delusional." Belgorov had been right about Sidorov's recruitment tactics. For a split second, through the blood pounding in her temples, she wavered. What if she pretended to agree as long as he gave her the letter back?

Too dangerous. He'd find her anywhere. And while he wanted her sober now to discuss his business, when she refused to reveal the results of the investigation—or confirm it if he'd got it out of Olga—his bodyguard would force that concocted drink down her throat. And there was every chance he would also discover her Star of David, tucked under her blouse.

Sidorov put the envelope back into his breast pocket and tapped on it.

Without warning, Brooke rushed out of the room. The bodyguard didn't come after her, but rather than feeling relief, she was rattled by Sidorov's confidence. What had she done? What hubris had led her to employ guerrilla tactics in an enemy territory? If only she could wrap things up, reach Belgorov, and get the hell out of this cursed country.

But she couldn't just leave Olga upstairs. They might poison her to death.

Following the smell of food, Brooke raced from the main floor down a flight of stairs leading to the basement dining room. She burst in and noticed the crowd was just sitting down.

She caught Amanda's eye and ran to her. "This is an emergency," she whispered. "Gather the others and come up to the fourteenth floor. On the double."

"Why?" Amanda asked. "What's going on?"

"Please. I need you all to come now."

Nearby, Russians who might have noticed her frantic state pretended not to see; they'd been trained over a lifetime to mind their own business.

She ran toward the elevators again, Amanda and some of the others at her heels.

When she entered Olga's office, Sidorov and his bodyguard were gone. Olga was lying face down on the floor. Desk drawers had been pulled out, a bookcase was tipped forward, and files and papers were strewn everywhere. Olga's samovar table lay on its side with its legs thrust out, like bloated roadkill. Behind her, Brooke heard gasps and shocked murmurings from Amanda and the others.

She knelt beside Olga. A puddle of vomit gelled next to her mouth and stuck to the ends of her mussed hair. She was unconscious but her pulse was accelerated. "Water," Brooke called out. "And please make strong coffee."

Amanda handed her a wet cloth napkin. She turned Olga over and began to clean her up.

"My God! Look at that!" Amanda cried.

On Olga's upper thigh was an ugly welt, the size of a quarter. A foot away lay Sidorov's half-smoked cigar. "Lucky they didn't kidnap her to finish the job," Brooke said as she removed Olga's shoes and tucked a soft, crocheted pillow behind her head.

"Who?" Amanda asked.

"Sidorov."

"Sidorov?" Amanda stammered. "How do you know?"

"He was here ten minutes ago. In this room." Brooke wanted to cry. This was a nightmare, and Sidorov was not done with them yet.

From the samovar came the hissing sound of boiling water. The scent of coffee rose behind Brooke.

"I don't get it. What's happening, Brooke?"

"You'd be safer not knowing."

"It certainly looks like *you* are not safe here," Amanda said. "You should leave as soon as the airport opens."

"I can't desert Olga and Svetlana."

"Svetlana? What does she have to do with this? Brooke, I'm afraid that you are over your head in something." Amanda lowered her voice. "Is the rest of the group safe from whatever you're not telling me?"

"If I were you I'd question Sidorov's agenda in inviting us all."

"Why? You need to level with me."

"I really shouldn't."

"I'll set up a meeting with Sidorov to guarantee our safety in the presence of some heads of American companies," Amanda said.

"Good. When?"

"As soon as possible. We're leaving the symposium now, anyway. We've been cut out of the agenda. Those bureaucrats hijacked our time slots with their nonsense."

TWO HOURS LATER, a cough ravaged Olga's chest. When the fit was over, she rubbed her eyes and opened them. She looked around her office. "What happened?" Her hand felt the couch on which she was lying, then traveled to her thigh, now bandaged. She groaned. "My symposium?"

"Some leaders of women's organizations took over and continued with the program," Brooke said. "How do you feel?" She handed Olga a coffee mug and two tablets of Tylenol.

"Where is my Dukat?"

Brooke pulled a cigarette out of a packet, put it between Olga's lips, and lit it. "Where did you hide the folder?"

Olga inhaled and tapped the back of the couch. "There's a zipper."

Brooke crouched. "It's still closed."

"Call Viktor, please," Olga said, and dictated his office phone number. Brooke dialed and handed her the receiver. Olga said only a few words in Russian, then handed the receiver back to Brooke, who hung up.

"Olga," Brooke said. "Next time you won't be so lucky. We need help." She paused. "There must be some sort of enforcement somewhere."

"Sure." Olga said in a rare moment of sarcasm. "Yeltsin made a big announcement about a division set up to handle mafia crimes. But—" She coughed.

"Let me guess: There's no listed phone number."

"No one believes it even exists." Olga sipped her coffee. "I know people in high places who can help."

"Make sure they get to Sidorov tonight."

Thirty minutes later, Viktor arrived. His face looked flustered. Brooke decided to let his wife do the explaining. She supported Olga's left side, Viktor the right, and they took the elevator down.

ON THE NINTH floor of Hotel Moscow, Brooke found Svetlana waiting on the couch right outside her room. She looked miserable.

Brooke sat down beside her. The deserted sitting area seemed safer than her own room. "Did you return the files?"

Svetlana nodded, staring at a handkerchief crumpled in her other hand, then broke into a sob. "This has been the worst week of my life."

Brooke patted her shoulder as an idea blossomed in her mind, exquisite in its simplicity. "Are you as fluent in German as you are in English?"

Svetlana nodded. "But I haven't met any German women yet."

"I'm sure they'll like you as much as American women do." Brooke smiled. "How would you like to live in Germany?"

Svetlana raised her wet eyes. "How is it possible? I could never afford the tickets—"

"Don't worry about that. The important question is, would you like a job in my firm's Frankfurt office?"

"Would I?" Svetlana's voice was laced with awe. "All my life I've dreamed of taking Natasha to a safe place where there are beautiful things, beautiful people . . ."

"Yes, you'll be safe there." Brooke smiled. "The boss is my friend. You're hardworking and smart, and he'll be delighted to have you." She paused to consider any administrative hurdles, but none seemed to come to mind. Russia no longer stopped its people from traveling, Germany didn't require a tourist visa, and Hoffenbach could take care of everything else later. "We'll leave tomorrow. Do you have a passport? I heard that all Russians have passports."

"Those are internal ones. They didn't want to issue me an international travel permit during Soviet times because of uh, a character flaw. But as soon as *perestroika* started, I applied for a passport, just as a test, and got it!"

"What character flaw?" Brooke softened her tone. "I must know; I'll be vouching for you."

Hanging her head, Svetlana murmured, "When I was fourteen, I was raped by five men."

God Almighty. "I'm so sorry. But how is that your character flaw?"

"The judge said I should have fought them off. Even my lawyer agreed that I needed to be reeducated. My father's punishment for raising such a daughter was to be reprimanded in front of the entire factory, and then they fired him anyway. He left my mother, saying she should have raised me better. Even my cousins stopped talking to me; they didn't want people to think that they were immoral too." Svetlana's face contorted in pain. "I ruined my family."

"Svetlana, that was Soviet injustice. So unfair! They blamed the victim and let the perpetrators get off scot free. You did nothing wrong." Flashes of her own "character flaw" crossed Brooke's mind. That was a failing the new partners at NHB— if they found out—wouldn't take lightly. Nor would her clients. "Where is your mother now?"

"There was a man in St. Petersburg who had an apartment, so she married him."

Brooke hugged Svetlana. "You're a terrific person, and don't let anyone tell you otherwise."

"You understand because of your own character flaw."

"Me?"

"Your Jewish gene," Svetlana said in a tone as if this fact was obvious. "But you are a very good Jewess."

"Svetlana, please. It's not a gene—and certainly not a flaw. In fact, I'm proud to be Jewish." This wasn't the time to reeducate her. "Go home to your daughter and pack."

"I don't know how to thank you."

*How about by stopping to be an anti-Semite?* Brooke touched her shoulder. "Don't say good-bye to anyone. Not even to people you absolutely trust. You'll call them from Frankfurt later this week. Okay?"

Having solved one problem, Brooke's worry dropped one notch. At the elevator she asked, "By the way, have you talked to anyone about our investigation?"

Svetlana shook her head. "Not with any Russian."

"Not any Russian? Any other nationality?"

"Jenny. I asked her advice."

Christ. Brooke pressed her palm on the wall by the elevator, and a protruding screw stabbed her. Jenny. The image of that Betty Boop flirting with Sidorov the night of the banquet loomed behind her eyes.

Svetlana added, "She told me to go for it. She gave me the courage—"

"Don't discuss anything with anyone—Jenny included—until after we leave. Promise me? Don't even tell your deputy director at the factory," Brooke said in a tight voice. It was too late to be angry with Svetlana, or even with Jenny. She just wanted it all to be behind her.

After Svetlana left, Brooke placed the call to Hoffenbach from the floor matron's room. "I expect to be on the Lufthansa flight tomorrow," she told him. "I need two more tickets. Put them in my name. I'll give out the identities when we check in." She paused. "Please meet me when we land, and can you please have a typed job description for a secretary who's fluent in German, Russian, and English?"

"I'm sure we can use those skills," he said, a smile in his voice.

Back in her room, Brooke showered and put on her jeans. She lit one of Amanda's candles, sat on the bed, and looped her legs in a lotus position. Within the hour, Norcress would give Olga the article she could use as the bargaining chip in her negotiation with Sidorov. Tomorrow, Svetlana and her daughter would start a new life in Frankfurt, away from danger. All was as good as it could be for the moment, except for the envelope in Sidorov's hands. There was nothing she could do about that; she wouldn't compound yet another monumental mistake in her life by being sucked into Sidorov's laundering machine.

DINNER WOULD HAVE fit right in at the gulag before an execution, Brooke thought as she munched on a sliced cucumber. A long evening stretched ahead. "Curfew is at seven o'clock," Aleksandr said. "Afterward, the army will shoot anyone in the street. I'll see you in the morning." On his way to the exit, he clutched his portfolio to his chest as if his prized leather possession would stop bullets.

"I have a travel Scrabble. Are you up for a game?" Amanda asked.

They settled in the ninth floor sitting area. At the end of the corridor, in spite of the curfew, moved shadows of loitering clients. Other than having glimpsed the girls at the doors to their rooms, Brooke hadn't encountered any in the elevator or elsewhere in the hotel, and now wondered if it was due to their different schedules, or whether the girls were being kept prisoner.

She was about to ask Amanda what she thought when Jenny showed up. She hugged Brooke like a long-lost relative, and started chattering about the day's failed symposium. Brooke's resentment of her melted. Annoying as Jenny was, she had no evil intentions; she couldn't have known not to trust their important host.

Seated on the sofa across from Amanda and Jenny, Brooke surveyed the seven Scrabble letters she'd picked. Focusing on trying to score the highest points was a good distraction from her worries. At that moment, Olga must be in the midst of negotiating for her life.

"I've got a bottle of Champagne in my room. Shall I get it?" Jenny had barely finished her question when her smile froze.

Brooke's head snapped around. Six militiamen in camouflage fatigues poured out of the elevator, their Kalashnikov assault rifles cocked and aimed at the women. Seconds later, the other two elevators opened, and a dozen more militiamen spilled out.

The Scrabble tiles dropped from Brooke's fingers. This was surely a mistake. It might be sorted out later—perhaps after one of these loaded Kalashnikovs went off.

With unexpected agility, Jenny vaulted over the back of the couch, pulling Amanda with her, and they disappeared behind the elevator bank. "Brooke, move it!" Amanda called out from behind the shelter. "Brooke!"

But Brooke was frozen in her seat. The large coffee table had prevented her from running after her friends and now she was staring into the barrel of a gun and feeling her eyes round with fear.

A loud bang jolted her. It was a door slamming down the corridor, not a gunshot. Amanda and Jenny must be safe in Jenny's room. Her own room was right behind the couch on which she was sitting. Shaken out of her stupor, Brooke sprinted.

Reaching the door, she fumbled with her skeleton key. She had never mastered fitting it in on the first try, and now soldiers in heavy boots filled the corridor, the rough wool of their uniforms brushing her arm. Why didn't they stop her? Pictures from her parents' lives ran through her mind as vivid as if she had lived them. Her fingers shook so much, she couldn't line up the long key. A dozen more soldiers streamed in from a fire stairwell. In the narrow hallway, their uniforms reeked of smoke and sweat.

Through the drumming of her heartbeat, she heard the saving click. The door opened. She darted inside, but just as she was about to slam the door behind her, a gun jammed in the opening. If she resisted, the soldier might pull the trigger. Panting, she let go and leaned against the inside wall abutting the door.

The soldier stepped inside, scanned the room, and threw Brooke a suspicious stare. His eyes inspected the length of her body, from the bottom upward, then down again, stopping at her chest. Brooke cringed.

To her relief, a voice shouted from the corridor and, looking once more around the room, the soldier left. Brooke locked the door and put her ear to it. A new terror, alien from the one she'd felt earlier, clutched at her. She strained to listen, afraid of hearing a machine gun blasting. Realizing that bullets could shatter the door, she moved deeper into the room.

The phone rang. Its trilling sound was otherworldly. Brooke lifted the receiver but refrained from saying "Hello."

"Are you okay?" Amanda asked. "Are you there?"

"What's all this about?" Brooke whispered.

"It looks like a military unit is taking over the hotel."

"Whose side are they on?"

"Beats me. The civil war must be spreading."

"It's supposed to have ended." Brooke pulled the phone with her as she peeked out the window. "The soldiers are out in front, thick as cockroaches."

"I'll come join you as soon as I can leave Jenny's room," Amanda said.

"Don't you dare!" Through the whisper, Brooke heard her voice getting shrill. "These revolutionaries hate Americans. They might shoot you."

"You may be right," Amanda said, and Brooke was surprised that for once, her friend accepted the severity of the situation. "I've tried calling Judd," she added.

He would know what men with Kalashnikovs were doing at Hotel Moscow. Right now Brooke would accept any available help. Yet what if the soldiers had come for him?

After hanging up with Amanda, Brooke dialed the embassy number. The line was dead. She sat down to gather her thoughts.

A faint *tap-tap* on the door brought her back. She waited until it was repeated. "Who's there?" she asked.

"Aleksandr."

Aleksandr had left the hotel more than an hour ago. How had he dodged curfew and then returned? Brooke opened the door.

For once, Aleksandr's face was tense. The pallid illumination of the overhead light bulb cast shadows across his high forehead. "Were you one of the three out there?" he asked.

"You mean one of the Scrabble players?"

He nodded.

"What about it?"

"You're in trouble. The militia wants to arrest and interrogate you."

"Whatever for? What have I done?"

"You've insulted the militia."

"Insulted? Like I insulted the silly receptionist?"

"The soldiers are here to protect you, yes? When you ran away, you showed distrust."

Protect her against Sidorov? "I distrust people pointing assault rifles at me." Brooke's body shook with rage. "This is insane! What was I supposed to do?"

"Honest people would stay in place. Russians don't run away like rabbits. They would look down, like this." He demonstrated a submissive bowed head. "They'd sit still until the soldiers tell them they could get up."

"Sure," she replied with sarcasm in her voice. She remembered the two men locked in the Jetway with her, their passive submission. "This is a hotel. And we aren't Russians. I don't believe for one minute that three women playing Scrabble insulted the mighty Russian militia." Suddenly she realized something she had missed. "The soldiers don't know who the three of us are. You weren't even sure I was one of them."

"They saw a woman with brown hair enter this room. They say two others escaped behind the elevator, right? Who were they?"

Brooke blinked. "You don't expect me to tell you that, do you?"

Aleksandr cleared his throat. "Jenny, she's—er—talking to the soldiers."

"What are you saying?"

"She didn't insult the militia. She opened a bottle of Champagne for them."

"Her methods are hard to emulate." But Brooke was relieved that Aleksandr didn't know that Jenny had fled, too.

Crimson spread over Aleksandr's face. "Do you have anything to give them?" he asked. "Vodka, maybe?"

Was he suggesting that Brooke, too, should flirt with the

soldiers? She shook her head, then recalled that Amanda had brought back from the symposium one of their boxes of chocolates. She retrieved it and handed it to Aleksandr.

"I'll try to negotiate with them," he said. "Otherwise they'll throw you in jail for three days."

"Jail for three days?" Brooke regarded Aleksandr. "First they wanted to interrogate me. Now it's jail? How do you know that? Who exactly said it?"

He looked down at the tips of his shoes.

In her head, Brooke examined the facts. When there had been no armed soldiers, he was petrified of the chef, kowtowed to the maître d', and coddled that silly front-desk clerk. Now, in a miraculous transformation, this wimp had turned brave enough to deal with over thirty militiamen carrying automatic weapons. What was going on here? One thing for sure: she couldn't—shouldn't—trust him.

She yanked the box of chocolate out of his hands. "Don't negotiate anything for me. Is that clear?"

# *Forty-three*

A N HOUR LATER, nothing had happened. Brooke's nerves were on edge as she continued to listen for heavy footsteps outside, so much like those nights in her childhood in Brooklyn when she had believed that the Nazis might come anytime.

She packed her carry-on bag just in case she was dragged to jail—or she needed to escape.

To her relief, Amanda returned. She reported that some soldiers were still on their floor and the adjacent ones. "They haven't harassed us."

"They're after me—according to Aleksandr." Brooke gave Amanda an account of their conversation. "

"Brooke, it makes no sense."

"You're looking for logic in a place where none exists." Brooke paced around the faded carpet. "Multiply that by ten when Aleksandr's in the picture. I must get out of here."

"It's curfew time. Where would you go? Anyway, the soldiers may have forgotten all about you."

"What if they haven't? Would you take that chance?" Brooke stepped to the window and confirmed that the soldiers were still in front. "There must be more to this. What did this militia come to protect us from?"

Amanda scratched her head. "What are you driving at?"

"I may not know the problem, but I know the solution. Dollars. These soldiers want money." She pulled some American bills out of her money belt. In one pocket of her jeans she placed several tens, and in the other fives. She rolled five one-hundred-dollar bills under the strap of her watch. She snapped her suitcase shut and shoved her coat and purse into her travel bag, then secured the bungee cord on the wheels. "I'm out of here."

"Don't risk it. Please. Maybe there's another explanation. At least wait until you hear what Aleksandr finds out."

Brooke's stomach tightened. "Right now I am sure of two things: One, that Aleksandr will screw up. And two, that I must take care of myself before he does." She hitched her bag over her shoulder and rolled her suitcase to the vestibule.

"Where will you go?" Amanda asked.

"Anywhere but here." A commotion in the corridor halted Brooke. She listened. Shouts, orders, heavy footfalls. Then a faint rapping on the door, followed by a little voice.

"It's Aleksandr."

Amanda opened the door. Next to Aleksandr stood a militiaman with decorated epaulets and medals on his chest. Past them, some johns were facing the wall, their arms raised. Soldiers pointed guns at their backs, while others emptied their pockets. Two young women in tiny Spandex dresses protested as they, too, were shoved against the wall.

Amanda clutched Brooke's arm to hold her back. "Aleksandr, what are these soldiers doing at the hotel?"

He entered with the officer and closed the door behind him, then addressed Brooke. "The officer wants to know what you're hiding."

"Hiding? As in counterfeit rubles?" Brooke asked.

He shrugged. "I'm only translating what he asked."

"For Christ's sake. You could have answered that I was your guest on a business trip." She opened her palm and showed the officer money. She gestured toward the street outside the window. "Tell him to escort me out of the hotel." Once she was far enough from the hotel, she would stop a private car. An enterprising driver might even take her to his home where she could use the phone to call Belgorov.

"It's curfew. You can't go out."

"Right now I'm safer in the streets than here." The officer's eyes were glued to her money. Brooke handed him the bills and gestured with her head. "Let's go." Ignoring Aleksandr, she lifted the handle of her rolling cart.

"I'm sorry." Amanda threw her arms around her neck.

Behind Brooke, the officer spoke. "He says you should walk naturally, no sudden movements," Aleksandr told her. "His soldiers are nervous; they've been shot at a lot in the past two days. They might shoot you."

"That's what I've been saying all along, but you've denied it."

"Don't go to a hotel, though," he added.

"Why not?" Amanda asked.

"The army is looking for foreigners tonight."

"Why?" Brooke asked.

"Parliament sympathizers. You know, criminals who came from the Republics. They stay in hotels."

"Can't they tell Soviet out-of-towners from Americans?" Amanda asked.

"Do I look like I came from one of the Republics?" Brooke asked.

"No, they know you're American. Though Mr. Kornblum, he looks Georgian."

Goose bumps crawled up Brooke's arms. "Mr. Kornblum isn't here. How do they know what he looks like?"

Aleksandr stared at his shoes. The officer picked up Brooke's suitcase, then opened the door for her.

The corridor was teeming with soldiers.

"I'll drive you." Aleksandr followed her to the elevator.

Where did he think she was going? "It's almost nine o'clock, way past curfew time. Did you forget that you'll be shot in the streets?" Brooke sidled closer to the officer, who pressed the elevator call button. He flashed her a polite smile, revealing the absence of several teeth, then waved and walked away before the elevator arrived.

"You don't know your way around," Aleksandr persisted.

Brooke enunciated each word. "Please get lost, okay?"

He blushed, and for a split second she even pitied him. "Sorry. You did your best, but I don't want your help," she said. "Thank you, and good-bye."

Just then, the elevator door opened. Inside, three more militiamen stood with their automatic weapons at the ready. Brooke glanced down the corridor in search of the officer she had bribed, but he had disappeared. She regretted having five bills ready, when perhaps one hundred dollars would have sufficed.

One of the soldiers held the elevator door open. Aleksandr stepped in and motioned with his hand for her to come. She bristled, but got in.

The elevator door swooshed closed. "Passport," a soldier demanded. There was a tuft of fine peach fuzz over his upper lip. Brooke tucked three five-dollar bills into her passport before handing it to him, then handed each of the other soldiers an additional five-dollar bill.

"Okay. *Dah.*" The soldier gave her the passport back as the elevator doors opened to the lobby. The place was crawling with more military. To Brooke's surprise, the soldier who had checked her passport lifted her suitcase and helped her out of the building. Bribing the militia had gotten her more service than tipping the hotel staff ever had. She noticed Aleksandr watching her being accompanied out.

Several camouflaged armored vehicles were parked in front of the hotel, and more soldiers scrutinized her with hungry eyes. Brooke kept her head high, walking as briskly as she could while wheeling her suitcase with one hand and pulling the overstuffed carrier with the other. Adrenaline rushed in her veins.

In spite of the curfew, the soldiers let her pass. She quickened her steps as much as her luggage would allow. Her arms and shoulders already hurt, and her heart had been in overdrive for almost two hours. She scanned the street for a passing private car, recalling her apprehension on her first day in Moscow that stopped her from getting into a car with a driver who didn't speak English. Now, compared to the mayhem in the hotel, a stranger seemed like a rescuer.

"Brooke," she heard behind her, and turned around.

Judd was walking toward her, smiling, as if nothing was going on.

"Thank God," Brooke breathed, pushing aside her distrust of him. At least he was an American—and right now the least of all evils.

His eyes took in her luggage. "Where are you going?"

"Away. Anywhere. Don't go in the hotel. They're looking for you."

"Me? Who's looking for me?"

"I'm not sure. Maybe Aleksandr, maybe the militia—"

"Hold on a minute. What are you talking about? What's with this schlepping of your luggage?"

"I'm running as far away as I can get before I'm stopped by flying bullets which, Aleksandr insists, target those defying curfew."

"Tonight's curfew begins at eleven."

"It does? When was it changed?"

"It's been in the news since noon."

The skin around her mouth felt taut. "Aleksandr distinctly said seven o'clock."

"Calm down." Judd touched her elbow. "Nothing's going to happen to you." He lifted her suitcase and led her another block.

She gave him a synopsis of recent events. "I've tried calling the embassy. There was no answer."

"They've been hiding in the basement for three days without a change of underwear. Today a skeleton staff finally started working again. If I drove you over there, someone will put you up for the night at the Radisson Slavyanskaya, which is where I'm planning to go."

His perfect pronunciation of the hotel's Russian name no longer surprised her. "What about the search for foreigners that Aleksandr mentioned?"

"That has nothing to do with you or me. Forget everything Aleksandr's told you."

"Wiser words have never been uttered."

He smiled, took out a car key, and opened the door to a Zhiguli. He placed her suitcase in the back next to a gym bag. Drained even of her curiosity, Brooke slid onto the tattered vinyl passenger seat. The car reeked of cigarette smoke.

"Sorry about the ambiance. My Bentley is in the shop." Judd rummaged through his gym bag and produced an airline-size brandy bottle. "You look like you could use this." He turned the ignition key and shifted gears.

The drink stung then numbed the cut on her tongue as it traveled down to her stomach. It melted into something pleasant and warm. "I'd like to check on Olga first," Brooke said, giving him the Russian's address.

"You still haven't told me what happened at the conference."

"It's a long story."

During the twenty-minute ride to Olga's home, Brooke answered his questions regarding the most recent events at the hotel. She wondered whether any of the women had told him about what they'd seen at Olga's office. "I've known all along that this hotel was a disaster waiting to happen," Brooke said. "Even so, I was unprepared. Not even Kafka would have believed my story."

"Yeltsin's brought in ten to fifteen thousand men, and they're as unpredictable as they are greedy. These troops don't report to anyone."

"What were they doing at Hotel Moscow?"

"Just what that officer told you: looking for parliament sympathizers. After Yeltsin suppressed the uprising around the parliament, thousands of the deputies' supporters dispersed. They can stay in only cheap Soviet hotels."

She hadn't made the connection when Norcress had mentioned it that morning. "Like Hotel Moscow?"

"Yup. Yeltsin is worried that these supporters might start further disturbances. He's rounding them up."

"Wasn't it obvious that I was an American and *not* a parliament sympathizer? Why was I intimidated?"

"A simple case of extortion." But the pulsating vein in Judd's temple, the one she had noticed before, made her suspect he thought there was more to it.

## ❧ CHAPTER ❧

## *Forty-four*

THEY DROVE A few blocks past a boulevard edging a wide lawn, behind which stood an imposing building. Though its facade was illuminated, its windows were dark.

"Moscow University," Judd said.

"There's no one here," Brooke said. "In my Berkeley days, students demonstrated against Vietnam. You'd think that with all that's going on, students would raise their collective indignation."

"Not if they stand to lose their spots. No freedom of expression here, remember?"

Judd slowed down by a plaza with scattered ornate lampposts, all lit. A stone balustrade was bathed in milky reflection. "Moskva River," he said, circling close to the railing.

Rolling down the window, Brooke breathed in the cool fall air. Everything was eerily quiet. She eyed an old couple huddled on a bench, then the panoramic view of Moscow past the balustrade. "It looks so normal. Is it safe to stop?"

"Sure."

A sense of freedom ran through Brooke as she yawned and stretched outside the car. Just minutes earlier, she had believed she was escaping for her life. She wrapped her coat over her arm. Judd followed her as they walked the few yards to the marble parapet and leaned on it, keeping the car and her luggage in sight.

"That long line of lights is the Kremlin wall." Judd's finger moved to the left. "We could see the parliament building if they had electricity."

A couple of late-pecking pigeons flitted nearby, hoping for a handout. A young man ambled past, settled on a bench under a lamppost, and retrieved a book out of his khaki canvas bag. An occasional Volga or Zhiguli passed by. It was strange to be so close to the threat at Hotel Moscow, yet so remote.

A gunshot brought Brooke out of her lull. She straightened.

"It's at least a mile away," Judd said calmly. "The water surface carried the sound. We're overlooking downtown." He looked at her. "Want to leave?"

Brooke shook her head. In the black ink of the river, the city lights flickered and danced. Her hand traced the lines of the marble balustrade. It was smooth and cold, richer than stone.

She straightened and put on her coat. "Talk."

He broke a twig off a nearby bush. "What about?"

"There's some explanation you need to give me. You've already admitted to being involved in some big mysterious scheme. Why don't you start by telling me how keeping your knowledge of Russian secret serves you."

"I give up." He raised his hands in resignation. "This is about to become public soon anyway."

"What is?"

"Brooke, I'm here on a project for the F.B.I."

"F.B.I.? You mean the C.I.A.?"

"F.B.I."

"That can't be. The C.I.A covers international matters."

"Let me backtrack. I'm sure you've heard some mutterings about lost nuclear warheads in K.G.B. suitcases." He stripped the twig slowly. "What's especially alarming about that is that the Russian mafia has gotten into the act. Its activities now extend around the globe. Mafia dons from Italy and Brazil, who already were in cahoots with one another to pool resources, are now embracing the Russians."

"So?"

"The F.B.I. handles the mafia at home. Russian godfathers—here they're called *krestniy otets*—are throwing a very long shadow abroad. Some have settled in the U.S., from Brooklyn to Miami. They're setting up drug-smuggling, forgery, and prostitution rings. Their money-laundering operations are of proportions we've never seen before. But most disturbing is the danger of the huge amount of radioactive material all over Russia. Combine it with military personnel whose salaries haven't been paid in months. Do I need to say more?" Judd tossed away the stripped twig. "Officers on the loose are a dangerous bunch. When Russia ceased to be a world superpower, these men lost their status and dignity. Many of them now sell nuclear material to the highest bidder, from plutonium stored in bomb-ready form to enriched, weapons-grade uranium. It's confirmed that the mafia, in turn, has already sold it to unfriendly countries such as Iraq, North Korea, and Libya."

"I counseled a woman, Irina, who had a business idea based on using stolen military supplies," Brooke said. "Speaking with her, it occurred to me that there are scores of radioactive sources in Russia—in shipyards, labs, reprocessing plants, and power stations. Is our government planning to monitor them all?"

"It's only a matter of time before these materials fall into the hands of terrorist groups."

"And the F.B.I., which has no experience operating outside the U.S., will beat the mafia on its own turf?"

"We're working with Yeltsin's government, which has been outmaneuvered at every turn, and therefore has accepted our help. In a couple of months, the F.B.I. will open an office in Moscow, and the Russian government guarantees to cooperate."

"Wow."

He smiled. "Luckily, Yeltsin has quelled the uprising, and he's still the president."

"What if he'd failed?"

Judd shifted from one foot to the other. "I would have had to operate undercover, which is why I've had to keep my identity secret until now."

Brooke's hair, swaying in the breeze, tickled her cheeks. She tucked it behind her ears.

Judd looked out across the river. His hand rested near hers, and she could feel its heat. She pulled her hand away.

"Is that where your 'mingling with the peasants' fits in?"

"I don't usually let people know about my grandparents. You've figured out that thanks to them I am fluent in Russian. I did a graduate degree in Russian Studies. I'm keeping my eye on some seedy characters who might be tempted to support their political causes by selling nukes from military bases located in their regions."

*Sidorov,* she thought. "Even with Yeltsin's blessings, you can't control activities in the far Soviet Republics—not even those still within the Russian borders."

"We can't sit back either." A frown crinkled Judd's forehead. "But as it turns out, I must return home immediately to deal with a personal situation there." His eyes hooked into hers. "Before I go, will you let me in on the real pickle you've gotten yourself into?"

Brooke put her hands in her coat pocket and felt the tiny plastic bag with the manufacturer's extra button. She fingered it, thinking. Could she believe that Judd wasn't one of the opportunists jumping on the mafia's bandwagon? She mulled over the information she possessed that didn't come directly from his words, but rather from his actions. "You wanted to tell me something about home," she finally said. " 'Fess up."

Judd paused, then looked toward the city line across the river. "My wife has left. Took off. Some old film job contacts called from California—they had a crisis in the middle of shooting. She decided that this was her break to get back to her career 'when all she did at home was carpooling.' "

"Maybe she has a point in wanting the satisfaction of working." Brooke looked for the pigeons, but they had vanished. "You don't sound overjoyed by her departure. Do you want it both ways?"

"I never held her back." His Adam's apple bobbed. "It's about responsibility. In what universe is it okay for a parent to abandon her or his children without making any arrangements? While I'm away? They're devastated."

"She left them alone?"

"The cleaning woman is supposedly staying over. She speaks only Spanish and they don't know her because until now she came only in the mornings, when they were in school."

"Your turn for 'Nutritious Meals 101' at Adult Ed?"

He smiled. "I'll be leaving on the first flight."

"You've just told me about the new Moscow office."

"I'll be working mostly in the States." He moved his hand, the tips of his fingers lightly making contact with the back of her hand. "It will be a very hectic time, but not enough to stop me from getting on with my life."

"It can't be this simple. And I'm not referring just to the physical demands of managing a home. It must be an emotionally difficult time."

"For my boys, yes. For me? It's inconvenient, but a relief. I stopped mourning the death of this marriage long ago."

The old couple that had huddled on the bench shuffled by, curled within their long gray coats. With their arms linked and heads bent close together, it was hard to tell where one person ended and the other began. Marriage and age welded into one.

Brooke couldn't meet Judd's eyes. His timing was still too inopportune—and not in sync with hers. Too many unresolved issues in her life needed to be untangled, mistakes that could neither be erased nor retracted. She pulled her hand away.

If she could only get that envelope back from Sidorov.

## ❦ CHAPTER ❦
### *Forty-five*

Outside Olga's building, Brooke told Judd that her visit would last only twenty minutes, and he agreed to wait in his car. Anyway, he said, her luggage must be watched.

Olga's leg was propped on a small pillow. An ice pack rested on her knee, and an unlit cigarette dangled from the corner of her mouth. Brooke couldn't see the burn under the brown skirt. Without lipstick or blush, Olga looked exhausted.

"I'm sorry about everything," Brooke said as she bent to kiss both of her friend's cheeks, Russian-style.

"You and I did what we had to do—when we could do it," Olga said. "There's a Russian saying, 'Walk fast and you'll overtake misfortune; walk slowly and it will overtake you.' We couldn't have moved faster."

Viktor served tea, and Brooke breathed in its aroma, trying to drown her misery. "Any progress regarding the negotiation with Sidorov?"

"A comrade who's close to Prime Minister Yegor Gaidar

is contacting Sidorov directly. Gaidar is the man pushing for drastic economic reforms with tough legislation and enforcement, and the case we've uncovered is exactly the type Gaidar wants to crack down on, especially when it involves a man of great influence."

"If Sidorov agrees to secrecy in exchange for your life, you won't involve Gaidar, right?"

Olga nodded sadly.

"Will you still run for the Duma?"

"Of course. I will give my last breath for the future of my country. As soon as I settle with Sidorov, I'll make my announcement."

Brooke sipped her tea. "When will you know if he agrees?"

"In a couple of hours someone will drive me to my dacha with Galina, my granddaughter. They will contact me there."

"What about Viktor? And your son and daughter-in-law?"

"It's a workday. They will join us in the evening by train."

"Sidorov must be able to find out where your dacha is. You need a safe hiding place."

"If the negotiation fails, we'll move elsewhere."

Will Olga hide in the village of her youth, among the old anti-Semites? Brooke took in a deep breath. "Why not go there directly? You need to rest your leg—"

"I'll rest in my grave."

Brooke fidgeted in her seat. Not knowing the geography of the region, she must trust Olga's perception of her own safety. "I'm leaving in the morning. Finally. We had a weird situation in the hotel tonight." She described the chain of events. "Can you make any sense of it?"

"Five hundred dollars?" Viktor exchanged a look with Olga. "It's a lot! The militia wasn't searching for your kind, so why were you threatened with arrest?"

"Could it be a simple case of extortion?" Brooke asked.

"If that were so," Olga said, "then after you paid, you could have either stayed put or moved freely to another hotel. Aleksandr said you couldn't, right?"

Viktor tapped the ashes off his cigarette into the ashtray. "Whoever is behind it is monitoring your movements."

"I imagine that it can only be Sidorov," Brooke said. But it had been Aleksandr who had behaved strangely. He had never shown eagerness for any task, yet tonight he had insisted on negotiating for her, then driving her. She had assumed that his offer stemmed from guilt over his failure to do better by her. But guilt about fellow humans had been conditioned out of too many Russians. And what did the militia have to do with any of it?

Brooke rose to her feet. Thankfully, unlike Delta, Lufthansa had a late-morning flight. There was nothing more she could do in Russia.

"Even if Norcress's article never gets published, Sidorov will know his machinations have been exposed." Olga's eyes twinkled for the first time since the day before. "Things have a strange way of leaking. Gaidar might force him to curtail his activities."

"Leave this one alone. Please," Brooke said. "You'll have other battles in the Duma."

"Freeing women's cooperatives from the mafia clutches is a very important battle. Thanks for showing us the way."

Viktor cackled. "Olga says that you're the Lawrence of Arabia for our women."

"I'll appreciate the compliment better in the desert of Manhattan."

"We'll find a way to keep in touch," Olga said. "Not by phone or mail."

"You must let me know the results of your negotiation with Sidorov," Brooke said. "Could you get word from wherever you are to my Frankfurt office? I'll be there for a couple of days." She pulled her notepad from her purse and scribbled the address.

"I will."

At the door, Olga hugged her. "When you return, I'll show you the beautiful side of Russia."

If there was one thing Brooke was certain of, it was that she would never return. "I cherish that matryoshka you gave me. It reminds me of you. Strong, nurturing, traditional. Women as the keepers of old values." With mist in her eyes, she added, "Feminine."


HALF AN HOUR later, Brooke entered the elegant lobby of the Radisson Slavyanskaya , with its polished marble floors inlaid in a sunburst design. In this oasis she was a refugee no more. The dread she had been carrying lifted from her shoulders and chest.

Judd said he'd wait at the bar while she went upstairs to freshen up. If it were up to her, she would have just ordered room service and hit the sack. But he'd saved her, and she had promised to share the rest of the story.

After days of mayonnaise-dipped and oil-soaked food, Brooke craved a plain pasta dish. As soon as the waiter walked away with their orders Judd asked, "What would it take for you to let me in on the mystery of what happened to Olga?"

Brooke summarized the reports she had shared with Belgorov and Norcress. Unlike in her accounts to them, she told Judd about the bomb and the crater in the street. "For the rest of my life I will carry with me the picture of that boy's torn flesh and bones."

He reached across the table and touched her neck, sending ripples through her. "That explains these little scratches," he said. "But where does Aleksandr figure in all of this?"

"Aleksandr? He has nothing to do with it."

"Don't be so sure." Judd's tone was reflective. "Remember those faxes he didn't send?"

"I thought he was just being lazy. What about them?"

"The cover page was in Russian. Since the very first morning, he'd been writing down his observations of you. Why? You weren't investigating anything yet." He smiled. "I don't think he was just a secret admirer."

"What did his notes say?"

"They recapped the business and finance topics you discussed. Your home phone number was there, which you noticed, too. Also, I wasn't sure of the context, but did he manage to get his hands on some letter addressed to you?"

The roots on Brooke's scalp contracted. "Oh, God." She clasped her hand to her mouth. "I thought I lost it at the customs office! But it was him! He stole it from my bag!"

*Wednesday, October 6, 1993*

## ❧ CHAPTER ❧

## *Forty-six*

SVETLANA SWAM UP from the depths of sleep, bolting upright in bed. With the bare walls, everything packed into her cardboard suitcase and a canvas bag, her room suddenly seemed alien. But then it all flooded back. She was leaving today with Natasha for Frankfurt—and a new life!

As much as she had fantasized about this moment while reading magazines, collecting tea bags, saving postcards, listening to Radio Free Europe, and obtaining a passport, now that it was upon her she felt woefully unprepared. She took out her collection of teas, no longer needed to bring the flavors of the world into her dingy room. Waiting for the water to boil in her electric kettle, she stared out the window at the wall of the neighboring building, imagining what uncertainties she would face in a foreign country, alone with Natasha, not knowing a soul.

She selected an exotic tea bag. Darjeeling. Or maybe she'd have the Orange Spice? English Breakfast tea was the fanciest name, redolent with the aura of British royalty. In a curious way, life had been easier with no such choices, when the hardships had been a cruel monotony. In its predictability, that life had been more secure than the one she was facing, brimming with changes.

She crouched on Natasha's mattress and moved a tendril of hair stuck on her daughter's lip. "Wake up, little lamb. We're leaving today. We'll be flying in an airplane. In Frankfurt we'll have a nice apartment and good food. We'll even buy you sneakers."

Natasha's eyes popped open, and she squealed with joy. "I want to tell Lyalya."

"She's sleeping." The young woman probably had just returned from her night of entertaining men. Anyway, Svetlana could not take leave from her neighbor. If she didn't need to keep her departure quiet, she could have sold her furniture and kitchenware, even extricated some money from Zoya for her room. She regretted not calling Katerina to say good-bye, but with money from her first paycheck, she would buy her friend a new silk blouse. If anyone spotted her and Natasha with the luggage, she'd say they were going to visit her sick mother in St. Petersburg.

"You must be a good student in Germany," Svetlana said. "When you grow up, you will be a Western woman."

"Half-Russian, half-Western."

Outside the building, Svetlana put down the suitcase. Beside her, Natasha stopped dragging the heavy canvas bag. Svetlana pulled her closer and together they took in the red glow of the leaves on the old oak tree. Regardless of what awaited them, it was hard to leave Moscow. Her gloomy city with its defiant spirit, so intemperate and uncaring, permeated with pungent smells and downtrodden people, still had, perversely, a comforting presence.

"*Proshchaniye.* Farewell," she whispered. "*Auf wiedersehen,*" she added in German.

OLGA PULLED DOWN her straw hat to protect her face even though the sun had just risen above the forest. The early morning was unusually warm for this time of year; just two nights ago, the clean scent of snow had whirled in the Moscow wind. Now, merely two hours south of Moscow, it felt like late summer again.

She knelt in the soil of her vegetable garden and groaned as sharp pain shot up from her knee. The cigar burn on her leg ached, and her temples still throbbed from whatever concoction Sidorov's man had poured down her throat less than twenty hours before. Her aging body could tolerate just so much. But she had missed her garden, and there was so much to do there. . . .

She took in a lungful of the rich, pungent smell of the moist earth. Her fingers buried in the soil, slipping below the surface where it was warmer. Tranquility settled over her. Her garden had been neglected, and brazen weeds had reappeared among her red cabbages. In the next bed, crowns of carrots and radishes already peeked out, almost ready for picking if she needed to move on as soon as the rest of her family joined her.

From behind the small dacha, she could hear Galina singing, her voice like little bells. Galina loved the rope swing that hung from the old chestnut tree. As soon as she was done gardening, Olga decided, she would go inside and peel an orange for them to share. Once, when she herself was a child, her mother had bought one slice of an orange for her birthday, but now she had the luxury of buying a whole fruit for her granddaughter.

On the other side of the fence, cars and trucks roared past. Two generations before, the dacha had been built at the edge of a forest. Then, twelve years ago, a new highway had been carved around the hill to the east and slashed through the forest. Luckily, their dacha hadn't been confiscated to make room as others had, though the shoulder of the highway swerved by their property line. Viktor prophesized that one day a drunk driver might crash right into their kitchen.

At first, Olga had missed the noises of the woods, the rustling, crackling, twittering, swishing sounds of dry leaves made by small animals, birds, and wind. Eventually, though, she had become accustomed to the hum of engines. Instead, she had trained her ears to hear the cooing of the pigeons that nested in her attic and flew in and out through the small window Viktor had cut. Some winters, Viktor killed pigeons for meat, and she cooked them with carrots and preserved grapes. The trick was not to get too attached to the birds; she had stopped giving them names.

Ignoring stabs of pain, she moved on to fertilizing each furrow with crushed eggshells she had collected. She paid no attention to the car that swerved off the road as it neared her small cabin. Only when it skipped over the bumpy shoulder and tore through the hedge did she lift her head.

A shield on the driver's cap reflected the sun. Was that a police officer behind the wheel? Why didn't he even try to stop?

## ❧ CHAPTER ❧

## *Forty-seven*

THE CONCIERGE AT the hotel arranged for a private car to drive Brooke to the airport, where she would meet Svetlana. Judd would be there too, as he had to make last-minute arrangements to get on the flight to Frankfurt connecting to New York.

Brooke stood at the window of her hotel room. In the courtyard below, three women sat on stools, their aprons sagging with the weight of potatoes and carrots, which they peeled into bowls, their quick chattering sounding like an argument. A boy ambled about, banging a stick on iron grates and low windowsills, ignoring the women's admonitions.

During the night Brooke had heard gunfire. Now everything looked so normal. Moscow. What a city of extremes, she thought, combining the shortages of a nation stuck in the hunting and gathering stage with the technological sophistication of a superpower; a city with political chaos equal to an underdeveloped

African nation's, yet whose people were educated and possessed a vision for the future.

An hour later, at the Sheremetyevo Airport bar, Brooke glanced around. What if Sidorov or his minions showed up? Beside her, Svetlana sliced a huge sandwich into bite-size pieces and fed them to Natasha. Brooke was afraid the little girl might get sick from too much food, as she herself had in her youth.

"We must head for passport control," Brooke told Svetlana. She downed the last drop of her cappuccino, the sweet taste of home in her mouth. She hoped that the area beyond the lobby would offer protection from Sidorov, yet knew that she and Svetlana would be safe only once the plane took off. "Ready?" Brooke rose to her feet and took hold of her rolling case.

To her surprise, Svetlana grabbed her hand and kissed it, tears streaking down her cheeks. "Before, I cried because of my troubles, now I cry because I'm so happy. There is a word in German, *Weltschmerz*. It means world-weary. For the first time, I don't feel that way."

"You'll have a good new life. You deserve it." Brooke took out a tissue and dabbed Svetlana's cheeks. "NHB is lucky to have you. Now let's go."

Svetlana touched her "Attitude Is Everything" button, prominently displayed on her lapel. "I will do anything they ask me. And even though I will be so honored to work at a German company, I will always admire Jews. Because of you, I'll tell everybody that Jews have good hearts."

Svetlana's continuing awe at discovering that Jews weren't the conniving, devious people she had been indoctrinated to believe annoyed Brooke. She would deal with it another time, after they had passed customs and she had located a working pay phone to call Norcress to find out the status of the negotiations with Olga. As she bent to pick up one of Svetlana's bags to help move her along, something Olga had said came back to her. "By the way, how long have you known Aleksandr?" Brooke asked.

"A few years, maybe. I met him when he worked at the Economic Authority where my friend Katerina works."

"When did he leave?"

"A year and a half ago he received an offer from EuroTours." Svetlana pulled out a Ziploc bag from her purse and slipped the remainder of the sandwich inside. "He's a good man. Doesn't drink. You saw that he wears good leather shoes and a leather coat? It means that he makes good money."

Brooke shook her head in amazement. The connections were so simple, so predictable. If only it had occurred to her to ask earlier. "What did he do while at the Economic Authority?"

"Special projects for Sidorov. Once Sidorov even took him on a trip to America."

"Yes, he showed me photographs of a supermarket."

Natasha pulled on her mother's skirt, then whispered something, causing Svetlana to blush. "Natasha says you are more beautiful than Cinderella."

"Thanks." Brooke kissed Natasha's head. "Let's go to customs."

"We want to go to the toilet. It's clean here."

Brooke sighed and put down her bags again, watching the ladies' room door as if she could protect Svetlana and Natasha. She was relieved to spot Judd approaching.

He looked sprightly and fresh, and gave Brooke a big smile. "Got my ticket."

She spoke in a low voice. "We're not safe here—not even on the tarmac—until the plane takes off. What if Sidorov's thugs show up? It's easy to check the flight manifest and find that we're on it."

"With any luck, Sidorov himself will show up."

"What?"

"Last night, he tried to get you into a corner, but you disappeared from under Aleksandr's nose."

Brooke glared at Judd. "I've just learned from Svetlana that Aleksandr has been in Sidorov's service all along. When did you figure out the relationship?"

"Not soon enough, I'm sorry to say, because you hadn't clued me in on your investigation."

"Was the militia working for Sidorov too?" Brooke asked. "Was the threat of my arrest a hoax orchestrated by him?"

"The militia search for parliament rebels and sympathizers was for real. But it's likely that once they were in the hotel, Aleksandr enlisted them for a little freelance job."

Brooke was surprised that she was still capable of being surprised.

"Being a woman with star credentials, you must have been Sidorov's best candidate for recruitment. That's why Aleksandr kept notes on you. But you got away." Judd regarded her, his head tilted. "His interest in you began even before Olga and you launched your investigation."

"He's the one who had arranged my visa in less than a day."

"Here you go, then. He's been trying from the start to find a way to enlist you into his service. That's why he's been following your movements."

"Why, then, do you hope he'll show up here personally?"

"Your findings about him have become my business because his international dealings must be watched. I'd like to hear what he'd want with you."

Soon, everyone would know the truth about her. She might as well tell Judd now. "Sidorov has something over me," she said, her voice cracking. "There are—there were—things in my life I believed had been buried." Her hand reached to her Star of David. "Twenty years ago I posed for *Penthouse* in order to pay for college. Sidorov got the photos."

Judd's Adam's apple bobbed. "I'm sorry. It is a shocker, but I understand." He looked away, then back at her, and his eyes behind the rimless glasses reddened. "God knows I did things in Vietnam that are far worse. Survival, or the perception of what we need to do to survive, can make us jump out of character, but it doesn't change who we are."

This was so much easier than she had feared. Relieved, Brooke studied his face, but then her eyes caught past him a small man in an Italian-cut suit entering the cafeteria. His graying hair was brushed back from a peaked hairline. It took Brooke a few seconds to place him. "Roman Belgorov? What are you doing here?"

As he had done at Zagorsk two days earlier, the Russian took her hand and kissed it. When he raised his eyes, his expression was grave. His dark gaze shifted from her to Judd, assessing him.

A sense of foreboding enveloped Brooke. "You can speak freely."

"I'm afraid I have bad news. Dr. Olga Rozanova is dead."

Brooke's skin went cold. She smelled the sting of the detergent used on the linoleum floor, felt the burning of a hangnail, heard the distant, irregular crackle of a P.A. system.

"This morning, a car crashed into the garden at her dacha while she was tending her vegetables," Belgorov continued. "*Looks* like an accident."

The words echoed in Brooke's head. Her body went slack and heavy, and she staggered to the nearby chair. Suddenly, it was twenty years ago. She was lying in a bed in a white room, panting, exhausted, her life slipping away with the distant wail of the baby she would never see. Nothing left but searing loneliness and hopelessness. Judd crouched by her chair and placed an arm around her shoulders. "Brooke, I'm so sorry."

She raised her eyes toward Belgorov. "How did you find out?"

"I was the one negotiating with Sidorov on her behalf," he said quietly. "I didn't know her personally before Monday, when you told me what was going on. I immediately contacted her through a mutual friend. As I told you, I work closely with Gaidar. I had hoped to begin a chain of releases from the mafia, which would maybe also uncover what happened to Yuri." His voice wobbled. "And I would have, if only that American journalist had not released the article in spite of—"

She bolted upright. "What?"

"The *Los Angeles Record* transmitted the article over the newswire before dawn."

The words hit her like a blow. Norcress. "I should never have trusted him!" she cried. "Olga's death is my fault."

"You took an enormous risk yourself. It could have been you," Belgorov said.

A sob broke from her lips, and she pressed her temples. "Olga said that she would rest in her grave," she murmured. "She never expected to get there so soon."

Judd must have signaled the bar because a small glass of vodka materialized. "Drink," he ordered.

"It's only ten o'clock in the morning." But she reached for the glass, noticing as she did how tightly her fists were clenched. She released them. Tiny crescent-shaped marks were etched into her palms. The sip of vodka she managed burned her tongue, throat, and stomach.

Belgorov pulled over a chair and sat down. "I want you to know that this chap, Norcress, called me. Apparently you had given him my number for Yuri's story. Thanks. He asked me to tell you that his editor had published the story against their prior agreement, that he was very upset and wanted you to know that he had kept his end of the bargain with you."

"What good does that do? Olga is dead."

"For whatever comfort you may derive from it, you'd be glad to hear that your investigation with Olga and the exposure were not in vain. As soon as the newswire story came through, Sidorov was arrested."

"But not before ordering Olga killed." Her throat felt scratchy. She took another sip of the vodka. "Since he operated with direct authorization from the Kremlin, his arrest might very well be a token gesture. Yeltsin will release him within the hour, I'm sure."

"One of Yeltsin's less endearing traits is his disloyalty to his friends and backers," Judd said. "People fall out of his favor as quickly as they come into it."

Belgorov added, "Right now, there's no one of authority between Yeltsin and Gaidar to countermand Gaidar's arrest of Sidorov."

"Is there any evidence to connect Sidorov to Olga's death?" Judd asked Belgorov.

The Russian shook his head. "It would be safe to assume that the car's owner won't be associated with him. In fact, his car was driven by a local policeman." He clasped his hands together on the table. "But thanks to you, Brooke, there's plenty to connect Sidorov to the terrorizing of women's cooperatives in the Moscow region."

"Even if he does jail time," Brooke said, "he's accumulated more dollars, yen, and deutschemarks than he knows what to do with. He'll resurface as an oligarch." Her voice gathered rage. "His political connections will still be around, and with so many power axes crossing, Gaidar will soon fall out of favor."

"Even in Russia it might be difficult for Sidorov to run for mayor of Moscow," Judd said.

"I must call Viktor."

Judd waved to Svetlana, who came out of the bathroom with Natasha, and pointed to the gate sign. "After we clear passport control and customs. I don't relish the idea of missing our flight." He picked up Brooke's and Svetlana's bags.

"Before you leave," Belgorov told Brooke, "I have something for you." His hand reached into the inside pocket of his suit jacket. Brooke's heart skipped a beat as she recognized the neat typing of her name and saw the red "Personal and Confidential" stamp. "It was on Sidorov when he was arrested. It's addressed to you."

Her tongue thick in her mouth, Brooke took the envelope and turned it over. The Scotch tape had left fraying marks, the tin clasp was broken. Sidorov must have had a laugh, and God knew who else had seen her naked body. "Thanks," she said with a tight smile. Whatever Belgorov might have seen of her younger bare thighs and breasts, neither his face nor his demeanor showed it. She tucked the letter into her purse and clutched it to her chest.

## ❧ CHAPTER ❧

## *Forty-eight*

**M**OUNTING THE STAIRS from the tarmac, Brooke stopped before entering the plane and turned her head for a last glance at Moscow's sky. A flock of ravens floated above. The last time she had seen ravens, less than a week before, she was fleeing the Gorbachevskaya Street Factory. She had thought then that that had been the worst scene she could ever witness.

Svetlana had been shocked by the news of Olga's death. Her Russian passport had allowed her fast process, and she had rushed onto the plane with Natasha.

Brooke settled into her window seat and placed her Walkman in the pocket in front of her along with the copies of *Business Week* and *Fortune* she hadn't opened all week. From across the aisle, she watched as Svetlana bravely steadied herself in front of her daughter, and Natasha accepted with delight a coloring book the flight attendant handed her. Brooke sent Svetlana a tight, sad smile over the child's head. She adjusted a pillow and lay her head back. Judd stowed his bag in the compartment above, sat down next to her, and took her hand. This time she let him.

After takeoff she asked, "Do you believe in life after death? Do you believe it when people claim they sense a dead person's presence?"

"The friends I lost in Vietnam just died."

"I feel Olga is close by." The awareness of it shocked Brooke. "I can't let it end this way. I don't want Olga's death to be for naught." She looked out the window. The sky above the clouds was bright and clear. She mulled over Olga's candor, her owning up to the collective guilt and shame, her facing uncomfortable truths about her family and her village. Olga had the courage to assume guilt for actions she had not committed. Perhaps it was time for Brooke to own up to her own momentous mistakes.

"Judd, what I told you earlier was only the second part of a long, ugly story." She halted, the words stuck in her windpipe.

"I'm listening." He brought up her hand and planted a kiss at the base of her palm.

She hesitated, and then the words rushed out. "I went to Berkeley at seventeen and lived in a commune. Seven months after it broke up, when I was a sophomore, I gave birth to a baby. They told me it was a girl, and I insisted that she be adopted by a Jewish family. This way at least, my role in perpetuating our tribe wasn't wasted."

Without speaking, Judd kissed each finger. His face was close to hers. He raised his face, and his lips sought hers.

The kiss took her breath away. "Thank you for not judging me," she whispered.

"But I do. And I find you an amazingly accomplished woman who's gone through a lot but never allowed it to defeat you."

"Don't we have to be strong and successful to show the *goyim*?"

He smiled. "As good a motivation as any."

"I did the other thing, the posing, to make up for the scholarship I lost while I was having the baby. I was depressed. My hormones were raging. There was no way to jump out of my skin and escape my misery. All I knew was that I had to pull out of the muck. And, of course, my parents could never know."

"That makes you all the more compassionate toward other women."

She stared into the void of the sky. "When Amanda suggested this trip, I thought I'd learn something about the new economy that would give me a leg up at the firm after the takeover. At best, I would collect some brownie points for next Yom Kippur. But now the joke's on me. I got emotionally tangled in the plight of the women I've met." She took a deep breath. "But the greater surprise for me is finding my Jewishness. I always brushed away anti-Semitism because I didn't want it to exist. It's easy to be liberal in New York, to consider prejudice a non-issue." She looked into his face. "How do you deal with anti-Semitism here?"

He took her hand in his again. "I try to ignore it, but it still hurts to be hated so much—and for reasons that never make sense."

"I don't want to be defined by it any more than I wanted to be defined by the Holocaust. I want my Judaism to be my choice—a spiritual me—not dictated by others' misguided view of me."

"Well, you fix the world as we're commanded to do," Judd said.

"I try to, but not very successfully." Brooke glanced in Svetlana's direction. The young woman had fallen asleep with Natasha's head in her lap, the girl talking softly to her stuffed rabbit. Svetlana's comments had merely represented the voice of millions of other Russians. "I hate to admit it, but anti-Semitism has brought to the surface my pride in being Jewish." She chuckled. "I love my DNA."

For a while, neither spoke. An air of understanding—rare, comfortable—stirred between them.

It was time she stopped running away from it all and confronted her mistakes. Brooke reached for the envelope. A cardboard piece kept the papers inside from bending. She put it down again, afraid to look.

Olga would have had the courage, she thought. Angling herself toward the window away from Judd, she turned the broken flap of the envelope and slowly pulled out the contents.

There was only one photo, and it stared at her: a light-skinned black woman in a graduation cap and gown. Brooke peeked again in the envelope. Where were the nude pictures? She checked the envelope again, as if someone had made a mistake. There was only a folded sheet of paper. No. Two full lined pages, written by hand in blue ink. She turned the photo over. On the back was written, "To Brooke, from Sage."

"Sage?" she murmured, disbelieving. Sage? They'd kept the name she had put on the adoption papers.

She turned the photograph over again. The young woman

peering at her had magnificently high cheekbones. The wide eyes were sprinkled with hazel. She was beautiful.

"Sage," Brooke whispered again. With trembling fingers, she unfolded the letter.

*Dear Brooke,*

*Although I often fantasized about what my birth mother was like, I wasn't looking for her. I have wonderful parents and two adopted siblings: a sister who is three years younger, and a brother who is only eight years old.*

*In preparation for my graduation from Reed College as a business major with an interest in finance (I've managed to graduate in three years instead of four with a grade point average of 4.0), I began looking for a job with an investment firm. I want to gain experience for a couple of years before applying to graduate school.*

*My mom once told me that all she knew about my birth mother was that she had been a student by the name of Brooke who grew up out East, and that she had wanted me placed with a Jewish family. I concluded long ago that my birth mother must have been white, but that wasn't much to go by if I tried to find her.*

*If you are my mother, and if I am like you, you can understand how thorough I was in my job search. As I researched the top thirty investment companies in*

*New York City, the financial capital of the world, I was astonished to come across in Norton, Hills, and Bridwell's annual report a woman named Brooke Fielding. I know it's crazy, but I found at the library a* Business Week *interview with a picture of you standing in your office, and I learned your age and that you had graduated from Berkeley. It all fit, but was still unrealistic.*

*After some deliberation with myself (do you also use big words?) I asked my parents' permission to contact the adoption agency. They are okay with my search for my birth mother. The agency representative would not confirm anything, but said that she would contact whoever was the right woman, if she were still alive. I left this letter and photograph with her and told her that if indeed you're my birth mother, she should send them directly.*

*What am I like? Probably a typical twenty-year-old, right down to my love of pop music and the suffering over boys. (I don't have a boyfriend right now.) I love dancing, and while in high school I belonged to a performing jazz troupe. I'm a bit more serious than my friends, though. I volunteer at a nursing home one afternoon a week, and since high school, I've been a Big Sister to a girl from a troubled home. She's doing great. Do you do volunteer work, too? It's okay if you don't; you are such a busy executive, you may not have any free time.*

*If you receive this letter and still decide that you*

*don't want to meet me, I'll try to understand, although I can't say that I won't be disappointed. The* Business Week *interview printed nothing about your personal life. Maybe you're married, have a couple of kids, and no one knows about me. I don't wish to break your life apart. But maybe you'll be willing to answer the million questions that buzz through my mind when I think of the woman who couldn't raise me. I hope that you'll respond, if only this once. (I know I'm supposed to ask for medical history, but that is only a cover for what I really want to know about you.)*

*As I said, if you decide you don't want to meet me, I promise to keep my distance, but I will always be proud that a woman of such accomplishments may be my birth mother.*

*With admiration and warmest regards,*
*Sage*
*(206) 555-1212*

Crying, Brooke reread the letter. The incredulity of it all spread through her, filling her with happiness and sadness at the same time. "Sage," she murmured the name of her daughter, "Sage." Her tears dripped on the photograph she tried to study but could no longer see. She touched the sleek, cold paper and broke into a sob.

Judd, who had been playing with Natasha across the aisle to give Brooke privacy, turned to look at her. Without attempting to wipe her tears, she lifted the letter toward him. This was the biggest moment of her life, the rebirth of her child—and in some way, of herself.

When Judd finished reading the letter, he pulled her as close as the tight space would allow and planted little kisses on her head.

"How selfish it was for me to imagine that these were the nude photos haunting me," Brooke cried. "Why didn't I wonder whether my daughter, who was now twenty, would search for me?"

"Why, really?"

A sad smile crept up her face. "I thought I was undeserving of happiness."

He kissed her again. "You'll have plenty from now on," he whispered.

She lowered her head to look at the photograph again.

"Well, what's the first thing you'll do when we land in Frankfurt?" he asked.

"Call her." She laid her head on his shoulder and listened to his breathing. "The timing of it all. One loss, one gain."

"Sage sounds like the kind of woman who may love to continue Olga's unfinished business," he said. "She doesn't carry your Holocaust *mishegas*."

"I don't know about that. Russia is such a dangerous place—and she is Jewish, after all."

He laughed. "Maternal instinct already kicking in? You'll do all right."

Her eyes were fixed on a pencil-thin gray light on the horizon that bifurcated the sky into two worlds, one above, one below. The top tier melted into the farthest reaches of the universe.

It all came together; it became one. Whole.

# Glossary

Note: Russian words used in the novel are transliterated to the closest English-speaking pronunciation.

*avoska*—string basket
*Bozhe moi*—My God
*chort*—a curse
*dezhurnayia*—hotel matron
*demokratia*—democracy
*keep-ya-tok (=kipyatok)*—boiling water
*Khrushchoby*—Khrushchev's slums
*krestniy otets*—Russian godfathers
*krysha*—private security unit
*leemon*—lemon
*mannaya kasha*—semolina porridge
*nichevo*—never mind, not important
*normalno*—normal
*offshorsky*—offshore
*pizda*—cunt
*po gblatu*—connections, in accordance with *blut*

*proshchaniye*—farewell
*Rossiya*—Russians' pronunciation of *Russia*
*sidyet*—a "sitting" job
*slozhno*—complicated, exhausting
*spasiba*—thank you
*tabletka*—a pill, a capsule
*uzhasno*—terrible
*vanna*—a large laundry tub
*vkusno*—yummy
*yob tvoyu mat*—a curse
*zhaba*—a toad

# Acknowledgments

To the hundreds of nameless Russian women in Moscow and St. Petersburg who listened to my presentations, attended my workshops, or sought my one-on-one counseling: Only teachers who touch other people's lives can understand how much you gave me in return.

To my closest friend, my lifelong gift, Bina Shif Rattenbach, and especially to her late mother, "Tusha" Eibschutz Shif, who told me so much about Nazi concentration camps, yet left unspoken spaces shrouded in shadows. To many other childhood friends in Tel-Aviv who are second-generation Holocaust survivors: I watched you and your parents as a child but only processed what I had seen and heard much later as an adult.

To the American Jews who similarly grew up in the shadows of the Holocaust, both friends and strangers, who initiated confessions to me because they sensed that I would understand: Please know that I listened.

To Sasha Chalif, founder of The Alliance of Russian and American Women, who organized a "citizen mission" in May 1993—my first journey into the lives of Russian women—and to journalist Rosalind McLymont, whose inspiring, flowery speeches matched those given by our Russian hostesses.

There is no one to thank at the U.S. Information Agency, now defunct, that sent me on my second trip to Russia that same year, in late September 1993. However, besides the dozens of women I met and whose hugs I still remember, there are David Kennedy Hunter, then at Moscow's American Embassy, and former U.S. Congressman Gary Ackerman, who helped me leave in haste after the uprising of the parliament against President Boris Yeltsin had run its course.

Most of my research was done in 1994, when trying to make sense of the chaotic events in which I had been caught, starting with my interviewing former U.S. and Russian security personnel. They were instrumental in giving me the lay of the land when little published material was yet available: Richard S., National Security Agency; Donna M., Central Intelligence Agency; and Anatoly G., former K.G.B. Businessmen Ury K. and Benjamin D. explained the convoluted Russian international trading practices, and architects Gerry B. and Robert S. gave me photo tours of communal apartments situated in former Czar-era mansions that they began renovating for a new class of rich Russian oligarchs.

Beyond the mountains of information parted by these professionals, there were the dozen former Soviet Union citizens, who were finally free in the United States and Israel to speak and share their stories, giving my story literary texture and depth. At that time, the late author Bel Kaufman (*Up the Down Staircase*) added her perspective of Jewish–Russian history.

More recently, as I reshaped the material into a novel, editor

Rebecca Stowe's sure-footed guidance was followed by talented writing buddies with red pens: Susan O'Neill and Victor Rangel-Ribeiro. Joining them with constructive suggestions was my writing group, Two Bridges, administered by Walter Cummins. Thanks, too, to Ada Samuelson for correcting my transliteration of Russian words.

Moving a manuscript from the bowels of my computer to the light of day is the triumph of my insightful literary agent, Marly Rusoff, and my brilliant editor at William Morrow, Katherine Nintzel. Kate and her talented team at HarperCollins/William Morrow—Jennifer Hart, Marguerite Weisman, Molly Birckhead, Shelby Meizlik, and Megan Schumann—wove behind-the-scenes magic and midwifed this novel into the world of readers.

And underpinning my literary and feminist endeavors there is always my Ron: You keep showing me by example how fulfilling a life devoted to causes can be, while the ocean of your love allows me to ladle into my fountain of creativity.

## About the author

## About the book

Insights,
Interviews
& More . . .

## Read on

# Meet Talia Carner

TALIA CARNER is the author of *Puppet Child, China Doll*, and *Jerusalem Maiden*, which won the Forward National Literature Award in the historical fiction category in 2011.

Her award-winning personal essays appeared in the *New York Times*, *Chocolate for Women* anthologies (Simon & Schuster), *Cup of Comfort* (Adams Media), and *The Best Jewish Writing 2003* (John Wiley). Her short stories have been published in *Midstream*, *Lynx Eye, River Sedge, Midwest Literary Magazine, Moxie, Lilith, Litro, Rosebud, Clackamas Literary Review, Two-Bridges Review, Confrontation*, and *North Atlantic Review*. Before writing fiction full-time, Carner worked for *Redbook* magazine, was the publisher of *Savvy Woman* magazine, and founded a successful marketing and consulting firm servicing Fortune 500 companies. She taught at Long Island University's School of Management and was a volunteer counselor and lecturer for the Small Business Administration. In 1993 she was sent twice by the United States Information Agency to Russia, and in 1995 participated in the NGO women's conference in Beijing.

Her addictions include chocolate, ballet, Sudoku—and social justice. ✑

© Steve Lars

For a more detailed bio, reviews of the novel, and the author's book tour dates and locations, please check the author's website, www.TaliaCarner.com.

# Talia in Russia

*October 1993: During Moscow uprising (Kremlin wall in the background). (Courtesy of the author)*

*May 1993: In Moscow's Red Square. (Courtesy of the author)*

**Talia in Russia** *(continued)*

*Preparing for a women's business conference. (Courtesy of the author)*

*At Troitsa-Sergyeva Lavra monastery, the ancient seat of the Russian Orthodox Church. (Courtesy of the author)* ✑

# Russia Then and Now . . .

By Talia Carner
www.TaliaCarner.com

*This essay was written in December 2011, twenty years after the fall of communism.*

WHEN THE ISRAELITES fled Egypt, they wandered in the desert for forty years until the generation born into slavery had died. According to God, only a people who had known a life of freedom possessed the strength to overcome the hurdles of building a new nation in the Promised Land, and would enter it.

I understood that wisdom when I journeyed to Russia twice in 1993 to teach women entrepreneurial skills. And I am reminded of my impressions at that time today when Russians are supposed to celebrate the twentieth anniversary of democracy. Instead they are taking to the streets to protest the autocratic regime that is all too similar to the totalitarian Soviet rule it had replaced.

In late April 1993, merely sixteen months after the fall of communism, I joined a group of American businesswomen to meet courageous Russian women who traveled to Moscow and St. Petersburg from areas as far as the Ural Mountains and from far republics whose names I had never heard. Suddenly we were no longer *The Enemy*. They watched with awe how we walked tall, strutted about with confidence, and punctuated our talks with smiles. (They asked why so many of us were in mourning or else why would we wear black when all the colors of the rainbow were available to us?) At the edge of their seats, they clung to every bit of information we could dole out. As we spoke through interpreters to groups and individuals about business plans, marketing strategies, and pricing policies or as we lectured about advertising, promotions, and selling tactics, they took furious notes. In turn, they asked tough questions to which we had no simple answers: from how to export their homemade, poor-quality products "to America," to how to launch a women's political party or start a women's bank

As hopeful and valiant as these women were, we hit a wall when we introduced the concept of networking. "Both of you. ▶

face the same problem motivating employees," I said to two students who had found themselves running bed and beer barrel factories, respectively, after a lifetime of working on the conveyor belt sawing and gluing lumber. But the two women glared at each other with suspicion. "Look, you live over six hundred kilometers apart," I explained. "There is no risk, and you can both benefit if you share ideas about ways to deal with business problems. You are not even selling to the same consumers!" But the women only shook their heads at my naïveté.

In a city that had never published a phone book, one's Rolodex equivalent had become a cherished commodity. It meant survival in a country that had never had aspirin or toothbrushes in its few stores. We soon learned that expecting our students to share any information—from a reliable printing shop to the name of an English teacher—was doomed. They balked at the notion that they should help a friend, let alone a stranger. They also asked why Americans smiled so much, finding this basic human gesture incomprehensible. And the idea of attempting to *connect* with strangers was outright frightening. It involved eye contact! Who could imagine what disaster a stranger might bring upon you?

It did not take long for me to grasp what had happened to the Russian nation on a deeper lever. Under a regime that glorified children turning in their parents to the authorities, where neighbors in hellish communal apartments spied on one another, where life's basic needs were in such short supply that stealing had become the norm, Russians had been conditioned into deep distrust. For seventy years, stripped of not just the right to practice religion but the social and moral values that we refer to as Judeo-Christian, Russians were unprepared for democracy that respected the rights of others, that set boundaries between the individual and the collective, that held random kindness in high regard, and that viewed cooperation as the route to strength. Russians had become adept at navigating the system without ever negotiating truce between individuals. Taking a cue from the corruption that invaded every Soviet institution, where apparatchiks openly enjoyed preferred treatment and flaunted their leather shoes and Rolex watches, the Russian masses emulated the only methods proven to work. Thus the curator of a geological museum invited me to her cramped apartment and, over a table laden with Russian delicacies and vodka, proceeded to offer me a business partnership in which we would privately sell the museum's semiprecious stones and rare geological rocks to American museums.

Privatization meant that formerly state-run large and small manufacturing plants gave ownership vouchers to all employees, who were wholly unprepared to operate these ventures. In a coat factory where I was training a small, newly elevated team, I explained the math of pricing a single coat: the cost of materials, the number of hours it took to create it (based on the seamstress's hourly salary, including benefits), and the fixed cost of running the place divided by the number of products expected to be manufactured. The suggested price I arrived at was by far lower than the thousands of dollars these women had expected *me* to pay for a coat. When I expressed to the interpreter that I was not buying one, she explained the team's dismay: What other reason had propelled me to spend two hours "negotiating" a price? It dawned on me that these women had never imagined volunteerism. Why would anyone do something for strangers without expecting to gain something out of it?

I also realized that while our children in the United States learned the basics of market economy when setting up their lemonade stands, negotiating allowances, and later working in fast-food chains that taught them customer service, adult Russians were strangers to the simplest market concepts. At a brush-manufacturing plant, for which the state had paid the bills, provided the raw materials, and then "bought" the finished product at a price it had set, the manager now placed the entire sum of utilities and building maintenance into the price tag of the first item to be sold. That first household brush was priced at the equivalent of tens of thousands of dollars. Since no one was buying it, the factory was stuck.

One night, after our group had paid the local tour agent— one of our organizers—for tickets to a ballet performance at the famous Bolshoi Ballet, we were taken to an unadorned building whose sign in Cyrillic script we could not read. My impression of being in the wrong place was sealed when the dancers came on ▶

stage. Although they were talented, we were clearly at a ballet school performance. After being pressed, the enterprising tour agent claimed that "it was the same thing," and acted indignant when we explained that not only she had committed fraud but also jeopardized her business's future by developing a bad reputation. Bad reputation? The stupid Americans had handed her whatever cash she had asked for! Now confronted, she was unremorseful about raking so much money into her pocket in a single evening. "You wanted ballet, I gave you ballet."

In spite of these experiences, there were women who admired what we did, who appreciated our gifts of lipsticks, condoms, and Tylenol in Ziploc bags. There were so many women desperate to provide for their children in a country where the majority of households were run by women because men often drank, beat their wives, and died of alcoholism at the average age of fifty-seven. I had never met as many bridge engineers as I encountered in one day in Moscow or as many female doctors as I met in one day in St. Petersburg. Yet bewildered by the fast-changing society, these highly educated women were isolated by the absence of a give-and-take social contract that could be fully relied on, and now lost after the state-run child care and meager medical services had been pulled from under them, leaving their children hungrier and sicker than ever before.

These brave women motivated me to accept an invitation by the U.S. Information Agency (USIA), which sent experts to all parts of the world, to return to Russia only six months later. Among other topics, I was assigned to conduct workshops about truth in advertising and ethical business practices and was given a budget for the translation of material to be printed in one hundred copies. Ironically, my Russian coordinator took the money for the translation, but it went up in smoke even before we left JFK Airport in New York City, my material never translated.

I landed in Moscow in October 1993, two hours after the uprising against President Boris Yeltsin had erupted. While our bus turned away from a bridge where peasants waved pitchforks and sickles, our Russian handlers insisted that we had misunderstood what we saw. As we watched the burning Russian parliament from a conference building's windows, our handlers pulled us away into windowless classrooms. As we received frantic phone calls from home detailing CNN broadcasts, our handlers called it Western propaganda. As we were subject to curfew, our handlers "forgot" their English to answer why the hotel was surrounded by soldiers. As I told the group that I had heard tanks rolling down our street, our eavesdropping handlers accused me of enticing disobedience and set me loose to be chased by the Russian militia so that my only choice was to escape Russia.

Even as the country fought for democracy, these English-speaking translators and facilitators, who must have read English literature and magazines, were incapable of releasing their tight-fisted grip on their charges to stop controlling the flow of information—or even of thought—and to permit us to speak freely among ourselves. Moreover, they were not embarrassed by their obvious lies. After a lifetime of bankrupt ideology and empty slogans, insincerity had long become the norm; no one believed anything anyway.

Russians still harbored the souls of embittered, subjugated people, a dispirited nation that had known no freedom, privacy, or choices. They were unprepared for democracy, freedom of the press, personal choices, market economy, and assumptions about transactions—be they social, economic, cultural, or legal—that shared the common concept of decency, if not rule of law. The regime that bloomed after the fall of communism embraced the same mind-set as its predecessor, using the former K.G.B. under a new cloak, revering bureaucrats-turned-oligarchs, and exploiting brutal tactics to silence criticism and opposition. Not unlike the Israelites wandering in the desert for forty years, Russians needed time to shed the old mentality of the oppressed until the younger generation raised in a much more open world would be prepared to claim what is rightly theirs.

That younger generation is now taking to the streets in protest.

*On November 3, 1993, at 2:48 P.M., three weeks after escaping Russia, Talia Carner started her fiction-writing career.* ∾

# Communal Apartments

"Kommunalaka," a Czar-era mansion converted into an anthill of communal apartments that allotted one room per family with up to twenty people sharing one bath, one toilet, and one kitchen.

*(Photo by Sergey Kozmin)*

*(Photo by Sergey Kozmin)*

*(Photo by Sergey Kozmin)*

*(Photo by Yevgeny Kondakov)*

# Talia Carner Talks with Lucette Lagnado

Originally from Cairo, Lucette Lagnado and her family left Egypt as refugees when she was a small child, an experience that helped shape and inform her recent memoirs, *The Man in the White Sharkskin Suit* and *The Arrogant Years*, both published by Ecco/HarperCollins. In 2008, she was the recipient of the Sami Rohr Prize for Jewish Literature for *The Man in the White Sharkskin Suit*, which has been translated into Spanish, Portuguese, Turkish, French, Hebrew, and Arabic. She is also the coauthor of *Children of the Flames: Dr. Josef Mengele and the Untold Story of the Twins of Auschwitz*. Lagnado, a cultural and investigative reporter for the *Wall Street Journal*, has received numerous awards for her reporting work. She resides with her husband, journalist Douglas Feiden, in Sag Harbor and New York City.

Here she discusses with author Talia Carner her journey in writing *Hotel Moscow*:

**LL: I love the name "Talia"—it is so exotic. Can you tell us a little bit about your past, where you are from, and how you came to have that name?**

**TC:** In Hebrew, "Talia" means "God's dew," as in "morning dew." When I was given the name, it was quite rare in Israel. Today, with its variation "Tali," it is probably as common as "Jennifer" is here. Since the 1940s, the Sabra (Israeli-born, so named after the prickly pear whose fruit is very sweet) pulled away from Diaspora and biblical names and created children's names that were descriptive words in the spoken language. My immediate family was secular, dominated by the maternal side, an Ashkenazi family whose ancestor, Rev Zalman Salomon, arrived in the Holy Land back in 1794. His son, Yoel Salomon, along with two other community leaders, built the first synagogue in Jerusalem since the Temple was destroyed almost two thousand years earlier. My family was educated—most of my mother's siblings had graduate degrees; her first cousin was a Nobel Laureate. My adoptive stepfather, an attorney, was born in Leningrad and arrived in Palestine at age seven. When I visited his birth city in 1993—by then renamed St. Petersburg—he had already passed away, but as I walked the streets, I narrated for him what I was seeing.

I grew up in Tel-Aviv among many friends who were born to Holocaust-surviving parents. There was a difference between my very Israeli parents and my friends' parents, who were often a decade older and spoke another language at home. They had survived the degradations and losses of the war, then crawled out of the ashes and created a second family with only one child who often had no grandparents, aunts, uncles, or cousins. Growing up as the generation after the Holocaust, we were all entrusted with the mission "to remember." At age ten, I went on a class trip to a nascent Holocaust museum, where we were shown lampshades made out of Jewish skin, and soap made out of Jewish fat. It stayed with us when we served in the Israel Defense Force, which is the true melting pot of Israeli society. During each war we were aware of the dire consequences of losing.

**LL: How do we get from your exotic background to Moscow and the setting for your new novel?**

**TC:** Since I have lived it, I don't see my background as "exotic." However, I can say that I always sought challenges, starting with my selecting a French high school in Tel-Aviv. It opened my eyes to another culture and, when I was seventeen, to my first trip abroad—one of many to come. In the army, my commander hand-picked his charges to work independently so he could study for law school, which he attended at night. It gave me enormous responsibility for people's lives, as well as reinforced my strong work ethic. Later on, as a young mother, I landed in Long Island, New York, and soon turned my classes at the State University of New York in Stony Brook into credits for a graduate degree in economics. I had started my career in advertising in Israel after graduating from the Hebrew University, but in the United States I incorporated it with marketing and magazine publishing. When I became the publisher of *Savvy Woman* magazine, I was the youngest publisher of a major magazine in the United States—and only one out of four women in that capacity at a time when even women's magazines were run by men.

By then I had developed an understanding of my own feminist ideas about women's rights, ideas that had germinated when ►

**Talia Carner Talks with Lucette Lagnado** *(continued)*

I was young, but for which I had lacked the vocabulary to express.
I soon fused my passion for women's issues with my career.
Among other things, I became a volunteer counselor for the Small
Business Administration's programs for women. That's how I was
recruited for my first "citizen mission" to Russia in May 1993 to
teach entrepreneurship to Russian women. I was so taken by the
valiant women I met—their no-nonsense, hard work, and stick-
to-it-iveness that reminded me of my mother and her generation
of Israelis who had established the country—that I readily agreed
to travel again in October of the same year. Unfortunately,
I landed in Moscow two hours after the uprising of the Russian
parliament against President Boris Yeltsin had erupted, and soon
I became caught in the mayhem. Now that's "exotic."

**LL: Lots of people with ordinary careers fantasize about the
novels they will publish some day. How did you actually make
the switch?**

**TC:** I was a storyteller. As early as second grade, I gathered a
selected group of girls at recess to tell them "my dreams last
night." And although I always wrote well in terms of stringing
words into complex sentences or constructing reasonable
arguments, I had never fantasized about becoming an author or
publishing a novel. Writing had never held the promise of
authorial magical dust because I led a busy and exciting life with
its own high points. Then, with no preparation or forethought,
I just sat down one day—November 3rd, 1993, at 2:48 P.M., three
weeks after escaping Moscow—and started writing a novel. I had
a story to tell. Russia in Soviet times—and perhaps still now, a
mere twenty years later—has been a society of female heads of
households with men gone MIA, due mostly to heavy drinking.
Besides struggling politically to regain the rights lost when
communism fell and the entire legal system was obliterated
(including medical care, school lunches for children, and political
representation in the parliament), women had to deal with blatant
sexual harassment. My fellow Americans and I watched
powerlessly as men of authority pounced on the women we
counseled. In fact we, too, were pounced upon, literally, by

passing strangers. Ads for secretaries required "long legs, no inhibitions." I wanted to capture this intolerable reality in a novel.

Within three weeks of writing, I knew that I had found a new calling. I had been running my own marketing consulting firm whose clients were Fortune 500 companies. Now I told my husband that I wished to be "a kept woman," and since it was December, I declined to accept new clients for the following year. I closed my firm's satellite offices, canceled four out of my five phone lines, and donated my suits to charity. Prior commitments to clients were executed for the next eighteen months by a skeleton staff while I continued to write feverishly, honing the craft of dialogue, scene building, characterization, and pacing. My last check was from Lincoln Mercury in July 1995. I never looked back.

In the process of publishing three novels, each dealing with a different social issue in a different setting around our globe, I realized that I think in multilayered plots painted on large canvases. I hold in my head a few perspectives simultaneously, from the psychological state of mind of the players, through the geographical setting, to the historical dynamics. This horizontal thinking underpins my writing while my story moves vertically to ratchet up the tension. Like in a dream, I am in the scene, feeling the emotions, seeing the sights, hearing the lines spoken, and smelling the scents, while the larger story unfolds. I close my eyes, and type along.

**LL: Your book has a wonderfully intriguing title, *Hotel Moscow*. Can you tell us how that came to be the name of your new work?**

**TC:** Actually, the working title of the novel was *Matryoshka Girl*, in line with the naming of my previous three novels. The novel is based upon material researched for my maiden effort mentioned above, a manuscript that was never published, telling the story of Russian women and their lives. *Hotel Moscow* is a different story, starring Brooke Fielding, a young, urbane, career-oriented Jewish New York liberal who's been trying to escape the legacy of her parents' suffering during the Holocaust. I wanted to juxtapose ▸

Brooke's feelings against the reality of unabashed anti-Semitism. Crossing her path with the setting of Moscow during the uprising of the Russian parliament against President Boris Yeltsin—in the confined setting of a hotel—gave me the tool to accomplish that.

The actual hotel where the story takes place is named Hotel Sputnik. My polls on social media revealed that neither word, "matryoshka" or "sputnik," was familiar enough. Since I believe in relating my message clearly, I changed the name of the hotel. *Hotel Moscow* hints at travel and a quest, at a mystery that unravels in a self-contained place, and, of course, at the city in a country that is on the news every day.

**LL: How did you do your research? Did this work require lots of travel?**

**TC:** In 1994, working on my first manuscript, I interviewed many Russians who had emigrated to the United States not long before and had fresh impressions of the trials and tribulations of living at the bottom of the food chain in a corrupt society. I also interviewed Cold War–era U.S. security personnel and attended lectures about the Russian politics of the time. Personally, while visiting Russia twice in 1993, I watched her women—probably the most educated group of women I had ever met—suffer the humiliation stemming from deprivation: the famous food lines led to empty stores, since basic consumer products had never been manufactured. Soviet Russia had been a superpower that cynically manipulated its people, toyed with their sense of worth, and deprived them of everything they wanted. The women were reduced to being hunters and gatherers almost like the African women I had counseled before them.

In Moscow and St. Petersburg I had visited small apartments, similar to the one described in *Hotel Moscow* as Olga's. But leaving Moscow in October 1993, at the Frankfurt airport, I met two American architects who had been hired by newly rich Russians to renovate old mansions that had been turned into anthills of rooms barely suitable for humans. I saw pictures of families—sometimes even three generations: an aging parent, a young couple, and a baby—squeezed into a 10-by-14-foot space.

I learned how typical these communal apartments were both through my subsequent interviews and my continuing involvement with Russian women helped by the Alliance of Russian and American Women—the organization with which I had visited Russia the first time, and which later built a "business incubator" in St. Petersburg. One of our recipients had grown mushrooms under the small table in her room; another had had to remove her sleeping cot just to make room for a sewing machine.

**LL: Did you have to go through many drafts to get to this finished product?**

**TC:** While I had done all the research twenty years earlier, writing *Hotel Moscow* from scratch was a downtime project while I prepared the release of *Jerusalem Maiden* with my publisher and then spent two years book touring, giving keynote speeches, chatting with book groups, blogging, and conducting media interviews. Even though I am now a much more experienced novelist, I still edit and revise ad nauseam. It is no exaggeration to say that I reread this version forty times.

I also faced an interesting challenge: Each of the protagonists in my previous novels was instantaneously sympathetic. In *Jerusalem Maiden*, for example, the reader immediately feels for a twelve-year-old who is supposed to be married off soon. And there was no problem evoking compassion for the Russian women who were secondary characters in *Hotel Moscow*. But how do I make the plight of a thirty-eight-year-old successful New Yorker worthy of empathy? How do I set up the story so that the reader will want to get on the journey with her? I knew where I needed to go—into the psyche of a second-generation Holocaust survivor who lived the experiences and the trauma as her own, whose existence to her parents was merely as a stand-in for all the children and relatives who had died. With every round of revision, I struggled with how much of Brooke's background to lay out and how much to let the reader extrapolate on her own When my editor at HarperCollins told me how lonely Brooke seemed to her, I knew that I had nailed the character. ▶

**Talia Carner Talks with Lucette Lagnado** *(continued)*

**LL: Unless you are superstitious, can you tell us about what you have in mind as a next book—another novel?**

**TC:** Being superstitious can bring bad luck! I already have a hundred pages of another novel, with the setting, characters, and their challenges in place. But another story is pulling me: the sequel to *Jerusalem Maiden*. Remember how the novel ended in 1924 and picked up as an epilogue in 1968? In order to write that epilogue, I had to work out in my head what had happened in the intervening forty-four years. Now I may just write the full story. It is complex and exhilarating, and requires tremendous research. In my writing, I like to explore how the forces that shape our lives touch an individual, and Esther was in the epicenter of major historical events. Since it will be a while before this novel is written, edited, and published, I can humbly suggest that readers feed their curiosity on my previous three novels.  ～

# Reading Group Guide

1. When Brooke first decides to go to Moscow, her goal is to gain expertise about the new market in order to save her job. Discuss the change in her goals once she arrives at the Gorbachevskaya Street Factory.

2. It's widely believed that friendship can transcend cultures. Can it really? Discuss Brooke's relationship with the Russian women she meets in light of her realization of their anti-Semitic past (Olga) or present (Svetlana).

3. How has escaping her sad home and the legacy of the Holocaust affected Brooke? Did she gain the freedom she sought?

4. With the fall of communism Russian women lost their rights and the safety nets of social services. Discuss what legal rights they had that women in the United States did not have and what rights we had that they sorely needed.

5. Corruption in 1993 Russia seems to have pervaded every sphere of life. Discuss what you've learned from the novel, what feeds it, and what, you believe, are the ways to rein it. Is it different from what we know of corruption in our own political, economic, or social systems?

6. In the novel, we get a glimpse of the living conditions of most Russians during communism when we visit ▶

Svetlana's and Vera's apartments. What, if anything, did you find surprising? In what other ways did you see the Russian government's indifference to its people?

7. Judd becomes Brooke's love interest, but it takes her time to trust him. Discuss your take on the development of their relationship. What is unique to them and where do you foresee it heading?

8. Brooke carries with her two secrets that threaten to destroy her career. Yet she is thrilled when one of those secrets is exposed. Does it have the potential to destroy her the way the other might? Are they viewed differently in the context of our current mores? What about your own social environment?

9. Svetlana commiserates with Brooke upon learning that Brooke works long hours, and believes that "they make you work so hard." Discuss the differences in career choices and work lifestyle for people living under these the two superpowers.

10. In spite of her high education, Olga is ignorant about the most basic business principals. The concept of capitalism is both revered and loathed. Discuss how a government-controlled market economy is different from an open market economy—research, pricing, distribution, promotion. Do you believe that government should stay completely out of the game or impose some regulations and controls?

11. When President Yeltsin was frustrated in his attempts to reform the old system and to pass new democratic laws, he fired the entire Duma, the Russian parliament whose members had been elected through a democratic process. (Or had they used their former power to be elected?) He eventually used the army to force them to leave the building and to subdue their sympathizers. What were his options before, during, and after the crisis? From what you know about Russia today, how have things changed?

12. Brooke is looking forward to meeting her powerful host, Sidorov, until she meets him. Discuss his character. What was his motivation in inviting the group?

13. Jenny is a colorful character who has taken control of her life and makes sure to be noticed. How is she perceived by her fellow American travelers and by the Russian women? What is her real motivation when she speaks with Sidorov?

14. The Russian male characters vary. Compare Aleksandr, Sidorov, Viktor, and Belgorov. What typifies each and what motivates each?

15. Judd tells Brooke about his father. How had Judd—a third-generation survivor of the Holocaust—been affected by his family history?

16. Brooke does not want her Judaism to be defined by the Holocaust or by anti-Semitism. Yet, has she found an answer at the end of this short visit to Russia? Did the past twenty years of running away from her legacy help her find a new way? What makes her Jewish?

17. Judaism in our open, mostly secular Jewish society is seeking new definitions, new grooves. Discuss what it means to you to be Jewish. If you are a nonpracticing Christian, what defines your Christianity?

18. When Svetlana expresses anti-Semitic opinions, Brooke's instinct to correct her is always pushed aside by more urgent issues. At the end, in spite of Svetlana's repeated remarks, Brooke does everything to save her. Discuss what this means in terms of Brooke's Jewish values.

19. Russian women seem to have strong opinions about femininity. What does the notion of femininity mean to them, and how much is it the same or different in your social milieu?

20. Olga gives Brooke a matryoshka doll. Discuss the symbolism of these nesting dolls both in the context of the novel and your own life. ❧

# Excerpt from *Jerusalem Maiden*

## Jerusalem

SEPTEMBER 1911/TISHREI 5672

ESTHER'S HAND raced over the paper as
if the colored pencils might be snatched
from her, the quivering inside her wild,
foreign, thrilling. All this time she hadn't
known that "blue" was actually seven
distinct shades, each with its own
name—azure, Prussian, cobalt,
cerulean, sapphire, indigo, lapis. She
pressed the waxy pencils on the paper,
amazed by the emerging hues: the
ornaments curving on the Armenian
vase were lapis; the purplish contours of
the Jerusalem mountains were shrouded
by indigo evening clouds. In this stolen
hour at Mademoiselle Thibaux's dining-
room table, she could draw without
being scolded for committing the sin
of idleness, God forbid.

A pale gecko popped up on the
chiseled stone of the windowsill
and scanned the room with staccato
movements until it met Esther's gaze.
Her fingers moving in a frenzy, she drew
the gecko's raised body, its tilted head, its
dark orbs focused on her. She studied the
translucency of the skin of the valiant
creature that kept kitchens free of
roaches. How did God paint their
fragility? She picked up a pink-gray
pencil and traced the fine scales. They
lay flat on the page, colorless. She tried
the lightest brown—

Her hand froze. What was she

thinking? A gecko was an idol, the kind pagans worshipped. God knew, at every second, what every Jew was doing for His name. He observed her now, making this graven image, explicitly forbidden by the Second Commandment, *Thou shalt not make unto thee any graven image, or any likeness of anything that is in heaven above, or that is in the earth beneath, or that is in the water under the earth.*

With a jerk of its head, the gecko darted away. Esther stared at the paper, her hand in midair. She had never imagined a sin like this.

Mlle Thibaux walked in from the kitchen nook, smiling. Her skin was smooth, luminous, and her brown hair uncovered, its coquettish ripples pinned by twin tortoiseshell combs. She picked up Esther's drawing and examined it. *"C'est merveilleux! Quel talent!"*

Esther blushed. The praise reflected what Mlle Thibaux's raised eyebrows had revealed that morning in sixth-grade French class when she had caught Esther doodling. To Esther's consternation, her teacher must have detected the insects hidden inside the branches and leaves. The teacher turned the page this way and that, and her eyes widened. She then asked Esther to stay after school, and Esther was certain she would be ordered to conjugate the verb "to be" hundreds of times on the blackboard: *je suis, tu es, il est, elle est*—Instead, Mlle Thibaux invited her to her apartment at the Hospice Saint Vincent de Paul, a palace-like building with arch-fronted wings, carved colonnaded verandas and balustraded stairwells. The teacher was a *shiksa*, a gentile. Newly arrived from Paris, she probably didn't know that while it wasn't forbidden in Esther's ultra-Orthodox community to decorate with flourished letters and ornamental shapes, drawing God's creatures was another matter.

Now, holding Esther's drawing, Mlle Thibaux smiled. "Here, try mixing these two colors." On a separate page, she sketched a few irregular lines with a pink pencil, then scattered some short leaf-green lines in between.

Esther chewed the end of her braid. Fear of God had been instilled in her with her mother's milk and in the Ten Commandments tablets displayed everywhere, from her classroom to the bakery. In addition, the Torah pronounced that any urge must be suppressed, as it would surely lead to ▶

sinning. The quickening traveling through Esther again proved that what she was doing was forbidden. Her mother said that Esther's harshest punishment for sinning would be failure to become betrothed at twelve, as every good Jerusalem maiden should upon entering her mitzvah age. Yet, as Mlle Thibaux handed her the pink and green pencils, Esther silently prayed for God's forgiveness and recreated the hues inside the gecko's scales. To her astonishment, they blended as a translucent skin.

A knock sent Mlle Thibaux to the door, her back erect and proud as no woman Esther had ever known. The teacher accepted a pail from the water hauler and carried it to the kitchen while Esther collected the pencils into their tin box.

Outside the window, slicing off the top of the Tower of David, a cobalt-blue sky hung low on the horizon like a wedding *chupah* with a ribbon of magenta underlining it. A flock of sparrows jostled for footing in the date palm tree, then rose in a triangular lace shawl formation before settling again. The warm smell of caramelized sugar wafting from the kitchen made Esther hungry for tonight's dinner, a leftover Shabbat challah dipped in milk and egg, fried and then sprinkled with sugar. Closing the pencil box, her hand traced its scene of a boulevard in Paris, lined with outdoor cafés and their dainty, white, wrought-iron chairs. Women wearing elegant hats and carrying parasols looped their arms through men's holding walking sticks, and the open immodesty of the gesture shocked Esther even as it made something inside her tingle. In Jerusalem, only Arab men, dressed in their striped pajamas, idled on low stools in the souk and played backgammon from sunrise to sunset. Their eyes glazed over as they sucked the mouthpieces of hoses coiled around boiling tobacco narghiles. Paris. Esther had never known a girl who traveled, but when she had been little, her father, her Aba, apprenticed at a bank in America. It was a disastrous exposure to "others," her mother, her Ima, said, because it filled his head with reprehensible new ideas, worse than the simpleton Hassids'. That was why Aba sent his daughters to a school so elegant that Yiddish was frowned upon. Most subjects were taught in English, and Esther mingled there with Sepharadi Jewish girls who spoke Ladino and Arabic as well as with secular girls—heretic Zionists all of them, Ima said—who spoke the sacred Hebrew.

"*Chérie*, will you light the candles?" Mlle Thibaux walked in from the kitchen nook and placed a silver tea set on a spindle table covered with a crocheted napkin. The high collar of her blouse was stiff over starched pleats running down the front to a cinched waist, but when she moved, her long skirt immodestly hinted at legs. Had she ever walked in Paris with a man, daring to loop her arm in his?

Mlle Thibaux smiled. "It's four o'clock—"

Four o'clock? Esther's hand rose to her throat. Ima, who expected her to attend to her many chores right after classes, had been laboring alone while Esther was indolent. Ima would be furious. "I must go home—"

Mlle Thibaux pointed to a plate with slices of glazed cake sprinkled with shaved almonds and cinnamon. "It's kosher."

"*Non, merci.* The neighborhood gates will get locked for the night." Saliva filling Esther's mouth, she gathered her long plaid skirt and backed toward the door. She had never tasted a French cake; it had been ages since she had eaten any cake. But Mlle Thibaux's kitchen was *traife*, non-kosher. Esther wouldn't add another sin to her list. "*Merci beaucoup!*"

She ran out of the apartment, down the two flights of steps, and across the stone-paved yard to the street facing the Jaffa Gate in the Old City wall, where camels awaited pilgrims and Turkish soldiers patrolled. Restless birds chirped in desperation to find shelter for the night. Wind rustled the tops of the tall cypresses and whipped fallen leaves into a spin. Maybe it would rain soon, finally replenishing the dry cistern under her house.

Running downhill, she turned north, her sandals pounding the cobblestones. At least she wasn't barefoot as she had been that morning, putting her sandals on at the gate to Evelina de Rothschild school to save the soles. She vaulted over foot-wide sewage channels dug in the center of the alleys. Then there was the open hill with only rocks and scattered dry bushes flanking the dirt path grooved by men, carts and beasts. Climbing fast up the path, she listened for sounds beyond the trilling of crickets and the buzzing of mosquitoes. ▶

In the descending darkness, a Jewish girl might be dishonored by a Turkish soldier or murdered by an Arab. Just on the next hill, the grandfather she had never met had been assassinated while inspecting land he purchased for the first Jewish neighborhood outside the Old City.

A scruffy black dog stood on a rock. Esther's heart leaped. Dogs were despicable creatures; they carried diseases that made people insane. It growled and exposed yellow-gray teeth. When Esther swerved out of the path, it gave chase. She screamed, running faster, the dog barking behind her. She grabbed the hem of her skirt, and her feet pounded on rocks, twisting, stumbling. If she tripped, she'd die. Now that the Ottoman Empire was crumbling and the sultan neglected his subjects, hungry Jerusalemites ate even rotting scraps of food, and starving dogs bit people. The Turkish policemen killed dogs on sight.

Was that the dog's breath on her heels? She gulped air. Her wet cheeks were cold in the rush of wind. A blister burned the sole of her foot. The dog must smell her sweat, her fear. She couldn't outrun it. Her punishment for drawing idols had come so soon! It had never occurred to her that there could be a fate worse than Ima's warning about failing to find a groom. To Esther, that threat had always sounded like a blessing.

Cold pain sliced her rib cage, and her

lungs burned. She could run no more. She stopped. Whirling, she faced the dog, exposed her teeth and snarled, waving her arms like the mad girl she'd become if it bit her.

To her amazement, the beast halted. Another snarl rose from Esther's chest, tearing her throat, and the animal backed off. She flailed her arms again, and the dog tucked its tail and slunk away.

Her heart still struggling to escape its confinement, Esther whispered a prayer of thanks and then fumbled for the amulet in her pocket to stave off the evil eye. Her pulse drummed in her ears. She broke into a trot. Five more minutes to Me'ah She'arim. Her inner thighs chafed over her belted socks, but stopping wasn't an option. Wicked winds—worse than dogs—gusted in search of a soul deserving punishment, one that had defied God. ◡